ALTERED STATES

Edited By

Ajax B. Coriander

ALTERED STATES

Edited by Ajax B. Coriander, Kodiak Malone, and Andres Cyanni Halden
Production © FurPlanet Productions 2016

Cover and Interior Illustrations by Kuma
http://www.furaffinity.net/user/kuma/

TABLE OF CONTENTS

To H.G. Wells

Who wondered what it would be like to lift beasts up to the place of men. We explore the reverse.

Finishing Touches

Ianus J. Wolf

Carefully making a few final strokes with the small brush, Henry stepped back to take in his work. The painting looked pretty good, all things considered, especially for what was relatively a rush job. Given a little more time, he could see little places where he'd like to do a few more touch-ups, but it had to be sent out tomorrow to be proofed in time for the book.

A week before, Ryan had called him in desperation to beg him to set aside everything and figure out a cover. The publishing house had a fantasy novel due to print in a little over two weeks and the previous cover artist had bailed over creative differences with the author. Ryan had ranted for a few moments about how this was why he hated letting authors pick an artist friend of theirs to do cover work, but at least he had a go-to guy like Henry Wilson that he could count on to do good work in a hurry so would he mind taking this on? Henry had taken the quick commission for a twenty percent bump in his usual price for rushing, and Ryan had sent him the manuscript overnight.

He'd skimmed it quickly for visuals that might work, checking a few post-it notes from Ryan and the author at various pages. The novel itself wasn't that inspiring, just another 'band of unlikely heroes quests to destroy the evil power' kind of thing. But now as he looked at his own work, he felt he'd managed to get a pretty good image of the noble citadel with banners flying and the silhouette of

9

the evil wizard's dark tower looming off in the background. Not bad for just about a week's work; as long as the publishing house and author approved it, he'd be getting a nice fat check in just a few weeks.

Leaving the painting to dry on the easel, Henry wiped the splatters of colors from his hands with a rag. The white tank top he wore to paint was starting to feel a bit tattered as he looked down at it; he might have to get another from the pack soon. At least the gray cargo pants would survive a few more rounds; he didn't have to hit a thrift store yet. Henry stretched his muscles, feeling just a little sore, but happy that he'd done good work and that he'd be bringing in some extra cash once again.

His artwork might not make them anywhere near the money that Carol did as a VP at Unidyne, but he was still managing to sell regularly between genre conventions, online sales, and a few different clients that trusted him to do quality work on a deadline. Carol never complained about the difference either, she was practically born for business and climbing corporate ladders. They were both satisfied, and while he'd at one point been worried about how much of the expenses she paid, she felt that their lives weren't broken and thus didn't require fixing. When he wasn't sketching or painting for a client, he at least tried to keep up the house.

From outside the studio he heard the sound of doors opening and closing that brought a smile to his face. Perfect timing to finish for the day, she was home. He could go greet her, but over the last few weeks there had been a routine she'd initiated that was kind of nice. She'd come in, pour a drink for each of them and bring them to wherever he happened to be. That was their greeting almost every evening. Soon enough there was a gentle knock at the studio door.

"Come on in," he said, still looking at the painting for anything it might need.

He heard the door open and Carol slipped in. "Oh, so you finished it, huh?" she asked as she stepped up beside him and handed him a wine glass.

Henry took his first sip while Carol took another step forward and looked over the painting. He always trusted her to give honest feedback, one of the things he loved about their relationship. As he took another drink of the sweet red wine, she made little noises of appraisal. He couldn't help his own admiring as he looked from the short cut dark hair with its vague hints of red highlights to the way the skirt suit framed her healthy body. Grinning to himself as his eyes traveled to bare notion the skirt gave of her round rump, Henry just thanked his lucky stars that they'd met and hoped he'd always feel so attracted to her.

"So I'm guessing that's where the stuffy elf and the gruff dwarf trade insults while someone hands them the quest, and that back there is where the evil Lord Fuckhead or something plots to take over the world?"

Almost snorting his wine for a moment, Henry nodded and gave a little coughing laugh. "Yeah, that's about the size of it. What do you think?"

She turned to him with a smile. "I think it's great, dear, has your style but fits the book the way you described it." Carol leaned forward, giving him a soft kiss on the lips and taking care to keep her suit away from his paint-stained clothes. "Want me to take it to be shipped on the way to work tomorrow?"

"If it's not too much trouble, that'd be great."

"Nah, you know they're on the way. It'll get out early and you can sleep in tomorrow. Then you can call Ryan and let him know you've saved his bacon and the painting is in the mail."

"Thanks, hon." Henry smiled. "Well, I think I'll slip into something a little less messy and we can see about dinner."

"I brought Chinese home," Carol said as she started to walk past him, "And just lose the clothes and meet me in the bedroom. I need to unwind, and the food will wait."

With a casual swat on his ass cheek, she sauntered out of the room. Feeling a little tingle up his spine, Henry turned just in time to see her heading towards their bedroom. He downed the rest of the wine and began tugging at his tank top. "Yes, ma'am," he mumbled to himself. Henry loved it when his wife took charge like that.

Still riding the afterglow, they made their way into the dining room, Henry in loose sweatpants and Carol in her thin white robe. He could still taste her on his lips, and he found himself yawning and occasionally licking them.

"Hmm, hope it hasn't gotten too cold," he said as they began to take apart the paper bag of white containers.

Carol settled herself into one of the chairs at the small table, a wide smile still plastered across her face. "I doubt it. Not the first time this has happened; it's usually fine."

Plopping down on a chair, Henry fished out the chopsticks and plastic utensils that had been tossed into a bag. They didn't bother with plates on nights like this, just shared from the box. He opened a few boxes in his search before he found his beef with broccoli.

"So how was work today?" he asked as he plucked a couple pieces.

Carol paused, swallowing a mouthful of lo mein. "Oh, long, taxing. But it was productive, worked out some details on the new product line. Don't feel like talking about it much now." Her bare foot stretched out, idly rubbing his shin. "Have anything planned next, now that the cover's done?"

He shrugged. "Nothing really. Probably do some house cleaning tomorrow, then go into the studio, see if anything inspires. Though this book is supposedly the start of a series, and if the author likes the cover, Ryan will probably be keeping me at the ready to do the next volumes. Of course, that'd still be a while off, but it's another commission potentially lined up. Maybe when I call him tomorrow, I'll see if he's got anything else. Help me remember to email him a picture of the painting before we wrap it up. "

"Sure. I imagine you'll think of something for tomorrow. Maybe one of those gothic pieces, those usually sell prints pretty well."

"I suppose those are good for a quick sale. But I really want to do some of my own work for a few days, something... I don't know, truly inspired. I'll take a little time with a canvas tomorrow. So, a little more True Blood after dinner?"

"Sounds perfect."

As Henry put away the leftover Chinese food, Carol set up the TV. In a few moments, he was stretched out on the chaise part of the sectional with her nestled against him in his arm. Life was good.

The discomfort woke Henry at about three in the morning. Drifting slowly up from the recurring dream of the moonlit forest, his hand went to his belly and moved up to his chest. With a wince he slipped quietly out of the king-sized bed, Carol barely stirring on the other side. The discomfort grew as Henry headed for the bathroom, feeling a knot twisting its way up his insides. As he closed the door and turned on the light, he nursed a silent hope that Golden Palace hadn't given him food poisoning.

Sweat broke out on his forehead, and Henry knelt on the cool tile floor. The discomfort rose but never crossed the line to true pain. Something roiled inside him, spreading from his abdomen up to his chest. He felt his muscles starting to twitch as a tremble ran through him, his skin starting to tingle and itch. Scratching and adjusting his eyes to the harshness of the light, Henry looked down at his arm as a dull ache continued to work through his body.

All along his skin, mingled with the thin dusting of hair on his arm, there were gray flecks that he could actually see growing into new hairs. As his finger ran over the surface, the new hairs continued to sprout, feeling slightly more course. Almost like fur. He scratched madly at the itching, feeling the first strains of panic as both arms were steadily growing a thicker coat of the strange fur. With the itch all over his skin, he stood up, scratching one place only to find another flaring up faster than his fingers could move. As he stood and moved his hands up to his face to scratch, he suddenly stopped.

In the bathroom mirror, Henry saw that his entire body was now almost covered in the new fur-like hair. Largely gray with some darker patterns, he watched as lighter colors filled in his chest, up his neck and cheeks, while a darker strip grew between his eyes. He began to call out for Carol, but all that came out was a high-pitched whimper as his throat caught and his face began to stretch forward.

What he saw in the mirror should have been agonizing, yet somehow there was no pain. Henry simply watched for several moments, feeling the subtle stretch as his mouth began to push out and elongate as if someone had taken hold of his nose and jaws and pulled them outwards. His teeth began to feel too big and slowly elongated in the mirror as his jaw stretched and thinned. Before long, as his mouth worked its way forward into a thin muzzle, he felt the rest of his skull sliding and gradually changing form, the furred skin moving to accommodate.

Gripped by a mix of fear and fascination, Henry pitched forward, leaning on the bathroom counter and watching as his head completely changed. The strange fur thickened and soon completely subsumed his normal short black hair. As the last of it disappeared, he watched his now fur-covered ears growing longer and gently sliding up the side of his head. The odd, uncontrollable stretching sensation continued as they took on a triangular shape and turned to fit at the corners of his scalp.

The volume on the world turned up as the two shapes slowly grew more convex atop his head. Steadily he could hear the water in the pipes of the bathroom, Carol's breathing in the next room, bits of machinery ticking and buzzing all around the house, and a host of sounds he couldn't even completely place. It was almost too much, and Henry brought his hands up to where his ears used to be out of habit.

Dream. All this has to be a dream. Going to wake up next to Carol in a bit and tell her all about it.

He whimpered again as he tried to figure out a way to shut his ears off for just a moment. Then he felt the tugging at his fingertips, distracting him from the sounds. His nails had already gone through their own changes as furred skin grew over the cuticles and the nails themselves pushed and thinned into short, blunt claws. Turning his hands over, he watched as his fingerprints were pushed away by course pads growing along his fingers and palms.

Feeling a stretching in his torso, Henry had a bad feeling about what would happen to his legs. It was only as he stood up again that he realized just how tired he was beginning to feel from all the work his body was doing. The strange canine face in the mirror blurred as he stumbled back a bit. Whatever was happening, he couldn't be found laying on the bathroom floor like this in the morning. Carol would freak.

His entire body seemed to be stretching now, and Henry had gained some height as he managed to hunch and weave his way out of the door and slowly down the hall. Already he could feel that now familiar stretching working its way through his thighs. It was getting harder and harder to stay upright as his legs and feet tried to slip into a new shape. As he reached the door to his studio, he could feel a warm comforting darkness trying to claim him.

Pushing the door open, he barely managed to close it and flip the latch as he almost fell inside. This would be nothing new; sometimes he woke early when he was inspired. Carol had found the door locked plenty of times and left him be. He just had to hope that she didn't get worried if she called for him and he didn't answer. But by now he was just too tired to care.

As the feeling of being pulled, twisted and reshaped finally began to ebb out of his body, Henry slipped down to the floor in complete physical and mental exhaustion. Still hoping that the whole experience might be some kind of dream, he curled up on the floor and sank into a black, oblivious slumber.

Warmth bathed his skin, pulling him up from the deep well of sleep. The feeling was more pleasant than usual as he gave a groggy stretch. The light in the room was brighter than expected as he turned on the hard floor. The lack of the bed brought memories trickling back as Henry pushed into consciousness. Had he dreamed and sleepwalked? He'd never sleepwalked in the past. With a twist of his head, he looked up to the high windows of his studio. The position and intensity of the light, it was probably about noon.

Henry's heart thumped in his chest. He remembered what he saw in the mirror, and his ability to deny it was dwindling by the second. As he began to roll to his back, pressure at his tailbone stopped him. Slowly, he craned his head around catching a look at the fur on his side and saw that the discomfort at his tailbone was... his tail. The new saber-shaped extremity thumped the floor once as the reality of his memories brought Henry completely into wakefulness.

For a moment, he began to try to get up too quickly, only to slip down into a heap again and thrash on the floor. He stopped and took a deep breath, and instantly the strong aromas of paint, canvas, wood, and every other material in the room threatened to overwhelm him. Henry had always loved the smell of his studio, that air of creativity that he felt, but all the scents had been turned up to eleven now. It took him a moment to focus again as he tried to separate out all the different smells and turn them down.

His mind of was racing. He thought to himself, "Okay... Okay, calm down. I won't get anywhere if I just flail around. Clearly I changed last night somehow. Carol hasn't seen me, nobody's seen me, don't panic. Just... assess the situation before I do anything."

Closing his eyes for a moment, Henry centered himself. Whatever he saw, he'd have to accept, no more denial. That would be a waste of the few hours he had before Carol got home to try and solve the problem. As he opened his eyes, he looked down his body.

His torso was slightly longer than it had been before, but displayed the musculature of his normal, human self. Looking down to his legs, he saw that they bent at new angles, which was why he'd had trouble getting up a moment ago. No, that wasn't quite right. There were no new angles, the old angles had just... moved slightly. His thighs were about the same length, but both his calves and feet seemed a little longer. And there was a slightly more pronounced bend at the ball of his foot. Maybe he could figure out how to stand if...

Suddenly a moment of terror gripped Henry that completely distracted him from his legs. He began to hyperventilate with a sound of panting as he realized he couldn't see his penis! It seemed just... gone amidst the thick fur. Frantically his hands went to his groin, searching. A moment of relief came as they felt his balls, about the same shape and size as always despite the fur, but for a moment he still couldn't find anything else. Yet it felt like it was still there.

That doesn't mean anything! People who lose a limb can still feel it tingling! Whatever happened, it took your cock! It took...

Then his hands brushed across something that gave him that same familiar pleasant feeling he remembered. As he looked down, he could see a fur wrapped nub at his crotch with a small hole. Using his fingers and minding the new claws on them, he pushed it down to reveal a pointed, bright pink head poking out. He breathed a sigh of relief.

Well it's there... sort of. Thank god. Wonder if this is what uncut guys feel like. Huh. Okay... point of business: stand and get to a mirror... if you can stop playing with yourself.

He found his fingers idly rubbing the furred nub and noticing just how good it felt as he experienced the beginnings of an erection in his new equipment. But there wasn't time for that now. He had more important matters like standing, getting to a mirror, figuring out if this was a hallucination... but the new sensations were amazing, a bit like the first time he had ever discovered that pre-orgasmic feel of touching himself.

Shaking his head before he started to pant, Henry pulled his new paws away from himself. Time to try standing up. He reached up to a sturdy shelf in the studio that was normally waist-high and began to pull himself up, trying to get the odd curve of his legs under him. As he drew up and tried to stand, he found himself wobbling and had to grab the shelf for support several times. He tried to remember the times he had painted canines before and the references he had used.

Toes. They walk on their toes. But you'll never be able to hold that for long or stand up that way. Hang on... try... toes and the balls of your feet... or paws... or whatever.

Feeling the joints of his new legs and adjusting them as best he could, Henry settled his center of gravity over the balls of his feet, keeping what was once the heel lifted. He took a couple shaky steps back from the shelf and kept his hands out. Stumbling just a bit, Henry moved back and forth a few times to get a feel for how everything sat. Soon enough though, he was actually able to stride forward and backward without much trouble.

Standing steady, he listened for a moment and for the first time took advantage of his ears. They perked up as he took in the sounds of the house. It was actually kind of interesting to hear everything that creaked or flowed in the walls or floor. He was satisfied that they had no pest problem at all, but the most important thing: Carol was definitely not home.

As he took a few steps to the door, something clattered behind him, making him whip around. A cup full of paintbrushes had fallen off a table. Could this be related to the change? Was it part of some bizarre haunting? Something else fell behind him and he turned again to see a closed bottle of paint rolling across the floor. Then there was another clatter at a table behind him. Was there a presence in the house with him? Stopping a moment, Henry craned his head back and felt an inner groan. His tail was swaying and knocking things over if he got too close.

I... am a moron. That thing's going to take some getting used to.

Concentrating on keeping the tail still, he unlocked the studio door and headed for the bathroom. Henry needed a mirror, needed to see just what he looked like. He paused for a moment, a bit nervous to really see, but he had to have some idea of the final results. He pushed himself in and took a good look in the mirror that spanned most of the bathroom wall.

His head was almost completely that of a wolf, as he'd seen the night before. The muzzle might have been a tad wider and longer, the forehead just slightly different in slope, but for all intents and purposes, his face and head matched every reference he'd looked at for a wolf. Except that he noted that the eyes in the head were his own, their same brown as before and for the first time had a moment of thanks that he was seeing the world in perfect color.

Henry followed from the face down to his neck, which sat like a human's, though was covered in the gray and white fur that now adorned his entire body. As he'd noticed before, most of his physique had not really changed either. His shoulders were still broad human shoulders under the fur, and his arms looked the same down to his wrists. Though his hands had more or less changed to paws, the digits remained the same, giving him another moment of gratitude that he still had working thumbs.

Twisting his torso a little here and there, he tried to see if his back had changed much and noticed how his tail moved as he did. He reached back and grabbed it with his left hand, pulling it carefully to get a good look at it in the mirror. The pressure could be felt where his back met his rump, but it wasn't that bad. Stroking a paw through the bushy fur there, he found it actually kind of calming as he examined a slightly long, but otherwise perfectly formed wolf tail.

As he brushed the fur and felt himself relaxing, taking in the whole picture of his new form, he found himself thinking about Carol. For a moment, he thought she might actually like him like this. But really, fantasy was one thing, having the unexplainable show up in life was quite another. Still, as he stroked his fur lightly he could picture her, almost breathless with excitement, laying back on the bed and just waiting for him to take her. He felt that fresh excitation in his loins as something expanded there, putting a nice pressure on that furred nub and opening it. He imagined Carol's scent, the sound of her voice as she begged for...

Henry's dozy reverie was shattered by a shrill screech that hit his ears like daggers twisting slowly into his brain. He clutched the points and closed them, trying to figure out what that unearthly torment was as it stopped for just a half a moment only to repeat at regular intervals. Then it came to him. That was how his basic cell phone ringer must sound to his canine senses. Wincing, he moved to the bedroom to silence the offending thing.

He picked it up off the nightstand next to his side of the bed and jammed a pawpad down on the volume button to stop the ringing. Looking at the screen, he saw that he had missed the call, but his first priority was to lower the ringer. As he set it to the lowest possible volume, Henry noted that he'd probably have to change it to something a lot less obnoxious and definitely lower pitched.

As the daggers receded and he could think a moment again, Henry came upon his next big problem. How could he communicate with anyone? Muzzles weren't made for talking and he owed Ryan a phone call. He could try to stave it off with email, but he and Ryan talked pretty regularly and it would get noticed. Plus, with a phone call planned today, if he didn't make it, Ryan was the sort to get a little worried about the cover. He might try to call Carol and see if she knew anything. And when Carol came home, how would he let her know what was going on? She'd come home to a monster, and when he tried to say, "It's me Henry!" it would likely come out as growls and snarls. This was not going to go well.

The phone rang again, and Henry knew it was probably Ryan checking on the status of the painting. Pacing the bedroom and trying to keep his tail from knocking anything over, he wished he could just do something simple like answer the phone.

"What am I gonna do?" he muttered to himself, bringing his furry fingers to his eyes out of habit. He stopped completely and blinked a few times. "I... I can speak?"

Henry rushed back to the bathroom mirror and looked once again at his lupine face, watching the muzzle move.

"Peter Piper picked a peck of pickled peppers." Perfect words, not a hint of a growl or whimper.

"Make your mouth round when 'o' sounds abound. I am a thistle sifter who sifts thistles." Not the slightest distortion as he watched the muzzle move in ways he'd never seen a dog be able to work. Whatever had happened to him, at least he'd been granted that.

Henry almost tripped over himself trying to reach the phone. The ID read "Ryan" as he'd expected. Despite the clumsiness with his larger paws and the claws getting in the way, he managed slide a pad along the screen just before his voicemail picked up.

"Hello? Ryan?" He held the phone to his head only to discover that it couldn't extend from his muzzle to his new ear. "Ah, crap. Ryan, hold on! Let me get you on speaker."

"Okay, okay take your time, no rush," Ryan said loud and clear from the phone. At least Henry's amped hearing would apparently be able to compensate for some people on the phone. Managing to get the phone to speaker mode, he held it a few inches from the tip of his nose.

"Ryan, you still there?"

"Yeah, I'm here. Hey, I thought you were going to call me earlier."

"Uh, yeah. I, uh... I slept in and... had some of the weirdest dreams."

"Figure that would be good for you, give you something to paint," Ryan said, "Speaking of which..."

"Yes, yes, the cover painting. Carol... Wait, let me check something." Henry looked out of the door of the bedroom and down the hall to where the painting had been wrapped to go. "Yeah, Carol dropped that by the shipper this morning."

"Wonderful, wonderful. Well, I got an email from the author when I sent him those pictures you texted me, and he absolutely loves it, wants you to do the rest of the series when he finishes them. So we get the painting, do a high-res scan, let the graphics guys add the titles and whatnot and you, my friend, get paid in a couple weeks."

Henry couldn't help but stare at the paw that wasn't holding the phone. Yeah, if I can ever paint again. "Oh that's... that's great, Ryan, yeah. Good stuff. Um, listen, I need to get a few things done around here, so you mind if I talk to you later?"

"No problem, no problem, I know how it is, you artists, always onto your next project, right? Catch you later, my man!"

"Yeah, good talkin' to you."

Henry hit the end button on the phone and sighed. At least talking wasn't a worry. In the whole conversation, Ryan hadn't noticed anything wrong. Then again, it was Ryan, and he wasn't the best test for this sort of thing. Still, Henry's own voice sounded natural enough to himself.

"So great, I can spend the rest of my life in my studio doing everything by phone. And talking to myself, apparently."

With the fact that he was walking and talking dimming some of the initial shock, Henry wracked his mind, trying to think of any reason for his change. Clearly this was actually happening and wasn't a dream or a hallucination. So how? If he had been attacked by something on a moonlit night, this would be easier, but he hadn't even had a dog bark at him recently. And as far as he knew, last night was barely a half moon. Plus in all the old legends, you turned back into a human at sun-up.

He thought about trying to search for answers online, then realized his claws weren't likely to be very good on a keyboard. He'd be looking at a few hours of careful hunt-and-peck and probably turn up little beyond the myths he already knew. That and a ton of crazy conspiracy theories that could actually be true or could just be the ramblings of shut-ins with too rich an imagination.

Then the thought occurred to him. What if he could transform at will? What if last night had been involuntary, but he could actually change back any time he wanted to with a little focus. That would actually be kind of cool, when he thought about it. He headed into the bathroom yet again.

Staring into the mirror, he tried to remember what it felt like to change. That stretching feeling, the expansion. He tried to picture the muscles and bones and what they must have done, then tried to visualize the whole process in reverse. He willed his face to contract in the way it had expanded, the same way he might will his arm to lift a weight. He gathered all his will, and when his concentration reached its peak... nothing. He still stared into the exact same wolfish face. Sighing, he turned away from the mirror.

So there was no changing back, no stopping time, no reasonable way to find out how this had happened. Now he just needed to think, and he did that best in his studio with a brush in hand. He had at least mastered standing upright and some communication with the outside world. Best to see if he could still do what he loved while he tried to figure out just what he'd do when Carol got home. Henry ducked into the studio and just barely missed slamming his tail in the door. That thing really was going to take some getting used to as he tried to stop it from swishing lazily behind him. He locked the door, tried to turn on some music at low volume, and set up for a new project. The smell of fresh paint and canvas helped clear his mind as he tried to summon up a picture to render.

A few hours later, Henry threw another paintbrush to the ground and knocked another ruined canvas off the easel. He stormed around the studio for a moment as he just couldn't get even the roughest figure to come out right. The fur was too slippery, making the brush slide around in his usual hold, and he just wasn't used to the sensitivity of the pads yet. This was getting worse all the time.

As he felt himself slipping from a borderline tantrum into a moody sulk, Henry heard the door open and the smell of perfume came into the house. Soon after that, he heard her voice echoing through the hall. "Hello! Hey, Monet, you still at it?"

Oh crap. The hits just keep on coming.

He looked to the locked door as the moment of truth came closer with every step he heard. What would he say? How could he hope to explain this to her when he couldn't explain it to himself? There was the knock at the door.

"Hey, hon, cover whatever you're working on and open up. Thought maybe we'd go out tonight if you want to get cleaned up."

"Um..." he called through the door, with no idea of how to start. He'd been so distracted by the inability to paint, he hadn't spent any time working on this moment. "I don't think that's a good idea. I... uh... don't feel so good. And something kind of... happened today."

"Oh," she said, sounding a little concerned, "What happened? Did that author nix your cover? If he did, he's a fucking moron, dear, and you know it."

"No, nothing like that, he actually loved it. It's just... my body... I don't think I can explain it, I just have to show you."

"Oh God, Henry, did you hurt yourself?"

"No," he took a step closer to the door and reached for lock, pausing at the handle. "It's just... something odd... I don't know how you'll react, but..."

"Look, you're not going to live the rest of your life in there, dear. Whatever's going on, just let me take a look. I promise, it'll be fine. Okay?"

"Okay, I'm going to open the door. It's just... try not to scream. Please."

Henry turned the latch and tugged open the door with his paw then stepped back into the studio on full display. Carol's expectant face looked in at him and her eyes went wide, her mouth dropping open. Henry felt his shoulders hunch just a little as she slowly stepped in, her mouth working with no sound emerging. His wife looked him up and down while he stood, waiting for her reaction. With measured steps and her eyes never leaving his frame, Carol walked around him. He even felt her hand brush the fur of his tail as she walked behind, and he tried not to feel the little thrill of pleasure that touch brought him.

"Oh... my... god..." she said quietly as she finished and stepped back around in front of him. Her hands went up to cover her mouth as she looked wide-eyed up and down. Henry cringed a little at what might be coming, wishing he knew how to control the fur trying to stand up on the back of his neck. Carol's hands slipped down to reveal the huge smile on her face. "This came out better than I could have imagined!"

As she rushed forward to run her hands through the fur of his chest and side, Henry just stood there agape. The world seemed to stop spinning. "Wha... Better than... Come again?"

"I've been working on this for months, but I was never sure if it was going to really work. It's a lot sooner than I expected. I thought I'd have to initiate the final process." Her nails quickly brushed through his fur to the skin of his chest. "But you look... incredible!"

Despite the fact that his body wanted to just roll back and bask in the pleasure of her scratching, Henry managed to focus on what he'd just heard. "You... you did this to me, Carol? Seriously?"

"Well, I had some help," Her fingers deftly walked their way down his chest to his belly, making Henry let out an involuntary rumble from deep within his chest. "I suppose I really should come clean about a few things. I didn't want to bring them up, because I never thought you'd believe me."

"I'm feeling pretty receptive right now." Henry said, trying to hold on to some righteous anger while the rubbing and scratching sent waves of pleasure through his body.

"Well, for starters, how much do you know about the occult? I mean, the real occult."

"Until very recently, I thought there was no such thing. So all I really know is stuff from horror movies and novels. And apparently that it's possible for a man to turn into a werewolf."

"Okay, fair enough. Here's the thing, I'm what you might call a 'witch,'" Carol said as she continued to brush her fingers up and down his belly and chest, "and I have been for a long time. Since I was about thirteen really, I've had a natural connection to forces... well, outside of what people think of as normal. I have a small coven that I work with, we help each other look out for our individual interests, keep the craft alive, trade recipes, that kind of thing. It's kind of been the secret of my success."

A day ago, he'd have thought she was joking, but now he couldn't deny the possibility as she so casually admitted to having strange powers that had apparently been used on him. "So you, what, just turned me into a freak on a whim? Was that the plan all along, since we've been together?"

"No, of course not! Look, I had the idea a little while back to kind of take things further with this little fantasy. So I talked to the girls about what I wanted, and we started working on it. Doing research, testing a few things out. There are only a few vague legends of this working at any time in history. We found out there was a potion with some specific herbs and a few incantations, and the best shot was for someone to slowly ingest it over time, for the body to be prepared."

It all clicked for Henry. That pleasant tradition of her bringing him a drink every evening the last few weeks. The dreams he'd been having lately. The way his senses had seemed slightly sharper. Even as her fingers worked wonderfully along his sides, he pushed her hands away and stalked past her, not wanting to look at her now. "So you've been dosing me with this stuff for weeks now, not sure if it would work? And if you came home and found me dead, what then? 'Oh well, guess that didn't pan out!'"

"Oh... no, Henry," Carol said, "you have to believe me, your safety was the first concern! I wouldn't have even tried if it was anything that could actually harm you. We tested the formula out first. Even at incredibly high levels, the worst you'd get is mild skin irritation for a week."

She came up behind him now and reached her fingers up to his ears where they joined his head. As the nails worked there, a part of Henry's brain tried to shut down. His mouth lolled open, and he couldn't stop a little groan from escaping. This was a kind of sensation he'd never truly experienced before that started at the base of ears and made his whole body tingle. Desperate not to give in, he turned now to face her so that she couldn't reach them as easily.

"That doesn't change the fact that you turned me into this thing, without asking, for your own amusement!" Henry said with a glare as more things were clear to him, the words coming out as a growl. "I just can't believe this. I wore those costumes for you and played the part whenever you asked! When you got that thing for me to wear on my dick with that weird knot thing, I felt a little insulted, but you told me it was just for the fantasy, so I did it! But apparently, all that wasn't enough, you had to change who I was entirely!"

"Look, Henry, that's not how it is. I love you, every bit of you," she said as her hands stroked up around his muzzle to his cheeks. "Honestly, you got so into it those nights that I thought this might be a nice surprise."

"A nice...? You thought...? I got into it because it was turning you on! You should have talked to me about all this beforehand!"

Carol put her hands on her hips now. "Would you have ever believed me? About any of it?"

"That..." Henry stopped, almost pointing a claw at her before his paw and face dropped with a sigh. "That's not the point. You still didn't have any right to just do this to me. I have my own life, even if I'm not a mover and shaker in the business world like you. So change me back, do what you have to do."

Carol took a step back and looked chagrined. "Yeah. About that..."

"Carol? You can change me back... right?"

"We... haven't exactly figured out a reversal spell yet."

With a loud groan, Henry tossed his paws up beside his head.

"Look, I didn't expect you to change this soon! We thought we had at least another few months to figure out how to reverse the transformation and do either one at will. The initial potion should have just started preparing your body. You must have had some natural affinity towards this, maybe... I don't know, a latent familial trait?"

Steadying himself on one of the shelves, Henry took a few deep breaths. "Wonderful. Just wonderful. So because you have this werewolf fantasy and happen to dabble in the dark forces without finishing things, I'm stuck looking like... like something out of The Howling."

"It's not all that bad," Carol said with a guilty look on her face, "I mean, the incantation made sure you'd be able to walk upright and to speak. And I made sure that you'd have your normal vision. We just need a little time to figure out a way to get you back and forth."

"Oh if you think there's going to be any 'back and forth' you are sorely mistaken! After this, I don't see how I can even stay..."

She stepped forward and put a hand on the paw that rested on the shelf as she looked up at him. Henry wanted to pull it away, but something made him stop as he saw her eyes shining, almost to tears. Somehow, when she looked up into his eyes, looking genuinely sorry, he still loved her. It was something he just couldn't deny, even in the most insane of situations.

"Please don't say that, Henry," Carol said with a deep breath, "I'm really sorry. I thought... I was so excited at the idea, and I thought that I'd be here to walk you through when you started to transform. I thought by then I'd have a simple antidote and a way to just reverse it at the end of the night. That it would just be something fun for us to play around with on occasion. I'll fix this, Henry, I swear. I love you... more than anything."

Henry sighed and just stood for a moment. Slowly, he reached his other paw up to carefully stroke her hair. "And I love you too. Damn it, I can't help it." He let out another breath and looked at her over his muzzle. "So what about my life now? How am I supposed to go out and do anything? If I have to meet with a client, how am I supposed to do that?"

"Well, to be honest, dear, when was the last time you really wanted to go out? I mean, there's nothing wrong with it, but you do tend to be a homebody anyways. You work with just about all your clients over the phone.. I don't remember you having an in-person meeting for over a year."

"I suppose that's true."

"So clearly, you won't have to adjust too much. I mean, I get it, you'll generally have to stay inside, which isn't ideal. But what we'll do is, we'll watch for opportunities, you know what I mean? If there's a particular convention in town or some reason people will think you're just in a costume. A really good costume. And we could throw a killer Halloween party this year. If it takes that long, of course." She gave him a hopeless little smile. "It's not much, but it's something, right?"

"It's a start I guess." Henry's posture relaxed a little bit, his tail falling from where it had been raised. "Still, it's more about if I wanted to go grab something from the store, or get out of the house, I could when I had to. What do I do now?"

Carol nodded, thinking for a moment. Idly she reached a hand out to stroke the soft fur of his belly again. "Okay, how about this? I'll take a couple days off work to get you set up here. We'll make sure you don't need anything in general, I'll stock the house with food and bring home dinner most nights. I'll give you one of my credit cards for emergencies if you need to order anything online. We'll take care of it."

"That... that could work." Henry felt half lost now. A low rumble emerged from his chest as he unconsciously leaned into her hand. Now that he wasn't fighting it so much, the sensation as her fingers brushed the fur there sent a little tingle of pleasure all through him. "Have to admit, that actually feels pretty nice."

"Well, I never could keep my hands off you." Her fingers dug a little deeper, and Henry responded with a low moan. "And this is just irresistible. Maybe I can show you a benefit or two of your current condition."

"Don't think you're getting off that easy. I'm still very annoy— oh... god..."

Almost falling over, Henry lost his train of thought as Carol's other hand reached up to scratch at his ear while she continued to stroke his belly. Caught off guard, he no longer had much choice to fight it as he let out a strange whimpering little yip of pleasure.

Trying to lean his body into both hands as her well-manicured nails scratched perfectly, Henry found himself in momentary bliss. It was as if she had found some itch he didn't even know he had and supplied just the right remedy.

"See? Not all bad is it?" she mused as she slipped her left hand over the top of his head to work at the other ear. Her right began digging long furrows through the fur of his chest and belly, Henry trying to keep his leg from moving as his tail swayed behind him.

"That's not fair," he muttered as his eyes drifted half-closed.

Carol's fingers worked, slipping occasionally to scratch the top of his muzzle before moving back up his head. His tongue flicked out and licked her wrist affectionately on instinct, loving the feel of her skin there.

"Maybe it's not," she said, "but I do feel like I should find some way to make you happy tonight."

Sighing, she leaned closer into him and rubbed her face into the fur of his rumbling chest. As Carol's hand slipped around his body and her fingers stroked a newly sensitive point where his tail met his back, Henry's eyes closed completely. He drifted on the pleasures of fingers through fur and his arms instinctively slipped around her, holding her against him. In his embrace, Carol moaned loudly and her hands stroked a little faster along his neck and back.

Inhaling deeply, he took in everything about her scent. The perfume, the growing arousal underneath, the basic smell of her. As it awakened old memories and new desires, he felt a stirring in his loins beyond what her continued scratching and rubbing had already caused. An expansion as the new equipment began to slowly push its way out of that little furry nub. As if on cue, Carol's fingers slipped down through the fur of his chest and abs and found the growing sheath, stroking experimentally around the rim as he felt the head beginning to emerge.

She buried her face in the fur of his chest as her fingers worked, inhaling his scent as well from the feel of her warm breath against his skin. With one hand at his side stroking and the other rubbing the sheath around his steadily growing member, Carol began to nuzzle her way down along the center of his belly. As she kissed his navel, a deep rumble built in his chest, sitting there and growing louder while she knelt before him.

"I can't lie... I have dreamed of this..." she muttered as she looked up at him, massaging the base of his shaft as it slipped out in front of her. Looking down, he could see his lupine erection glistening, the familiar sensations of arousal tinged with a freshness he'd not known since adolescence.

Saying nothing, he simply panted in response. It seemed to be all he could do at the moment, and she giggled coquettishly as she leaned forward. With a deep inhale of the strong musk that wafted from his manhood, Carol took her first taste along the underside of the shaft. A tremor ran through his whole body as Henry felt that warm wet stroke along the sensitive skin and heard her moans. It was like the first time he had ever been touched by a woman all over again. Eagerly she lapped at him with long, slow sweeps of her tongue, clearly enjoying the fresh taste and texture of what he had become.

Paws reached to stroke her hair as Henry whimpered and tried to hold himself together. He felt he could lose control at any moment and climax too soon. Then as her lips opened and slipped around the vulnerable skin, humming in pleasure as she suckled, he lost all focus. Every inch was susceptible to the pleasure that had previously been at his head. He felt something pushing out and expanding at the base, different than the build of an orgasm. Before he could look down to see, Carol's lips brushed against that pressure, she moaned loudly, and that was all he could stand.

The climax rocked his entire body, making him push his hips forward at her lips. As his blood pounded in his ears to the beat of the rushing waves, he thought he heard her gag once and tried to pull back. This was greeted with more moans and the smell of her arousal rising in the studio as his seed shot recklessly into her mouth. He hadn't even had a chance to warn her, but from the sounds and the scent, Carol had no complaints.

As the intense waves finally subsided, Henry leaned on the shelf and tried to steady himself. He looked down to see the base of his member swollen just outside that nub of fur and Carol's lips still wrapped around the upper half, her eyes slightly glazed as her hand rubbed between her legs with her skirt hiked up on her hips. She slipped back and leaned onto her feet, eyes closing as she licked her lips and softly stroked herself through dark blue panties.

"Mm... better than I imagined..." she moaned as her fingers worked.

Henry blinked, trying to remember where he was and if he still had feet. "Sorry that... uh... didn't last long. Was a bit intense."

Opening her eyes, Carol righted herself and gave him a sly look. "Oh, I don't think you're completely spent for the night." She stood and ran her fingers along his chest once again. "Follow me, and let's see if we can get you started up again."

Still dazed from the intensity of the climax, Henry followed along as she took his paw and led him back to the bedroom, leaving her shoes behind in the studio. Her other hand was already working frantically at the buttons of her suit coat and her blouse as they walked through the door of the bedroom. Carol stepped to the foot of the bed and began to strip before him as Henry began to come back to himself.

She practically tore the coat away and flung it across the room, followed soon after by the blouse, as if the two were stifling her. Her breasts were framed in the soft, dark blue material that matched her panties and as she reached down to begin removing her skirt, Henry couldn't help reaching out and wrapping his fingers around the supple mounds, squeezing them and rubbing across the erect nipples through the fabric.

"Hm. This might help," he said with a grin as Carol shimmied her hips gently to let the skirt fall to her feet. She moaned at his touch and began to settle herself back on the bed, his paws following her as she did.

He couldn't really kiss her as he wanted to, but leaned in to test a soft lick over her face. When she responded with a pleasant shiver and sighed, he slipped his long tongue over to her ear and let it caress the delicate lobes. Gasping and giggling, Carol reached between her breasts and unhooked the bra, letting it fall back onto the bed as she leaned down into the mattress.

"Please.... Henry.... please, here..." she moaned out as a hand cupped her breast and lifted it towards him.

Letting out a low rumble, Henry obliged, sliding his muzzle down to her chest and letting the tip of his tongue flick the erect nipple before bathing it in long, steady strokes. Carol writhed on the bed, her right hand kneading the breast his tongue was lapping while the other slipped down into the thin band of her panties. Gasping and arching her back, she released her own high pitched whimpers as he moved his tongue to her other nipple and repeated the delicate treatment against the hard nub and the soft flesh.

Hips bucking against her fingers, Carol began trying to slide the underwear down her legs, barely making any progress as the intoxicating scent of her arousal filled the room. Beginning to feel his own stirring again at the touch of her skin, Henry growled lightly through his muzzle, the sounds much more natural in this state, and nuzzled down along her belly. Panting and sweating, Carol's fingernails dug deep into his back and raked through his fur as she threw her head back.

As he reached the thin elastic where her other fingers still fumbled, he gave a husky, "Allow me."

"Oh... oh yes... God, yes!" Carol whimpered as her hands moved to grip the sheets.

His nose rubbed her navel as he slipped down and hooked his long canines under the band. Holding her legs steady with his paws, Henry carefully pulled the panties down her thighs, his fur brushing the sensitive skin as he went and eliciting a high breathy cry from his wife as he worked his way down. Paw pads and claws gently rubbed over her skin, making Carol squirm on the bed even more, her hands balled into fists. He held her ankles steady and carefully pulled the silky fabric from around her feet, only to whip his head and toss the underwear aside.

Gently Henry began to set her feet down at the edge of the bed. His tongue licked at the skin of each shin a few times, finding that somehow her essence seemed to fill his senses there. Carol's thighs spread, and she begged once more as she looked down her body to where he crouched.

"Please," she muttered, the need plain in her eyes as her fingers went automatically to her sex, slowly rubbing the engorged nub there. "Oh please."

Something changed within Henry in that moment to match the change without. The sight of her pleading for release, the rich aroma of her desire, the sounds she made as she hovered at the precipice of her pleasure all made him crouch lower, rumbling and groaning as he sniffed his way towards the welcoming lips of her center. Nuzzling her inner thighs, he let his fur brush over the skin of each one, moving his head from side to side as he steadily homed in on the flower of her sex. He listened and delighted in the sounds she made, each moan and cry like a symphony as he teased closer and closer, tormenting her almost to the point of breaking.

Finally his tongue made its first slow stroke of the puffed lips, tasting her essence with low growl of pleasure as she squealed on the bed. Feeling his arousal grow again, he delved just a little deeper, pushing his long tongue against her nether entrance, letting the pressure build without entering for several strokes. His nose pressed against her with each lick, bathing in the scent of her as her hips began to buck. When he could resist no longer, his tongue slipped into the deep channel of her sensitive passage, tasting even more of her fluids as their flow increased. He could tell she was close now as his paws gripped her hips and ran up and down the sides of her buttocks with the rough pads and soft fur mingling. Deep within her, his lapped and flicked at every surface as little growls and moans of pleasure escaped him. Her fingers brushed his nose as they rubbed the small button of her bliss, and Henry pushed forward, letting the back of his tongue rub against that nub as his teeth just barely grazed her skin.

Carol exploded in that moment. The tangy, musky fluids gushed over his tongue as she rode to the heights of pleasure, crying out and panting as her legs slipped under his arms and wrapped around his back. His tail wagged and batted at her toes, only seeming to fuel her pleasure all the more. Her heels pulled at him as his tongue continued to explore her depths and he felt a new full erection at his groin, her attentions spurring his own desires in the midst of her climax.

Henry's paws squeezed her rump as they pressed into each other, listening to the heaving, shallow breaths as the multiple jolts of her fist orgasm began to subside into low aftershocks. His tongue began to leave her, his muzzle slipping away from her hot, wet cleft. Slowly he began to stand as her legs allowed him some movement, panting in his own need now. The swelling feeling at the base of his shaft had returned and he looked to see an odd swollen ball of pink flesh behind the hard, dripping shaft pointing towards her.

Still panting in the aftershocks, Carol's eyes fluttered open and looked at Henry. At the sight of his arousal, she frantically turned herself over so that she was bending over the bed, raising her hips up before him.

"Knot me, Henry! Oh please god knot me now!"

He needed little encouragement as he took one stride forward and gripped her hips once more. With a quick smooth thrust of his own hips, he plunged into the heat of her center, releasing something between a growl and a howl as her warmth surrounded him. He pumped into her with a steadily quickening rhythm, rocking Carol against the bed as he felt and smelled her rising once more towards a peak of bliss. Just below his gut, he could feel something roiling and bubbling up as well. It would not be as quick as before, the climax was building slowly now as he rutted faster and harder, letting this animal nature take over almost completely.

With every hard push, Carol squealed with delight, barely bracing herself against the passion of his movements. Henry grunted, growled, and panted as he drew closer and closer, now teasing her with that bulbous knot at the base of his member. She was panting in eager anticipation, once again at the very edge of the most intense delight. Feeling that roiling climax almost ready within himself, Henry pulled back once and slammed forward, spreading her lips wider to accept what she had begged for.

He felt her once again pushed over that edge as her fantasy was truly satisfied, his wife giving another high-pitched cry that slipped into a low moan. Her sex squeezed tight around the amazingly sensitive flesh of the knot in the throes of her second orgasm, milking him and forcing Henry to try and hold himself back to savor the moment. As her own orgasm began to taper down, he released his and pulsed deep into her. Squeezing her rump and yipping with every little spurt, it was a few moments of utter bliss at the culmination of their coitus.

When the pleasure and the flow finally began to subside for him, he realized she was in the grip of a third climax as they remained tied together. His panting slowed as he tried to remain standing, letting her slip slowly back down from her pleasure. Sweat beaded all over her skin as she began catch her breath, and Carol simply gave little trembles after a few moments.

"That was... amazing..." she muttered as she smiled over her shoulder to where Henry was still stuck within her.

"Uh-huh," Henry managed, tugging gently and making her squirm as he waited for his erection to shrink back down, "Though, um... we seem to have a complication."

Carol chuckled, "It's okay. Just follow my lead."

Twisting a bit and taking their movements slow, they wound up laying on their sides in the bed, his arm draped over her. The feel of her snuggled against him made his tail gently thump the bed as he began to feel the knot finally diminishing.

"So," he murmured against her ear, "We really going to live like this from now on?"

"I can think of worse things," Carol patted his paw and pulled his arm against her body as he softly slipped out of her. "I know the situation's not ideal, dear. And that's my fault and I'm going to try and fix it. I swear. But until then, we'll make the most of it and I'll do whatever I can for you. I love you."

"Love you too," he said as he felt himself beginning to doze. "This could all work out."

Stepping back from the canvas, Henry admired the image, looking between the mirror and the painting and opening his jaws just a little to check the look of the character. His tail swayed back and forth behind him, and he dipped the brush into his palette to add a few details to the werewolf.

The first couple weeks, he'd had to somewhat relearn how to hold the brush for the best results. But after five months, he was finding that in some cases the paw pads gave him better control than his fingers had previously if he held them just right. The studio had been adjusted so that his tail wouldn't knock things off of shelves as he had during those early days, and a few other odds and ends to account for his height and the way he had to hold himself. Now he was finding he was just as productive as ever, and if he needed anything to help that, Carol always took care of it immediately. Life in the new body was going all right.

Initially there had been some tension between Henry and his wife. When he thought a few times that he might not be able to paint again, he had been bitter about the change and how she'd tricked him. Of course, he couldn't safely leave on his own, so he was somewhat stuck with her. There were definitely times, no matter her protestations of love, that he wondered if he'd been reduced to just a pet. After the first night, they hadn't been intimate again and it had taken a day when he finally produced a decent canvas with the paws for him to let Carol back in and enjoy some affection between the two of them. After that evening, Henry had started to live his life again, at least on some level.

Socially, things hadn't been as bad as he'd expected. When the odd convention was in town, he and Carol would go and get out of the house for a bit. A pair of tattered shorts was all it really took and everyone wanted to get pictures of his "costume" or "suit" as the case may be. And of course, as promised, Halloween had been a blast. They'd thrown their first house party in months and everyone had asked him how he'd made such a life-like outfit. Greeting the few kids that came to the door to trick-or-treat was actually a lot of fun.

With a final few brushstrokes, Henry felt more than satisfied with the art for the gothic horror novel. Especially with plenty of time to work on it, since it was for an author for whom Ryan had recommended Henry since the earliest concept stage. The preliminary sketches had been met with a great deal of enthusiasm, and the writer in question now wanted Henry to do the covers for all his upcoming books.

The loose smock had caught most of the paint splatter, but Henry was still going to have to shower now that he was done for the day. He slipped it off and hung it on the back of the door just as he heard Carol coming into the house. She no longer brought him a drink every day, but her coming into the studio was still one of the best parts of the evening.

As the door opened, he saw her smile and refrained from bounding up to her and hugging her. He had what she'd come to call "painter's paws", and she wouldn't want her work clothes ruined. So he settled for leaning out as she came in and getting a kiss on the nose while he returned a little lick to her chin.

"Mmm, hey hon." Henry leaned back and playfully gestured between the painting and his own lupine face. "Well, what do you think? Huh?"

Smirking, Carol rolled her eyes. "Yeah, good likeness. You're Rembrandt with fur."

"Well, I do have the best model since Pickman."

"Pickman?"

"Sorry, I forget you never read Lovecraft."

"No, not really my style, dear," Carol said as she actually took in the painting, "It is really nice work, I have to admit. I like the

background too, though I think a few of your trees could use just a little more detail, even if they are shadowed."

"Thanks, I'll have to keep that in mind and come back to it tomorrow. Just have to get it shipped off next week. I have a little time to make sure everything looks the way I want it to though."

"That's good to hear." Carol paused, her face falling just a bit. She reached into her purse and looked at him. "Look, Henry... I have something for you."

His ears came up a little as they often did now when he was listening. "Oh? What is it?"

"Something I've been working on the past few months. With the coven." She pulled a decorated vial out of her purse containing a clear liquid with what looked like flecks of glitter. "I know... I know you weren't originally happy with how this change happened. And even after that first night, I started trying to figure this out. It really wasn't right, the way I did this to you. So we made this after a lot of research. If you drink it, it'll turn you back into your old self."

Henry wasn't sure what to say as she put the vial into his paw. He'd adjusted well to his new body in the last few months and felt like it was part of him now. Yet the allure of being able to take care of his own business, to go out to eat, all those little things he'd taken for granted before were a draw.

"But there is a catch to this," she said with hand on his chest, "If you take this right now, it's a one-way ticket. I'll never be able to turn you back into this body again. The shock to your system the way it's made could very well kill you if I tried. But this is safe and if you really want to, you can change back now. Otherwise, it could take a year or two for us to come up with a way to get you to go back and forth. It's proving a lot more complex than we thought. I'm sorry."

She leaned up to him now, heedless of the paint on his fur. Rubbing her cheek against the side of his muzzle, she kissed the corner of his jaws. "I really enjoy you being like this, but I wanted you to have the choice. Just remember, I'll love you no matter what you look like."

As Carol stepped back and looked at him, waiting, Henry wrestled with himself. He had really enjoyed the times they'd had together the last few months. The new sensations, the strength he felt, the raw increase in their lust for each other; all were wonderful. Yet there were all the other things he missed, such as a walk in the park and being able to go outside in general. But if he could be happy, and they could be happy together, wasn't it worth the sacrifice?

He stood for several moments just thinking, going back and forth over whether or not to turn himself back. Several times he told himself to just bolt the new potion and not look back. Other times he thought it would be better to smash the bottle on the ground in a dramatic gesture and pull her into his furry arms and tell her how much he loved her and would stay this way for her. But melodrama wasn't his style and wouldn't be practical. Finally Henry took a step forward and put an arm around his wife.

"Here's what we're going to do. I'm going to go put this in the fire safe. We're going to keep it if there's ever an emergency, if I need to take you to the hospital or something like that. And someday I may decide to take it anyway, and you should be ready for that." He paused and smiled as best he could at her. "But for now, you keep working on that other version of the potion or the glamour thing. I'm happy, we're happy, and for the moment, that's enough."

Sighing, Carol leaned up and kissed the tip of his muzzle. "Have I mentioned just how much I love you?"

"Love you too," he said with a squeeze. They looked into each other's eyes, and with a playful little growl, Henry picked up his wife and carried her to the bedroom.

A Mile In Their Paws

Richard Coombs

I suppose I should start this off with a fairly simple greeting. Hello, whoever you are. My name is Heelo Cartix. This is the story of my journey.

My journey requires a small preface. After all, I think it would be very bad form to just throw you into the thick of my experiences without some form of context. As a self-trained wizard, I have learned the importance of providing context to some, if not all of my writings. As such, I shall begin my tale about a day before the rather amazing event happened.

It was a dark afternoon. It had been raining, and the wind was whistling outside my little window. As such, I was forced to surround myself with candles as I poured over notes from old bastards far more experienced than I. I refuse to say they were smarter than me, as they had gone through this exact same sort of experimentation during their younger days. Probably their older days as well, but I really didn't care. If I could just piece all of this together, I wouldn't have to worry about losing my youth at all. I would be forever immortal in the eyes of the entire world.

I wasn't getting old, by any stretch of the imagination. In fact, during the time of my research, I was only twenty summers, and quite proud to be a pinnacle of good looks in a field that was populated by the decrepit, the warped, and the ill-favored. I pushed a few brown locks from my eyes and turned the page of an old tome, being as careful as I could. The entire book felt as though it would turn to dust if I looked at it the wrong way.

I had been studying magic for three years when I began to study animals vigorously. Not for companionship, of course. I hated animals, unless they were sitting dead on a plate in front of me. It was their abilities I was interested in; their hearing, their vision, their ability to sift through scents. The lizard's camouflage, the wings of an eagle, the gills of a fish—the possibilities were endless! Thus, I had made it a goal to look over every text I could find on the subject of the natural world, be they written by those skilled in the magical arts or not.

And that's where I was at that moment, pouring over texts of varying ages and complexities. The candles were a very poor source of light for this, but it was enough for me to at least see what I was doing. Flame made me nervous around so much parchment, but it was a risk that I was willing to take in the name of progression. Every word I read, every fact I stored within my mind was just another small step towards success. That was the only thing keeping me from collapsing in my exhaustion. Perhaps I was too wrapped up in my work now and then, but wasn't that true for everyone?

Anyways, I had been hard at work for a long time. My studies on the old Druidic practices had provided me with what I believed to be the final breakthrough. The book talked about needing a part of an animal, but it was not specific. I assumed that any part would do. Paired with all my other research, I believed I had finally found a recipe for a concoction that would give me the desired effect. The rest of the ingredients were fairly common, things that I could easily procure on my own around my hovel. I was busy congratulating myself on a job well done when I heard something skirting across the floor. I looked down and saw the cat that I allowed to live in my house, and his food dish, which he had pushed across the floor, to my feet. I crossed my arms, wondering why I even bothered keeping this stupid feline around when all it did was eat and sleep.

"I've already fed you," I stated, glaring at him. "Go elsewhere for your meal. Chase some mice or something."

Its tail swished from side to side, and he kept looking up at me with that disturbing, blank look that every cat had. I hated it when he looked at me like that. I grabbed one of the candles and threw it at the animal.

"Away with you!" I snarled. "Go and find your own meal, and don't disturb me again!"

I had missed him, and he turned tail as soon as I had raised my hand. He dashed to the far side of my hovel, letting out a hiss and hopping up onto the windowsill, where he would lay and just look about. I was half tempted to throw a second candle at the animal, but I thought better of it and just decided to finish up my research for the night. I took up my quill and began to write out a complicated sequence of symbols, measurements, ingredients, and other such items that I won't bore you with. This tale is not meant as a cure for insomnia, and going into the specifics behind my craft would only bore you poor, simple folk.

When I finished, I leaned back, casting my tired eyes over what I had written. Then my view broadened to my research as a whole. I felt quite elated, but in my elation a conundrum emerged. An animal. I needed an animal, a part of one, for me to get the spell to work, and a full moon to work by. The moon was no problem: that would be tomorrow night. But the animal? That might be a bit more of a problem. I looked at the cat, who had decided to amuse itself by grooming its privates, and I just grunted and looked away.

No, I would not use that stupid cat. I wanted a true animal. I wanted something cunning, intelligent, fast. I considered the selection of fauna I knew was around this area. I didn't want anything that was too difficult to catch, nor did I want something that was already domesticated, their natural gifts dulled by a life of leisure provided by other humans. I postulated on each of my options in turn, weighing their merits, how easy it would be to acquire a 'part' of them, how dangerous they were, and so forth. At last, I decided to settle on a fox. Yes, that would be the perfect creature for the first experiment I was planning. They were relatively common around my home, and they kept stumbling into the traps that I used to catch rabbits and other creatures foolish enough to walk right into a pair of large, metal jaws.

I finally let myself rest after that, getting up and dragging my tired body to the well-worn cot that served as my bed, flopping down on it and letting out a sigh. I felt something jump down against my back, and a few claws gently poking into my flesh. I tensed and sat up, looking over my shoulder. The cat had launched himself down from the windowsill, all the way to my back. I glared at him and reached behind me, batting at him, rather hard. He hissed and jumped away from my hand, retreating again.

"Damn beast," I cursed again, laying my head down and closing my eyes. As I felt the haze of sleep rolling over me, I thought about getting rid of the animal. But as he was the only bit of companionship I had, little as it was, and I wasn't prepared to become a full-fledged hermit just yet.

I let sleep take me, my mind wandering in every direction, away from my plights and my triumphs, and towards the morning, where I would gather the last of what I needed. Soon, nature's secrets would be secrets no longer.

The following day I was up with the sun, dressed as casually as was possible, in a simple white tunic with dark green pants. I had taken the time to pack a small sack of minor items that may have proven useful in a pinch. After all, better safe than sorry. I had also taken the precaution of outfitting myself with a small dagger. I was no great fighter, but I always felt better having something close to defend myself with.

Not that there was any real danger out here. These woods were about as domesticated as they could be without just being another town. The worst that one would find out here was the occasional bear, or for the really unlucky, a lone, desperate bandit. Today was not one of those days, though. I went deep down into the woods where I had left several traps, hoping to catch a bit of meat for my pot. Today, though, I wasn't so much interested in meat as I was in fur, a paw, a claw, an eye, something that a fox—or baring that, any animal—could give me.

The first few traps were fruitless. One was still set and nothing had wandered into it, and two others had been triggered, but the catch was gone, along with the bait. I was starting to get a little disheartened, as I only had a few other traps to check. Even if there was something in there, there was little chance that it would be the specific animal I was looking for. If I failed that day, it would be another whole month before I could attempt my spell. The full moon was tonight, and only tonight. I didn't want to have to wait a month; I wanted to try out my spell right away.

Impatience aside, it was hot, and I did not react well to temperatures outside of my comfort zone, which at best was room temperature. Thus, I was irritated. I don't know why I bother to include such facts. Perhaps by doing so you won't find me such a monster when I detail what happened next.

My fourth trap was also empty, save for a few tufts of rabbit fur that I didn't even bother to gather. Now, with only one trap left, I started to lose hope. Then I heard whimpering. At first I was just thinking it was my mind making up things, but as I drew nearer to the final trap, I realized that whatever was making that sound was not in my head, but was an actual creature. I was elated. It wasn't another rabbit, that much was for sure. Now I just had to pray I hadn't trapped a dog, or another stupid farm animal that had thought it was a good idea to cut from the herd and head out into the forest for new grazing lands.

It was not.

As I pushed my way through the undergrowth to the tiny clearing where I'd set my last trap, I saw not one, but two foxes. One had a back leg caught in the trap, and looked as though it had tried to jerk its paw free by force, as the metal jaws had worn a deep gash into its leg. The other fox was pacing about the trap, observing it, looking for a way to get the trapped one out. It wasn't about to happen, though. I took a step into the clearing grinning, and they both noticed me. Of course, I wasn't really making an effort at being subtle. The trapped one panicked and redoubled its efforts in trying to get free. The other laid its ears back against its head and let out a threatening growl at me, baring its fangs. I raised a brow as I realized that I was dealing with a pair of mated foxes.

I approached slowly, keeping my eye on the free fox. Last thing I needed was to be bitten by a potentially diseased canid. I circled around, trying to get closer to the trapped fox, but its mate circled with me, always staying between the trap and me. I had little time to play such games, so in an effort to scare off the beast, I drew out my dagger and brandished it, giving it a few swings, hoping to intimidate the little beast. It was not impressed. In fact, I think that my action might have had the opposite effect, as its fur began to prickle, and the growls got even louder, and far more threatening. For such a small creature, it was trying its best to look big and tough.

But I needed to get a part of them. I had to have a piece of the fox for the spell, and I had to have it by that night. I threw caution to the wind and began to walk towards them, every step full of determination and fearlessness. The fox still refused to move. I was barely a step away now and I tensed as the fox let out a little bark. The one in the trap was still writhing and whimpering and yipping, very loud now. I ignored it and focused on the little bastard who stood between me and my trap.

I closed the gap and gave a little kick forward. It wasn't a very hard kick, but hard enough to let it know that I was bigger, and stronger than him. The toe of my boot connected with the side of its head and it yelped, but the impact didn't make it run, as I had anticipated. Instead, it took a moment to shake its head and then lunged forward. I tried to move out of the way, but it caught me on the leg and it bit down, hard. I cried out as I felt its teeth sink down past the soft fabric of my pants, down into my flesh. I glared down at it and twisted my body around, shaking my leg back and forth, trying to get the little red rat off of my leg. It only clamped down harder, and I could feel the warm trickle of my own blood dripping down my leg, the liquid of life seeping into my pants, staining the dark green with crimson.

I shook harder, and after I realized that it was doing nothing but encouraging him to mutilate my poor leg further, I stopped and reached down, grabbing him by the tail and yanking hard. I think I had found a rather sensitive area, because it let out a loud yowl and released my leg. But I didn't release its tail. I pulled it up, holding it at arm's length and level with my face. It was enraged now.

I was as well, as the pain trobbed in my leg. My other hand clenched around the dagger that I had drawn. I'd made sure to sharpen the blade to hair-splitting fineness, to the point where it could probably sever a finger at the joint with a single quick cut. At this time, it wasn't a finger I wanted to cut. Quick as a flash, I brought the knife up, pressed it against the base of the creature's tail, and I began to saw into it, ignoring the squirming and shrieking the fox gave in protest. I just kept cutting deeper and deeper into the fox's tail until at last, it came loose and the poor beast dropped to the ground, still shrieking, and I held its tail in my hand.

I smirked and gave the bloodied fox another kick, this one in its side, and it finally began to retreat, hobbling off. I let it, my rage subsiding, satisfied that I had taught the animal a good lesson about who was superior. I sheathed my bloodied blade and examined the limp tail in my hand. It would seem that I had what I came for, albeit I hadn't planned on taking so much at once. I turned back to the trap, intent on letting the other fox go, provided it wasn't as feral a creature as its mate, but discovered to my bewilderment, that all its thrashing had worked. A trail of blood led from the trap out into the underbrush. Bits of fur, and even a claw from the fox's back paw had been torn from its body. With my prize in tow, I left the bloodied trap and began to head back to my home. I was quite thankful to whatever deity had given me exactly what I needed at the moment. I was also about to learn that the cosmos has a damn annoying sense of humor.

At this point, I must confess that I felt no guilt for the act I had just committed. The fox was nothing more than a means to an end, and at the time, if I had needed something more than just its tail, I would have no qualms with eviscerating it and taking what I needed from its carcass.

But I digress. The sun had finally set, and the moon was shining bright above me. I had gathered the necessary ingredients and had prepared a clean space outside of my home, around back, to make the potion. I ground each of the herbs I needed to a fine mush, dumping each of them one at a time into the small cooking pot that hung above a small fire pit I had dug for this express purpose. The evergreen branches I had thrown onto the fire were raising a huge cloud of smoke, but that was what I wanted. Every action that I took was something that I was sure would result in the spell, the potion that I wanted.

Bit by bit, piece by piece, a little bit of everything was sacrificed. The herbs and evergreens to signify power over nature. A few drops of my blood as a signifier of my life. The fox's tail as an offering. Finally, I just needed to mix it all together and concentrate upon what I wanted from this potion. I stirred the pot, slow and steady, one hand holding the spoon and the other hovering over the bubbling pot, concentrating, letting my energy flow, pouring my power down into the pot, and chanting in a long-dead language.

The pot gave a small rumble and began to pulse with a soft, incandescent glow. I continued to chant and stir, but soon the liquid seemed to be hardening, as it became harder to churn it. The glow became brighter, and a breeze began to force the smoke to disperse. Then, when I could no longer stir, I removed the spoon and tossed it to the side. It was ready. I grinned down at what I had created and watched as it bubbled and began to shrink. The contents were soon nothing more than a soft, malleable blob. It hissed, and steam rose off of it. I lifted the pot from the fire and set it down on the ground, letting it cool. I began to throw some dirt over the fire, letting it fizzle out until nothing remained of it save for a few embers, straining to keep themselves alive as their brethren died around them.

Now, with the pot cooled and the fire out, I reached into the pot and gripped the small, green substance that I had created. It was soft in my hands, still warm from the fire, and it slipped and stretched as I lifted it out, something that was halfway between a liquid and a solid. I rolled it about in my hands a bit, pushing against it, compacting it, until I had a small ball about the size of one of my hands. Then, I raised it to my mouth and began to eat it. The taste was horrific, much like plucking ordinary grass from the ground and shoving it down your throat. Not just grass, but dry grass. Dry grass from a cow pasture. I felt myself reflexively gag, but I forced the bile back down and continued to eat it, taking as large a bite out of it as I could each time. I don't think I even took that much time to chew the little globules that I was gulping down. Almost as soon as they were in my mouth, they were down my throat.

And then it was gone. I licked the last of it from my hand and took a few deep breaths. Nothing was happening. I grew a tad concerned. Usually, these sorts of spells took effect almost instantaneously after the last of the mixture had been consumed. Had I miscalculated? Were the texts inaccurate? Worse, was I going to have to wait another whole month just to try again? The prospect was disheartening, to say the least. At the moment, I was more concerned, though, with the potential side effects that the botched spell could have on me.

I was about to find out. My stomach gurgled and I felt a terrible pang surge through my abdomen and up my chest. My heart clenched, and felt as though it were trying to force it's way out past my ribs. I clutched at it, gritting my teeth. My vision tripped between focused and blurred. My head swam as another jolt of pain began to swirl around my insides, this time spreading further along my body, up through my chest to my limbs, my neck, all along my back and sides. If I had been in any sort of state to compare it to anything, I would have said that it was probably what a tree felt as it was eaten away from the inside out by all the insects that called it home.

I crumpled to the ground, panting harder, still squeezing my hand over my heart. At this point I was panicked, convinced that I had inadvertently gotten myself poisoned by my bravado. That, of course, was not the case; otherwise I wouldn't be here, telling you this story now. But at the time, I really did feel like I was dying.

My vision blurred completely and as the sensation of pain overtook every nerve of my body, I felt consciousness slipping away from me and every breath became labored. I tried to cry out, tried to call for help, tried to get the attention of someone, anyone. Even if I had managed to force the scream trapped at the bottom of my throat out into the world, there was no one around who could have heard it. The nearest village was a mile away and those superstitious xenophobes wouldn't have done a thing to help a magic user.

So I lay there, gasping out what I thought was my last, and I resigned myself to my fate. I stopped the fighting and the struggling, rolling myself up onto my back so that I could observe the stars as the last of my life was forced from my body. In one final act of defiance, to show how upset I was with the whole situation (to put it mildly) I raised my hand up and made a nice, rude gesture to the entirety of the cosmos.

I was very gratified to see that I was still alive. My feeling of touch was the first thing to return to me. Smell and taste came next. Then I could hear again. Sight returned not long after. As sight returned, I realized that there was light outside of my eyelids. I opened them, instantly regretting it as I realized I was staring straight up at what I could only surmise was the noon sun. I rolled over, onto my stomach and let my eyes open, bit by bit, now that they weren't in danger of being assaulted by the cruel rays of nature's gaze.

Just from that alone, I had gathered that I had been asleep the entire night, and had probably missed most of the morning as well. My body felt stiff and sore, and I had no appetite to speak of, but other than that, everything felt as though it was working fine. But my clothes felt very uncomfortable, for some reason. I forced myself to sit and groaned. Not only did my clothes feel very uncomfortable, almost like they were constricting me, but my shoes felt strangely loose as well. I frowned and looked down, wiggling my feet a bit. My shoes flopped from side to side, almost like my feet weren't there at all. My eyes widened and I reached down, grabbing for my shoes, but stopped when I saw my hands. Only, they weren't my hands. They looked kind of like my hands. Only they were covered in red fur, with claws. I turned them over and the other side, my palm, was covered with white fur. It was like the pattern of...

No, I thought I must have been delusional. I raised these strange hands to my eyes and began to rub, telling myself that after I took them away, everything would be just fine again. I counted to three, stopped rubbing, and pulled them away. When I opened my eyes again, I felt my blood running cold. They were exactly the same.

My pulse quickened and I pulled off the shoes, revealing that my feet had also been altered. They were now more like paws than feet. I ran my hand up my leg and actually found the entire makeup of my lower body to be different. I had haunches, for one thing, and I could feel a coat of fur brushing up against the legs of my pants. As I shifted, I found that something near my backside was pressing against the pants as well. Fearful for what I might find, I reached around myself, pleading to no one in particular to not let what I was feeling be what I thought it was. I reached down below my waistline and gripped at what was there.

It was a tail.

I let out a loud howl. Not a yell, but a howl. I ran back towards my house, leaving everything else behind, tripping over my own feet numerous times as I struggled to get used to the balance of my new form of locomotion. After discovering that bending forward helped

53

lend a tad more balance to my paws, I scrambled inside, pushing aside stacks of books, papers, a cauldron, and a chair as I made for the mirror. I slowed as I approached it, afraid of what I was going to see. With ever increasing nervousness, I forced myself in front of it. What I saw there wasn't my usual wonderful features. Instead, I had a bright red fuzzy face, with a slightly long nose, very canine in look, with puffs that pushed out from each cheek. My mouth was now stretched into a long, thin line, inside which was a set of very sharp looking fangs. My eyes, which had used to be a deep brown before, were now a gentle gold. My ears had moved to the top of my head and stood straight up, now just two cute triangles. Well, I would have called them "cute" on someone else. Right now, they just terrified me.

"What's happened?!" I shouted at myself. "What went wrong? I'm a... a damn fox!" I looked down at myself, pulling my tunic open at the neck, peering down. As I had thought, the rest of my body was also covered in a thick coat of fur, most of it red, with my stomach a bright, puffy white. I tore my tunic off, both to get a better look at what had happened, and also because the fabric rubbed unpleasantly against my new coat. Tossing it to the side, I observed my body. My build was roughly the same that it had been before the transformation, save for the obvious. You know, the paws, the ears, the head, the claws, and so forth. I wrung my hands together, trying to order my thoughts. "Alright," I said to myself, "Get a hold of yourself, Heelo. All I have to do is get together all the spell reagents again and mix it in reverse order and that will be that!"

"Oh, I don't think that'll work," came a voice from behind me. I whirled around, flicking my head back and forth. Out of some sort of strange, innate instinct, I laid my ears back and felt my lips peel up into a small snarl. But I saw no one there. No one but the stupid cat, sitting upon my cot, grooming its paw.

"Who's there?" I asked. "What do you mean that won't work? Whoever you are, what do you know about magic?"

"Apparently, more than you," the voice taunted.

I looked around, but still saw no one. "Who are you to insult me in my own home?"

"It's my home too, fool."

I blinked. My eyes slowly edged down until I was looking right at the cat, who was now just looking at me. "You?"

"It appears you aren't as dense as I thought. And for all these years, I thought you were both dense and cruel. Turns out I was only half right." The cat's mouth never moved, and yet somehow I could hear a voice emanating from it, as though ever little movement that it was making was somehow forming a word all its own.

I growled at it, once again more out of some new instinct rather than meaning to. "You!" I shouted, pointing an accusing finger at it. "You did this to me! What did you do to my spell?"

"I didn't do a thing, fool," it said again, purring in a way that made it sound like it was laughing at me. "Don't you see that you got exactly what you wanted?"

"What I wanted?" I asked, my fur bristling in my agitations. "I wanted to gain the senses, the powers of the animals. I wanted to unlock nature's secrets! I didn't want to become a filthy animal myself!"

The cat gave another purring laugh. "Poor, stupid human," it said, its tone one of mock lamentation. "For all your study, for all the pooling you did over those musty, old tomes and that acrid paper, and all the notes that you took, you really didn't think of the one primary matter involved in alteration." It paused so that it could lick its paws again. "You cannot gain anything unless you give something away. You wanted something we animals have? You wanted something the foxes have? The only way you're going to get it is by giving up a piece of your humanity."

"How was I supposed to know this would happen?" I shouted. "Nothing in the texts said anything about this!"

"It's called common sense," the cat said. "Quite sad how you humans always pride yourselves on your advanced intelligence, your bipedal movement, and your damn opposable thumbs and yet you have no concept of the obvious. You had to unlock a part of the animal within you if you wanted what an animal had. If you ask me, you deserve what you get for what you did to that poor fox." It looked at me again, and this time its eyes looked far less than blank to me. Now, they held the unmistakable tinge of accusation, of judgment. This stupid animal had the audacity to look at me as if this was my fault! I was shaking now, and I could feel my tail standing up in the back of my pants. The cat was giving me what I could only describe as a sneer.

"I have eyes. I have ears. I see everything that you do in and around this shack. I stick by what I said. You've only let what was on the inside, out. Congratulations, you monster."

I wanted to tear the creature apart. Why I didn't, I don't know. I would certainly have felt justified in doing so. I had enough frustration to work out. But no, I just stood there, shaking in rage and fear. But I let myself calm down. I had to think. I had to plan. Regardless of what that stupid cat said, something must have gone wrong. All I could do was try to reverse the spell.

"All I have to do is get together all the reagents," I assured myself. "Then I just cast the spell again and it will be alright." I made for the door.

"Wait!" the cat shouted at me.

I stopped, the sudden halt causing me to lose my balance. I fell forward, becoming intimate with the dusty ground. I growled and rolled over, sitting up. "What?" I snapped. "Want to taunt me some more? Care to place more blame on me?"

"No, this is far more important than that," the cat said. It hopped down to the ground and pushed its bowl towards me. "You haven't fed me yet today."

The sun had started its descent by the time I had gathered everything again, save for the part of the animal that I needed. With everything stored at my home, and a well-fed cat sleeping on my cot—I had found that he was much quieter when he was full—I

set out for the final item that I needed. Rounding the traps yielded nothing. When I came to the trap that had held the foxes before, I looked over the bloodstains, and the trail left behind. I suppose I could have tried following it, but there was no guarantee that the trail would lead me to them, or that it would hold up until I could find their den.

Then, something amazing happened. For the first time I tried sniffing the air. I don't know why I hadn't thought of this before.

Probably because I was still thinking as a human. Probably because the excitement and terror of what happened that had made me forget about the whole reason I had started this fiasco. The senses. The powers that animals possessed. I breathed deep and I finally noticed the world around me. I noticed things that I never had before. Thousands of different odors filled my mind. Some were very familiar, others so foreign I had no idea where they could have come from. I tried concentrating on one at a time, sifting through each smell, letting myself gain familiarity with every single one of them.

When I started to recognize a few of them, and could sift through them easily, I bent before the trap and slid a finger down over the bloodstains. The feeling made me tingle and I shifted my weight from foot to foot. My feet, or rather my paws, felt so sensitive, so well balanced, that I felt I could never fall again. At least, that was what I felt at the time. I'd tried putting back on my shoes earlier, but they were too loose on my new paws to bother trying to wear them. I lifted the blood to my nose and got a good whiff of it. The smell was strange, a mix between sea salt and pine needles. I took another sniff, followed by a third, letting the smell engrain itself into my consciousness.

When I had it memorized, I bent down and began sniffing around the ground, sifting through all the different scents until I found the exact match to the scent of their blood. It was a little muffled, having had a full day to just lay there and permeate, but enough remained for me to follow it.

I found that I was just as easily able to balance on all four of my limbs as my two feet. The palms of my hand felt just as sensitive and attuned to where I was stepping as my paws did. As I kept my nose to the ground, following the acrid scent of fox blood, I felt my ears flicking from one direction to another, unconsciously, listening for anything that could be a threat. I apologize for my rather simple descriptions here, but it is so difficult to encapsulate in words what this was like, to feel like I had peeled back a whole layer of the world and revealed everything that was hidden underneath.

So I kept on. The further on I got, the more the scent mixed with others that the foxes emitted. Their fur, their breath, their... ahem, musks. I memorized them all and just kept following the trail. It twisted and worked its way in a convoluted path, over a small stream and through a few bramble bushes that I was forced to go around, for the sake of my hide. The trail I followed also started to mingle with the remains of other trails they had walked. I must have been close to the heart of their territory. It became harder to sift through to the freshest trail.

I lifted my head to sniff up in the air, hoping to catch a whiff of them on the breeze. As I did so, I noticed for the first time that the sun was much lower than I had thought. Yet my eyes hadn't been affected. I glanced around a few times and discovered that, even with the rapidly dimming sunlight, I could still see just as well as if the sun were up at its highest point.

Then I smelt it. I had finally found them. There was no mistaking it; the scent was far too prevalent and fresh. I made my way down a small hill, and into a little cluster of trees. Their den was close. I began to shift from one tree to another, finally coming to one that had partially been uprooted, most likely from some old storm when it had been younger. I peered down under its roots, squinting, trying to make use of this new form of night vision I had been gifted with.

It was lucky that I had done so. Otherwise I probably would have been given quite a nasty bite on my nose. I jerked my head back, just as one of the foxes lunged from their hiding place, snapping at me with a snarl, and surprising ferocity for a creature so small. I suppose when someone comes invading your home, you feel a great need to defend it. I backed away, rubbing my nose, just in case it had grazed me. It hadn't, so I decided to try my own bit of intimidation. I raised my lips up into a small snarl of my own and laid my ears back, getting down on my haunches and raising my fur up, trying to make myself look bigger. Well, I was already bigger than them, so that didn't really matter. Maybe more imposing would be the better term to use.

Anyway, my point is, I wanted to scare the little thing. Then, much like the cat, it started to speak. Or should I say she? The voice was unmistakably female. "Go away, monster!" she barked.

I was caught off guard, having forgotten for a moment that I could understand them. I shook my head and resumed my snarl. "I'm not a monster," I said. "But if you don't do as I ask, then I'm going to get very nasty."

"No!" she hissed defiantly. "You will take nothing more from us!"

I blinked. "Nothing... more?"

"Don't play stupid," she said, still standing in front of the entrance to her den. "You may look different, but I know for a fact that you are the one who hurt my mate! You took his tail, you mangy creature!"

I tensed, feeling something heavy resting upon my heart. But why? And what was I feeling? Was it guilt? Could I actually be feeling guilty about what I had done? Oh, I had surely paid for it with this accursed form, but I had felt nothing but satisfaction in taking the creature's tail before.

I had no time to dwell on this. I wanted to get a piece of her—please don't twist that into something perverse—and reverse this damn spell. "I don't care if you think of me as a monster. I need a part of you to reverse my spell," he snarled.

"It's no concern of mine what you've done to yourself," she countered. "I don't care if you want to turn yourself inside out, you aren't getting a single piece or part of me or my poor mate."

I heard another form approaching the entrance to the den. The female shifted, and a second fox appeared.

"Sheeku," he said, for it was definitely male, "What is happening?"

"He's returned for more," she growled, flicking her head towards me. Her glare bored deep into my head. Her mate joined in, and I felt very small all of a sudden, smaller than the cat I had treated so badly, or even the field mice that he fed himself on.

I shifted a few times where I stood. I couldn't exactly figure out what to say. But why was I trying to say anything? They were just animals. I should have charged them, grabbed one of them, and taken what I needed by force, but I just couldn't. It was like I was talking to people.

And that's when it hit me. I was talking to them. I could hear the hate in their voice. I could see the fear, the hatred, the emotion in their features now. I understood them. When I had been human, I had always viewed them as beasts, unintelligent, driven completely by instinct, unable to comprehend anything that we humans were capable of. Now, talking to them, seeing the pain that I had caused, being able to understand them, I understood that they could voice their thoughts in the way that a human would.

Don't lecture me on how animals always show us their emotions in different ways either. I never thought, before this, that those emotions could really be felt on the same complex level that I had felt them on. My ears fell again, only this time it was in sadness and shame.

"I..." I struggled to find something to say, something that would help me to defend myself, make me sound less selfish and more of the scholar and revolutionary I had thought of myself as being. But nothing came to mind. I could have spouted off anything at that point, but none of it would have been a viable excuse. So, I went with the truth. "I wanted to have what you have."

That did little to placate them. The female, the one that had been referred to as Sheeka, took a few steps towards me, her teeth still quite bared. "And so that gave you the right to cripple Moski?" she asked.

I fiddled with my hands a tad. "He seems to be doing fine now."

"After a long while of trying to learn how to balance again," he hissed. "If you came here to apologize, you're doing a piss poor job of it."

I sighed and got down on my knees, leaning forward so that I was at eye level with them. "No. I came here to take more," I said. "But only to revert to my original form."

"Oh, well, if that's the case, I suppose it's okay," she said, turning around flashing her tail at me. "Would you prefer to gnaw my tail off here? Or did you want my head?"

I felt my heart sinking. "I don't want any more trouble." I felt very foolish for a moment, actually saying this to a fox. But at this point, I didn't see them as just a fox. Their hate was real. Their sorrow was real. I could not bring myself to view them as the animals they had once been to me. "What I did, I did out of ignorance, and a lack of understanding. I ask for nothing if you are not willing to give it. You will not see me again." I looked at her back paws, and saw the torn fur, the scar left by my trap. "Is your back paw all right?"

She hissed at me. "What do you care?"

"Pay him no more mind," Moski stated. "We must sleep, dear one. There will be much hunting tonight, if we are lucky. I only pray that I can still pounce as I once could."

I cleared my throat. "What I mean is," I ventured, "I can try and heal you."

Their ears perked up a little. "Beg pardon?" Moski asked.

"It is a small thing," I said. "I've studied enough magic to know some basic healing spells. While I cannot regrow your lost tail, I can at least heal your mate's scarring, and perhaps ease the pain I know you must be feeling."

The foxes observed me for a moment, trying to decide whether or not I could be trusted. I guessed that they were leaning towards distrusting me, and I couldn't blame them. I would have just left if they wanted me to, though.

Both foxes sat at the edge of their den. "What will you do?" Sheeka asked.

My own tail stood up a little (I had cut a hole in the back of my pants to give it room to breathe) and I took a step towards the side, picking a few leaves from the bushes.

"It's a quick and painless spell. A few small words from me, invoking the blessings of the nature goddess, and you should be left with little more than a scar where the wound was." I drew closer to them and they retreated a step. "Please," I said. "What I did, I did because of ambition, of a feigned sense of importance in myself. I did not respect the forces I was using, and in turn, they saw fit to punish me like this. If I cannot be granted by human form again, then at least allow me to try and make up a little bit for what I did."

Sheeka looked between her mate and I. "The decision rests with you, my love," she told him.

Moski seemed to be considering his options. His expression was blank, and his body remained motionless, save for the gentle swaying of his tail. "You are certain that my tail cannot be brought back?"

I shook my head. "I am not a surgeon, and limbs or appendages are not as easy to heal as a cut, a gash, or a scar. Even the best of healers would gawk at the task of making a limb regrow without the original. Even if I had kept your tail, I wouldn't know how to reattach it."

"I see." He closed his eyes and yawned, letting his tongue roll out of his mouth. I suspect that he didn't really understand the finer points, but got my message just fine. Everything else was just boring. "Then heal us as best you can, monster."

I cleared my throat again. "I do have a name, you know."

"We don't really care," Sheeka countered, turning and giving me access to her injured leg. I drew closer, moving slow so as not to appear threatening to them. When I was close enough, I reached down to examine her leg. I heard Moski growling and I forced my ears and tail down, taking a submissive look, hoping to placate him. His growls didn't cease, but they did grow quieter. The female let out a few growls of her own, mixed with nervous whimpers.

I frowned as I looked over the wound. I could see the start of an infection from the wound. I took the leaves I had picked and, being as careful as I could not to irritate the leg, I wrapped the wound in green, muttering to myself as I did so. Then, I started to chant, as I rubbed the leaves along her fur with one hand, the other being used as a focal point for transferring my own power and energy into the injury. The leaves started to emit a soft glow, same as the mixture had when I had ingested it. This continued until the glow dimmed, fading from the leaves. I removed my hand and they fell to the ground, losing not only their magical glow, but also their green luster, crumpling into the dull red and brown associated with the autumn months. I smiled at my handiwork. The spell had been flawless and there was little left of the injury, save for a bit of surface scarring that probably wouldn't be visible at all once her fur grew out a tad.

"How does it feel?"

"Numb," she answered, taking a few steps, hobbling when she put her freshly healed paw to the ground. "Now, not only can I not feel pain, but I can't feel anything."

Before they could start growling at me again, I raised my hands to defend myself. "That is supposed to happen. It's basically just like lying on your leg for a long time and having it go to sleep. It should wear off in an hour or so, I promise."

Moski snorted and trotted up to his mate, laying down to get a closer look at her leg, licking at where the wound had been. "The monster was at least truthful about being able to heal you, dear one. The wound is gone."

"I am glad," she said. "But your tail..."

"I will have to be satisfied with having him heal what is left of it." He wiggled the little nub that was left of his long, bushy tail and I felt another pang of deep guilt rip into my heart. Moski approached me, turning away and sitting, letting me see the damage I had caused.

The stump was scabbing over nicely, but parts of it looked quite bad, like a single touch would reopen the wound and more blood would flow. I picked another leaf from the bushes and pressed it against the end of the stump, taking a deep breath. I felt myself weaken a little, having never tried to cast two spells like this at once. The amount of strain that it put on my body was something I hadn't considered. With my breath growing heavier, I rubbed his former tail and started to chant.

Sure enough, it had the same effect, completely covering the wounded area, leaving no trace save for the small scar, and perhaps the fact that there was no more tail aside from the small nub at the base of his back.

"It is done," I told him with a light smile, my breathing heavy. I felt like I had been out chopping wood all morning.

The fox stood, wiggling the stump. "Numb," he said. "But painless." He lifted his head in a show of pleased pride. "It seems you aren't quite as worthy of the title of monster as I had first thought."

"Perhaps I am," I said. "What I did, I do regret now. Healing a stump and a leg is hardly a way to make up for what I have done." My ears stood. "Please, allow me to do one last thing for you before we part ways?"

"What is that?" Sheeka asked, her voice lacking that dangerous edge she had displayed the entire time I had been talking to her.

"Allow me to hunt in your stead. You both seem tired. I will bring you something to eat so that you might both rest."

The two foxes regarded me with strange expressions, as though they had not understood any of what I was asking. "You would hunt for us?"

"I don't think either of you would have successful hunts tonight. You are still learning to balance properly without your tail and your mate will take another hour to regain feeling in her leg. By then, I'm relatively sure that the woods would be crawling with creatures much more dangerous than I." I sat back and let them consider my offer.

They looked to one another, their eyes doing all the talking. Then, they both retreated to their den again. "We accept. But you had best bring us something substantial. You ruined our hunt for the whole day."

I nodded. "Consider yourselves fed," I promised.

Two hours yielded nothing. My delightfully attuned senses had led me to a few rabbits, some small birds, and even a field mouse or two. Any one of these probably would have made a fine meal, but I had walked away empty handed. These creatures had senses, much like mine. If they hadn't seen or heard me coming, I'm pretty sure they could smell me. So they ran, and I wound up with nothing. I actually did manage to apprehend a rabbit, but before I could strike a killing blow and return to the foxes in triumph, the poor beast let out a string of pleas and howls and whimpers, its words so laced with fear and agony at the very thought of death that I couldn't bring myself to strike it.

So, I had let it go, wondering how anyone could kill when they could understand what was being said. Then I remembered it was about survival. Animals fought, hunted, killed, in the name of proliferation, and I suppose that was true of humanity as well, even if we came up with fancier ways of describing our animalistic traits. I pondered this as I made my way back to my hut, tired and disappointed, intent on just grabbing something from my storeroom and hoping that it would be good enough for the foxes. As I walked in, the cat met my gaze from across the room.

"I see you're still neither man nor beast."

"I see you still haven't let out all of your sarcasm for the day."

The cat licked its paw. "Well, it's so rare that I get to have someone who responds to my sarcasm. You're a lot more fun to taunt when you actually understand what I'm saying."

"Hmph." I walked in and sat down for a moment, mopping my furry brow.

"So, what happened?" it asked. "Did you not find the piece you were missing?"

"I found it." I sighed. "I just couldn't bring myself to take it."

"Ah, I see. That sense of guilt that you humans have is getting to you."

"You are saying that animals have no concept of guilt?"

"Not as you know it. We don't feel bad for much. We can't afford to. Our survival is based upon the strength of ourselves and the strength of our mates and offspring."

"It is the same with humans."

"No it's not. You have the entirety of your race to turn to. You appeal to their sense of charity, you guilt them into helping when there is nothing to gain for them. Even if they do so grudgingly, another human will do it, because of their humanity."

"Are you saying that it is wrong that we care about one another?"

"No. But it is not our way. The wilderness is harsh to us, and we must be harsh in return. We don't build lavish shelters like you humans do. Those of us that do make homes do so for functionality more than comfort. Even then, there are many differences from animal to animal." It got up and stretched, walking towards me. "I am merely saying that we are all similar and yet different, and that is how it should be. Don't think too much about it. If you were meant to know the answers, they would be available, but even the vast knowledge that humans accrue cannot give you the answers you seek." It rubbed up against me. "Answers just lead to more questions. If you spend your whole life trying to understand everything, even the obvious, then you're going to grow old far before your time."

I let out a small bark of laughter and ran a hand over the cat's head, something I had not done for a long time. My tail was waving back and forth now, and I felt the tip brush along my back as I did this.

"You're quite wise," I complimented. "How did you get this way, cat?"

"Life," it answered simply. "I just live as I must, even if it means putting up with you. And I do have a name, you know."

My ears flicked. "I don't recall ever giving you a name."

"You didn't. But I always had one. Humans aren't the only ones with names."

"Very well, then. Since I have the opportunity now, may I hear your name?"

"Depends. Are you going to start feeding me regularly now?"

I huffed a little, but smiled. "Sure, I don't see why not."

The cat nodded. "Very well. My name is Thorn."

"Thorn?"

"Yes. My mother gave birth in a rose garden and I was the first of the littler to appear. So she called me Thorn."

"It's a rather gender ambiguous name, isn't it?"

"Does that matter?"

"Well, it would be nice if I could tell."

The cat blinked. "You really don't know if I'm a boy or a girl?"

"Um, no," I answered, ears laying back. I rubbed the back of my head in embarrassment.

"I've been living in this hut with you for two and a half years!"

"Yes, well, it didn't really matter much to me, and I certainly didn't go looking."

"I'm a girl, you jackass," she hissed, pulling away from me and walking away, tail flicked in the air in annoyance and prideful dominance.

I gave a soft smile. "Well, so sorry, madam. Next time, I'll be sure to treat you like the elegant lady you obviously are."

She just snorted and made her way over to the window sill. "See if I'm ever polite to you again," she muttered.

I just laughed, and stood up. My rest was over. I had one last thing to do before I could finally afford to relax. I went to my personal storeroom and began to rummage around, looking through my stores of food, hoping that I had something that the foxes would appreciate.

I didn't know how late it was, or early as the case may be, when I returned to the fox's den, retracing my own scent back towards the den. Their scent had faded, but mine stayed strong. I'm embarrassed to admit it, but my scent was quite unpleasant. Maybe it was just the fur or something, but it reminded me of fermenting fruit. I made a note to bathe thoroughly when this was over.

I had a sack of foodstuffs slung over my back, from a few meats I had been preserving from a previous day's trappings, and some fruit and roots I had harvested on my own time. I stopped a few hops from their den and set the bag down, giving a small whine. Their heads popped out from under the roots, sniffing the air.

"You returned."

"As I said I would," I told them, smiling and drawing closer with the bag. "I think there will be enough in here to last you for a few days, at least." I emptied it next to their lair, and then backed away again, out of respect.

The two foxes began to drag the food down out of sight, bit by bit. While Moski focused his tasks on getting all the food he could, Sheeka regarded me with strangely warm eyes. I wasn't accustomed to such a gentle look from a fox.

"We thank you for your assistance."

"I was pleased to give it. I only hope that you two will be all right from here on out."

"We will manage. Life is full of tragedy, but it is full of happiness as well. We are still alive, so we will continue to live as we always have. And what of you?"

"What of me?" I repeated. "I think I will continue to live the life I have as well. I thank you both for helping me to see what was in front of me for a long while. I might have lost my physical humanity, but I'm starting to enjoy my place between man and beast. You're all certainly better at conversation than some of the humans I've met." I laughed.

They gave a few small barks of laughter as well. "Now you're starting to think like a fox," Moski complimented. "You might have made a decent kit, if fate had played out in your favor."

"I think fate did. I just didn't realize it yet." I stood up and bowed with a light flourish to them, twirling my tail. "Be well, my friends."

"You as well," Sheeka said. "Just don't come around here unannounced again. And watch where you put your traps, please."

"I will," I promised. "And I also promise, no more spells that require fox parts as ingredients." I gave another little bow before I turned and began to hurry home. My heart felt lighter, my head felt clearer, and it seemed as though the entire world finally made sense to me. I felt whole, and I felt complete. I suppose all I really needed was to walk a few miles in another's shoes... excuse me, paws, to really find the answers that I was looking for. Suddenly, recognition didn't matter too much.

Do you know why? Because I was happy, comfortable and content. In the end, I think that's worth a whole lot more than anything magic or fame or recognition could ever provide.

Richard Coombs

LEVERAGE

Ajax B. Coriander

Private Daniel McCall panted as he hid behind a Humvee in the storage hanger. His stomach lurched, he felt so hungry; if it wasn't for the fear surging through his veins he'd be doing anything he could do to find food. The kangaroo couldn't believe how bad things had gotten in just a short time. He looked down at his body, everything had started to change since his infection. His legs were shorter, and his stomach was thicker, he hadn't gone full tilt yet, but he already knew his fate if he didn't escape the base.

He would have given anything for a gun at that moment, but the new Colonel in charge of the base had made sure to gather all of those before he'd started infecting "volunteers." The kangaroo felt his body shudder, and he fell over onto the ground and began to writhe in pain. His stomach felt like it was hollow, as if it was trying to eat itself as he saw his rough fur start to fall out, quickly being replaced by something softer, smoother.

The panic began to rise in him, tears forming in the corners of his eyes. He didn't have a lot of time left. It'd be happening soon. So soon. He forced himself on his feet, and he peeked over the hood of the Humvee to make sure the hanger was still empty. He walked over to one of the workbenches along the wall, tools and greasy parts strewn across it. He'd always hated taking those automotive repair classes in high school, but now he was so glad he had. He

73

grabbed a worksheet off of the bench and looked over the notes; he found a vehicle that's only problem was a bad battery and his tail began to wag. He paused and his brow furrowed as he noticed his long tail wagging behind him.

"Well...that's new," he mumbled before he shook his head and got back to work.

He grabbed a tool box and a crow bar. He dashed over to a humvee, and used the crowbar to force the hood open.

"If only I had some keys," he grumbled as he yanked out the vehicle's battery. He could hear shouting from outside, and an icy chill ran through his body. He stayed still and listened for a moment.

"They spotted one of the fatsos trying to break into the mess hall."

"The colonel wants us over there ASAP, if this one slips through us we won't get any of those new rations for a month!"

"We better hurry, then."

Daniel sighed in relief, the mess hall was all the way on the other side of the base. He dashed over to the other Humvee and this time he went over to the driver's side window and used the crowbar to smash it open. He was a little worried about someone hearing him, but it was worth the risk. He reached in to pop the hood, but his arm didn't reach.

"Oh god, no, no, no, not yet." The kangaroo said, his eyes filled with tears again. He should have been able to reach it no problem, but his arms seemed shorter for some reason. He unlocked the door instead, and he yanked it open, popped open the door and pulled the hood release. He quickly moved back to the front of the car, using the toolbox as a stool as he put up the hood.

He swapped out the new battery for the new one, grabbed a set of wires from under the hood, used a wire cutter to split them, and touched the ends to the battery. It sparked, once, twice, and then the engine roared to life. The kangaroo's tail wagged again— the sensation was still so strange.

He shook away those thoughts; he needed to focus. He slammed the hood shut and went to go get in when one of the side doors burst open. His ears went up and alert as he looked at the scared looking rat that ran in. He was in nothing but his underwear, and his changes were farther along. He was short, round and pudgy; his whole body looked soft and squeezable. The rat tripped and fell on his face. He screamed out in pain and then a voice rang from outside.

"He's in the repair hanger! Send a squad over!"

Daniel could hear footfalls coming towards the open door, and he cursed silently. He slid the crowbar into his waistband just in case he needed it later as he hid behind the running car again. He still hadn't opened the garage hanger door; he toyed with the idea of just ramming through it, but that would just lead to him being chased down. They'd know he was trying to escape like that, he'd wanted to be subtler otherwise it was a guarantee he'd be caught.

The kangaroo peaked around the Humvee, and watched as two of his former fellow soldiers burst in. They had to duck to get under the doorway as they strolled over to the rat as he tried to get up. Daniel recognized one of them, or at least he thought he did. The badger looked sort of like Private James, but he was so different now: he'd gained two feet in height, his former soft body had packed on massive amounts of muscle. His fur looked course and he had a thick auburn-colored beard.

He watched as the badger walked up to the rat and put a booted paw on the rat's back, easily holding him in place. The badger gently pressed the talk button on the radio on his shoulder and spoke into it.

"We have a Chub Variant in the repair hangar. Send up a retrieval team while we sweep the area."

"Please!" The rat cried, "Guys you know me! Don't do this. I... I don't want to go to The Room, just let me go, I... I'll just disappear. C'mon, we're both soldiers."

"Shut up," the ferret growled, "you're not one anymore. You're weak, and soft." The ferret crouched down and looked the rat in the eyes. "And you're only good for one thing," the soldier grabbed a handkerchief from his pocket and stuffed it in the rat's muzzle before using a zip tie to keep his mouth shut. He took another set of zip tie cuffs and secured the rat's ankles together, then another set for his wrists so he couldn't escape.

The ferret that was with him nudged the badger with his elbow. "Why is that Humvee on, James?"

James looked over and noticed the broken window. He put his finger to his lips, and then he used hand signals to gesture they might have another Chub Variant in the hangar with them. Daniel saw this, and mentally cursed. The kangaroo snuck towards the door he'd left propped open with a small rock, just in case he had to make a quick escape, and silently slipped out before they found him.

Daniel glided between the hanger and the building next to it, trying to move as quickly and quietly as he could. He tripped, falling and having to hold back a scream as his bare hands caught his fall on the rough old concrete. He sat up and looked at what he'd tripped over, and it'd been his own shoes. He moved his paw back and forth watching as his boot moved like it was two sizes too big now. He cursed under his breath and he crawled against the wall of the building next to the hanger. He quickly untied his boots and then yanked the laces as tight as they would go, before tying them back together. He noticed that his arms were shorter too, the cuffs of his sleeves going past his palms. He looked down at his pants and sure enough the same had happened to his legs. He didn't have time to spare, so he rolled them up, jumped back up and got back on the move.

He needed somewhere to lie low as he thought up a new escape plan. The kangaroo's mind raced as he ran between the cluster of brick buildings, and then he remembered a place. The old K-lab that was cleared out and set to be demolished. He saw a four-way intersection of alleyways, and he took the left route, gravel kicking up under his feet as he made the sharp turn. He ran as fast as he could, but he felt slower, more sluggish than he used to be, the constant shifting of his hands inside his boots didn't help either. He came to another intersection of alleyways, and he made a right this time. The soldier slowed down. He peered out down the alleyway, spying the large fence and the patrolling guards that kept him trapped in a place he once felt so safe inside.

Daniel bit his lip and his tail thrashed behind him in rage. He got close to the wall of the K-lab; it was an old brick building that leaked heat like a sieve, and had pipes that always seemed to leak, hence the reason it was to be demolished. He glanced around, looking for something he could stand on to see inside the window that was just out of reach. He spotted a pallet leaned up against the wall under one of the windows and he went for it. The kangaroo hopped to it, and he made sure the pallet was steady, before using the slats as steps and climbing up it to peer into the window to see if the coast was clear. The kangaroo felt his stomach lurch as he saw what was inside.

Chained to the walls were Chub Variants, some cuffed, others swollen from where they'd been smacked/beaten. Some were fighting against their chains, trying to yank them from the concrete walls they were bolted into, others seemed to have given up and were just sitting on the ground looking off into space, and some were sobbing as others tried to comfort them. He watched as the metal door that lead to the room swung open, and a skunk was dragged in. The skunk's face was covered with cum; he had long streaks of it down his back, and rump. The soldiers dragging him locked him into one of the empty sets of chains, and they turned to an otter on the wall. His eyes filled with fear and he begged for them not to take him, but they grabbed him, and used their superior strength to drag him out. The kangaroo's ears laid flat to his skull and his tail wrapped around his leg.

Daniel stepped down and sat on the pallet for a second, his back leaning up against the bricks. He felt numb. If he didn't get out of there soon, that would be his fate. He couldn't let that happen. He had to escape. He wanted to save them, but he couldn't. He was outnumbered. The only thing he could do now is run. He took a deep breath and headed towards another building, a set of offices that he figured would be unguarded. The new Colonel had made up some lie about a gas leak and sent most of that staff home two days ago before the chaos began.

He used the alleyways to stay out of sight and slid into an exit door that he knew had a broken lock and alarm. He'd always catch the technical staff smoking here for that very reason. Sure enough he was able to slip inside and into a stairwell. He made his way down them into the basement that was used for storage. He came to the end, and it felt like his body was about to give up on him. He felt light headed, and his vision was starting to blur. He just felt so hungry. It felt as if he hadn't eaten for weeks. He put his hand on the wall to steady himself and try to let the feeling pass.

"Stop right there!" He heard a voice shout, and he lifted his head to see the outline of someone in the darkness. He couldn't see them, but he could see the outline of a gun in his hand.

"Fuck," he cursed. This was it. He was done for. Soon he'd be in that room just like everyone else, with no hope of escape.

The figure's head cocked to the side, and he asked, "Wait, are you a Chub Variant?"

"You know I am, just get it over with..." The kangaroo shouted, his body too tired to move. He'd been running on fumes, and his body had finally drawn him to a stop. The figure in the shadows stepped forward into the light, and a wave of relief washed over Daniel as he saw the short chubby figure standing there. He held a black stapler in his hands, it was open so it'd take the shape of a gun in the darkness.

"Oh thank god," the skunk said with a breath of relief, "I had no idea what I would have done if you'd been a Muscular Variant." The skunk was nearly naked, the only thing left on him was his boots and thin white underwear. He looked over the kangaroo in front of him, the soldier's body shaking. "I'm guessing you've been ignoring The Hunger?" The skunk said as he walked over to the kangaroo. The skunk wrapped an arm around the kangaroo's waist and Daniel wrapped an arm around the Chub Variants' shoulders.

Daniel leaned into him, and he nodded. "I am... but I can't eat. If I do, I'll only change faster."

"You'll pass out if you try to ignore it any longer, and then you'd be easy pickings for those bastards," the skunk said and he felt the urge to nuzzle the kangaroo's muzzle so he did. The kangaroo sighed contently at that and he squeezed into the skunk, finding a comfort in his scent and his soft pudge.

"I know," the kangaroo said as he felt a lump forming in his throat. "I... I just can't. I don't want to lose who I am. I've already held out so long, maybe if I can just go a little longer I can turn back."

"That's not what will happen. The change is inevitable, you will become like me, it's just a matter of time. The question is if you'll go the easy way or the hard way," the skunk explained with a sigh as he helped guide Daniel to a makeshift bed he'd made between two rows of file cabinets and behind a desk. He laid the kangaroo on the blanket bed and sat on the floor next to him.

"Yeah, and how do you know that," the kangaroo said defensively as he sat up and leaned against one of the file cabinets. Clutching his stomach that still felt like an infinite black hole that was trying to consume him.

"Because, I'm Doctor Comstock," the doctor said, "I was the first doctor to discover this virus. I was the first responder when the first set of barracks was infected. I was infected just like they were, and then the Lieutenant Colonel John went crazy and kept me locked up while I," the doctor shifted uncomfortably, and his eyes looked away in shame, "did some experiments against my will. Trust me, if you don't eat to fight the change, eventually you'll pass out and your body will die trying to eat itself. It's not an easy thing to see."

"I'm Daniel by the way, and it's just Colonel know, he gave himself a promotion when he and his goon squad overthrew the acting Colonel. I overheard some guards talking while I was hiding in the ceiling of one of the buildings. The old Colonel turned into a Chub Variant from what they were saying, and the new Colonel has plans of making him into some sort of pet," the kangaroo responded. Part of him wondered if he should be angry at the doctor for working with the mad Colonel but as he looked over the skunk's soft pudgy body, short muzzle, and how weak he looked, he knew the doctor had no other choice.

"Sounds like something he would do. He'd been ranting about making a whole army of super soldiers out of this infection, and going on about "Making America powerful again". Hell, the second he found out the infection was transferred through bodily fluids, he jacked-off one of the guys and drank it right there in front of me just to gain the power he craved. I managed to slip out when he did that, and I found my way here. That was three days ago. I've used a radio to listen to the chaos outside."

"Yeah, that's how I found out a lot of info too, for a while a few Chub Variants were squawking back and forth to each other, but one by one their voices faded, and soon I was the only one left," the kangaroo said his voice cracking up. "But," the kangaroo's ears folded back, "there has to be some kind of cure or something to stop this right? There has to be a way to keep me from turning into one of you," the kangaroo said, more begging for an alternative than asking.

"There's nothing I can do. The virus is alien in origin; it's like nothing I've ever seen. It does share some common traits with Earth viruses, which is why it can infect us, but I wasn't able to really study it before I escaped." The skunk moved beside the kangaroo on the makeshift bed. "It doesn't change you that much. I'm still me, I just look a little different. And I have the libido of a teenager, and an attraction to guys." The skunk looked over the kangaroo, "I'm sure you're already feeling that. It's the first thing that happens, you just get so horny and all you want to do is fuck or suck someone off regardless of the sexuality you had. I know for a fact it even happens before infection, there's something about a Variant's pheromones that makes it your only thought, and Chub Variants have an even stronger set of scent glands."

"Yeah, I noticed it a little..." The kangaroo said as he felt the inside of his pants starting to shift as his cock grew along the inside of his pant leg.

"And it does have some perks. Here, give me your tail," the doctor said, and the kangaroo did as he was told. "The change affects different species in some ways. Badgers and wolverines get crazy amounts of endurance, skunks like myself get extra potent scent glands, and anything with a long tail gets extra joints in their tail." The skunk said as he started to move the kangaroo's tail in ways that it never should have bent. "It'll get even more flexible when you complete the change, and the fur near the tip will change and it'll allow you to grip onto things. I never got a chance to study why, but it's impressive." The skunk felt the urge to nuzzle Daniel on the cheek, so he did. "We also do some strange canine things, like the way our tails wag, our ears lay back, and some other basic traits. I'm not really sure why."

"Well, that is kind of cool," the kangaroo admitted as he started to flex and curl his tail, trying to figure out just what he can do with it. "So I have to go through the change then? There's no way out?"

"I'm sorry, no," the doctor said as he nuzzled the kangaroo, "If you think you're ready, reach forward with your tail and open the middle cabinet's bottom drawer," the Doctor Comstock whispered into the kangaroo's ear.

The kangaroo's tail reached forward, the tip resting on the bottom drawers handle, and then pulled it open. Inside was an assortment of high protein food, beef jerky, spam, sardines, peanut butter, and others. The kangaroo's stomach growled, his body shuddering, his mouth watering as he looked at that food like a man who had been lost at sea.

"Eat, give into the hunger, just let yourself give into the change," the doctor nibbled at the kangaroo's ear, "those are Doctor's orders."

The last shreds of Daniel's will broke. The hunger inside him was just too strong, he used his tail to grab the jerky first, opened it up, and started to eat.

"There you go," the doctor said as he rubbed the kangaroo's leg. "The virus also seems to mutate the bacteria in your stomach as well, it turns up your digestion by a factor of 40 until it's gotten everything it needs. You're able to absorb something the second it hits your gut."

The pain in Daniel's stomach started to fade as he ate handful after handful of food, his body absorbing it, taking what it needed and urging him to take in more. He finished off the first bag in no time, his body starting to expand, getting thicker, starting to strain against the buttons of the former beanpole of a man's shirt. The Doctor moved between the kangaroo's legs, and he started to unbutton Daniel's straining shirt, revealing his silky soft light brown belly. The skunk ran his hands across it, before leaning in and inhaling his rich, earthy scent.

"I wouldn't want you to burst from these clothes, that's what happened to me, and it was rather uncomfortable," Comstock said as he helped the kangaroo slide off his shirt as the kangaroo ate. The protein in the food broke down, turning into the building blocks he needed. His whole body tingled as he felt himself changing, his body rearranging, his bones thickening. He felt the waistband of his pants start to tighten, and the doctor undid it for him. He leaned down and nuzzled at the kangaroo's belly before working the soldier's pants down to his knees to give him the room he needed to grow. He slid off the kangaroo's boots next, working off his pants, and leaving him in just his underwear and dog tags. He reached into the kangaroo's tight dark green briefs and pulled out the kangaroo's pulsing cock and balls. He watched as it throbbed, his length starting to shrink as his balls started to grow. The shaft went from easily nine inches to five, and started to thicken. The doctor knew his balls would be around tennis-ball-sized when they were finally done.

The doctor watched as the kangaroo started to lose height, going from six feet down to five. He saw his body straining against the underwear around the kangaroo's waist, the pair made for a much smaller man than he was becoming. The doctor had been lucky; he'd already been pudgy before his change. He felt bad for the kangaroo as he realized it was too late for him to take them off. He rubbed the kangaroo's belly, watching as his hips expanded, the elastic creaking, before the underwear finally failed and it burst into several pieces, falling all around him. The doctor saw the changes start to level off, the last thing to change was Daniel's face. It retracted a bit, becoming shorter and a little more round. His ears grew bigger as well, which overall gave him a cuter appearance.

Daniel finally calmed down and set the jar of peanut butter he'd been eating with crackers down. He grabbed a towel lying on the floor and wiped off his muzzle. He looked down at himself, his hands sliding over his soft silky fur; the body he used to pride for being so thin and fit. He looked at his tail, and he flexed and curled it as if it had no bones at all. He was able to make it look like a corkscrew, he was able to curl it like a chameleon's tail; it seemed longer than it once had been, and it was fluffier.

The pulsing between his legs drew his attention and he looked at his stout cock above his massive set of balls. He couldn't help it as he reached down to stroke his shaft. His whole body shook as he did; it was like being touched for the first time, his flesh so soft and his fingers sliding over it as massive amounts of pre started to drool down it. His nose twitched and for the first time he could smell his own scent, it was rich and almost sugary, and the more he smelled it, the more he wanted of it. He breathed in and then he noticed the doctor's scent. It was musky and rich like his own, but it had spice to it instead of sugar.

Daniel's eyes traced over the doctor's body, looking at his cute black rounded ears, his soft doughy body, and the way his cock was throbbing and leaking pre from the tip was making the inside of the doctor's white underwear almost transparent. The kangaroo's body urged him to reach out with his tail and pull the doctor against him. Their bellies pressed together as their cocks pressed against one another, separated only by thin fabric.

They looked deep into each other's eyes, and they both knew what they needed. They needed to be together and join as one for a couple of brief moments. Comstock pulled down his underwear, freeing his throbbing cock and letting the elastic band rest behind his heavy balls. Daniel leaned forward and his lips met the doctors, their lips tingling as they pressed into one another, the skunk cocking his head to the side as his large fluffy tail waved behind him. Daniel slid his hands to the skunk's waist and he held onto those soft sides as Comstock put his hands on the file cabinets behind them to steady himself as both of them gave into their new urges. They didn't think about how they'd been straight before their infection; the only thing that crossed their mind was the need for one another.

They shifted, the kangaroo laying on his back as the doctor laid on top of him. Daniel wrapped his now shorter legs around the skunk's waist, holding onto him with all his might as that skunk thrusted forward, slowly fucking his throbbing stout cock against the kangaroo's. They moaned into each other's muzzles as their tongues tenderly danced with one another, the skunk's ass rising and falling as he ground their precum-covered shafts into one another.

Daniel slid a hand over the skunk's body, and he pressed his hand into the center of Comstock's chest. He pushed him up a bit, their kiss breaking, before Daniel looked up into his brown eyes. His eyes were filled with need, a vulnerable need that could only be shared between the both of them in that moment as their worlds fell apart around them outside.

"I," Daniel said as he tried to find the words, "I need you to be with me. I need you to be inside of me."

"Alright," the doctor leaned in and kissed the kangaroo on the cheek, making him giggle and blush. The kangaroo got a confused look in his eyes, and the doctor chuckled back. "Oh, and you'll giggle like that too. We all do for some reason."

The kangaroo just nodded, and the doctor grabbed a pillow from the pile they were laying on, and he gently lifted the kangaroo up so he could slip it under his lower back. He looked into the kangaroo's eyes again, and he shifted his hips, so his stout cock would slide between Daniel's soft rump. He leaned down and whispered into the kangaroo's ear, "just relax." Daniel took a deep breath as he felt the slick head of Comstock's cock slide against his pink pucker, and as he exhaled he felt the doctor slowly push forward.

Daniel squeezed onto the skunk's pudgy belly as he felt a thick stout cock slide into him for the first time. He shuddered as he felt his cock rubbing into that other man's belly as the skunk sank deeper and deeper inside of him. He expected there to be pain, but it was as if he was made for this. The skunk's cock just glided in, the massive amounts of pre making it even slicker than silicone lubricant. His tight ring squeezed around the doctor; he looked up and the doctor had his eyes closed tight as a look of pure joy came across his face. Those velvety insides of the Private wrapping around his shaft, making him feel like a virgin again as he finally bottomed out inside of him. He held his cock there for a moment, and he looked down at the cute kangaroo below him.

"You doing okay?" The doctor asked as his balls churned against the kangaroo's taint.

"Yeah, it feels really good actually," the kangaroo admitted with a blush.

"Good, you feel nice too, just so you know," the skunk leaned down and gave the kangaroo another long slow kiss as he just held his cock inside him. The two of them taking comfort in something both of their bodies so badly needed. The skunk started to slowly, gently, slide his shaft in and out of the kangaroo below him. His hips softly patted against that light brown upturned rump, the Private underneath him shuddering as the pleasure spot inside him was stroked by a cock for the first time. It felt so good. So right.

They heated up the small space, which was lighted only by a dim lantern that cast a soft yellow light over them inside the little hide away that they hoped would keep both of them hidden and safe. Daniel wrapped his tail around Comstock and he squeezed him right around the waist as a spike of pleasure surged through them. He could smell their scents getting stronger, swirling in the air as they let themselves get lost in their pleasures.

Daniel could feel his cock leaking like a faucet as it laid trapped between their bellies, each soft thrust of the skunk above him would stroke him, bringing him just a little closer to cumming. Daniel set his hands on the sides of the skunk's soft belly, slowly kneading it, making the doctor groan into his muzzle as they kept their lips pressed together as they came together as one. Comstock's thrusts started to grow a little faster and deeper, and it made Daniel shudder below him, his new body shaking underneath the doctor with his every thrust.

Daniel felt his orgasm building within him, each thrust stroking his cock and prostate at the same time, overloading him with pleasure. He didn't dare break their kiss as he felt his new huge orbs start to pull up tight to his body, and his cock pulsing as he grew close. He wanted to just throw his head back and cry out in ecstasy, but he didn't want to risk anyone hearing him outside. So he just held onto the doctor as tight as he could, and as he felt his cock twitch and start to spew cum between them, he kept locked in that kiss letting his cries of pleasure be muffled by the soft lips touched to his. The doctor followed him soon after as he felt the kangaroo's ass start to pulse around his cock, as if trying to milk him of all his cum. Either way, that's just what happened. His cock twitched inside of Daniel and jet after jet of hot sticky cum began to pump into the Private beneath him.

They stayed still, the skunk's muzzle buried inside of Daniel's neck as he slowly let his cock go soft, before it finally slipped out with a dribble of cum going with it. Doctor Comstock rolled off the kangaroo and pulled him close, the two of them looking into each other's eyes as the sticky mess Daniel had made matted the fur of their bellies.

Neither of them noticed just how strong their scents had become or how far it'd traveled as they stayed cuddled together, both too tired to even speak. They were so lost in each other they didn't hear the sound of the door on the level above opening or the heavy footfalls coming down the stairs.

"See! I told you I smelled something... Yeesh, it's like a whole brood of them is down here fucking," a voice said from the darkness.

Their eyes snapped wide open and their ears jumped up and alert. The doctor quickly fumbled for the lantern and turned it off. Casting them into darkness. The two of them got on their hands and knees and listened to the sounds of the soldiers.

"Alright, you were right," a second voice said in a hushed town, "but keep it down, I'll make a call, and we'll wait until we can get backup." The second voice said.

"Pfft, have you seen how weak they are? We could take a group no problem. Hear that, you little tarts? We're coming to sniff you out," the solider said before they saw a beam of a flashlight graze across the ceiling, adding just enough amount of light for them to see each other.

"Follow me, quickly," the skunk whisperer.

The kangaroo didn't protest he followed the outline of the skunk in front of him. He felt his paw hit the crowbar he'd taken from the repair hanger, and he grabbed it with his tail. He slid his tail between his legs and wrapped it around his thigh with the crowbar to keep it in place. The two of them crawled under the desk that acted as an entrance and quietly made it through a maze of office equipment. The beam from the flashlight occasionally filtered through the towers of chairs, the forgotten rusting metal desks, and stacks of old computers.

"Why don't you just come out and make it easier on yourselves and suck my dick and let me fuck that little ass. You know you're going to get caught eventually. You might as well get used to it," the soldier said as he worked his way through the stacks of office equipment.

The two of them made it to a far back wall to where Comstock had stacked desks, crates, and chairs into makeshift platforms that led to one of the windows that opened to the outside. The two of them started to slowly climb up it.

"Oh lookie here, I found your little love nest. It still smells so good, I can tell the two of you must have just fucked. Such a shame, you're only going to tire yourselves out before we show you your new place in life," the voice teased.

Daniel and Comstock carefully made their way up the stack towards the window. Daniel made it to the top first, and carefully, slowly, unlocked it. He put his hands on the glass, and he pushed it open. A loud rusty creek echoed through the basement, and a bright Maglite shone right on him.

"Fuck, get through the window," Comstock yelled. Daniel grabbed the crowbar from his tail and tossed it in the alleyway. He went to leap through the window after it, but he'd miscalculated for his new size and got stuck on his new girth. He tried not to panic, but that was hard as he raked his fingers along the gravel in front of him. Looking for something, anything to grab onto as he desperately tried to wiggle out of the window frame.

"Oh look at that ass wiggle! I can't wait to burry my dick in it, look it's even been lubed up with cum!" A voice from inside taunted.

Daniel felt Comstock start to push him from the inside, groaning as he grabbed a hold of the kangaroo's hands and pushed as hard as he could. The kangaroo worked with him, and he felt his body finally start to give way and then with a groan he finally popped through the window frame. He scrambled to turn around,

"Quick, give me your hand!" The naked kangaroo said as he reached through the window frame. Comstock grabbed his hand, and the kangaroo yanked back with all his might. Daniel looked into the basement, watching as a hand reached up and grabbed the skunk's ankle, pulling back.

Daniel quickly planted his feet in the ground, and he pulled with all his might, using both his hands to tug on the doctor's arm. Tears formed in the corners of his eyes as he felt the doctor's hand slowly slipping from his grasp. The doctor looked back at him with eyes that pretended to be happy, and he smiled.

"Good luck," the doctor said as his fingers slipped from Daniel's hands. The kangaroo saw him jerked to the basement ground and bound out just like the rat from the hangar had been. Tears streamed down his cheeks as he saw the soldiers trying to scale the make shift steps after him. He pushed out of the way just as a hand reached for him and almost grabbed him by the tail. He scrambled, grabbing his crowbar with his tail as he ran naked across the alleyways. The stones cut into his feet, but he ignored it as he ran as fast as his legs could take him. He tripped over a storm drain cover, and he held back a cry of pain as his toe throbbed in pain, knowing the second he did there'd be a horde of troops down on him. He looked at the lid and then the crowbar in his tail.

His eyes scanned the alleyway and he spotted a rock about the size of a shoebox. He grabbed it and placed it next to the lid of the storm drain lid. He shoved the crowbar in the right spot in the lid, leaned it across the rock so he could get leverage, and then with all his might he pressed down. The lid popped open. He rolled the rock away, grabbed his crowbar with his tail, and then quickly descended the steps into the dark concrete corridor. He closed the lid behind him as before he dropped to the ground, he heard someone start to shout above him.

"Where the fuck did he go! You guys were supposed to be watching the exits!" A voice from the basement growled.

"We were! We never thought one of their fat asses could squeeze through a window," a voice yelled back.

"Well you thought wrong, dumbasses! Now head down the left at the branch and I'll take the right," the voice from the basement shouted.

The Private's bare hands came to rest on the damp concrete below his feet, and he staggered backward until he hit the wall behind him. He sank down, and sat on the concrete. He pulled his knees up, and buried his face in his hands. Tears fell down like rain into his hands, his teeth firmly on his bottom lip to keep sound from coming out, knowing they'd find him if he dared cried. He felt so helpless. So weak.

He couldn't do anything for Comstock, and he couldn't do anything for himself. He thought about giving them what they wanted. Just giving in and being locked in that room with the others, before being dragged out to be used until he was a sloppy mess, being thrown back into his cell, and having to wait for it all to happen again. Being forced to do things over and over again until they broke him and he looked as hollow as some of the Chub Variants did when he'd spied on them. The only thing he was good for now was sex, he knew that's what they wanted him for, that was the only thing he could do for them with this new body.

A thought started to play through his head, and he sniffled. He poked his head up, and he sniffled again as he looked at the crowbar in his tail. He turned it back and forth with his tail, it moved so smooth. He lifted his tail up and smacked it against the concrete, watching as spider web cracks spread out beneath it.

No.

He wasn't weak. He wasn't as strong as them sure, but he was stronger than he ever used to be. And now he had other gifts. Things that he could use to his advantage. He stood up, and he twirled that crowbar with his tail. He couldn't save everyone, but he could at least try to save a few. What kind of a soldier would he be if he left his men behind? He needed to save as many of his people as he could. He had an advantage that the Muscle Variants didn't. They wanted him unharmed, what use was he to them if he wasn't? He on the other hand didn't need to worry about that. A smirk grew across his face, and he wiped the last of the tears from his face on the back of his arm. He started to walk his way down the concrete corridor towards the buildings where the Chub Variants would be.

He made his way towards the closest storm drain access cover, and he climbed up the ladder. Up till this point he'd been assuming he'd be too weak to open it, but as he pushed it felt almost light as it lifted up under his fingertips. He stuck his head up and peered out from under the lid and looked around to see if he could see anyone down the alleyway. He pushed it aside and crawled out.

He looked out in the darkness around him, the moon hidden behind the clouds keeping even those shimmers of silver light locked away. He squinted, noticing that along with his changes his eyesight had gotten worse. But as his ears swiveled back and forth he realized his hearing range had increased. He remembered what the doctor had talked about, and he lifted his nose and sniffed the air. He could pick up the dark deep musk from a Muscle Variant somewhere, but it seemed far off and out of his way.

He walked down the alleyway and he spied the pallet that was just under the room where the other Variants like himself were being held. He picked it up and carried it to the corner of the building. And he stopped as he heard voices coming from at the end of the alleyway he was about to turn into. He stopped and listened.

"Frank! You can't do this! You have to see how fucked up all this is, right?" A voice shouted.

Daniel gently sat the pallet down and he crawled onto his belly, so he could peek around the corner without being seen. In the street in front of the building he saw three Muscle Variants kneeling with their arms zip tied behind their head.

"You have been found enemies of the new state," a soldier standing behind him said as three more kept rifles pointed at their heads.

"Go fuck yourselves! I'm not going to sign up to overthrow the government I signed on to protect," a soldier in the middle shouted, before a rat standing behind him used the butt of his rifle to smash the back of his head making him cry out in pain.

"That government is weak! We're going to make America powerful again with our strength!" The rat hissed.

"You can't do this! Not only is that treason, but you're keeping people prisoner, someone is going to find out about this!" The first one that had spoken shouted again, "I don't care how cute they are or how fucking awesome they smell, just because you want to use them doesn't give you the right!"

"As I was saying," the soldier reading the orders started to read louder over their voices, "the new Colonel, John McClintock has found you guilty of treason and conspiracy to overthrow the new state, the sentence for which is death." Daniel watched as the rifles were raised. His body tensed and he got to his feet to help, but before he could, the speaker continued.

"Gentleman—ready, aim, fire!" and then the sound of three loud pops from the gunfire echoed across the base. Daniel leaned up against the brick wall behind him as he heard three bodies fall to the ground and then laughter as they were dragged away.

He clenched his fist; they didn't have the luxury of not getting harmed that he did. He couldn't save them, but he could save someone else. He'd wanted to go around the side and use one of those back wall windows, but he was going to have to settle for one on this side. He adjusted the pallet and crawled up. He was so thankful he could reach the window with his new height. Daniel peered inside to make sure it was empty, nothing but forgotten dusky beakers, microscopes, and discarded papers seemed to inhabit the space. He pushed the window open, cringing as he expected a creek, but he got lucky with this one. He managed to wiggle through, hanging onto the side as he stretched his tail down to steady himself on the counter below. He slowly, quietly lowered himself down.

He walked towards the door, looking out the window to the brightly lit hallway. In front of him was the L bend where one hallway met another. He slowly opened the door and looked down. He saw two guards posted out in front of where the Chub Variants were being held. For his plan to work, he'd need something first. He waited until they were both looking away and he dashed into the hallway in front of him. He rounded the corner, and he saw a third guard with his back turned towards him walking in the opposite direction. He smirked and started to slowly walk up behind him, his bare hands being an advantage to him this time.

He got a few feet from him, and then he stopped and put his hands up. He put on the best fake smile he could muster and he finally said, "Hey."

The guard reached for his gun, and he spun around. He looked at the chub variant, and his hand moved towards his Taser instead.

"How did you get out of your cell, cutie?" The badger said with a predatory grin.

"I didn't, I decided to turn myself in. I never would have made it on my own, I'm just too weak," the kangaroo lied. "Besides," Daniel seductively looked the Muscle Variant up and down, "I couldn't stop thinking about you big strong men. I bet it must feel so good to have one of you slide between my lips and breed my muzzle..."

"Well," the badger puffed out his chest, and he chuckled, "I know how you guys always need a hefty helping of cock. Otherwise why would your scent drive us so crazy?" The badger said before gesturing to his crotch, "I mean, look, all it takes is smelling you and I'm hard as a diamond."

The kangaroo giggled as sincerely as he could, "aww you're just saying that big guy. But I'll tell you what, why don't you come over here and I'll suck your dick before you lock me up. It'll be our little secret. I wouldn't want such a handsome guy have to feel all frustrated as he's taking me in after all. That would just be rude."

"If you insist, cutie," the badger unzipped his freshly made pants, and he started to walk forward as he pulled out his dick.

Each step he took closer made Daniel's tail grip harder on the crowbar hidden behind his back. He waited until that badger was just a pace in front of them, and then in one fluid swing the crowbar came from behind the kangaroo's back and slammed right between the badger's legs. He began to fall forward, and Daniel took the crowbar and used his tail to swing it into the badger's head, knocking him out cold. Daniel caught him before he hit the ground and drug him into a supply closets nearby. He stopped for a moment, thinking about how he'd just done one of the greatest movie clichés and shrugged.

He worked off the guard's belt, his shoes, and his pants. He put on the soldier's shirt, rolling up the sleeves. It was long, but that played to his advantage because it covered his stomach. The guards pants slipped on with ease, their waists were about the same size because of the height and muscle mass difference. He did need to use the guard's knife to cut off some of the length so he wouldn't trip. He slipped the shoes on; they were massive. He had to pad the toes with the guard's socks just to keep his feet from moving around, but at least they protected him from stepping on anything unpleasant.

He wasn't dressing up to pretend to be a guard, he knew the second he saw how tall he was they'd know what he was, but he missed having pockets and a belt to hold things, like a firearm. He checked the clip to make sure it was full before he grabbed the Taser with his tail. He gave it a testing squeeze, watching the electricity arc. He went to leave when he spied the crowbar lying forgotten

94

on the floor. Part of him wanted to leave it, but he couldn't bring himself to do it. It had become his symbol, it was something by itself was useless, weak, but with a little leverage put in the right places it could be strong. He picked it up and tucked it in his belt. He took a deep breath and headed out of the supply closet.

Daniel ran down the corridor as quick as his short legs could take him, the overhead lights whizzed by in almost hypnotic flashes. His heart pounded in his chest, and it combined with the sound of his boots pounding against the floor. He held his tail up high behind him, keeping it steady as he gripped tightly onto the Taser in it, the gun in his hand feeling heavy as he hoped his plan would really work.

He rounded the corner, the soles of his boots skidding with a loud screech as they scuffled the slick floor. He cleared half the distance he needed to, before the soldiers guarding the door finally noticed him. They stood up and aimed their firearms right for him, then the beaver guard shouted:

"Halt or we'll shoot!"

"Wait!" The rat guard standing next to him said, "He's a Chub Variant, orders are to use non-lethal."

Daniel smirked as he watched them fumbling for their Tasers as he closed the distance1 and felt goosebumps prickling his fur as he reached the final few feet. He saw one of them free their Taser and before he could get it up the kangaroo spun, the Taser in his tail arching as it came in contact with the closest guard. The guard shuddered and dropped to the ground. He trained the gun on the other guard.

"If I see you reach for your gun again, I won't hesitate to shoot. I don't have orders to keep you alive, but I'd prefer to do so." Daniel took a firing stance, so he wouldn't miss if need be. "Now, slide your guns and Tasers over to me. Slowly," he ordered. The rat grumbled but he did what he was told. The guns and Tasers slid over to Daniel and he smirked.

"Alright, now strip off your clothes, and your buddies. Then zip-tie him up," Daniel ordered.

"If you wanted to see us naked you didn't need to go to all that trouble, we would have done that for you gladly for a piece of that cute ass," the rat said with a cocky grin.

The kangaroo let out a soft growl, "Another comment like that, and the next Taser shot will be to your balls."

A look of fear came across the rat's face, and he settled for stripping off his clothes until he was bare, he did the same to his friend, using plastic zip-tie cuffs to lock him in place.

He stood there naked, and he glared at the kangaroo holding the Taser, "now what?"

"I'm going to thank you for your compliance with a kiss somewhere I know you'll find electrifying," the kangaroo said with a smirk.

The rat looked excited at first, but then the look quickly faded to one of annoyance. "You're going to tase me in the ass, aren't you?"

"Yep," the kangaroo replied.

The rat sighed and got on his knees and positioned himself so he'd fall onto the other soldier he just tied up. The kangaroo kept a bead on him as he walked to the rat's side and tased him right in the ass. The rat shook before passing out on the beaver.

Daniel quickly zip-tied the rat, and he grabbed the both sets of keys the guards had from their discarded clothes. He unlocked the door, and pulled it open. Inside the smell of sex, cum, fear, and tears washed out. He looked at the Chub Variant's inside, they were attached to the walls by crude chain collars that went around their necks and wrists. He tossed the sets of keys to the two closest Chub Variants.

"Quick, unlock yourselves and then start getting everyone else, we're getting out of here," he said. His eyes scanned the room, looking for Comstock, his ears folding back as he realized he wasn't there. "Wait, is this everyone? Has anyone seen a skunk named Comstock?"

"No he must not be with our group," the sea otter who seemed a few years younger than Daniel said as he helped a mouse from his bonds.

"Wait, what do you mean your group? Isn't this everyone?" He said, his tail deflating as he looked at the fifteen faces in the room.

"No, we're group 7 of 9 ," a raccoon replied helping a badger to his feet, his knees wobbling. "They have us positioned all over the base, there's a few groups in the mess hall, some in headquarters, a few in the barracks."

"I heard one of the guards talking about a bathroom where they have one of us strung up like a urinal slash gloryhole," a panda said with a shudder.

Daniel thought about just leaving them the keys and telling them his escape plan, but then the radio on his shoulder squawked, "7th Squad, what's your status with the Special Rations? Over." He reached up to grab the radio to reply with an all clear when a stoat stopped him.

"Don't! They have code words, they'll know we escaped," the stoat desperately said.

"7th squad come in. Over," the voice squawked again. There was a pause, and it squawked again, "Are you two sucking each other off again? Take the dicks out of your mouth and replay or I'm sending the assault division over there to whoop your asses, over."

The kangaroo felt his heart sink in his chest. The base was too big to search for the Doctor, and if he didn't leave right now he and the rest of them would just be rounded up and put back into the concrete cell. He fought the lump in his throat and the tears wanting to well in his eyes. He had to help these people, he had to be as strong as he knew he could be. He had to be confident or the rest of them might break. He took a deep breath, and he pushed the thoughts of the doctor away, no matter how bad he wanted to run out into the night and find him. He watched the last person was unlocked from the wall.

"Alright, everyone able to walk?" He asked. Everyone nodded their heads yes. "Then follow me, and grab what you can from the guards on the way out, I don't know what we'll need," Daniel said. He peaked around the corner, and the coast was clear. He signaled for them to follow, and they made their way down the hallway to the lab he'd broken into.

"Alright, when you get outside, lift up the storm drain lid and pile inside," he explained.

They all hurried out of the window, doing as they were told, until he was the last one left in the lab. He looked at the door that lead into the hallway, he felt his heart urging him to go out it and look for Comstock. He almost went for it, but as he heard the clatter of boots of the assault team, he knew that wasn't an option. He climbed on the counter and out of the window. He and the rest of them followed the storm drain to outside the perimeter where they slipped into the woods.

Daniel took one last look at the military base as they crested a hill; it was brightly lit, search lights mounted on helicopters buzzed around looking for them, as soldiers scurried around, he couldn't make them out because of his eyesight, but he was sure they had to be.

"I'm going to come back for you doc. I promise you that," Daniel said before he and the other disappeared into the night.

Ajax B. Coriander

ON COMMON GROUND

Whyte Yoté

He had picked this particularly remote road for a reason. Pockmarked gravel and washed-out washboard notwithstanding, it was far in the way he wanted and near in the way he needed. His nondescript four-door sedan would need new shocks sooner rather than later, but the price was one of many paid over the years... and that price was non-negotiable.

As he bumped and bounced along, the soft soothing sounds of Eighties easy rock crept from the radio, calming and familiar. Earlier that evening he had taken his Wellbutrin to keep from buying a pack of cigarettes, and his nitroglycerin to keep from having a heart attack. He had not, however, taken his Ambien to help him sleep, because this night nothing would be able to keep him in bed.

The moon simply did not allow it. One time he had tried to fight it off and had almost paid the price with his life. A single night per month had suddenly seemed not so bad after all.

After negotiating an S-bend and crossing a covered bridge he extinguished the car's headlights. A momentary darkness quickly turned a desaturated tapestry of blues through which he had little trouble navigating, as he fully expected. It meant things were progressing as normal.

Thick trees gave way to a clearing where the washed-out track turned to twin lines of compacted dirt surrounded by waist-high grasses. A solitary oak on the hillside marked the end of his journey, silence filling the cabin after he killed the motor.

He pulled down his sun visor and flipped open the vanity mirror. Vertical pupils glowed back at him, surrounded by yellow irises. He didn't have much time.

Running a hand through his receding hairline, he unbuckled his belt and spilled out onto the soft ground, paunch-first. He looked up to see the icy glow behind slow-moving clouds, a very minor delay that wouldn't last long. The dirt on his palms and knees went ignored while he fumbled at the trunk lock with shaky hands.

Quickly he took stock: a change of clothes for the office tomorrow morning, his toiletry kit for stopping by his gym on the way to work, a gallon of water, beef jerky, chocolate milk. Perfect hair-of-the-dog, as he called it. Years of trial and error had revealed the ideal morning remedy.

His back began to itch as soon as the t-shirt left his body. Soon would come the cramps and pain; all bearable, never acclimatable . His shorts and briefs came next, the former folded neatly and the latter crumpled and thrown on top as the task became too difficult. He gingerly untied and remove his shoes so his new claws wouldn't destroy them. And as soon as the trunk lid shut he doubled over, collapsing onto his side.

The clouds had moved on.

With a will that defied his new mistress he managed to deposit his keys inside the bumper, tucked safely in a plastic alcove. This final task completed, he lay, relaxed and naked, and let the change take him.

Only a true masochist would enjoy the entire process; there is no getting used to the change, there is only growing a certain tolerance for it.

As he lay behind his car, moonlight like pins and needles on his skin, he tried to fight the natural urge to resist the sprouting fur, the restructuring of muscles. Most of a year learning meditation taught him enough mindfulness to accept reality and let it wash over him like a forest stream, but a day job in middle management sought to thwart his mental gains.

His extending tailbone forced him onto his side, the pain of it bursting out through his skin and sprouting reddish fur supplanted by overwhelming warmth radiating from his roiling gut. Around him the grass and trees brightened, their shadows in stark contrast under the moon's intense gaze. He dug his claws into the soft earth so his limbs wouldn't flail as the joints broke themselves into angles unattainable by humanity.

A flickering on top of his head accompanied a new rush of sound, new ears homing in on whatever caught their attention. After the initial rush of endorphins wore off, he settled down to let the wave take him through. The hot flash turned to a warm glow, his pelt thickening. Once his feet had finished their journey he ventured to stand, getting to a crouch before becoming dizzy.

The rest allowed him to surf the remainder of the change: redistribution of body fat, muzzle pushing out, genitals growing and rearranging themselves. With nothing better to do, he calmly watched his flaccid member grow a foreskin and draw up to attach to his lower belly before being covered in creamy fur. He idly scratched himself, the new heft of his endowment no surprise after all these years.

His first snout-breath of air was necessary, the second invigorating. The third he held as he stood to a new height on spring-like legs, powerful and dedicated to one purpose and one purpose alone.

He stepped out into the night.

One never knows just quite how conducive the night is to running unless one is built for such an aerobic and engaging activity. Taking an afternoon constitutional is all well and good, if one wants to settle for a light breeze and blisters on one's feet.

But the forest becomes entirely different—sometimes seductive—place come nightfall. Even on a stagnant summer night, heavy with the humidity and the day's latent heat, those in tune with the song of Nature can enjoy the soul of the earth, the scents and histories of almost everything around them fed through nostrils sensitive enough to detect even the ages of the trees through which they effortlessly bound.

That is, if one dares to run fast enough.

Running is not a problem in the least for our protagonist, who just so happens to be indulging himself thoroughly on this night. Who knew that a relatively inconsequential investment banker, struggling snail-like up the corporate ladder, would have such a wild streak in him? Not this man as he is most of the time, when the moon isn't calling out his name. This man has nothing more than vague memories of his time spent naked, running through the night, as this fox has snippets of cubicles and minivans and deadlines coursing through his. They are but distant notions of another world, far from the cares of this sleek vulpine as he perks his ears to better navigate a thick copse of trees.

Paws and feet alike strike the ground at intervals, propelling his gloriously lithe body to and fro through darkness flooded with argentite light. All things are blurs passing by the peripheries of his sharp yellow eyes; the unmoving things dark shapes while living creatures incandesce in greens, teals, oranges, reds. None of this matters, though, to the two-legged fox who passes them at breakneck speed.

Barely above the roar of the wind in his tall ears he can hear his heartbeat hammering in the back of his head. He draws in air through moist flared nostrils with the excitement of a child at play. For a few hundred yards he changes pace, taking the ground in giant leaping bounds, employing his tail as a rudder for balance.

Now something else comes across his nose, almost imperceptible next to the air and moss and patchy fog. In his zealous lust for speed the fox has ventured farther than on previous excursions, and now he's come across a stream. Whereas dew carries a fresh, innocent scent, and fog its still, slightly dirty aroma, running water takes everything it touches and turns it into a low-lying cloud of refreshment that pervades for quite a distance.

His curiosity piqued, he slows to a walk, breathing deeply but hardly winded. He can pick out individual scents again, and for the first time since his transformation his stomach rumbles at the light tones of salmon and other fish, just under the surface of this stream. Returning to a trot, he anticipates catching a midnight snack.

Twigs and leaves from seasons past crackle under his pads, loud against the drone of crickets and faraway traffic beyond. Stands of evergreens give way to deciduous, and finally the werefox breaks into a grassy meadow bathed in moonlight. His feet sink deeper into sandy soil the closer he gets to the source, but his purchase remains solid.

A sparkling blanket of stars stretches across the horizon as far as the eye can see now, until the moon overpowers it all at one end of the sky. The air is alive with insects, snakes and small animals darting out of his way, a microcosm of activity. Amid all this grandeur, the fox makes his way to the edge of the grass and down a steep cliff leading to the rocky shore. One simple leap and he lands, his legs flexing to absorb his weight.

First thing: a nice, cool drink. Crouching at the water's edge, the fox bends...sniffs...and snorts in disgust. Too much sediment. The center of flow is clearer anyway, and all the better for fishing. He wades in up to his knees, bends again and laps away to slake his thirst. He takes the opportunity to relieve himself as well, basking in the naughty freedom.

On to dinner. Using the wonderful—if temporary—gift of night vision, the werefox tracks several tasty-looking fish, some of them swimming right between his legs without noticing what he is. He becomes indecisive, and then finally just grabs for one with claws at the ready. It slips away, its wriggling body a mockery of his lack of prowess. The next one almost topples him over so he crouches down, wincing when his sensitive flesh dips into the cold flow.

It's just a game, not the end of the world. But while he's in this form it seems a shame not to take advantage of his physique. What kind of a fox can't catch a fish?

His eyes narrow, tapping into nonhuman instinct. Wait, watch, plan... wait, watch, strike! A slow mover, unaware of its perilous position, winds its way closer. The fox's paws come down on either side of its body and he snaps them closed, his claws sinking into its scales. When he brings it up he lets out a yip of triumph, freeing one paw while the creature remains skewered on the claws of the other. Unfortunately, its wriggling throws him off balance and he falls head over tail into the stream.

After being swept down a few dozen yards he digs his feet into the mud and stands, the fish still attached. He crawls up onto the bank and discards the body before shaking himself thoroughly to a damp floof. If he were a wolf, he might howl, but he is a fox and thus too refined for such things. So he sits with the fish in his lap and proceeds to devour. The man in the back of his mind offers a revolted gag, but he's not the one in charge. Satisfied, he lies back in what remains of the gloaming to rest and dry off.

The silence and privacy don't last too long, though. Somewhere upstream and on the opposite bank, a flicker of motion—a simple tac-tac-tac of claws on rocks—draws our fox's attention. Eventually it piques his interest and he gets up to walk along his side of the stream, keeping downwind so he can close the distance without being detected.

He reaches a bend, and to his pleasure the thing on the other shore hasn't moved. The gentle night breeze is slack but adequate enough to carry scents across the water. He raises his muzzle and takes in a musk not unlike his own, stronger and more pure. Hints of roots and damp soil and dried leaves all overlay that same undertone the fox can smell on himself. It's wilder and sharper than the cologne-laced scent he carried with him through the change.

There is a tod on the other bank, the remnants of a fish beside him while he dozes, a twin in spirit if not in form.

So much fun to be had in a running partner, he thinks. All the times he's gone out to the forest and run his heart out, and no one with whom to play. Not that he's ever looked, but now that the opportunity sits just a few yards from him the thought is more than tempting. He wonders if he'll be able to communicate with the little guy. This is the first time he's encountered another fox on his moonlit escapades. There's no harm in trying, so he makes his move.

Reluctantly, he crouches into the water again, shuddering in the cold despite his fur and the warmish night. He must move with the greatest of care so as not to startle the tod, and he succeeds in getting to the other side without being noticed. Tendrils of jealousy creep around the periphery of his mind at the sight of three fish carcasses and a dry pelt with the exception of four wet paws; this fox is an expert fisher.

Creeping low, our fox crawls up alongside the tod until his shadow blocks the moonlight. Gathering up his courage, he bends down and says, "Hey." His transformed larynx is scratchy and full of phlegm, and he coughs.

The tod's eyes fly open, his body up and stiff as ice, his hackles on end. For fear of scaring the thing further, the werefox lifts one five-fingered paw and waves. With a scattering of leaves and fish, the tod is gone.

The chase begins.

All I wanted was some fun, he thinks. I just wanted to play with you, you stupid skittish animal! But then again, what else could he have expected to happen after waking up a sleeping creature with a whisper of guttural English in its ear? At least this way, if he doesn't catch his "prey," he'll have gotten some exercise in the process.

He takes off after the four-legger, claws shearing away great clods of earth, eyes trained on the small body ahead of him. He is at a disadvantage in the speed department but his strides are long, keeping the gap fairly short. The trees surround them again in a flash, and it's all our fox can do to change direction every time he sees the tod dart away.

"Come back here!" he shouts, but it does no good. If anything, it's more confusing. There's too much debris in the way, too many things over which he can trip and fall and lose his quarry for good. Even in daylight the other fox would be nothing more than an orange blur.

Across another small clearing they run, pseudo-predator and prey, back into the forest again after a sweep through knee-high timothy. Whether the tod intends to keep going through the trees or double back to the stream, he won't be able to get away. Exhaustion is a faraway thing compared to the adrenaline pumping through our fox's made-for-speed body.

The scent of water approaches again. Eyes darting from the flicker of a fiery tail to the moon above, the fox keeps pace, watching his target falter, change direction and falter again. They hit the clearing and race along the shore before the tod makes a jump for the other side.

His legs betray him. Only halfway across he comes down into the water, kicking and attempting to swim in the swift current. The two-legger keeps pace, stepping ahead of the little guy and picking him up by the scruff of his neck. He squirms, yapping, whimpering, spraying water all over the fox's belly. His bared teeth and plastered ears are less than threatening.

"You didn't really think you could outrun me, did you?" the fox asks. Abject fear hazes the creature's eyes before he seizes and becomes too hot to hold. The fox throws him onto the shore with a yelp.

In a bed of steaming grass, the tod quivers and begins to change shape. His body seems to lengthen and triple in size, new fur seeming to fill in as the skin stretches. A low groan of pained pleasure comes from that small muzzle, rapidly lowering in pitch.

The fox steps back and watches with startled interest. He's always wondered what he looks like when the change overcomes him. It has always been that haze of emotion. This tod seems to slip into his new larger form with practiced, awkward ease, ending up somewhere between feral and were rather than were and human. His fingers are short and half-formed, his legs compact and suited for four-limbed travel. He's some kind of wereferal, a reverse lycanthrope. He's fascinating.

As soon as his transformation completes he's on his feet again, loping backwards to escape. But our fox has questions, curiosity and size... all three of which make getting away moot.

This time the tod relents right away when grabbed by the scruff and held up on tiptoe so he can't move away. He is half-led, half-carried away from the stream's muddy sand to a patch of grass, where he lands on his back, supplicating silently with the occasional whimper. His muzzle forms silent words no human can make, but our fox understands them in a way he can't understand himself. He hears noise and thinks words.

"Don't kill me," comes a soft, almost delicate voice—the kind of voice one might expect from a fox. "Please." Killing was never in the cards, but this little troublemaker doesn't know that.

"Why shouldn't I, when you put me through so much trouble?" asks the fox, looming menacingly enough to keep dominance but not to scare the thing shitless. This gains a wince and more trembling. It's apparent he can't gather his thoughts so soon after

changing, a sympathetic reminder of when our fox first encountered the power of the moon. He sits down next to the tod while
he recuperates. All the tod does is spread his legs and turn his
throat.

"I don't wanna die," he speaks carefully, the words catching in
his quivering throat. He's too scared to say anything else. Honesty
spurred by fear isn't always trustworthy, but that is not likely the
case here.

"What makes you think I wanted to kill you?" the fox asks. "I
would think you'd be more curious than anything. I know I am." He
becomes aware that he's scritching the side of the tod's belly with
an idle paw, and the little guy is making some kind of odd purring
noise despite his vulnerable position. He takes his fingers away.

The tod's eyes flutter open, as if emerging from a trance. They
shine in the moonlight like peridots. "I... don't know. You were
chasing me, so..."

"Never mind," the fox chuckles at the naïve logic, and the tod
rolls onto his side to face him.

"I never saw a fox like you before." Those glinty, nervous eyes,
darting up and down his slender, seemingly stretched body,
lingering in a few places. Locker room comparisons, even in nature.

"I've never seen one like you either." The prospect of making an
acquaintance sets his tail to flicking. Running alone has its privi-
leges, but there is something to be said of companionship. "You live
here in the forest?" It seems obvious, but necessary, to ask.

"Yes. Down the stream a ways and through a ravine. I got a den
I sleep in. Lots of warm leaves." Absent of fear now, his words take
on more confidence; his scent has improved drastically as well. Our
fox realizes he's yapping. "Where do you live?"

"Hmm..." The answer is there, clear as the day that shines on
his boring, doughy human body. Will this tod even know what
he's referencing? "In the city. Pretty far away, in the suburbs." He
doesn't even know how that last word will translate into fox-speak.

A wrinkled snout and short snuffling are response enough. "That
smelly place? With the noisy shiny boxes rolling around?" The tod

shudders. "Hurts my nose just thinking about it. How can you live there?"

In his current form, our fox doesn't rightly know. "I don't look like this when I'm there."

"Why not?"

"The same reason you don't look the same as you used to." The tod considers this with a nod, exchanging a shared knowledge of this small corner of the arcane

"I do that sometimes, when I get scared."

"Me too." Our fox nods, not bothering to elaborate on the different sources of their respective shifts. He doubts the tod would know about lunar shifts and lycanthropy, at least not in those terms.

"Right. We're both foxes!"

"Riiiight," our fox just agrees. If the tod knew he was a human at his "day job," he might not be as personable.

Ears flat, the tod narrows his brow in thought. "Why were you chasing me, anyway?" An innocent enough question. He must be only a few years old. In fox years, anyway.

The fox shrugs. "I was lonely." Then his ears start to burn with the embarrassment of what he just said. Oh well, too late now. "I wanted someone to play with." The conservative man in his mid-forties stays quiet, muted by transformation. Maturity has taken a back seat to more basic needs.

"You wanted to play... with me?" asks the tod, pointing to himself with a stubby finger in a comical way. His whiskers twitch in flattery, a raspy tongue wiping the whole of his snout in a single motion. "I can't remember the last time someone played with me."

"Long time ago?"

"Yeah."

"There must be other foxes around here." It's a forest, for God's sake; how hard could it be to find another fox? He thinks. But the little guy is shaking his head slowly, forlornly.

"Nobody who wants to play, not really. But I love to have fun!" Brightening again, selling himself in a positive light. "But there's

111

only so much you can do in the forest by yourself." He relaxes as he speaks, his posture supporting his weight.

"Don't I know it," our fox agrees with an empathic smile. "I've run all over this place and not seen another fox. But now you're here. Hopefully not afraid of me anymore?"

"No way! This is gonna be so much fun! Who gets to go first?"

"Um...well..." the fox stutters, not quite understanding. He contemplates the night sky and its diamond-dotting of stars. What are they going to do? They could run together, play in the tall grasses, play with each other's balls...

Wait. That last one is a bit odd. But...looking down at the little tod before him, he sees why his mind strayed in that direction. The delicate muzzle wears a new look, much different from the trepidation it had before. His eyes, his sparkling eyes, reflect the soft light from above, and they are looking at our fox's own with a combination of desire and questioning, the lax crescent of a smile stretching the side of his face.

Mouth agape in the midst of forming a word now forgotten, our fox stays still and tries to cope with the fact that the little fox is gently nudging the bottom of his scrotum with a foot, his toes rolling each orb to and fro, guileless and naughty. He has simply lost the capacity to answer.

The little guy continues his suggestive rubbing and says, "You did say you're from the city, so you might need it more than I do. I did it earlier today, but I don't know about you."

"Done... done what?" Even though he has a pretty good idea anyway.

"Played by myself, silly! You know, like mating, only without a female. You never done that?" The difference between "by myself" and "with myself" is obviously lost to the tod. Tilting his head like a puppy, the little fox curls and uncurls his toes, massaging our fox's sheath now. He can't believe this not-so-innocent misunderstanding.

"Sure, all the time, but... is this what you meant when you said 'play'?" Just to make sure.

"What else would I mean?" Gut roiling, our fox considers how the human inside him would react to a proposition from another male. It's never happened before, except for one case of mistaken identity, so there's no precedent. The feeling manifests as nothing more than slight indigestion. It seems like a perfectly reasonable request, and perfectly innocent. Nothing inherently wrong in that. His wife and kids would have different opinions, but they cease to matter when the full moon rises.

Whatever reason he may have to refuse, the attentive stroking of his bits is the first intimate touch to his vulpine form, and it feels amazing. The smooth sliding of his member against his sheath is pleasant and moist and raw, the skin tightening up as he gets more aroused. Why the hell hasn't he at least jerked off before now? He was too busy running around to get off? That will have to change from here on out.

He did want a playmate, didn't he? It's all in good fun, after all.

Our fox answers by relaxing, leaning back and letting his groin shift forward enough to put additional pressure against the footpaw. It curls around his balls, underneath and over again, then directly against his sheath, which has already filled substantially.

"Okay."

"Yay!" the tod barks, moving away to jump to his feet in a semi-feral stance. No arousal on him yet. "So who's going first?" His energy seems boundless.

What do I do? he thinks. I'm out of my league. He isn't even sure how it will feel once he gets going. "Why don't you take the lead, and I'll follow," he suggests, paws on hips. "Show me how you do it."

"Okay! I know a better place than these rocks." The tod takes his paw and leads him higher, away from the babbling stream and through a thick stand of trees before they break out into a field of long, wavy grass. They meander for a hundred feet or so before the smaller vulpine crouches on his knees, motioning for our fox to follow.

"Whaddya wanna do?"

The fox merely shrugs, afraid to initiate, not really knowing how. "Whatever. You know more than me."

"Oh, okay." Beaming proudly, the tod scoots closer, his tail counterbalancing his knees, his smaller bits showing mild interest but remarkable control compared to our fox's maleness, already poking through its sheath and even more exposed once it's taken into a delicate grip and squeezed lightly. Pleasure steals the voice from the werefox's muzzle, and he closes his eyes to take in every bit of feeling from that stroking paw. He hears a giggle.

"What?"

"You seem to like that," says the tod. It's incredulous to think anything to the contrary.

"How could I not?" asks our fox, taking a glance downward to see the tapered red tip of his cock staring proudly back at him. Sticky fluid already adorns his sheath and the tod's short fingers. He's never made precum as a human, even when edging. "I've never done this as a fox, though."

"Oh. I'm a fox no matter what, though when I change I can use my paws instead of just my mouth. What are you when you're a not-fox?"

"Promise you won't run away?"

"Why would I run away?"

"I'm a human."

The tod's paw pauses in its movement, but only for a few seconds while its owner thinks. "You don't seem so bad."

"Come visit me at my job." The sarcasm doesn't seem to translate, and the little fox's face shows it. Our fox finds himself envious of such innocence. "Anyway, it's not that bad."

"How is it? Playing, I mean?" This has to be the oddest sexual encounter our fox has ever had, aside from the time he ordered an escort and ended up in a spirited debate over the validity of religion in politics.

Still stroking the emergent shaft, the tod squeezes further down, where it seems to be swelling faster than the rest of him. Then his knot pops free, surprising him even though he knows what canine anatomy looks like anyway. Seeing it on himself is another matter.

His tail thumping the grass behind him, he begins, "Well, it's kind of boring. The woman...female...is usually on her back, with the male on top facing her."

"Facing?" It isn't a stretch to think the missionary position is a new concept to a creature that's used to mounting doggy-style because, well, he's styled like a dog.

"So they can look at each other while they're, uh, mating. It's more intimate." Realizing he should at least reciprocate something, the fox sets a paw on the tod's slender hip, scritching the fur there and getting another odd churr in return.

"Mmm, hee... what's intimate?" The word is pronounced carefully.

Our fox's exasperation doesn't last long when he concludes that concepts like love and intimacy are complex compared to mating. "Let's just say it feels better."

"Okay. Do you wanna show me intimate?" the tod pushes, arching his back and pressing his rear into our fox's paw, encouraging because he doesn't know better.

"I'm not sure I... oh, man..." The paw is now in direct contact, almost overpowering, the pads soft and warm and light and moving at the perfect pace. The human side of the fox's brain faintly registers pangs of guilt over adultery and immorality, but it's like trying to hear someone yelling across a lake. A bigger part—the foxy part—is conscientiously reminding him that he should be giving back in equal measure.

So it's not surprising when he finds his paw between the tod's legs, exploring the soft bits and smiling at the squeal he gets in response. It's a whole lot easier than he imagined.

His fingers curl underneath the small sac while his palm grinds against the swelling flesh above. A rush of taboo excitement flows through his body, extinguishing any second thoughts he had. He may not be supposed to be doing this, but he's not supposed to be running around at night all covered in fur, either. But it feels good, and best of all, it feels right.

Two male foxes masturbating each other: what could be more natural?

The tod has a lustful look in his eyes, pure attraction based on sexual arousal. He grinds upward on his knees, into our fox's bigger paw, and he gets rubbed harder as a result.

"Wow, wow..." The words come out as squeaks and mrowfs but hit the fox's ears as English. He's not used to such an open and eager partner.. Soon both their lengths are equally exposed, each enjoying the other's presence and building pleasure.

"Have you ever had someone do this for you?" our fox queries, noticing the tod's quick buildup but keeping his paw where it is.

"No!" Losing his grip on the fox's cock, he falters as he struggles to keep his hips from thrusting. "I've h-had a muzzle before, and that was nice."

"I can imagine," says the fox, imagining what a long warm muzzle must feel like compared to a human mouth. The added musk shared between them is nearly driving him crazy now.

The little fox's tail goes still, his ears flicking front ways and back, struggling to hold back his imminent loss of control. No more words; his arms are raised in a useless defensive position with his head tilted up. Small puffs of almost-steamy breath escape his muzzle; the scent of fox is everywhere around them.

"Oh!" And that's all there is to it. Like an implosion within his body, the tod slouches down, then pitches forward onto all fours on the grass. He thrusts once and holds his hips in that position, quivering with the effort of holding still while his cock spasms. The grimace on his snout belies the ropes of almost luminescent seed forming a rudimentary tic-tac-toe grid on the ground.

The fox stops and just squeezes, an odd sense of satisfaction filling him as he watches his little friend empty his balls. He lets go after a few more seconds, putting the paw between his own legs to play idly. He looks down at the seven inches and bemoans his transformation back to his human form. Five inches...no sheath... no knot...nothing.

"Where did you learn to do it like that?" the tod asks, collapsing onto his right side.

"Like that? That's basic...er, where I come from. Practice, I guess."

"I liked it. Like, liked it a lot. I can't wait to do intimate again. When do you have to leave?" There's a trace of genuine regret in his voice, and more than a trace in our fox's thoughts. But first things first.

"That wasn't too intimate, what I just did to you."

"Really?" the tod gasps. "What's real intimate like, then?"

The fox falters, looking for simple words and concepts. "You have the bodies of both partners," he dives on in. "Usually they're connected so they can both feel good at the same time."

"'Cept you're inside me!" exclaims the tod, sitting upright in a sparkling moment of clarity. "I've done that before, but I didn't know what it was called."

"Oh, so you have mated with a female."

"No," says the little fox, almost sadly. "None of them find me attractive enough, and they weren't in heat anyway. A coupla tods didn't care about it too much, they played out of season all the time with each other. Couple wolves, too." As much as the man inside the fox might not want to think about all this male-on-male romping in the woods, the fox is harder than ever, dripping into his paw.

"Interesting." The fox thinks this over, trying to figure out what to say without sounding desperate. Not that he's desperate, just really horny. "So, you're up for a little more?"

The tod's tail begins to wag in tandem with his own and answers with a nuzzle under his chin, making him hum before he can hold it back. How embarrassing. The paw cupping the bundled fur of his retracted sheath is electric, the stubby fingers exploring with dexterity not possible but for the change.

"See how I can grip it with my new paws?" he asks, holding the fox's erection out for them both to see. A dull heat begins to build between his legs, tension like a trebuchet. He looks down and sees the tod's pads shiny with pre as he grins and keeps stroking.

The two stay that way for a long while, holding each other in the moonlight, the pressure slowly rising but never crossing the threshold, not that it needs to be crossed just yet.

"Can we be intimate now?" asks the little fox, idly stroking and licking his fingers in a way that's innocent and sexy at the same time. He doesn't wait, letting go and positioning himself on all fours with his tail raised, as comfortable as if he's done it a thousand times before.

Our fox can't deny it's an enticing sight. His heartbeat pulses in his ears like waves upon a beach, washing out the night sounds as he gets to his knees with his shaft in his paw.

What the hell is wrong with me? The human voice asks.

Go for it, the fox's conscience urges.

"You don't have to be on your knees if you don't want to be," he says, his throat clicking drily.

The little fox looks back over one cocked shoulder, the white tip of his tail snapping like a flag in the wind. It's almost too sultry. "How do you want me?"

"On your back," says our fox, crawling over to his friend to help him into position. It's a bit awkward, but he eventually gets the tod onto his back, which is easier in his were form than it would be otherwise. His legs splay open, revealing his groin, which is still miraculously soft despite our fox's full member resting between the creamy-furred thighs. Its tip hovers an inch from its target, just waiting.

"Don't be mad at me," the little fox says.

"About what?"

"I'm scared."

"You don't want to?" He searches the tod's eyes, which flick this way and that, unsure.

"I do. But... go slow, okay? You're the biggest tod ever." It's the kind of erotic anxiety that communicates a desire that much more strongly, the kind of sign that says, "Do it to me and take my fears away."

"Sure." The tod's blind trust touches him deeply. "I've never done this before, so that kind of makes two of us."

"I thought you said you had."

"Not with another guy. Definitely not another fox." One more look into the tod's eyes and he puts a paw underneath his rear, pulling it up and inadvertently penetrating the little guy. Prepared to apologize, he's surprised (and pleased) to hear only a long, drawn-out moan escape the other vulpine's muzzle. Then the smaller body goes rigid and our fox settles down to further.

The feeling of the tight warmth surrounding his cock makes him wonder how he ever thought straight sex was the best type of sex to have. He wonders how he'll feel in the morning, or for the rest of the month. For now, this is what he's doing and there are no regrets.

Squirming, the tod appears to be in the throes of some very good sensations, and for a moment our fox envies his ability to enjoy such treatment. But then he sinks a couple more inches under that tail and lets out his own moan into the night.

A rainbow of expressions crosses the tod's muzzle, none of them negative. The flattened ears are to the side in supplicating bliss, inch by inch, until just the knot remains. Only then do his eyes cloud over.

"What's wrong?"

"Is it in? I mean, really in?" Our fox nudges further, his knot pushing up against the tod's compact sac. He even pushes a bit more after that, feeling the hole stretch to accommodate him before settling back again.

"All the way."

"Mmm, I missed this," murmurs the tod, perhaps remembering some other encounter. Our fox trembles with the effort of holding his kneel. He shuffles into a more upright position, all the while buried to the hilt and amused at all the noises coming from his little partner.

Slowly but insistently our fox begins a gentle thrusting, savoring every new feeling he gets from the tight space into which he's crammed himself. Keeping a consistent cant to his hips, he maintains a slight angle for the benefit of both his knees and the tod's back. Still, his legs burn with the effort.

"Ah, ah!" grunts the tod, baring his teeth in enjoyment of the slow fucking. His rear twitches around the intrusion, echoed by similar movements of his tail. Each little motion, each withdrawal and further thrust, elicits a different reaction, and he wishes there were just a little bit more to give. At the ends of his thrusts he hits the hard knob of the tod's prostate, watching each time as a little spurt wets the heaving belly below him.

"Did it ever... feel like this before?" our fox manages in his panting. He's losing the battle to keep from climaxing; it's all about slowing down the inevitable rather than avoiding it.

No answer from the tod, whose ears are back in submissive concentration, barely keeping his eyes open. They look at each other, but they're a million miles away. Squinting, wide, squinting again, his tongue lolling, he tries to form some sort of coherent answer but the ability to speak has escaped him. The flesh between his legs has risen up and out without help from either fox's paws.

An evil grin comes across our fox's face, and he licks his lips while he bends toward the length. He's too wrapped up in feeling out the situation to fall prey to pure lust, but all the same he wants a taste, just to see what it's like. He sticks out his tongue and gives the thing a long, loving lick from base to tip. It's comfortably warm, a bit salty, coppery and inoffensive to his palate. He licks it again, making the little guy wriggle around, arms flailing to either side.

"Nnuh...uhhn...huh! Yip!" Several spurts of thickly-musked fluid coat the roof of his mouth, filling it well despite it being the tod's second round. He lifts up just in time to see the other fox's head arched back, ears digging into the crushed grass, the rest of the watery fox cum coating his chin like spider webs. Several shots drape themselves over the tod's muzzle while the others taper off and coat him the rest of the way down to his groin.

Our fox licks at the essence on his tongue and palate. Potent, warm and flavorful, he knows it wouldn't appeal at all to his other self. It might even disgust him. Yet it slides down his throat easily.

His willpower on its last legs, the fox grinds his hips downward, making the tod squeak and writhe in his own juices. He wonders if he can try for a tie, but looking for permission only gets him another vague smile.

There's only one way to find out, so our fox bears forward and down, spacing his thrusts apart and putting more pressure at the end. Each time the tod's mouth widens in silence just a little bit bigger, and after only a few thrusts half the knot's in and there's no stopping now. On the next he stops and holds himself there, pushing, feeling the stretch of flesh around him, and with a couple spasms it slides down the opposite side, locking him in place.

His hackles stand up, his body turns cold. He doesn't even have to keep pumping. It builds and builds inside of him in a slow but inevitable wave until it all rushes back out in spasms as he fills the little fox with his pent-up essence. He wants to hump, needs to hump, but he can't move one bit. If he did, he might kill, or at least injure, his friend. All he can do is gape at the tod's grin as his balls empty themselves into that twitching tailhole.

The act completed, the tod sighs in the satisfaction of afterglow. Soon his eyes close and his breathing becomes deep and regular.

"Hey. Hey, you can't fall asleep on me. We have to get unstuck." The little guy only murmurs unintelligibly and tries to roll onto his side, tugging at their joined bodies. He's too far gone to feel anything. Our fox's knees begin to ache, and he hunches over in as comfortable a position as he can muster. Snug in the twin embraces of the tod's body and hole, he finds himself nodding off as well.

Suddenly something sharp and scratchy is tickling his ear, but he can't quite pull himself awake to brush away the annoyance. His dreams are many but they are unremarkable, all carrying the innate sense of wilderness and abandon, plus a generic eroticism he can't explain. Fleeting images stab at his subconscious, none of them explicable or particularly memorable.

It all turns orange. It's the orange of sunlight behind closed eyelids, but it's also the bright orange of fox fur.

The first thing he sees is grass, stomped flat, and the annoying tickle is still in his ear. Turning his head to alleviate it, squinting in the early morning sunshine, he has a moment of perfect clarity when his brain tries to tell him where he's supposed to be, as if he'd planned it. But then he can't remember why he would be here, or where here is, and panic stabs at his chest. Rolling onto his back, he realizes he is stark naked and sits up.

After the rush of blood in his head subsides, he takes stock of the clearing: just enough space for a couple bodies and nothing else. That's when he spies the fox.

It—well, him, judging by what's between his splayed legs—is lying on his back, out like a light, snoring softly. He's about average size for a fox, but the thought of what he's doing here leaves a bitter taste in his mouth. What is that stickiness, anyway? A part of his mind starts rushing to put pieces together, but he won't allow himself to entertain them as true. Not yet. He has a feeling, but feelings aren't facts.

He rolls to his knees, which protest loudly and painfully. The grasses slip along his bare pink skin scratching it.

"Ow."

The fox is up at once, skittering to the edge of the clearing and watching the heavyset human with suspicious curiosity. Equally curious, and despite his bewildered state, the man has an almost irresistible urge to want to touch the creature, to sit with it and pet it like a small dog. He holds out one pudgy hand, unaware that he looks a complete fool, and beckons it closer.

"Come on...I won't hurt you...come on," he singsongs in the most harmless voice he can muster, and the tod actually seems to obey him. Nose twitching but tail warily tight between his legs, the fox pads through the grass, slitted yellow eyes all over the place. It sniffs carefully, seems to recognize his scent for some reason, and even licks at his fingertips.

"See, I told you," repeats the man, and the tod, emboldened, makes a circle around him, testing the ground and his body for scents. As he completes the circuit, the fox darts between the man's legs, nudges its snout under his balls, and licks the head of his flaccid penis, all within a single second. When he darts out again and sits facing the man, he's showing pink from a compact little sheath.

"Oh, God. Oh, no, I didn't," says the man, burying his face in his hands. He feels a mixture of disgust, incredulity and leftover horniness all rolled up into one, and he takes a few seconds to imagine what this little fox is telling him happened last night. He prepared for the change, like he'd done every month but there is always that nagging doubt about being able to remember what took place as the fox.

"So now I'm screwing the wildlife," he chuckles, amused at the full-mast boner he now sports thanks to the feral fox. He tugs on it, all five inches of its taut circumcised skin, and wonders if it was good at all. But a male? That just raises more questions without answers.

"Well, whatever we did," he says to the fox who listens with perked ears, "it must have been worth it. Thanks, I guess." He stands up, and after one more glance at the funny pink-skinned thing towering above him, the tod scampers off, russet tail like an antenna parting the grass in long leaping bounds. "I just wish I could fucking remember what I do during the full moon."

At least he recognizes where he is, and thank God he didn't end up too far from the road. Judging by the angle of the sun, he has about forty-five minutes to get to work. It's Wednesday, the most boring day at his firm as far as workload goes. He'll be able to make it, if he hurries out of this field and gets to his car.

Starting through the grass, careful not to let the stalks stab his feet, he picks out the most direct route to his car and follows it as best he can. Last night's clothes will hide any dirt he collects on the way, and there's a shower in his building to change and get rid of everything else... including the odiferous stickiness on his chest and head.

I bet no one else at the office has to deal with this shit, he sulks, but then smiles to himself as his mind wanders to all the possibilities of last night. Huh. A male fox. Am I a weregay too?

He'll probably never really know, and that strikes his funny bone. He shakes his head and strikes out, an overweight, middle-aged naked man walking through a field from one life to another.

CORP VALUES

Apollo Wolf

T he first time Adam came to, he had the distinct impression of floating. More than that, he was floating somewhere outside of his body. It was rather disorienting to have self-awareness with none of his other senses. There were no sounds or smells; even his vision was a diffuse white glow. He had no idea how long he had hung suspended in this state because time didn't hold much meaning for him like this.

Fortunately, the second time he regained consciousness it seemed he was back in his body. He was first aware of the steady beeping of a heart rate monitor somewhere off to the left of his head. He laughed inwardly and thought, at least if I can hear my heartbeat I know I'm still alive. The air around him had a definite astringent note to it, a sterile quality bordering on overpowering. He could detect warm sheets and bedding surrounding his body and found that other than an extremely dry and gummy sensation in his mouth he felt entirely normal. He worked his tongue around a bit and yawned as his eyes fluttered open and he realized there were several people hovering over him around his bedside.

"Sergeant? Staff Sergeant Wentz, can you hear me?"

"Reading you loud and clear doc. What happened? Where am I?" Adam said stretching a bit and working the feeling back into his limbs. As he did so he took note of the collection of medical staff and other field officers surrounding him.

"You're in the infirmary, it was close and we thought for a while we were going to lose you. We're still trying to assess what went wrong with the test," Doctor Grant said as he reached over to feel Adam's neck and physically checked the strength of his pulse as if the monitors were not accurate enough. "You've been out of it for nearly two days."

"Damn, I'm sorry the test didn't work doc. I feel fine now though," he said, reaching up and rubbing his eyes.

"That's just it Sergeant, we think we were successful in several aspects of the protocol," The doctor said before pausing for an uncomfortable period of time, "There just appears to be a few unanticipated side effects."

"That's great what parts worked?" Adam asked excitedly before the last parts of the doctor's statement caught up with him. "Wait, what sort of side effects?"

Adam reached up to scratch his head and stopped suddenly. Something didn't feel right, his buzzed hair cut was completely missing, and his scalp was completely smooth. He moved his hand down to rub his jaw and he realized if he had been in bed for two days he should have a significant amount of beard growth by now, but instead of any fuzz his jaw was smooth as polished marble.

"What the hell?" He mumbled as he pulled his hand away and noticed that there was something wrong with it too. More precisely there was something wrong with the color. From his fingertips and up across his palms and halfway to his elbows the skin was a bright snowy white but when he turned his hand over the back of it was a rich glossy black. His gaze followed the black up along his forearm and to his biceps. Then when the doctor pulled back the sheet and Adam had to choke back a gasp. His chest was same shiny white as his palms while his sides and obliques had taken on the same jet black hue as his arms and shoulders.

Doctor Grant sighed as he handed over a small mirror and Adam looked at his face in the reflection. The change in color had taken place on his head as well, the white ending just underneath his chin while with the exception of two large white spots on either side of his temples the rest of his face and scalp were completely black.

"Well shit," Adam swore.

Alpha Company Barracks – One Week Before the Experiment

"Attention on deck!" a strong voice called out just before the room became a blur of controlled chaos with the Marines quickly stashing whatever they were doing to stand at attention at the foot of their racks.

"Alpha Company present and accounted for, sir," Staff Sergeant O'Donnell reported back when all the men were assembled.

"Thank you Staff Sergeant. At ease, gentlemen," Colonel Richts answered back before striding fully into the room. "I've just been given new assignments for a select few of you. If your name is called please gather your belongings and report to motor pool on the double for immediate transport."

Sergeant Adam Wentz listened carefully as the Colonel started reading out the names and quickly realized he was only taking the very best. Corporal Frank Dawes, perhaps the best marksman on the base; Private First Class Jose Benitez, young kid but built like a tank and the current record holder for the company bench press competition; Sergeant Jamal Cooper, one of the fastest guys around and only seconds shy of a four minute mile. Wentz knew he was good but would never measure up to these guys physically; however he did have the edge mentally. Perhaps the smartest Marine in his unit, he took to tactics like a duck to water and could outperform the desk jockeys in the pentagon when it came to a winning war game strategy. Supremely confident, he wasn't the least bit surprised when his name was added to the list of those called.

The colonel dismissed them after about a dozen names were read and Adam moved quickly to transfer his gear from his locker to a duffle bag. He set aside one fresh uniform before packing the rest and quickly changed into his service Charlie's, making sure that his perfectly creased olive green pants and button down short sleeve khaki shirt was completely in order, before setting out across the base to the motor pool. The other two companies on base also had some members selected and soon close to forty Marines were milling about waiting for their next set of instructions. Adam was glad to see that among the cross section of the best Maries the base had to offer was his best friend, Carter.

Sergeant Reginald Carter had been Adam's closest companion since basic training and they were lucky to have been stationed in nearly identical posts for so long. While Carter might not have been on the same level as Adam intelligence-wise, as Adam himself was keen to remind him from time to time, he was about as sly as they come and if he couldn't think his way out a problem he wasn't above tricking his way out of it. He was also an avid tri-athlete and had qualified for the Ironman the past three years running. Plus, he gave one hell of a good blow job.

"Shit I thought this was an elite group, how the hell did the craziest Marine in Bravo Company make the cut?" Adam joked as he walked up to Carter and shook his hand.

"Wentz you son of a bitch I should have known you'd show up here, you're always tagging along after me," The other said grinning broadly.

"Yeah right, I think you've got that backwards on who's following who. So you have any idea what's going on here?" Adam asked.

Carter shrugged. "None at all, Colonel Richts pulled us right off a training exercise and sent us packing so it must be pretty important."

"You know what that means don't you, the Colonel didn't have a choice so he probably doesn't even know what's up. This has special ops written all over it."

"Just great. You know how much I love a good secret."

"Yeah, I remember that," Carter said with a wry smile and a wink.

Infirmary – One Week After the Experiment

Adam was starting to get used to the changes in his appearance. At least he no longer startled himself whenever he caught sight of his reflection. He was still confined to his hospital room but he was up and moving about again. Given the opportunity to examine his body at length, which the doctors had done repeatedly themselves, he found that the changes to his skin extended all the way down to the soles of his feet, which happened to be just as white as his stomach. His legs were mostly black except for the insides of his thighs where the white coloring took over and spread north up over his crotch and blended in with his abs. He found there wasn't a single hair left on his body, not even an eyebrow, which made his skin feel all that much smoother.

His new skin did seem to be tougher and thicker with a bit of a rubbery feel to it too. The slick glossy sheen of his skin was especially prominent when he was soaped up in the shower. In fact, it was only in the shower, under the steady deluge of water, that he felt the most comfortable. He had taken to jumping in the shower repeatedly throughout the day, for no other reason than being wet just made him feel better. The big difference was now he preferred his showers on the cold side. Lying around the dry air of his hospital room left him feeling tight and constrained in his own skin. More than once he had lost track of time only to find he had been standing under the relaxing stream of cold water for more than an hour.

Naturally, it was during one of these extended showers that Adam finally took note of the other changes. He was certain the doctors had mentioned it along with a few other details, but he was so caught up with the fascination over his skin tone that he hadn't really paid attention. Now as he ran his hands over his smooth skin it was easier to measure up the exponential growth in his musculature. He had always been in good shape and of course, all the physical training he got in the corps only increased his overall physique. He might as well have been a ninety-eight pound weakling compared to the way he looked now though. Adam figured he was a good half-foot taller and had added another fifty pounds of solid muscle. He had never possessed great definition before, but now he was positively ripped, maybe it was the contrast between the black and white on the surface, but he found ridges of muscles he never knew he had previously.

He finished washing up and toweled off, he had pulled on a pair of his old jogging shorts and he was still examining himself in the bathroom mirror when the door opened behind him. He was becoming accustomed to these unannounced visits by members of the medical staff so he didn't even pay any attention to the visitor.

"Jesus Wentz! What the fuck did they do to you?"

The familiar voice of his best friend startled him out of his self-examination and he spun in place to face Carter who was standing on by the door with his mouth agape and his eyes wide in shock.

"Carter, what are you doing here?"

"I've been trying to figure out what was going on, they hadn't given us any information about you since you went with the Doc last week. I slipped one of the orderlies a hundred bucks and he got me through security. So what's the deal, what is that, body paint?" Carter said stepping closer.

Wentz had to smile at his friends efforts to check up on him though he wasn't sure how he was going to react to the changes in his appearance. "Unfortunately no, it's not paint. It's a side effect of the treatment; Doctor Grant hasn't had any luck in figuring out how to reverse it yet."

Carter walked up close still staring at him, his eyes traveling up and down Adam's altered physique, "Well it's weird but I gotta say it might be worth it considering how huge you look now. How do you feel?"

"I feel great, I just wish they would let me out of this room so I could get a bit of exercise, I'm getting a bit stir-crazy in here," Adam said as he paced to the other side of the room and flopped down in a chair.

"Maybe they don't want to freak out the rest of the guys. Those docs always underestimate the Marine's resolve for an assignment. Besides, most of the guys wouldn't mind that much if they had to shave their heads like that," Carter said taking a knee in front of Adam.

"Yeah, well, I didn't shave it. That part of the side effects, I lost all my hair, on my entire body." Adam said with a shrug.

"Really? Can I feel it?"

"Sure, why not. Every nurse and doctor in this hospital has."

After days of constant examinations Adam thought he was getting used to being pawed over but there was something different in Carter's touch. His large and rough calloused hands felt hot against his own smooth skin and his fingertips felt surprisingly gentle as they moved over him. He started by laying his hands on top of Adam's scalp, running softly over the top of his head and down the back of his neck. His powerful grip massaged his upper back and shoulders before slowly squeezing down on one of his biceps and across the length of his arm. Adam tried not to laugh at both the slight tickling sensation and the look on Carter's face as he bit his lip and slowly placed his palms flat against Adam's chest. Carter firmly gripped Adam's wide pecs and let his thumbs rub across his slightly hardened nipples. Adam shuddered and was certain if he still had hair it would be standing on end along with a nice set of goose bumps as the incredibly sensual touch of his friend drifted lower to his abs.

He thought Carter had gotten enough as he pulled away only to have him drop his hands down to Adam's calves and move their way slowly up his legs. Adam squirmed a bit as his buddy was suddenly moving his hands up under his shorts, letting his fingers trace around his heavy ball sac and his steadily thickening cock.

"Whoa, we don't have time for that Carter," Adam said as he only halfheartedly tried to push him back.

"I just wanted to see if you really were completely hairless," the young Marine said with a mischievous grin while he continued to cup his friend's balls. "Besides, it's been almost a week, you telling me you haven't needed this?" He added suddenly wrapping one of his hands around Adam's swollen shaft.

Adam tried and failed to suppress a moan. "You know I do, but right now? Like this?" he asked, fighting back the urge to pump his hips up into that strong grip.

"Why not? I think you look kinda hot like this."

"But one of the doctors could be in at any minute," Adam's protest sounded weak in his own ears.

"So? When has the threat of interruption ever stopped us before," Carter stated with a mischievous smirk.

"Well somehow I don't think the nurses here would be as accommodating as that waiter in Cabo San Lucas." Despite himself, Adam felt his hips start to thrust his hips into Carter's grip.

The other marine simply smiled up at him. "Are you kidding, have you seen some of the nurses around here? A few of these guys are damn hot. Makes me wonder what it takes to get a sponge bath around here."

"Still, the docs come in to check on me all of the time," Adam said as his resolve continued to ebb away.

"Then there's no time to waste," Carter said as he slowly started stroking his friend's cock while moving in closer to place his mouth around the swollen head of his prick as it tented out the thin running shorts.

Carter had no sooner kissed the tender knob of flesh when the door rattled and the handle started to turn. He quickly, though reluctantly, released his hold on Adam's dick and jerked back as if jolted by an electrical shock. He stood and took a quick look around before making a dash to the bathroom and taking cover behind the shower curtain.

"What's up doc?" Adam said shifting in his seat and crossing his legs to try and hide his now prominent erection.

"How original, Sergeant," Doctor Grant rolled his eyes as he closed the door behind him. "Still feeling ok?"

"I'm telling you doc, I've never felt better. I wish you guys would let me go back to the rest of my unit at least."

The doctor shook his head from side to side as he stepped up next to Adam's chair, "I think that would be inadvisable at the moment, we are still trying to assess the nature of these changes in your appearance." He reached over and again felt the side of Adam's neck to measure his pulse. "Are you sure you're feeling okay? You look a little flushed and your pulse is quite high at the moment."

"What, oh yeah I was just uhh, doing some exercise, you know push-ups, crunches, jumping jacks stuff like that. I'm getting a little restless in here all by myself." Adam lied convincingly tough he was sure he could hear Carter snickering a bit in the bathroom.

"Hmmm, I suppose we should see about arranging for some more activity for you. It would be a good opportunity to test the intended effects of the procedure."

"Sounds ok with me."

"Very well. I'll make the arrangements," Doctor Grant said as he turned to leave.

"Oh hey doc, before you go, what about some visitors?" Adam asked hastily almost standing up before he remember his still throbbing cock, "I've got some friends who came here to the project with me and I'm sure they're concerned about me."

For a second it looked like the doctor was going to shake his head no again, but he paused instead. "We may be able to get clearance for a few of them, but we want to make sure these results stay classified for now."

"Trust me doc, I guarantee some of these guys know how to keep things quiet," Adam said for the benefit of Carter who was listening in as much as to reassure the doctor.

"That's good to hear. Nurse Wheeler will be in shortly to get today's blood sample, make sure you notify me if anything changes in your condition."

"I will doc, thanks."

The doc left and Carter sauntered back out of the bathroom, "So where were we?"

Adam couldn't help but laugh. "Damn dude, you are unbelievable. Maybe we should wait until you get clearance."

"I thought I already had your clearance for this?" he asked playfully, giving Adam's crotch a gentle pat.

Adam had to fight hard to keep his hips from rising into his buddy's touch. He desperately wanted to continue but knew discretion was of more importance at the moment after all the nurse could come in to draw blood at any moment.

"Fuck, you know how bad I need this right now? But you could get seriously busted if you're caught here now, then what will I do for fun?"

"Have it your way, spoil sport." Carter said backing off, though his own bulging fatigues clearly indicated how badly he wanted to continue. "I guess I should get back the barracks, were hitting the obstacle course again tonight, everybody is still trying to beat your time."

"Not gonna happen dude," Adam said with a grin.

"We'll see. Maybe some extra body paint will help me beat your time. Seriously though, you really do look fucking sweet like this." Carter said once again groping his own crotch for emphasis.

"So glad you approve. Just keep it quiet for now and don' tell the other guys about me looking like this, ok?"

"Why not? It won't matter at all. Black, white, blue, or purple you're still a Marine bro. Semper Fi."

SIX DAYS BEFORE THE EXPERIMENT

It was a long bus ride, one that probably seemed even longer than it actually was owing to the blacked out windows that prevented them from seeing where they were going. They had been given no further instruction back at the base other than to board one of the three busses that were waiting for them. After eight hours of non-stop driving they could have been just about anywhere. Disembarking from the bus into bright sunshine and cool air gave them no further clues to their location except to find themselves on a standard non-descript military base surrounded by forest. They had just gotten settled into their barracks when they were called to attention by a large impressive looking Major.

"Gentlemen, I am Major Dawes. You have all been selected for participation in a top secret program called Operation Jonah. This program will test you. Mentally and physically. It is our goal to select the very best of you to become members of a new special ops team that will have better capabilities than any existing unit in the world. For the time being we must request that you refrain from making any inquiries about the project and no communication off the base will be permitted. For now I suggest you grab some chow and get some rest. Your training starts at O-Five Hundred tomorrow. That is all."

"Wow that was certainly informative," Carter whispered in Adam's ear as they stowed the rest of their gear by their bunks.

"That wasn't meant to be informative, numbnuts. It was a challenge. Of course the rest of you will have to settle for fighting it out for second place." Adam said confidently, puffing out his already impressive chest a bit.

"In your dreams pal, I'm gonna smoke your ass this time. You know I'm a better marksman then you so I've already got that in the bag if they score us on that."

"Dude you only beat me last time because you had me so hungover from the night before. Even so, you still only got me by ten points."

Carter shrugged, "A win is a win my man."

Wentz and Carter weren't the only two marines to figure out the challenge and most of the talk around the mess hall seemed to center on who was going to be best of the best. Adam mostly let Carter handle the bragging. Boasting in front of his pals was one thing but he preferred to keep a low profile around the others, at least until he was blowing past them at every obstacle. After dinner one of the other Staff Sergeants formed up a platoon for an evening run around the compound. The open roads around the base yielded no more clues to their location with mile after mile of trees being the only thing visible, not a single car passed them the entire run.

One thing Wentz truly appreciated about the military was a never ending supply of hot water. No matter which base, ship, or outpost he had been stationed on, there was never a shortage of steamy water for a very long shower. There was something about a travel day that made him need the therapeutic cleansing of a good hot shower more than other days. After being cooped up for hours on a bus and then a vigorous run, the strong pulsating stream from the showerhead felt as good as ever. He had closed his eyes and was just letting the water cascade down his chest and shoulders when he sensed somebody taking the free stall right next to him even though the rest of the large shower room was completely empty. He didn't even have to open his eyes because he knew it could only be one person.

"That took you a little longer than I expected, Carter," Adam quipped as the water continued to massage him.

"So sorry to keep you waiting, I had to ditch a few guys before I came over. Didn't think you would want an audience," Carter said, starting the water in his own shower.

"We can't all be former porn stars like you, man."

"I hardly think a pair of amateur DVDs before I enlisted qualifies me as a star."

"Well you sure suck dick like one. So are you going to get over here or just talk all night?"

"Just waiting for your order Sarge."

INFIRMARY – EIGHT DAYS AFTER THE EXPERIMENT

The next morning Wentz woke up almost as horny as he had been when he had fallen asleep the night before.

"Damn you Carter," he swore under his breath. He rolled over onto his back and ran his hands down along his smooth glossy skin until he finally reached his straining prick. He gently wrapped his hands around his shaft and slowly pulled up along his shaft and back down, sighing in relief and satisfaction. He picked up the pace and was soon pounding away on his rod, but no matter how hard or how fast he went he just couldn't make himself cum. He produced a ton of pre and his slick skin burned with well lubed desire, but he just couldn't manage to climax.

Adam continued to jerk off for what seemed like an hour until he finally noticed some change in the sensations coming from his groin. His hand was still flying up and down his shaft and his balls at long last felt like they will tensing up ready to cum. He felt his sac pull in close to his body, but it didn't stop there his nuts continued to contract until the sensation was coming from inside his crotch. Adam propped himself up on one elbow and looked down and was mystified by what he saw. His balls had pulled up completely inside his body—only a large bulge noted their location. Despite his shock he still couldn't stop stroking his meat; it was like his hand was glued to his sensitive flesh even as it glided up and down the smooth skin.

Next thing he knew his cock itself started changing. While it had changed along with the rest of his skin it had previously been as bright white as the rest of his belly but now it was gradually becoming a very deep shade of red. The red spread all the way up to the tip but that wasn't all. His cock seemed to be getting longer as well. As Adam tightened his grip on his rod the faster it seemed to change. It was like his dick was molding clay in his hands and he continued to stretch out and reform his shaft. In a moment his cock had completely altered in appearance. Now a prodigious ten inches long and tapering to a point at the tip, it also had a distinct bend to it, curving up and then out to for a slight S shape. Just as horny as ever Adam felt as though he could finally manage to cum. Just then there was a knock at the door.

Swearing, Adam reluctantly pulled his hands off his dick and quickly rolled onto his side and pulled up the sheets to cover himself just in time. His cock pulsing, just needing a few more strokes to climax, but it would need to wait.

"Ah, good morning Sergeant. I hope I didn't wake you?"

"Not at all Doc, I've been... I've been up all morning." Adam said with a slight grin.

The Doc launched in to his usually morning battery of questions about how Adam was feeling today. He did his best to stay still on his side and stay covered up as he willed his erection to go away and was surprised when it started to work and his felt his stiffness subside. He could even feel his cock relaxing against his body as he calmed down. For a moment he debated telling the doctor about the latest changes right then and there, but with his hands still feeling wet and sticky from his pre he decided there would be time for that later.

Eventually the doctor finished his daily inquisition and got up to leave, "I do have some good news for you. I received the clearance needed, so I have a visitor for you. I briefed him on what to expect, but all the same I would not be surprised if your appearance was a bit of a shock, so I wouldn't take that personally."

Once at the door he motioned outside, "You can come in now."

Adam had little doubt as to who it would be and he wasn't disappointed.

"Oh wow, Hey Wentz, how're you feeling man?" Carter said as he came in, faking the appropriate amount of surprise to fool the doc.

"Carter, damn man it's good to see you." Adam said starting to feel horny again just from Carter's mere presence and started wishing the doc would just leave. "So what do you think, you like my new color?" He asked conversationally.

"Well it is different, the doc tells me they aren't sure how far the changes extend or if they'll be able to reverse them yet." Carter responded, clearly anxious for the extra company to leave as well.

"That's what they tell me."

"If you gentlemen will excuse me," the doctor said politely, "I have some additional tests I need to check up on. Try not to stay too long Sergeant Carter, he still needs his rest."

"Doc I've been telling you I've had enough rest, I need some action now," Adam complained as the doc retreated from the room and shut the door.

"So you need some action do ya, I guess I arrived just in time," Carter said with a smirk.

"Man you have no idea. Hell, part of it is your fault for getting me worked up yesterday and then leaving."

"If I recall correctly it was you who kicked me out," Carter said crossing his arms.

"Yeah, well, I couldn't think of how to pass you off as another Doc if the nurse walked in, especially if you had my cock in your mouth."

"Speaking of which," Carter licked his lips as he stepped closer to Adam's bedside.

Adam quickly felt himself getting aroused again and despite how much he wanted to just let his bud go at it, he felt he deserved at least a bit of warning first.

"Carter, wait. There've been a few more changes, something I haven't even told the Doctor about yet."

"Really? Like what?" Carter said with a gleam in his eye like a kid on Christmas morning.

"My junk... well here see for yourself," Adam shrugged and threw off the sheet.

"Holy shit! Your cock is gone!" the other Marine gasped.

"No it's not," Wentz said, reaching down to his groin, "it's just— oh shit, it is!"

Wentz felt around the mounded bulge of his groin, the touch of his fingers against his smooth skin arousing him further despite the shock at finding his equipment missing. When Carter added his own hands to the mix it only got worse. It only took a moment though for a thin vertical slit to open along his crotch and the pointed red tip of his cock started to re-emerge. His sigh of relief quickly became a shudder as Carter wrapped his fingers around his altered shaft coaxing more of his impressive length to protrude.

"Damn dude this is so fucking... so totally fucking..."

"Weird?" Wentz offered as his buddy stuttered at the bizarre appearance of his meat.

"Hot!"

Carter had both hands wrapped around Adam's cock, stroking up and down the prodigious shaft. Adam lay back down against his pillows, his hips gently rising into his friend's touch as his dick began unloading large amounts of clear fluid. He had to admit there was something arousing about his new appearance even more so since Carter seemed so into it. His friend's strong hands worked up and down the curves of his prick even as he climbed up onto the bed with Adam. Now hovering just above the pulsing spire of flesh, Carter ran his tongue over his lips again before pulling the tip of Adam's prick into his salivating mouth.

The changes to his penis must have made it more sensitive than before and Adam had to grab a pillow and hold it over his face to keep from yelling out too loudly. Pleasure coursed through his entire body as inch after inch of his member disappeared down his best friend's throat. He had let Carter deep throat him before, but the sheer size of his cock was taking it to a whole new level. Carter was more than equal to the task though and with practiced pace he kept Adam hovering right near the edge of climax without sending him over.

"Why'd you stop?" Adam all but whined.

"Because I want to see this monster shoot, that's why."

Carter's hand was soon flying up and down Wentz's well lubricated shaft while he reached beneath him with the other to squeeze his firm ass and probed his friend's sensitive hole with his fingers. Now Adam was torn, he wanted to prolong this bliss for as long as he could but he also felt the desperate need to cum building in his balls. Soon it was too much; he was no more able to stop his orgasm as he could stop the sun from rising. He gritted his teeth as his body jerked and he did everything he could to keep from unleashing a primal shout that would probably draw the attention of every living soul in the hospital. As it was his hips bucked and his already massive prick thickened beneath Carter's firm grasp before launching a steady stream of thick white spunk. His buddy grinned in triumph while bringing his hand up to deflect a second blast splattering the bed and Adam's chest with his load.

Adam could barely breathe as he collapsed on his hospital bed, sweat still rolling off his glossy black skin and a splattering of his seed blending in with his white chest and the sheets. Carter sat back with a satisfied grin spreading wide across his face as he gave Adam's dick a long slow pull collecting some of the remaining fluid that still leaked out and sending shivers of ecstasy up and down Adam's spine. Those shivers quickly turned to astonishment as they centered directly between his shoulder blades and it felt like the already uncomfortable mattress was starting to stab him in the back.

"Oh fuck..." He muttered trying to prop himself up a bit.

"Don't tell me you're ready to go again?" Carter asked sounding hopeful as he paused from licking his fingers.

"No, it's my back. I think I'm laying on something."

"Well here, let me have a look," his buddy said as he grabbed him around a bicep and pulled him forward to look at the mattress. "I don't see anything man."

"Are you sure, It felt like something was jabbing me between my lats." Adam frowned, sure he had felt something.

Carter just reached down and rubbed his hand over the slightly damp sheets, "Nothing dude—uh, oh..."

There was something about the change in the tome of Carter's voice that instantly raised Adam's level of concern. "What? What is it?"

"Well, it's not something on your bed; it's on your back." Carter reached around behind Adam and slid his hand up along the small of his back and when he reached the spot where he had felt the strange sensation pushing into him there was something different about the touch. Like it was farther out than it should have been.

Wentz jumped out of bed, nearly knocking Carter over in the process. He darted into the bathroom his semi-hard cock still bouncing off his stomach and he made it across the room in just a few leaping strides. He angled the medicine cabinet mirrors around slightly so he could get a clear view of whatever it was that was on his back and his eyes widened in surprise at the sight. Directly between his shoulder blades a large lump was swelling outward beneath his skin. Even as he watched the mass continued to throb and grow extending outward by a couple more centimeters. Aside from the strange pulsating of its motions there was no pain associated with its expansion though, only when he reached back and tried to press it back into his skin did he feel the slightest twinge like he had while lying in bed.

He was still examining the steady growth when he spotted Carter looking over his shoulder who like Adam wanted to see what this new development entailed. He gently ran his hands over Adam's smooth black skin starting from the uppermost extent of the protrusion just below Adam's neck, and down along its side to where it ended about midway down his back.

"Does it hurt?" Carter asked.

"Not at all, actually. Just feels different is all," Wentz responded honestly.

"Do you want me to get the Doc or anything; they may need to check this out."

"Are you kidding? Right now with my dick still hard and you and the rest of the room still reeking of my jizz? I don't think that's a wise strategy."

Carter laughed at that, wrinkling his nose at the strong musk that floated around them both, "Yeah I suppose I should defer to your tactical genius."

"Don't worry, I'll get the Doc to look me over soon enough so he can tell me that he still doesn't know what's happening to me. In the meantime let's get this place cleaned up a bit before anybody comes back."

THE GYM – FOUR DAYS BEFORE THE EXPERIMENT

"Come on; let's get this place cleaned up a bit before anybody comes back." Wentz said as he surveyed the mess around him.

"Are you sure I can't do it once more for you?"

"I don't think so Corporal, I'm totally drained and you need your rest too."

"Sure thing, Sarge. Thanks again for working this over with me," Corporal Teague said, wiping some of the scum from his face.

142

"Don't mention it, and if any of the other guys ask just tell them you got roped into maintenance duty," Adam said with a sly grin.

"Oh don't worry, I'm not telling anybody about this until I can do it in front of the entire battalion."

"I can't wait to see the looks on the rest of your squad when you shove it right in their faces." Adam offered, thinking about how well Teague just did.

"I'm sure they'll be shocked when I blow right by them."

"It's about time that a few of those guys learn that size doesn't matter, I'm just glad I was able to offer you a few pointers on how to perform better."

Teague continued to put away the equipment while Adam straightened up around the general area and made sure everything was just as they had found it earlier. When they had both finished it was impossible to tell anybody had been there at all.

"Thanks again for showing me how it's done Sergeant Wentz." Teague offered, holding up his arm to fist bump his fellow Marine.

"My pleasure. By the end of the week we'll have you kicking this obstacle course's ass in record time." Wentz complimented the smaller man while wiping some of the dirt and sweat off his own face. Teague might not have had the power and size of some of the other guys brought in on this duty assignment but Wentz was quick to recognize the passion and determination he had to give it his best and that was something he admired about him and one of the reasons he offered to give him some extra training in their off hours. The Corporal had improved by leaps and bounds since their first attempt, and this time he only fell once, smearing his fatigues and face with muck.

"Same time tomorrow then?" the Corporal asked, finding a towel to clean up a bit with.

"Actually we'll need to push it back and hour, I have a tactical briefing tomorrow at 1900."

"Roger that. 2130 then."

Wentz watched him go and smiled to himself. The schedule they had been given the previous morning hadn't afforded him a lot of leisure time, but in reality he was happy to use his free moments to help out a comrade who deserved it. He knew that being cooped up on a base as isolated as this he would get a little stir crazy otherwise. He was already bored with the training sessions that they had three times a day and the classroom evaluations were a joke since he figured he could probably sleep through them and still pass the exams they had been given with ease.

True to his earlier confidence, he was the only one to make it completely through the obstacle course on the first try despite the non-standard setup they had devised. He had spotted Teague struggling with it though and getting no support from his squad which pissed Wentz off. He immediately pulled him aside and offered to help him with the challenge so long as he kept if to himself. Hell, Wentz hadn't even told Carter what he was up to because that loudmouth would whine about why he wasn't helping him out.

Sure enough Carter was the first person he ran into as he made his way back to the barracks.

"Hey Wentz! Where've you been? I've been looking all over for you!" Carter called out as he jogged up.

"Oh I had to go down to the motor pool to help with some maintenance on one of the Humvees," Wentz made up on the spot.

"Huh, I was just down there and didn't see you."

"Must have just missed me then, what's up?" Adam asked trying to redirect the conversation.

"I've been trying to track you down to let you know that Major Dawes wants you to report to his office ASAP. Guess you're in for it now." Carter laughed.

Wentz just rolled his eyes and shrugged, "Maybe he needs some input on how to get rid of you, not that I could be of any help in that department, I've been trying to get rid of you for years."

"Just one more failure for you, man."

"Tell me about it, guess I better head over. I'll catch up with you later."

"Good luck."

Wentz headed over to HQ on the double though he regretted not having a chance to clean up a bit more. Keeping the Major waiting any longer than he already had been was a greater concern than a dusty uniform though. In no time he was outside his office door where he knocked loudly.

"Enter!" The deep voice called back from inside.

Wentz marched in and snapped to attention. "Sergeant Wentz reporting as ordered, Sir!"

"At ease, Wentz. Have a seat," the Major responded from across his massive desk.

Standing at ease before taking the offered seat, Wentz relaxed a little on hearing the Commanding officer's casual tone, "Thank you, Sir."

"You've really gotten off to a fast start these first few days. I figured it would take three weeks to identify a suitable candidate."

"Thank you, Sir."

"Your runs through our enhanced training course were superb, you've aced every evaluation you've taken and I have been very impressed by your leadership skills. I'm especially pleased with the work you've done with Corporal Teague."

The confusion must have shown on Adam's otherwise impassive face.

"Yes, I am aware of the extra training you've arranged for him. As I said you seem to be the perfect candidate and since we are under a tight schedule stepping up the selection process is the most logical choice at this point."

"Pardon me, Sir. But the selection process for what exactly?"

"Sergeant this is all highly classified. We are developing a test program in a joint operation with the Army, Air Force, and Navy to develop select squads of extremely specialized and elite personnel. I'd like you to be our first candidate. You'll receive an immediate promotion to Staff Sergeant and upon completion of this program you'll be given your choice of any duty assignment."

"I'd be honored, Major." Wentz felt himself beaming.

"There is more to consider before you accept Sergeant. In order to take part each candidate will be required to undergo some experimental medical treatments designed for complete physical and mental augmentation. These treatments are not without risk and therefore this program is entirely voluntary and you can back out now with no negative repercussions."

Wentz scratched his head at that one. This sounded like a once in a lifetime opportunity, but did he really want to voluntary make himself a human guinea pig? "What kind of augmentation are we talking here Major?"

"The procedures are designed to increase your overall physical strength, stamina, and agility. In addition you addition your cognitive abilities for reason and tactical planning with be greatly enhanced."

"I see. Well Sir, the Corp hasn't done me wrong this far so I'm in."

Major Dawes grinned and nodded his approval, "I figured as much, Staff Sergeant. We'll need to get started immediately though." He pressed a button on his phone and moments later an older man in a doctor's coat strode into the room.

"Staff Sergeant Wentz, this is Doctor Grant, our project leader."

INFIRMARY – NINE DAYS AFTER THE EXPERIMENT

"Doc, I'm telling you I feel just fine," Adam complained as he lay on his stomach on the examining table.

"I heard you the first time, Sergeant," The doctor said dismissively as he continued to prod his fingers into Adam's skin. "However since you chose to ignore my instructions, I have opted to ignore your input as well."

Wentz twitched a bit as he felt his body poked again, "It just started as a little swelling Doc, I didn't think it was a big deal."

"And now that you have what appears to be a dorsal fin, what does your expert medical opinion tell you now," Doctor Grant quipped as he took a measurement of the still growing appendage protruding from the marine's back.

He had no comeback for that rhetorical question. By the time he and Carter had gotten themselves and the room cleaned up the growth on his back had extended outward by at least five inches and it was fairly evident what it was becoming.

After Carter left, Adam decided to lay down in bed where he managed to fall asleep and when the Doc came back on his rounds the next morning and walked in to discover a ten-inch fin sprouting from his back, he was upset to say the least. In the flurry of activity that followed, much to Adam's embarrassment, the alterations to his crotch were also discovered and made very public to the rest of the attending medical staff. The in depth examination that followed that revelation tested Adam's humility even though he found that he was extremely proud of his new endowment and by the end he didn't mind showing it off a bit.

"I've requested all along that you notify me immediately of any physical changes."

"Doc from the very first needle you stuck in my arm you told me to expect certain changes to my appearance, but not to be alarmed by them as the procedure was perfectly safe. Has that changed now?"

"No, I don't believe you are in any danger, however I still need to document as much as possible if there is any hope of replicating or reversing the changes." He said as he jabbed a needle directly into the fin to extract a blood sample.

Adam flinched from the piercing bite of the syringe again finding himself in silent contemplation. He looked down at his arms and the smooth glossy black and white skin that now covered them. So what if it can't be reversed, Adam thought to himself. He was taller and more muscular now, and still growing stronger by the day. The changes to his crotch had taken some getting used to but clearly they weren't adversely affected. Sure he was getting a fin and god knows what else, but how bad could it be?

"You can sit up now; we're finished for the time being," the Doctor said as the rest of the medical staff retreated with their various blood and tissue samples.

"They won't cancel the mission because of this will they; I mean the other tests will go on won't they?"

"I have not been fully briefed on their progress but my understanding is that the other services have orders to proceed with their test protocols. We're still evaluating whether or not we can make another attempt with next candidate here."

"Wait, what about me, I'm not ready to give up here!" Adam said feeling his anger rise slightly.

"Nobody said you were being eliminated, the task at hand was to form an elite squad and despite your current physical appearance you are still expected to be able to take command of that squad."

"Good, because I'm starting to think you don't need to change me back."

"That's not entirely your decision to make, but I am glad to hear you are taking this so well. Now, is there anything else that you've noticed that you would like to report?"

Adam thought it over as he sorted through the different sensations his body was sending him. He realized his feet were a little numb and this actually concerned him a bit. "Yeah doc I think something may be happening to my feet."

Doctor Grant bent down to examine them and again started his poking and prodding. Adam listened as he made his usual grunts and noises as he looked him over, trying hard not to squirm as he tugged on his toes and cause a bit of a tickle along the soles of his feet. "Hmmm this is rather interesting."

"Oh shit, Doc, don't tell me I'm going to lose my legs now too!" As much as he liked these changes he didn't think he was prepared for something like that.

"No, I don't believe that is indicated Sergeant, but you do appear to have some webbing forming between your toes and a small fin growing along the back of your heel."

"Really?" Adam said, lifting his foot up into his lap as he sat on the edge of the bed. He hadn't noticed how much lager his feet had become and sure enough he found his toes were all connected together by a thick membrane of black tissue giving them a much more flipper like appearance. Accompanied by the three inch triangle of cartilage poking out the back of his heel he determined his feet would definitely help propel him faster through the water given the chance.

"Yes really, now I've had a pool on standby since you requested some exercise time, I'd like you to try it out and see how these new additions to your anatomy work while in an aquatic environment," the doctor said as he stood up and took a few notes.

"Alright doc, I'll do anything to get me out of this room."

BARRACKS – THREE DAYS BEFORE THE EXPERIMENT

"So when are they supposed to start treating you like a lab rat?" Carter asked from the top bunk.

"What? How the hell do you know about that? It's supposed to be top secret," Wentz said trying to mask some of his surprise.

"I have my sources."

"Yeah, well, I don't know what you've been told, but I don't think lab rat is what they have in mind," Wentz said rolling over in his rack and tossing aside the magazine he was trying to read.

"Right. I've even heard about that kiddie pool you've been playing in, which would probably mean something more aquatic in nature, dolphin training maybe?"

"You are unbelievable you know that, you're gonna end up facing a court martial one of these days for sticking your nose where it doesn't belong."

"I doubt it, but if I do you can be my character witness."

"What character?" Adam scoffed.

"Har-har, so what are they doing to you?"

"You know I can't tell you that."

"Yeah but I bet if I we snuck into the lab you could show me?" Carter kept on pressuring him.

"Are you crazy?"

"Not when I'm on my meds. What would you say if I told you I've got a copy of the passkey to let me into the lab?" He asked, waving a red plastic card in front of Adam.

Wentz sat bolt upright almost hitting his head on the bunk above him. "How the hell did you get that?"

"Again, I have my ways. So what do you say? Want to take me for a tour?"

It took almost another hour of arm twisting to talk Wentz into going over, though he still insisted they wait until after lights out to even try it. Adam half expected the passkey Carter had to fail and bring a swarm of MPs down on them any moment. Surprisingly they got through the security checkpoints without a hitch and they were quickly surrounded by the array of strange equipment that Adam had been getting very familiar with. The medical equipment still gave Adam the chills with the vast collection of tubing, dials, and glistening steel needles. The first several rounds of treatment hadn't hurt anymore than a routine inoculation, but there was still just something imposing about the set up. The strangest piece of equipment was the large submersion tank standing in the corner.

It was completely filled with startlingly blue water; the clear glass tank churned and gurgled slightly as small bubbles rose from the bottom as well as the multitude of apparatus and attachments that lined the corners of the device. Wentz had undergone scuba training years ago and while this was reminiscent of that experience it was completely contrary to anything he had experienced before. Immediately after the first series of injections the Doctors wired him up like a Christmas tree, attaching electrodes to almost every inch of his body before having him step into a modified swimsuit that held his genitals in suspension and a breather mask that completely covered his head. He was then submerged in the tank for hours on end where his biggest challenge was keeping from becoming overly bored. The increasingly fishy smelling air he was forced to breathe was unpleasant at first but he gradually became accustomed to it.

Doctor Grant had explained to him that the injections were a combination of hormone supplement designed to stimulate muscle growth and genetic manipulators to enhance his overall DNA structure. His periods of suspension inside the tank were supposed to electrically stimulate tissue growth, though he argued that strenuous exercise would probably achieve the same results. After a day and a half of this treatment he was starting to wonder if this medical mumbo jumbo was just some bullshit psychological experiment. Still if this is what it took to make his way rapidly up the ranks he was more than willing.

"So what is it they are trying to do to you with all of this junk?" Carter asked looking around at the impressive looking equipment.

"No idea, but so far the only side effect seems to be that I feel horny all the time."

"Hmph, weapons grade Viagra maybe?"

Adam had to stifle a small laugh, "Anything's possible I guess, but this seems like overkill for that project."

"Yeah, especially since you were pretty much horny all the time before this."

"You should talk, but since you bring it up, just being in here is really getting me going again. What do you say, want to help a guy out?" Adam said giving his crotch a firm grope and feeling his cock become satisfyingly swollen.

"I thought you'd never ask."

Carter went to work fast, dropping to his knees and pulling apart the fly of Adam's fatigues. His warm hand swept inside to grab at Adam's cock through his briefs, tugging and pulling on the already swollen shaft. In due course he massaged it free of its confines and Adam felt the hot breath of his friend blowing across his stimulated skin. He wished he could explain why he was so aroused at the moment, but there was just something about being around all this equipment that was letting Carter get to him more than usual. After just a few minutes of effort Carter had Adam's cock deep in his throat as the vacuum of his maw intensified the tight feeling around his dick. He had loosened his pants the rest of the way and let them fall noiselessly to the deck as Carter ran his strong hands up along the back of his legs to prod at Adam's ass with his fingers even while Adam gently thrust into his hungry mouth.

It was such a rush, such an illicit thrill, to be doing this in the lab that it didn't take Wentz long to reach the edge of his resolve and he let loose with his seed into Carter's throat. With Carter's usual skill he made sure not to not waste a drop and that Adam's orgasm came to a full stop before he slowly withdrew. Standing up Carter held Adam tight, grinding his own swollen groin against Adam's still sensitive prick.

"I think you should let me fuck you," he whispered softly into Adam's ear.

Adam felt a chill run up his spine as the notion of that thought filled him up. His initial shock at the request dissipated and left him feeling curious. Carter had never come close to suggesting this. All the times they fooled around it was usually Carter going down on him or mutual hand jobs, Carter never even offered to let Adam suck him off. His own cock was rock hard again and his knees shook at the possibility so in the end he simply looked into Carter's eyes and nodded in the affirmative. Carter gently turned him towards the tank before unbuckling his pants and fishing out his erection. He pulled out a bottle of lube and slicked up his rod. Adam exhaled as he felt a gentle pressure slide against the puckered hole between his cheeks. Carter pushed forward slowly into his friend, the head of his cock sliding in with ease. He started to slowly push in and out.

With each gentle thrust Carter pushed in deeper and Wentz gasped at the sensation of his best friend filling him up. He did his best to concentrate on the gently floating bubbles rising through the tank in front of him during the twinges of pain, but mostly he focused on the pleasure spreading him wider and wider. He felt his friend's hips slowly smacking against his rear, their bodies meeting, mixing with the sounds of the bubbles finding their way to the surface of the tank. He groaned, his balls swinging softly between his muscular thighs as his cock twitched, throbbing against his abs. This went on for several minutes, until Carter reached around and stroked his buddy's shaft, slowly pumping it as his cock stroked long and deep at that pleasure knot inside of the Sargent.

Adam's face twisted up in pleasure and his fingers gripped onto the tank, as he moaned and a thick load of his cum shot across the glass in front of him. He heard the man behind him groan, and he shuddered as he felt a warm sensation start to pump into his ass, drippling out and sliding down over the back of his balls.

It was several minutes before both of them, gasping for air, could disengage from each other. Carter found a towel to clean up with and handed it to Adam and he wiped off the tank.

"That was incredible," Adam confessed. "But we should head back before we get caught."

"You worry too much, but alright."

Testing Pool – Ten Days After the Experiment

Adam sat at the edge of the pool and felt the warm water swirling around his toes. It turned out his new glossy skin was better than any swim suit for its ability to allow him to glide through the water and also acted as compression for his muscles. His feet had become much more like flippers and with the stability offered by the small fins on his legs and the large one on his back he was able to cut through the water like a torpedo. He had been at it for several hours before even taking a break and he was starting to feel just as at home in the water as he was on land.

"Don't you know it's dangerous to swim without a lifeguard present?"

The voice behind Wentz made him jump, falling back into the pool with a pronounced splash. When he resurfaced and stopped sputtering from the large gulp of water he had taken in he smiled at the sight of Carter standing there in nothing but a tight black and white speedo.

"Jesus dude, you scared the crap out of me. What'd they let you back in here for anyway?"

Carter shrugged at question and Adam's startled response, "Eh, I talked the Doc into letting me hang out with you a bit more. Told him it was important for your emotional stability."

"And he bought that?" Adam said with a chuckle. "Nice swimsuit by the way, not exactly standard issue but I like it."

"I figured you would, I'm just trying to blend in with you." Carter dove in the pool next to him. "So let's see what you can do."

Carter pushed off hard against the wall and shot down the length of the pool. Adam knew a challenge when he saw one and was quick to pursue. With just a few kicks of his larger feet he caught up with his friend and shadowed him stroke for stroke for a few seconds. Then he really poured it on, streaking through the water, feeling his body cut through the small waves and currents like a knife. With a graceful flip turn at the far end he was soon circling back past Carter only to reach the starting wall just as the other reached the first turn. They stopped and stared at each other from across the distance, Carter with an impressed smirk on his face.

"Now you're just showing off," he remarked.

"That's right. You impressed yet?" Adam laughed.

They swam back towards one another, meeting in the center of the pool where Adam circled his buddy a few times, letting his dorsal fin break the surface of the water. He had been practicing and now found he could hold his breath for much longer than he ever could before. Staying under water, he made several more laps of the pool around Carter before he bothered to surface.

"Ok, I am impressed." Carter said when Adam finally came to a stop in front of where he was treading water.

Adam floated in close and wiped away some of the water beading up across the glossy black skin on his head. "You know, I told the Doc that I wasn't all that concerned about him finding a way to change me back. Do you think I should be?"

"I think I've already shown you my approval, unless you wanted another demonstration." Carter offered, pressing their foreheads together before kissing him.

Wentz could feel the warmth spreading through his body at the touch despite the coolness of the surrounding water. Most noticeably around his groin where he detected the subtle swelling of his changed genitals as Carter thrust the ample bulge of his own speedo against him. He was certain that Carter would have been more comfortable to swim back to the pool deck to continue their activities but he surprised Adam by slipping his rapidly stiffening cock out of his swimsuit right there in the water.

Adam didn't have to worry about a suit himself since he had been swimming in the buff and he was much more prepared this time around when his fellow marine floated around behind him and nestled his hard dick in the crack of his ass. His own body seemed much more buoyant now and he didn't have to work as much to float there and enjoy the experience. Carter's strong arms wrapped around him and rubbed across his smooth white stomach before finding purchase on the red mast of flesh that had extended from his crotch.

Carter entered him and Adam groaned in pure pleasure, more easily accepting the length of his dick this time around as he gradually thrust into Adam's ass. The semi-weightless sensation of floating in the pool seemed to slow Carter's efforts and gave Adam that much more time to enjoy every exquisite moment of it. He let himself float freely, Carter ridding atop him like some bizarre sort of raft. Adam let his body shift forward as Carter pounded into him, his buddy still keeping a firm grasp on Adam's cock, working it in time with his gentle yet powerful motions. By the time Carter was unloading his sperm deep inside of him, Adam's own shaft buzzed with a copious amount of spunk as his load was deposited into the depths of the pool.

Adam was almost completely numb with satisfaction, noticeably so right above his ass. The odd sensation intensified and it was almost as if his spine was stretching, extending further away from his body. It wasn't until he glanced over his shoulder to look at Carter that he found out why. Several inches past his dorsal fin a large mass of his own black skin was stretching outwards, thickening as it elongated. It was a curious feeling, like a mix between a severe muscle cramp and the pins and needles sensation you get when your foot falls asleep. Carter withdrew and moved back slightly as this new growth continued to expand, the strangest look of amusement on his face. Fins sprouted from the tip of the growth as it grew in girth, and in mere minutes, Adam had a fully formed tail extending from the small of his back and the upper part of his ass. The smooth white of his crotch extended down along the underside of his new tail, almost to the fin while the upper half remained as glossy black as the rest of his backside. With scarcely a thought he was able to flex it up and down sending a wave of water crashing into Carter's face.

"Well that's different," Adam laughed.

"If you think that's something you should see your face." Carter said wryly.

It was only at that he realized that the tingling he felt in his throat was not just a giddy thrill about growing a tail. The pulsing numbness was spreading up along his neck and through his jaw, gradually spreading across the rest of his face. His tongue felt thick and heavy in his mouth as he worked his jaw up and down, his sinuses popped and his nose felt like it was completely congested. Wentz startled slightly as he struggled to draw a deep breath only to feel a rush of air across the back of his throat coming from a whole new area of his neck.

Adam looked down at the surface of the pool and he could tell there was something different about his appearance but he couldn't see it clearly enough. He ran hand across his face and his nose and mouth definitely seemed swollen. With a quick flick of his tail and a kick of his flippered feet he exploded through the water and leapt fully out of the pool in one swift motion. He landed heavily on the deck, the weight of his new tail feeling even more apparent on his backside now that he was out of the water. He trotted over to a stainless steel equipment cart and tossed the tools off the top to stare at his reflection in the metallic surface. He was getting used to the strange black and white coloration but what he saw now was certainly no longer human. His nose was gone and in its place his mouth had stretched out into a thick almost beak-like distension. Adam's ears had receded to the point where they were just small indentations in the side of his head and if he was not mistake he also now had a blow hole at the crest of his skull.

Carter had pulled his speedo back on and climbed out of the pool to stand beside his stunned friend. "You still not interested in them trying to change you back?"

Adam blinked and looked over his reflection, rubbing his hands over his face and down his chest and arms. Water steadily dripped off his smooth skin and he admired the striking patches of black and white that covered his body. He felt his brand new tail flick slightly and his massive dorsal fin twitched as he looked down at his still erect and oddly shaped cock. All things considered though he felt right like this, like this was the way he was meant to be.

He took a deep satisfying breath as he looked up at Carter. "Actually, yeah I am sure. I mean I'm stronger, faster, and a better swimmer than I was before, so why not stay this way? I'm sure the Marines could use a few Orcas like me in spec ops."

"Is that what you think they made you?" Carter asked still smiling a lot.

"Well the Doc told me they used killer whale hormones in their formula after my skin color changed. Do you think I should change back?"

Carter shook his head. "Actually I was wondering what else they could do for me. Just because they promoted you to Staff Sergeant is no reason for you to start to thinking you're better than me."

"That's not just what I think, it's a fact of life bud, especially now," Adam said standing up to his full height and flexing his impressive muscles.

"You know I think I should go get the Doc, there's defiantly something wrong with your mind now," he laughed.

"I probably should let him know about this right away, he was pissed enough the last time and that was just a fin, now I have a tail."

"I can go find him for you. In the mean time you should see about getting rid of this unless you want somebody other than me to examine it," Carter said giving Adam's semi-erect cock a gentle squeeze before kissing him on the cheek.

"No, I think I'll save that honor for you," Wentz chuckled as Carter turned to head towards the locker room. The Orca's new face twisted into a grin, "But first... There's something I want to try out."

Before he got out of reach though Wentz grabbed him by the arm and pulled him back, falling backward so they both landed in the pool with a tremendous splash.

Adam dove underwater, circling around Carter as he sized up his prey. With every flip and turn he became more accustomed to using his new tail to help propel himself through the water. Eventually he came in close enough to bring his beak into contact with Carter's bulging speedo which was failing miserably to conceal the aroused state of his prick. It was incredible how the taste of the water across his tongue was almost like pulling in the masculine scent of his friend.

Adam yanked the thin spandex swimsuit down his legs before lashing Carter's cock with his tongue which was longer and thicker than before he had changed. Adam could hear Carter's moans coming from above the surface of the pool as his mouth engulfed the entire length of his shaft in one fell swoop. All Carter could do was to try and tread water as Adam bobbed in and out on his erect cock. Adam knew it would take longer to bring Carter to climax since he had shot a full load into him only minutes before but he wasn't in much of a rush. Underwater, every sensation was amplified for him. The pool currents rippling across his fluke and throbbing cock, the taste of his best friend filling his mouth, and the touch of Carter's quivering hands rubbing over Adam's glossy smooth skin all made the moment of Carter's orgasm just as enjoyable for him as it was for Carter judging by the muffled cries he heard from above the surface.

Wentz drank down every last drop of Carter's seed before he released him. Slowly floating upward, he let his dorsal fin breach the surface first before exhaling in a powerful blast from his newly formed blowhole.

"Holy shit man, how long can you hold your breath?" Carter panted out, still coming down from his orgasmic high.

"I had had it up to ten minutes the other day, but I feel like I can go twice as long now. Of course the better question is; how long can you hold yours?" Adam hinted ominously.

Wentz floated upward on his back, exposing his throbbing cock to the air just enough to give Carter a hint at his intentions and give him time to take a deep breath. Flipping over and swimming underneath him, Wentz maneuvered behind his fellow marine and wrapped his arms around Carter before gently pulling him beneath the surface. This time the grunts and groans sounded entirely different to Adam since they were both underwater. It had taken him a while to decide that he was ready for this and he only hoped that Carter was just as ready. The pointed tip of his cock zeroed in on Carter's rear and the tight warm embrace of his hole gradually replaced the cool water around Adam's shaft.

Holding him tightly, Wentz drove into Carter repeatedly, pushing the length of his orca-like cock deeper into him. He was very careful to stay close to the surface, bobbing upward often enough to make sure Carter was able to breathe at regular intervals. Adam loved the touch of his friend's body against him, radiating heat into the water surrounding them. Even floating in the pool Adam felt like he was in complete control of his new body. A subtle flip of his tail and his dick was in Carter to the hilt. A slight adjustment of his fins and his throbbing member rotated slightly causing Carter to gurgle with ecstasy.

Adam was nearing the limits of how long he could hold his breath, the air burning in his lungs only increasing his need for release. He wanted to finish before he surfaced though. He slammed against Carter, the pace of his thrusts quickened and in moments Adam's climax shot through him like a bolt of lightning. He held onto Carter as his entire body tensed up and he concentrated the full force orgasm though his pulsing cock. Several long, pronounced jets of cum erupted from his shaft into Carter as his skin tingled from the tip of his tail to the point of his dorsal fin. Floating in the water only amplified the euphoria he felt at that moment. He released Carter who drifted up off of his manhood towards the surface of the pool. Adam rose slowly, again blasting air through his blowhole as he drew in fresh oxygen.

"Fuck Wentz, I don't think I've ever had anyone pump me so full. You think that's just part of the changes they made to you or are you just better underwater?" Carter asked, gasping for breath.

"More adverse side effects, I guess," Wentz sighed.

"Adverse my ass. We're gonna have to do that again."

"Maybe tomorrow," Wentz grinned. "In the mean time you were supposed to be fetching the doc so they can have their turn probing me for the next few hours."

"My way would be more fun but ok. First things first though. Where's my swimsuit? Carter asked with a laugh as he climbed out of the pool naked.

Adam chuckled as he dove to the bottom of the pool to retrieve Carter's hastily discarded speedo, tossing it to him as he surfaced.

The young sergeant pulled the suit on before heading to the locker room; he wanted to shower off before getting the rest of the medical staff involved. Carter was only under the steady jet of water for a minute when the water started to feel too warm for him. He didn't think he had turned it up that high. He slowly dialed back the controls, each time still feeling like it was too hot. Soon he was standing under and icy spray of cold water. He simply figured it was the residual heat from Wentz's load in his rear that was keeping him warm. It was at that moment that a peculiar sensation rippled through him. He groaned aloud as he sank to his knees on the tiled floor, his cock had quickly become rock hard and was straining beneath the thin spandex of his swim briefs.

160

Hearing his cries, Wentz had come running from the pool, his heavy flipper-like feet slapping across the tile floor as he ran up to the prone figure of his comrade.

"Carter! What is it, are you okay?" Wentz yelled out as he shut off the shower.

"I don't know man. I just started to feel real... aaaargh!" Carter cried out again as he arched his back. His cock was jutting out in the speedo like a tent pole as it swiftly started to spasm depositing a thick wad of spunk that seeped through the black spandex and streamed down his legs.

Wentz gasped. Not at the sight of his friend shooting his load, he was used to that. Rather, he was shocked by the steadily darkening color of Carter's thighs as his skin gradually changed from a bronze tan to a steadily darkening, glossy black. Carter pitched forward, panting as he knelt on all his hands and knees, still ejaculating into his speedo. Now Wentz could see the color change wasn't limited to his Carter's legs it was quickly spreading outward from the small of his back as well. The changes didn't stop there however, as a bulge formed between his shoulder blades, in moments the pointed tip of a fin could be seen expanding outward from his back.

"I think I better go get Doctor Grant instead," Wentz offered as Carter's changes seemed to be slowing.

"Yeah, I think it might be explanation time, for us and for damned sure them." Carter agreed as he rubbed a hand across the black skin that extended down to his knees.

TEST LAB – TWENTY DAYS AFTER THE EXPERIMENT

"Staff Sergeant Wentz, Sergeant Carter, stand easy," Major Dawes addressed the two of them as they relaxed from standing at attention. "I am very pleased with how well the two of you have conducted yourselves during these test trials. I know things have been hard for the both of you and I appreciate your dedication to the corp."

Wentz could feel Carter next to him doing his best to stifle a laugh at the pun the Major unknowingly delivered. Wentz shot him a glance and Carter quickly wiped the smirk from his orca-like beak. Since their night in the pool, Carter had spent his time alternating between being submerged for hours at a time in the tank in the corner of the lab and being screwed by Wentz in every way imaginable. The strangest thing was that both activities were being done under Doctor Grant's orders.

Not surprisingly, the doc was none too thrilled with Wentz's changes when he had burst into his office that night, the addition of a tail was probably what really threw him. Nor was he exactly pleased with the method of exposure that triggered the changes in Carter.

Doctor Grant was very determined that this program succeeded though and was willing to keep the true nature of Carter's inclusion confidential. Under the doctor's supervision, Carter's transformation progressed rapidly and he now stood next to Wentz fully changed into the perfect orca Marine. Well, maybe not quite as perfect as Wentz who still felt he was bigger and better in multiple ways.

"With your help we believe our test protocol has been successful and is well ahead of the soldier augmentation programs developed in the other service branches." Major Dawes continued. "Doctor Grant has reported that he believes he is ready for a full scale test and we will be selecting additional candidates to form a full squad. That is, if you two feel ready to proceed."

"Yes, Sir!" Wentz responded immediately.

"I'm prepared to do whatever it takes." Carter added, again trying to repress his smile.

Even Wentz felt a thrill at that thought and stoically kept his face impassive.

"Very well then, Doctor," The Major said, turning his attention to Grant who was also keeping his best poker face, "you are authorized to proceed with your next batch of selections. Please keep me posted on your progress."

"Yes Major," Doctor Grant responded as the officer excused himself.

"So Doc, who do you want us to fuck with next?" Carter laughed after Major Dawes was out of the lab.

"Sergeant Carter," the doctor turned to face the second orca, "as much as I appreciate your enthusiasm, I am still trying to conduct a serious genetic modification program here. I had anticipated that the mix of hormones may have amplified the test subject's libido, however I had not surmised that the DNA adaptations would have reacted so aggressively in his reproductive system. If I had known that Staff Sergeant Wentz's ejaculations served as a triggering agent for alterations to his genetic structure I would have chosen a more structured method then to have the two of you fornicating in every corner of this facility to achieve results."

Wentz felt his skin warm as he blushed, though you couldn't see the effect on his new dark skin. He did feel bad about causing so much difficulty for the doc but he wasn't about to complain about the results. He glanced down at the floor and let his gaze drift back up along the length of Carter's thick tail as it jutted out from the modified fatigues they both wore in the presence of the top brass and additional medical staff. If it hadn't been for Carter, the doc would have never discovered that the formula he had injected into Wentz was so aggressive that it has turned his sperm into a potent delivery system for the new DNA he now possessed.

"Sorry doc, I just want to do everything I can to help out," Carter apologized.

Doctor Grant shook his head, "I appreciate that. The difficulty is that your transformation raises more questions for the program than it answers right now."

"How do you figure doc?" Wentz asked.

"First, Staff Sergeant, the introduction of your DNA into another subject—" the doctor raised an eyebrow, "repeatedly— altered his genetic structure. While the samples you have both provided have been helpful we now need to determine if Sergeant Carter's DNA is just as aggressive in another host."

"Great! Who did you have in mind?" Carter asked, slapping his hands together and grinning again.

The doctor had obviously decided the best course at this point was to attempt to ignore Carter's commentary. "We also need to ascertain if the initial serum we used on Staff Sergeant Wentz will have similar effects in others and if they too will need the hormones produced during coitus to physically change."

Wentz understood where this was going and while he was more composed he was getting just excited as Carter and could feel the swelling starting to stir in his crotch again. "So how would you like us to proceed, Doctor Grant?"

"You will be in command of this unit Staff Sergeant I will leave the decision up to you. I began administering the serum I used on Adam to Corporal Teague yesterday. Meanwhile, I had a lengthy conversation with Private First Class Benitez and Sergeant Mears who I had identified as the most suitable candidates for the alternative type of, ahem... DNA transmission, and they both seemed quite eager to volunteer. In the meantime I will be in my office when you're ready to make your first report Mr. Wentz."

Carter was already stripping out of his fatigues by the time the doc had reached the door, "So you heard him, command my unit."

"Damn it Carter, you're lucky you look good in black or I would just do this without you."

"Even you wouldn't be so cruel, Sir." Carter responded in mock indignation.

Wentz glanced over at the mirror on the wall opposite them and took in their black and white reflections while letting his tail flex slightly, "Well it sounds like I might need to break this slowly to Teague. For now, I say we go see if Benitez and Mears are ready for a new kind of service to the Corp."

THE WICKED WORLD
OF CHARLES JACKLYN

Roland Jovaik

C harles dismissed the cobwebs and dust bunnies that littered the floor of his dimly lit laboratory as he paced behind his desk, russet tail twitching restlessly. He had burned through hundreds of combinations and none of them unlocked the secrets he searched for! They refused to take hold or have any effect at all. Things were starting to look hopeless. There had to have been something he hadn't tried yet.

He rubbed at the bags under his eyes with closed fists. His ears drooped and his posture sagged with defeat, while his hands shook like a man suffering opium withdrawal. How could the pursuit for eternal happiness leave a man so withered and frail?

Friends and colleagues alike had told him he needed rest. They begged him to stop his tireless pursuit, but he would have none of it. They knew nothing of his plight, not that they would understand if he told them. He would continue his torturous journey without aid.

Success was palpable. He could taste success just as vividly as he could taste the other failed concoctions on the tip of his tongue.

Vials sat near the edge of his desk, filled with specific measurements of only the rarest herbs and chemicals. All of his calculations told him that this was the final concoction. The elixir of life.

The final result when mixed together looked like nothing he'd ever seen. It glowed dimly, casting eerie shadows in the absence of light.

"This is it," he muttered.

All the naysayers, all the ridicule. He would prove them all wrong with this.

There was no doubt in his mind. He swirled the contents of the beaker and tilted his head back, gulping it down without a second thought.

The taste was bitter and unpleasant, like medicine.

Charles waited, counting on some sort of sign to come forth and yield results for his painstaking work. Nothing.

The weary fox slumped in his chair with a palm on his forehead, his tail hung limp between his legs. Nothing worked. Maybe it was best he give up and heed the advice of those around him. It was a tireless pursuit and Charles had run out of ideas.

Charles' footsteps echoed beyond the darkness. The empty void seemed to stretch on forever, threatening to engulf him at any time. A dim halo of light radiated from his paws as he stepped forward.

"Hello?"

There was no echo. Nothing around him for his words to bounce off of. Yet he could feel someone watching him.

A pair of glinting yellow eyes blinked in the distance.

Charles balled his paws in front of his chest. "Who's there?"

A chortle echoed in the distance, quickly filling the space around him. It sounded like his own voice, but much deeper, and much more menacing.

"Show yourself! I'm not afraid!"

"But you are afraid." Charles could hear the saliva dripping from the voice's jaws as it drawled on. "You've opened the door Charlie, and once it's been opened there's no closing it. I'm comin' for ya Charlie."

The yellow eyes disappeared from sight and Charles whipped his head around and swiveled his ears, hoping to catch sight of the perpetrator.

"Show yourself!" Charles backed up in circles, not risking to leave his rear exposed for longer than a split-second. His tail thrashed around, the fur on his neck standing on end. "I don't know who you are, but I'll find you!"

"You don't?" The voice seemed surprised over this. "I thought you had more wits about yeh than that, Chah-ley." There was a noticeable emphasis when the voice drew out the fox's name.

"How do you know who I am?"

"You'll find out soon enough, Charlie."

Charles heard a snarl come up from behind him. He turned around just in time to see the large snapping jaws of a ferocious beast, gleaming white fangs closing around his head.

Charles awoke with a crash as he fell from his chair. Several items fell from the desk and broke against the hard floor of the basement.

"Charles!" A worried cry came from upstairs.

"I'm alright," the fox called out, holding a paw to the back of his head. He rubbed the spot that he was sure he'd hit when he fell back, but there was barely a bump, let alone any twinges of pain.

Charles stood. Much to his surprise, he was uninjured. The same could not be said of the chair. Two of the legs had snapped and the back was beyond repair. No matter.

Looking down at the chair, Charles realized he didn't just feel good, he felt great. Better than great.

His senses were heightened. He swore he could pick up smells from the whore-house, nearly a city's distance away, and he was overflowing with energy. His limbs ached with the need to do something.

Charles looked to the heavy, ornate wooden desk. He wondered if he might have the strength to move it on his own. He hunched down and placed his paws underneath the desk and heaved. The desk moved easily, as though it were a children's toy.

He marveled at his own actions, until it dawned on him that he was supposed to be approaching this scientifically.

He laid the desk down, his papers fluttering as it landed against the floor with a bang. His newfound power made it difficult to judge his own strength accurately.

"Charles?" Jessica called down again.

The stairs creaked with Jessica's stomps downstairs. She held her blouse up as she poked her muzzle downstairs. Her tail was bottle brushed and her ears were perked in alarm. "Charles, what in the lord's good name are is going on down here? Are you hurt?"

"No, I'm fine Jess. Thank you." Charles examined his paws.

Charles sat back down in his chair, looking to the desk and then to his paws. He flexed his fingers, inspecting them. Nothing about his outward appearance had changed, but it felt like a fire was roiling inside of him.

"Charlie."

Charles bolted upright in his chair, shaking free of his daze. He turned to Jess.

"Charles, I asked if you were you all right."

"I'm sorry," he muttered. "I did not hear you. I'm fine." He turned back to his papers and took a sip from his tea cup, ignoring the spill that he'd made from moving the desk. He choked and spat the bitter dregs back into his cup. The tea had gone cold in his absent-mindedness.

Jessica placed a fresh kettle next to Charles' notes, the steaming pot smelling strongly of persimmons. Somehow she knew when he preferred a fresh spot of tea or a day-old biscuit. He much preferred them that way. "*They go better with the tea,*" he would always reply.

"It is no surprise. Your head has been in the clouds, more than on your shoulders." She sat on the corner of his desk, mindful of her tail. She crowded a stack of papers together before minding herself with her hair, red locks twirled around her finger as she spoke. "Some days I fear I'll find you as dead as the silence you surround yourself in. I cannot always be around to feed and water you, you know."

She smiled. Her attempt at a joke. Charles managed a sideways grin and shuffled the rest of his papers back into their proper order. "Noise detracts from the conscious thought," he said simply. "And my body will surely tell me if it requires sustenance, although I fear I may have forgotten how to operate the stove."

Jessica laughed and rested a hand on Charles' shoulder with a squeeze. Her warm smile relieved some of the worry in Charles' face. "Dinner is almost ready. Take a break, you've been hard at work all day."

Charles rubbed the sleep from his eye and squinted down at his papers. What once resembled his notes merely looked like black smudges on a page now. Perhaps she was right. A fresh cup of tea and a warm meal would set his mind straight.

When Charles reached out to grab the desk again, he found it sat as heavily as it did before he drank the serum. The effects had already worn off.

Potent smells of a freshly cooked meal set Charles' nose twitching. Not once had he noticed the smell of Yorkshire pudding and prime rib in the air, nor the undertones of fresh beef gravy. All the more reason to take a break.

It was hard for the fox not to concentrate on his work, but as his gaze fell to Jess' lovely hips rocking back and forth like a well-timed metronome, it helped to put his mind at ease and concentrate on... something else.

Charles thought back to when Jessica first moved in with him. What started as a need for extra help around the house had evolved into a more casual affair as time passed. In between work, the two of them found each other exchanging timid smiles and sideways glances when they thought the other wasn't looking.

Jess was being especially forward about her flirting tonight. It wasn't hard to imagine what lay beneath that sultry tail. The things he could do to her tickled his deeper, more carnal sensations.

With the back of his thumb he wiped the drool from his lower lip, unable to hide his perverted grin. Fur prickled, and his senses spiked before Charles found himself disgusted by the impure thoughts flooding his mind. He prayed Miss Valentine had yet to notice and willed himself to normalcy, feeling the hair on his arms fall from their tensed positions.

Charles instead focused his attention to the savory scents of roast beef and Yorkshire pudding. It tickled his nose and sent his tail wagging.

The fox took his seat at the dark mahogany dinner table, brushing his tail out of the way. Not another word was uttered as he dug into the lavish meal that Jess had prepared. The meat was only slightly overcooked, the pudding a little doughy, and the gravy could have used more salt, but it was everything compared to the stale, toasted bread (the very extent of his culinary abilities) that he ate on a regular basis.

"You have certainly kept yourself busy these days," Jess piped up, interrupting Charles' silent fortitude.

"Life's secrets do not yield to the lazy," he muttered. Charles did not want to get into more detail than was necessary. Not when more than half the town already thought of him as a laughing stock. He doubted the vixen would understand anyway.

Jessica's tail whipped past his nose before she trotted off to the stove with a giggle and a spring in her step. Charles stole a sideways glance at Jessica's swinging hips.

"Keep showin' off yo'r tail like that and I'll have ta bend yeh over tha counta, li'l miss."

The crash of a dish rang in Charles' ears. Jess spun and pressed herself back against the counter. "Mister Jacklyn!"

Charles bolted from her chair, keeping his head down as he rushed past her and towards the bedroom. "I, I'm sorry Jessica, I'm afraid I don't feel quite right. Thank you for dinner, it was delicious."

The door slammed shut behind him and he threw himself onto his bed, tail cowering between his legs as he dug his nose into his pillow with ears slicked back. What had come over him at the dinner table? What had compelled him to say such an uncivilized thing? They were friends, and nothing more. Of course she'd been offended by such a crude and vulgar comment. He hoped she would have forgiven him by the time morning came.

Long, drooling fangs plagued Charles' vision, and slack-jawed laughing followed him wherever he ran. The voice wasn't coming from any one direction. It surrounded him, followed him. The feeling was reminiscent of the strange dream he'd had shortly after taking his concoction.

"This again," he grumbled. "Show yourself, coward!" Laughter echoed back at him. "I've told you once already, I am not afraid!" He bit his lower lip, hoping the voice wouldn't be able to tell he was bluffing.

"You can't lie to me, Charlie." A trill of a growl echoed in the darkness. "Because I am you. And I know when yo're lyin'." The voice laughed again.

Charles backed away from where he imagined the voice could be coming from. No matter how many steps he took, it didn't feel like he was getting anywhere.

"The night has come Charlie. It's time t'let the wolf out. Ready or not, 'ere I come."

The floor opened up beneath Charles and the darkness consumed him as he fell.

Charles screamed, falling to the floor with a painful crash. He sat up, throwing his blankets and pillow back onto the bed.

The gibbous moon outside his window filled his room with an eerie silver glow. How long had he slept? It was well past midnight.

"But the night is still young, Charlie."

Charles shook his head. He was talking to himself now? Preposterous. All of those late nights really were getting to his head. However, under the light of the moon, he felt more alive than he had in years. The world was his for the taking.

Floorboards creaked beneath his paws as he stepped into the kitchen. Even in the low light, Charles could see perfectly well, as though it were bright as day.

The streets were sparse, littered with only a few shady characters as Charles stepped into the night. A swift autumn breeze nipped at his nose. When his trench coat wouldn't close around his waist, he let it fall open as he padded down the city streets. For whatever reason, the rest of his clothes seemed to have a tighter fit on him than usual as well.

Further down the street, in the dim light of the gas lamps, Charles saw a short, fat, hunched-over figure bumbling his way around. On a second glance, the grey muzzle and wiry tail looked familiar.

"Henry!" Charles called out and waved.

The meek wolf looked up, paws wringing against each other. He froze in place when he saw Charles.

The fox stepped forward, extending a paw to shake hands.

"Stay back!" The wolf yelled, frightened and clutching his cane. The bowler hat he wore nearly fell off his head he was shaking so much.

"Henry, I—"

"I don't have any money! Just leave me alone, whoever you are!"

Before Charles could get another word in edgewise, Henry had run off into the night.

Charles scratched his muzzle trying to figure out what had happened when he noticed something peculiar about his paw. He yelped in surprise when he realized that his hands and claws had grown in size. They looked like wolf paws. His muzzle felt broader, too. On top of it all, he noticed that his heightened senses had returned. He had been too drowsy to notice it until now.

"What in the blazes," he muttered, staring down at his paws. He would be sure to document all of this when he got home from his walk.

The brothels were bustling as he waltzed further into town. He glanced into each one he passed, intrigued but not tempted enough to venture into one. He was about to turn back for home when a sweet cinnamon scent wafted past his nose.

A white vixen stood next to a dimly lit sign that read "The Red Curtain." Her fur was neatly trimmed, and her breasts were supported by a deep red corset.

"You look thirsty, darlin'. Why don't you come and settle in for a spell? The beer's watered down, but the company will keep you warm on a night as cold as this one."

Charles glanced back at the whore that stood in the doorway. The red, low-cut corset that hugged her breasts and her short dress, showing more than just a bit of ankle, suggested that she required a little warming herself. Likely one of her well-practiced selling points.

Charles offered an apologetic smile and tipped his muzzle to the mistress. "I'm afraid I partake of neither of the services you offer. Perhaps the next person you come across will be more receptive."

"Oh." Disappointment tainted her voice. "If anytime, you need a friend..." Her words trailed, her gaze slowly turning away.

C'mon Charlie, live a little.

"Miss."

The vixen turned her head, eyes sparkling with desire.

"I've changed my mind."

The main dining area was dimly lit by candlelight. A doe stood on stage, svelte red dress hugging her frame as she sang sultry tones to weary men. Her fur was beginning to gray and Charles could tell her ears no longer stood as tall as they used to. Her voice was scratchy, withered by nights of smoking and days of drinking.

She must know little else, he thought to himself grimly.

"This way, Love. Take a seat."

The seats were cracked and frayed. Flickering candle light may have even hid the small blemishes, were it not for Charles' supernatural eyesight.

The brothel had a distinct, musty smell, covered up by the scent of burning candles, cigarette smoke, and the spicy cinnamon-like perfumes that the whores wore on themselves.

Charles leaned back against his seat, eyeing the dancer on stage. Her ears flicked with each twist of her hips, the doe making sure that everyone in the crowd was had a good look.

He jumped, his focus broken when he heard a tap on the table. He looked to the shot glass in front of him, then to the side where the temptress had taken her seat.

"A little something to warm your blood, handsome," she said with a grin on her slender muzzle.

He had been so entranced by the evening entertainment that he barely heard the vixen leave, or come back, not even with his supernatural senses.

He looked down at amber liquid. The smell alone burned his nostrils.

"I don't normally—"

A growl within Charles' own mind silenced him. He looked back to the glass, feeling compelled to accept the Vixen's offering.

He reached out a paw and lifted the shot to his muzzle, allowing the potent smell of distilled spirits to sting at his muzzle.

"Where's yours, Love?"

The vixen reached up to brush a bit of fur out of her eyes. "I don't normally drink with the patrons."

"One drink won't hurt yo'r pretty figure." Charles leaned in, his free paw brushing up against the fox's leg, teasing her dress up just a little bit.

The vixen's ears slanted back and she looked away for a brief moment.

"Or we can get right down ta business if you prefer." Charles' squeezed her thigh.

The vixen jumped and tried to hide the fluster in her muzzle. "One drink couldn't hurt..."

Screams punctuated the banging of the headboard against the wall. The nameless vixen shredded the sheets beneath her with manicured claws as Charles thrust himself between the whore's legs. Her legs hung around Charles' shoulders, jerking up and down as Charles thrust himself upon her.

The growls that escaped his throat did not feel like his own. His urges and actions all seemed driven by an underlying force, something he couldn't quite comprehend. His thoughts were fuzzy and it was hard to concentrate on anything other than the attractive vixen beneath him, his ears twitching to the sound of each of her squeaks.

With large, drooling fangs, Charles' raked his teeth against the vixen's neck, prompting the vixen to drag her own claws against Charles' sides.

"No marks," she protested breathlessly.

Charles only growled in response, his thrusts quickening and his bites and claws becoming more aggressive, the closer he came to climax.

The nameless snow-white vixen cried out as Charles thrust harder, grinding his thickening knot against her sex, popping inside with a throaty growl.

It wasn't long after that, the fox's passage tightened around his cock like a vice, and Charles' painted her insides with his seed. His knot tied them together in a fleeting moment passion.

Now that the heat between his legs was beginning to subside, Charles found he was able to think with a little more clarity, about where he was and what he was doing. His eyes widened and he tried, against his better instincts, to pull out of the whore he'd tied with.

"Oh, honey, that hurts." She winced, her claws digging against his shoulder.

"I, I have to go. I have to get out of here."

There was a 'pop' as Charles managed to free himself forcefully from the vixen beneath him. She cried out, cursing loudly to the air as she pressed her thighs together.

"Sorry, sorry," Charles stammered, pulling his pants on as quickly as he could. "I can't stay here. Thank you," Charlie stammered as his ears flushed. "For your time," he finished, shame flooding his features.

The vixen continued to curse him as he fled upstairs and out into the street. He didn't look back. He couldn't stand to think about this extreme lapse in judgement. A whorehouse was so unbecoming of him. He never would have done something so careless before tonight. What was wrong with him? The transformed paws, his lack of inhibition. Was the serum doing this to him? Were the effects permanent? This all called for more research back at home. All the more reason to get back as soon as possible.

Charles squinted as the sun began to peek over the horizon. How could it be daytime already?

Tomorrow would be a long day.

Morning came early for him, much earlier than he ever felt reasonable. A loud clatter woke him from his slumber. Past the bleary papers and quills stood Jessica. At least he was fairly sure it was Jessica, standing with her crossed arms, an even crosser frown. Her ears twitched with irritation.

"Good morning," he managed before stretching with a yawn. "A bit early for tea, isn't it?" Charles yawned as he tried to rub the sleep from his eyes.

"Hmph, early indeed," she spat. "Maybe for you, Mad Hatter. Going out late, staying out all night! Don't even have the decency to let me know you've made it back in one piece. You will be the death of me, that much is certain. I hope it was worth it. Enjoy your tea, Mr. Jacklyn."

She left as quickly as she had come, storming up the stairs with her russet tail lashing about.

Charles fished out his pocket watch. Twelve forty-five. He had not remembered falling asleep at his desk, much less getting back to it after his walk from the night before.

Had he blacked out during the night? He couldn't remember getting home, but he definitely remembered leaving the brothel.

He recalled having felt different and much unlike himself. What was happening to him? Perhaps the visions in his dreams were a telling of things to come. The thought struck fear into him.

He rubbed at his temples, yearning for something stronger than the tea laid before him.

"You know how women can be, Charles. Go out for one night on the town and they get their knickers in a bunch."

Charles sipped his tea with pursed lips, letting the strong scents of black tea tickle his nose and bring him back to the waking world.

"I suppose so," Charles nodded to the wolf sitting across from him. Henry and Charles had met during a tribunal they both attended in regards to one of the fox's more risqué experiments; an elixir that would grant any one person extraordinary abilities and rid them of strife.

Henry had been assigned to represent Charles' defense. Despite an amazing argument, Charles was black-listed from continuing his experiments publicly. That did not stop the two from conversing and becoming close friends after the hearing was over, however.

"Women only seem to complicate matters," Henry continued, reaching a paw out towards Charles' black paw. Charles receded, stumbling for a lump of sugar to drop in his tea.

Charles interrupted the silence with a cough. "This is not the business that I met with you today to discuss, Henry. You remember the tribunal?"

Henry nodded, hiding his grey-speckled muzzle behind his coffee cup. The wolf always took his coffee the same way; black, sweetened with just a pinch of sugar.

"I think I've found a breakthrough."

Charles flicked his ears to the sound of crashing porcelain against the table.

"You're not serious! Surely you remember the tribunal's decision. It's mad!"

Frustration furrowed the fox's brow. He placed his teacup down and pinched the bridge of his hose. "I thought you of all people would understand my plight. I only want to help people, not condemn them."

"Surely you respect their decision, Charles. Nobody is questioning your motives, but a line of ethics has to be drawn."

Charles felt his hackles begin to rise, his paws clutching the side of his teacup. "Who's side are you defending, Henry?"

"I'm not taking sides, but perhaps the tribunal was—"

"Enough!" Charles stood from his chair, slamming his cup down with enough force to shake the table. "I thought you would understand, but I was clearly mistaken. I will do this without your help."

"Charles, wait!"

The house rattled as Charles threw the door shut behind him. With a deep sigh he stepped out into the street, ignoring the gawking stares.

Sun was beginning to set when Charles opened the squeaky front door to an empty dining room. He peered inside, cautious to the women scorned that may be lying in wait.

"Jess, I'm home."

Jess's door at the end of the hallway slammed shut, disturbing the curtains with a sudden gust of air.

"Still mad," he grumbled. It had been a long day anyway. Perhaps, he thought, he should retire early.

Charles shot straight up out of bed, wide-eyed and panting. *Those damn dreams again*, he thought. He looked out of his bedroom window to the light of the full moon. With little cloud cover, it shone almost as brightly as its own small sun.

Thanks to his nightmares, Charles had lost any inclination he had to go back to sleep. The more he glanced out his window, the more compelled he felt to take a long moonlit stroll.

He stepped into the dining room, surprised to see Jessica on her perch as she listened to the radio. She barely glanced his way, growing jaded to his bizarre antics, but still too caring to leave.

"Where are you going? It's awfully late." Her voice wavered. It sounded like she'd been crying.

"I'm going for a bout of fresh air. I wish to be back before sunrise."

"Of course, Mr. Jacklyn. Heaven forbid the sun touches your dry, musty fur, for fear that it might combust into flame."

For the sake of avoiding another one of Ms. Valentine's screaming matches, he forced a smile as he stepped out the door.

The smell of autumn was rich, notes of falling leaves and the oncoming seasons brushing past him in the wind. The cold air nipped at him from the moment he stepped outside. It buried itself deep beneath his fur and refused to lose hold. He cursed under his breath and huddled in the warmth of his coat. His bushy fur only went so much to insulate him from the cold. The seasons were early, and his winter coat had not been fully realized.

Sparsely placed lamps did little to light the streets under the shine of the full moon. They only seemed to add to the eerie nature of walking the streets at night. In spite of it all, he knew there was no reason to be afraid. Stories of boogeymen in the dark were merely children's tales, to scare them into behaving. They were not real.

A wind blew past Charles that sent a shiver down his spine and made him walk faster down the lane, coat clutched to his chest.

His late night walk brought him off the main streets of Leadworth, down toward an even darker landing that bordered a stench-filled river, a fine mix of water and raw sewage. It was as close to serenity as he could get near the busy streets of London.

He stuck his hands in his pockets and looked out over the river. If he tried hard enough, he could smell the faint scent of burning gas over the potent filth that floated by.

The scuffle of rocks woke him from his trance.

"Well, well, what 'ave we 'ere?"

Charles turned to meet eyes with the first of turned out to be three larger individuals. Though they looked taller and broader than the average fox frame, their sharp, angular muzzles were distinct. Their features were well-hidden in the stark contrast of the moonlight and the darkness. Not one of them looked to be less than two-hundred pounds, and they varied quite drastically in height. One at least a head shorter than Charles', another a head taller, and the other in between. The menacing grins on their muzzles told Charles they meant to do him harm.

"Good evening... gentlemen." He swallowed the lump in his throat. "I was not expecting company tonight."

Charles raised a black paw in the air. The brass finish of his walking cane shone with the moonlight, an item that had remained hidden under his jacket until now. "I don't want any trouble."

The three men towered over Mr. Jacklyn. Each one wore a stupid grin. The tallest one appeared to be their leader. His face was sunken and pale against the moonlight. "Well that's just too bad."

Charles' fur prickled under the light of the full moon. His back lurched forward and the fox let out a cry as an unbelievable pain coursed through his body.

"Please," Charles choked, clutching his cane with shaky paws. What was happening to him? "I do not want to cause harm." Something warm dripped down his paw. Blood, from digging his claws into his palm due to nerves.

The smallest of the three thugs piped up, his voice nasally and high-pitched like claws on a chalkboard. "Hey, this bloke says he won't do us any harm if we leave 'im alone!"

All of the foxes' laughed amongst themselves, scratching at their arms as their tails twitched erratically back and forth. Charles recognized the behavior as a symptom of cocaine. He could easily pick out the drug's potent effects. It was unlikely that they would leave of their own accord.

Charles bottle-brushed tail curled against his leg and the hackles on his neck raised. He raised his cane in the air, fearful that if it came down to defending himself, he would lose.

The tallest fox approached with a twitch in his eye while scratching at his left arm. A half-circle formed around him as they closed in. Charles looked from the tallest fox to the short one on his left. When he looked to the right, the third fox was missing.

Charles' world went white he fell to his knees. Blood splattered the ground in front of him when he coughed, and his limbs shook, struggling to keep him supported.

"This is gonna be easier than I thought," one of the foxes growled above him. He hadn't the wherewithal to tell which one.

Sleep tugged at the edges of Charles' mind. He was most certainly concussed. Whatever they hit him with had been hard, and he could feel blood dripping down his neck. As his vision blurred in and out of focus, he saw that his claws were growing larger and his fur was changing color, becoming thicker and longer.

"What the hell's happenin' wit''im?"

His ears twitched at the confused ramblings of the three muggers.

When Charles' vision returned, he could feel the rest of his body morphing in tandem. Pain seared through his back as it grew longer, threatening to tear itself from its weak, fleshy prison. The world grew blurry again as his muzzle stretched out before him.

He prayed for something to strike him down, to make the suffering stop.

Charles felt another presence invade his mind. It was strangely familiar. He froze when he a chuckle, the same laugh that plagued his sleep. The wolf from his nightmares.

The laughter only became louder, drowning out his thoughts. He was coming for him.

"Stop it!" Charles shouted, startling his attackers. "Stop what you're doing and get out of my head!"

"This is getting' freaky Boss," the smaller one squeaked. "Maybe we should—"

"Shut it!"

Charles clutched his head and kicked at the ground, ears flattened against his skull. The cackling voice was deafening.

A darkness surrounded the fox, pushing him to the very edges of his mind. He fought against the mysterious force, but something in his mind slipped and he fell screaming into the dark abyss.

A sickening crunch cascaded up the fox's spine as it twisted in ways that should not have been possible. Russet fur was swallowed up by an ever-expanding coarse grey coat. His senses grew sharper.

Night might as well have been day, and the mixture of poor hygiene and drugs on the thugs became painfully apparent to his over-sensitive nose. His limbs grew thicker and longer until nothing about his form was familiar.

When he stood, dragging his knuckles against the ground, the muggers flinched. They certainly didn't seem very intimidating now. The wolf wiped drool from his chin. His muzzle crooked into a sloppy half-grin as he stared down the three vulpines.

Shredded clothes hung his beastly frame. The only article survived was the jacket that stretched over the wolf's hulking shoulders.

The beast lunged forward, flaring his arms out.

With a fright the thugs fell back a step and the wolf howled with laughter, holding his belly with a paw. He held a tight grip on his walking cane, each of the thugs keeping a wary eye on it.

"What a pathetic lot you pigs are," he scoffed, letting drool run down his jowls as he spoke. "Run along, then."

None of them moved. The wolf snarled, giving them a long, hard stare. He snapped and the group took another two steps back. "Oy, what do you lot want? Piss off!"

The middle-sized fox was the first to dare take a step forward. "'Ey you, what 'appened to that otha bloke we was ruffin' up?"

"Otha' bloke..." The wolf trailed off, confusion twisting his features. "Oh, ol' Charlie! Sorry, he can't come to the door right now, but I would be happy ta take yo'r names and have 'im get in touch as soon as possible," he finished with a sneer.

"E'nuf 'a this!" The leader lunged forward with his fists balled, aiming right for the wolf's muzzle.

In one deft move the wolf lifted one end of his cane, deflecting the attack and throwing the fox off balance while using the other end of the cane to knock him square in the muzzle.

Everything felt like it was playing in slow motion. He extended his arm and smashed his fist against the would-be assailant's nose, sending the fox reeling sideways. He fell like a limp rag-doll. If he was still conscious, he didn't dare get up.

"Two against one hardly seems fair, doesn' it?" He threw his cane to the shortest, who caught it with less than an air of grace. "Much mor' fair," he laughed, throwing his head back.

"Why, you," The smaller vulpine took a running start, cane in hand. "You'll be sorry for mockin' us!"

The painfully inexperienced fighter went down with a punch to the ribs. Winded and short of breath, he fell to the ground, allowing the wolf to grab his cane back from the pathetically weak grasp.

The last fox standing did not dare take a step closer. He was visibly quaking and keeping his distance. "What kind of monster are you?"

The wolf barked with laughter, paying no mind to the drool and spit that sprayed from his muzzle, or the look of disgust on the fox's face as a good portion of it landed on him.

"I ahm so much worse than a monster, Sweet'art." His lips curled up into a vicious smile.

The fox kept himself on the offensive. "What's your name?"

The wolf's muzzle flashed confusion once more before he switched back to that knowing smile that spread from ear to ear. "I don't 'ave one."

The nameless beast took a step forward, and the frightened fox took a step back. Another step forward, another step back. Clearly outmatched, the last standing vulpine continued to slowly retreat before he broke into a full-out sprint.

The wolf was quick in pursuing him, dropping to all fours and keeping up with ease. There no doubt in the wolf's mind that he could catch such slow-moving prey. With a leap the fox was pinned under his weight, struggling helplessly as he gasped and called for help.

"No one is comin' to save you, Dahlin'. Now, let's 'ave a little fun, shall we?"

The fox shrieked into the dead of night and was quickly silenced.

The world slowly came back into view. Jessica was cleaning dishes and preparing what looked like breakfast. A fresh batch of toast sat before him and the sizzle of what he presumed to be fried eggs came from the stove to his left.

What had happened last night? The world had fallen away from him, and the rest of the night was a black spot in his memories. Something deep down told him he didn't want to remember. His body felt as though a carriage had run him over and came back around a second time to finish the job.

A paper lay on the table, headline reading "Three found dead near Leadworth Creek. Police investigating suspects."

Charles shifted in his chair and tried to stand. Bad idea, he thought as he held his pounding head. Keeping still offered no relief, and every smell was an assault on his senses.

He didn't remember drinking last night. Was that why he couldn't remember what happened?

"Sleep well, did you?" Jessica could not hide the snark in her voice as she set the steaming plate in front of Charles' muzzle. He had neither the will, nor the energy to grant her the satisfaction of any well thought out retort.

"I fear I may not have slept at all, M'Dear. Dreadful night, I fear. Very dreadful." He cradled his head, focusing on the lull of the radio to keep his mind off of his inner turmoil. "Is it morning already?"

"Morning?" She laughed. "You haven't moved since this afternoon! Blundering in here and passing out right where you were, sleeping like the dead. It's nearly evening."

Charles held his head once more, uttering curses at all the surprises that wanted nothing from him but pain. "I fear something awful happened last night."

"Maybe the radio's been soaking in through that thick noggin of yours while you were asleep. There's been a murder."

"Murder?" Charles sat upright in his chair, then cursed at the sudden movement, holding his temples with both paws. If he strained hard enough, he could remember three mysterious figures under a full moon. To recall anything more was too painful for him to muster.

"A ruffian," she confirmed. "Above-average height and stature, found out near the lake in County Square."

Another painful burst of memories came rushing to the forefront of the fox's mind. He had visited the lake last night. While he knew nothing of the finer details, his instincts told him this encounter with the three gentlemen from last night had not been one of civility. If only he could remember anything more, but he was sure it had been one of them, absolutely.

"Any witnesses?" He quizzed, nursing a bit of his toast. "Someone must have heard something."

"No witnesses."

Charles' breathed a silent sigh of relief.

"Though they did find fur on the body."

Charles dropped his fork and sputtered, forcing the mash of eggs and toast from his windpipe.

"And the constable believes they may be able to track down a scent they found on the body."

Charles had to fight the overwhelming urge to vomit as his stomach tied itself into knots. What happened to him last night? He knew, deep down, that he'd played a role in this murder. If he concentrated hard enough, he could make out a face.

He pushed the dinner plate away and excused himself.

"Charles, don't you dare waste a perfectly good meal!"

"I'm sorry Jess, I must go."

He left the shouting vixen behind and braved the fading daylight, his coat wrapped even more tightly around his torso. Was it the serum that was causing him to lose his memory, to become so uncharacteristic of himself? He'd known there would be risks of performing tests on himself, but he never imagined they could be so dire.

It briefly crossed his mind that he could end it all and this problem would sort itself out. Death seemed like an enviable option. For even if he found a way to reverse the condition, he knew at his core that he sat at the center of the foul play that had occurred last night. Blood that was spilled could not be un-spilled, and his paws ran red with it now.

"Charles!"

The shout broke him from his dire thoughts. He looked to see who had called him, unable to make out any discernible shapes.

"Charles!" Henry's hand shot up amidst a crowd of people as he ran towards his dear friend. It would be so easy to lose him, to feign ignorance, but his legs would not move.

The short, portly wolf came to a stop before Charles, doubled over and out of breath. Charles laughed and put a shoulder on the out of shape canine, grown heavy from too much eating and a life of paperwork.

"Charles, thank goodness. I feared I had lost you."

"Fear not, for I am found, Henry." For a flickering moment Charles regretted waiting up for the wolf. Normally he found himself in good company with his friend, but not today.

"I was deeply afraid something had happened to you." There was a wavering in the wolf's voice as though he had thought the fox for dead.

"I know not of what you speak" Charles lied, hoping that his friend might change the subject.

"Have you not heard?"

Charles shook his head.

He leaned in, pressing himself to Charles ear, his voice hushed in a whisper. "There was a murder last night, a fox. I feared for your life. I prayed, 'say it isn't so!'" he exclaimed in a dramatic display, his flailing arms nearly knocking Charles to the ground.

With a step back Charles laughed, giving himself a pat on the chest as if to demonstrate that he was still flesh and blood. "I am still here, old friend."

Henry threw himself at Charles, his chest heaving against the small, slender fox.

He braced against the impact of the wolf's embrace and gave a reassuring pat before returning the hug, unsure of how else he should console his friend.

The hug stretched into being uncomfortable, and Henry reluctantly relinquished his grasp when Charles eased him away. Henry wiped his cheeks free of any tears and took the chance to steady himself.

"I'm sorry," he muttered.

"No apologies necessary," Charles assured.

"I—I do not know what I would do without you, Charles," the chubby wolf stammered. "I really—"

"It came as quite a shock to me as well." the vulpine interrupted, smoothing out his attire. "To think that such a travesty could happen on our side of the world."

"I thought word had not reached you about the murder."

Curses, Charles thought. There was no hiding it. In the face of his current predicament, he had started losing faith in himself. What better confidant than his dearest friend?

He breathed a heavy sigh. "Henry, I must speak some dreadful news with you. Perhaps you would have me over for tea?"

Despite Henry's house being more than a twenty minute walk away, it was still a better alternative to his own. He could not imagine burdening Jessica with these troubles.

Silent tension killed his early attempts at conversation as steamy wisps rose from their cups, filling the air between them. Charles gripped his teacup with sweaty paws, distracting himself by smelling the subtle hints of honey and cloves.

"What news did you want to speak of, Charles?"

Charles tapped his claws against the porcelain, resting his arms back onto the table. He thought carefully of what he was about to say next. If he gave away too much information, he was sure to put Henry in danger as well.

"I fear I've done something awful, Henry."

Henry placed his cup own and tilted his ears forward "What do you mean, what's happened?"

"I can't tell you right now." His ears deflated. "I can't say I'm sure myself, but if my suspicions are correct, I fear I'm in a good bit of trouble, dear friend."

Henry folded his paws in front of him, furrowing his brow. "I know when you're keeping secrets, Charles."

The fox pursed his lips, letting his tail curl around the back of his chair. "I can't say with certainty what's happening but..." His claws scraped against the porcelain teacup. "I'm frightened, Henry."

Charles flinched when he felt Henry's paw on his. His ears slid back, but he did not withdraw. The fur on his neck stood on end. Even now he heard the menacing laugh of the wolf in his dreams.

His mind raced with the possibilities of things to come if he could not quell the beast's influence within him. He shuddered to think of the damage it would cause.

"Tell me what ails you, my friend." The wolf's paws squeezed tighter around Charles'.

Worry creased the fox's features. He thought hard about how much he could truly tell him. "I fear I am losing control, Henry. A fearsome power dwells within me."

"What do you mean? You're speaking in riddles."

There was only one way that Charles could think of that would guarantee a resolution. It chilled him.

"I fear the tribunal may have been right. I am in over my head." Charles breathed deep to steady himself. "You must promise me something, Henry."

"What promise might that be?" The wolf's ears flicked, showing his uncertainty.

"Promise me," he urged. "You must promise me you will do as I ask. This is not a task that can be done by any one person but you."

Henry hesitated, squeezing a tight paw over Charles'. This time he pulled his paws away. "I promise." Though the wolf did not sound confident, it mattered little.

"The person you see before you may not be around much longer. When that day comes, and you will know when it does, you must promise me that you will end it. End it all and put me out of my misery."

"You can't expect me to!"

"This is not a negotiation, Henry!" Charles slammed his paw onto the table, spilling his tea. It ran down to the floor. "It must be you. You are the only one that I trust who cares enough to carry out such a deed."

"Surely there is another way," he pleaded, rising from his seat. "Charles, if you would only tell me what is going on, maybe we can..."

Henry's voice died away as Charles woefully shook his head. The fox's ears had drooped and his paws were now completely still. "The time will come, and you must. Promise me, Henry."

Charles forced himself to ignore the pain behind his dear friend's eyes.

"I promise," he muttered in defeat, his paws balled up at the side of the table.

With a paw on the wolf's hand, Charles tried to offer comfort. Henry remained wordless, staring into the fox's eyes. Henry drew forward and pressed his lips to the fox's muzzle.

Charles jerked back slightly, taken aback from the unexpected advance. The kiss left a tingle on his lips as he inhaled the wolf's soft, dusty scent, like the smell of old books. "Henry," he whispered. "I..."

There was pause between them as Henry stared with tender, brown eyes. Henry squeezed at the fox's black paw, and he hesitantly squeezed back.

Only now did the wolf's desire reach his nose. He was unsure what to think of the situation. Charles had always viewed the wolf as a friend, but it was only clear to him now that Henry had always wanted something more.

He felt the warmth of the wolf's paws against his, the comforting scent of his excitement combined with stale tea, and his kind, greying features. No matter how crackpot Charles' theories had been, the wolf had always stood by his side.

A light shiver tingled down his spine when Charles thought about lying beside the wolf. The pursuit of science was a lonely journey, with little opportunity for intimacies, and it made Charles think back to how many other signs he had missed over the years.

"I cannot lose you, Charles," Henry whispered, tears staining his cheeks.

Charles' gaze drooped downwards, along with his ears. He didn't feel worthy of the wolf's affection. "Henry, I..."

His voice tapered off when Henry leaned in for another, more assertive kiss. The wolf's broad tongue begged permission, and Charles accepted, his features lightening as he let his worries fade.

All of the extended hugs and gentle touches made sense to him now. His friend had always showed such concern for him and now he understood why.

Somewhere along the way he had grown to depend on Henry, looking to him for guidance and comfort in times of need, such that the lines between friend and lover had been blurred long before he even realized.

After years of companionship, it only felt right that he have this moment with his oldest and dearest friend, before the inevitable. He did not have to sleep alone tonight.

Henry tugged at the fox's paw, gently urging him towards the bedroom. The wolf's ears were tilted back and towards the side.

Charles smiled at the wolf's bashfulness and trotted along behind him.

Clothes fell to the floor, each of them making half-hearted efforts to hide their bodies from each other as they exposed themselves.

Henry's belly obscured his waist a little bit, and even more so when he took a seat on the bed. Charles stood with his slender frame exposed, his fur hiding his gaunt-like figure.

Charles leaned down to place a paw on the wolf's belly, approaching the problem like he would a lab experiment. Henry smiled nervously, reclining to encourage the fox to lay with him.

He knelt atop the wolf, fumbling his claws through the wiry fur of his belly, venturing in for another kiss. Henry parted his muzzle, allowing their tongues to caress each other.

Saliva mingled and Charles felt a growing need between his legs. It twitched against the wolf's soft stomach, aching for attention.

Henry reached a paw down and closed his digits around the fox's needy shaft, pumping and stroking with a notable lack of practice. It made Charles shiver all the same, the scientist whining for more against the wolf's muzzle.

Charles reached behind him and cupped a paw around the wolf's sac, rolling it in his digits with careful calculation. Henry moaned back into the kiss, his own erection fully realized.

Minutes of playful touching, intimate kisses, and sensual moaning made Charles' loins ache with unbearable need. He broke away from the kiss and moved down the wolf's body, bringing his nose tip to tip with Henry's wolfhood.

He gripped the wolf's hips firmly in his paws and opened his muzzle, tongue extended for a taste of his shaft. It wasn't unlike the musk that wafted past his nose, setting his senses tingling. He gingerly opened his muzzle further and took the wolf in his mouth, dipping down between his legs and taking the whole shaft into his muzzle, using his tongue to caress the underside of the shaft.

Henry gripped the sheets and tensed, his thighs squeezing gently at Charles' muzzle. He continued, getting a thrill from making the wolf squirm. His head bobbed, tongue and lips teasing the wolf's shaft. Charles moved his hips against the sheets in an attempt to alleviate his own burning sensations.

The length twitched in his muzzle, and the wolf's knot grew. Henry clawed at the sheets with mixed whines and growls, his legs kicking against the sheets.

Charles recoiled when the first hot sticky spurt hit the back of his throat. He closed his eyes when the second one got him right in the muzzle. Charles breathed deep through his nose, inhaling Henry's rich dusty old book scent. The salty taste of the wolf lingered on his tongue, fueling the aching need between his own legs. He caressed the wolfhood with his tongue, fluttering over the length as a tingle rushed through his body, something he'd never felt before with any other person.

Henry arched, moaned, and collapsed against the bed with heavy breath. Charles slid from Henry's slowly softening flesh, and the wolf below him gave a soft shudder of pleasure. The fox sidled up beside his lover, erection nudging at the wolf's side. For a moment he wondered if thinking of Henry as his lover was overly selfish of him, though he decided it was much too late to worry about that now, covering his mouth with a paw as he yawned. Such trivial matters could be put off 'til the morrow.

Henry turned his head, gazing at Charles with a lopsided grin. The two pressed muzzles together and Henry's paw found his way down to Charles' shaft.

The fox gasped and gave an instinctual hump against the paw, pent up from so much foreplay.

Charles inhaled the wolf's dusty scent, drinking in the musk that painted his belly, alongside the strong aroma of his own arousal.

Passion peaked and Charles clutched his lover's hips with a throaty growl, his shaft twitching as he thrust against the wolf's paw, shooting hot strands over his own tummy.

Exhausted and breathless, they lay side by side, with Charles administering a final kiss before they fell asleep in each other's arms.

Freedom! Sweet, tantalizing freedom. The wolf could practically taste it on his lips, along with a musty wolf aftertaste as he threw the sheets back. Charles' fuzzy memories lingered in his mind. He looked over to the chubby wolf, remembering the ragged moans and the warmth he'd caressed with his lips.

"Sorry, Love," he mused to himself, "yo're just not my type. Too fat around the middle," he finished with a laugh. Without a second look back, he dressed himself and set out down the street, to the infinite possibilities of the night.

The nameless wolf found himself skulking the streets of less reputable parts around town. His aimless wandering had brought him back to a familiar place; The Red Curtain. It wasn't coincidence, he thought, that he'd found his way back this way. A place for harlots and mischievous gentlemen was exactly the kind of place he wanted to be.

Among the whores on stage and the sex-workers in the back, many souls were busy putting aside their morals and their wives for the night to have a little one-on-one with the "help", who were more than enthusiastic to return the fleeting affection. At least they pretended to for the right price. Everyone sitting on the other side of the flaking red paint of those large double-doors were comfortable, because no self-respecting man would dare speak of entering a whore house, especially one as dingy as this.

The venue tonight was especially busy, half filled with the upper-class, drinking to forget the long week. The other half was filled with the lowest society had to offer, those who dared not socialize anywhere else.

He fit into neither of these categories, but was more than happy to fill the space in between. Hormones were ripe in the air. Despite their differences in class, everyone here all had one thing in common; a need for sex.

Jeers, shouts and hollers filled the room as a vixen with deep red fur danced around a chair onstage. Her skirt showed off more than just a little leg, and mascara ran in dark lines along her muzzle like a mask. Some of the men in the club were more occupied than others. Some of them, the wolf knew, didn't come for the main attractions, but for the activities that went on behind closed curtains.

Tonight, one fox in particular caught his eye.

"Enjoyin' the show, Sweetheart?" He took a seat next to the younger gentleman, as though the spot had been saved especially for him.

"I beg pardon? Oh, yes, of course."

The canine only grinned, smelling the rising interest that came from within the fox's trousers.

The petite vulpine squirmed uncomfortably under the gaze of the imposing figure, eyes darting back and forth between him and the scantily clad vixen on stage.

"Shorely you didn't come for the strippers and whores here, Love. You obviously have no interest in that."

"I—I beg pardon, Sir," he repeated. His feigned offence lost all merit when the canine watched the fox's tail twitch with uncertainty behind him, betraying his expressions.

With the reach of a paw, he grabbed the fox under the tail. It would have been considered a bold move, had he been anyone else.

The fox jumped and stifled a yelp, but he could not hide the fluttering of his ears. There was no mistaking the potent smell of his arousal now.

The wolf winked. "What d' ya say we find a place a little more private?"

The two of them slipped away to a room hidden safely behind the curtains of the burlesque stage. The only sign that they were there the shadows cast on the curtain by the dim lamplight, coupled with the desperate squeaks and moans from the small, slender fox. Like the wolf, this fox had no name. Not tonight.

Fabric tore as the fox dug his claws against the mattress and bit into the pillow to muffle his cries. The nameless wolf drooled onto the fox's back as he watched the thickness of his length spread that tight ass wide open.

The wolf's mouth moved to the back of the fox's neck. The equally nameless fox cried out into the pillow gripped between his teeth as those sharp teeth tugged at his scruff. The wolf gave little regard to the fox's comfort, only paying attention to the tight confine's under that bushy red tail.

"Quit makin' so much noise," the wolf growled above the fox. "They might think yo'r screamin' bloody murder in 'ere." The wolf grinned to himself, wondering how long it would take for someone to find a body in one of these rented out rooms.

The tip of his cock arched inside the fox's rear, his swollen knot forcing him to keep his full length out of the fox. He growled under his breath, as he pressed harder with each thrust, nudging the fox's tight ring. The nameless wolf felt the fox's ring give way, and he slipped from tip to base within the fox. He leaned over, pinning the fox to the bed, feeling him shudder and squeeze around him as the vulpine squirt his load into the bed beneath them.

The wolf growled and bit the fox's scruff again, spit and drool soaking the fox's neck as his hips slammed into the fox as he unloaded under that fluffy bottlebrush tail.

The wolf snarled as he felt the last few drops of his orgasm spill out under the fox's tail. Holding the fox down by his shoulders, he tugged his knot free from the fox, ignoring the high-pitched yelp. With his sexual appetite sated, he hungered for something more.

He dressed, leaving the fox panting and laying in his own mess. There was no need for goodbyes. He would never see the effeminate vulpine again. He slapped a handful of silver pieces onto the counter on his way out, enough to pay for time spent and the damaged bed.

It was cold, and the night was bitter. Unlike his weaker half, he reveled in this, thrived on it. Never was an individual more suited to weather cursed by so many. His jacket hung loosely over his shoulders, and he spun his cane with a paw. It was truly a splendid night to be alive.

Elated as he was, something about the night troubled him, a thought in the back of his mind, threatening to push itself to the forefront. He could not place his finger upon it, but it nagged at him from a distance. He muttered and cursed under his breath, ignoring those who thought him mad as they passed by on the street. He would remember, eventually.

Later, he thought. *Later.*

Now was the time for blood. Since his first taste down by the river, he hungered for yet another opportunity. He would find his way back to that strong iron taste, the sharp metallic smell. Of that, he was sure. He scoured the darkest corners, the slums of even the lowest marks in society. He would find his next target.

A stout fox dressed up in spades knocked into the wolf, turning on his heel after making contact. "Watch where you step!" The fox spat and dusted himself off. "What warrants such haste at such an incredulous hour?"

The wolf turned, teeth bared and lips turning up into an unsettling grin. "Lookin' for a bit o' trouble, are we?"

"What do you speak of?" The fox questioned, tail lashing about behind him.

The aristocrat did not have a chance to react when the wolf struck him to the ground.

"Such gall," he spat, "that you would 'ave the nerve to run into me and blame my footwork!"

"You're mad!" The fox shuffled back, trying to keep his distance from the snarling, drooling wolf. "Stay back. Help!"

He raised his cane high above his head and swung with tremendous force.

The canine's brass cane clattered to the ground when a force struck him in the side, throwing him off balance and saving his latest victim from mortal peril.

"What in the blazes! Mind yo'r business!"

A short, chubby wolf steadied himself, panting hard and out of breath. He had likely run some distance to get there in time, and his exhaustion prevented him from seeing eye-to-eye, though something seemed oddly familiar about his attire, and he smelled strongly of sweat and dusty old books.

"My business is what I choose to make of it, *Sir*. Standing idly by while you strike a helpless bystander does not sit well with me." He managed to right himself fully now, his chest still heaving.

The beast growled and spat. As desperately as he wanted to strike down this new bystander, something stopped him. Visions from earlier that night slowly made sense of the situation. The portly middle, the dark gray and white speckled fur. Charles' beau, the one he had left at the house!

"What the 'ell are you doing here?"

"*That* is none of your concern. Step away. The constable is coming."

The beast turned his head as he heard a whistle coming from down the street.

Cries rang amongst the houses as the chubby wolf was struck down. The unnamed canine grabbed his cane back and disappeared into the shadows, like a creature of the night.

This was one of the rare mornings when Charles awoke in his bed. His head pounded with the potent aftermath of too much drinking. It was becoming a disturbingly common tactic for his other half to drink away the memories of the night previous.

He'd gone to the sink to wash and only then did he notice the blood on his jacket with more crusted splotches mingled within the fur of his paws. With a strangled gasp he plunged his hands below the water, scrubbing his fur free of the speckles of blood that marked him. The jacket would be burned. There could be no evidence. *Not another murder. Please God, no,* he thought.

There was no questioning it now. He could not rest until a cure for this wretched disease was found. He would not rest nor sleep. The snarling beast of his subconscious could not be allowed to surface again.

What if there is no cure? What if this is just your true nature creeping out, taking over? The voice in his head was tainted with that of his inner demon.

No, you will not sway me, he told himself. A cure had to exist. He would find it or, at the very least, he would die trying. He signed a cross on his body and prayed that it would not come to that.

He rushed down to his lab, where his notes and experiments created a barrier of comfort around him like a ward.

Scarcely more than a few hours into his studies was when Jess came downstairs, her tail twitching frequently and uneasy. Worry was etched on her muzzle. The air reeked of fear as she approached.

"Mr. Jack—Charles, Constable Riley is at the door. Shall I send him down?"

Charles's heart leapt into his throat. Had his beastly half left a trail that lead the police right to him? It was a dreadful thought. Surely not even he was that reckless.

He hoped.

"I will be up in a minute. Thank you, Jessica."

Charles put down his pencil, entertaining the fleeting thought of setting fire to the whole damned house. If they smelled something awry, it was over.

Waiting for him as he approached the top of the stairs was Riley, a well-known and respected individual of the town's peace-keepers.

Charles faked his best smile.

"Mr. Riley, what a surprise it is to see you this early in the morning. Can I interest you in some tea?"

Riley shook his head and removed his hat, his canted ears showing the slightest signs of remorse as he regarded Charles.

"I'm afraid this is a matter of business, Mr. Jacklyn. Do you have an alibi for your whereabouts on the night that one Arden Goodwin was murdered?"

Jessica stumbled back against the counter with a gasp at the surprise that Charles was a suspect in such an investigation.

Oh lord, oh lord. "I don't understand, Constable. Am I suspect?"

"We have scent trails and traces of fur leading back to this address. We will need alibis from both you and Ms. Valentine, detailing your whereabouts on the day of the murder." Riley opened his notepad, looking to Charles for an answer first.

"I was here all night, Constable. I believe Jessica can attest to this."

Charles turned to Jess, shooting a pleading glance at her.

"Charles, what—Oh, yes, of course. He was here with me all night, Constable. Always stuck in his papers, you know."

Riley laughed and jotted some notes down on his pad. "Of course. You know we could use a mind like yours on the team, Charles?"

It was Charles' turn to laugh, more out of derisiveness than good humor. "You lot get along fine without me. Now if there is no further business, I must be getting back."

"No, not at all. Sorry to bother you."

Charles closed the door behind Constable Riley and breathed a sigh of relief.

Jess tapped her foot while leaning against the kitchen counter, glaring right at Charles.

"You had better tell me what that was about," she chided. "Or I will bring Constable Riley right back in here and tell him exactly where you were not that night."

"Jess, I assure you this is not what it appears. I was at The Red Curtain and must have had a few too many, for I do not remember—"

A knock at the door interrupted Charles' during his explanation.

"Oh thank goodness!" Charles rushed to see who it might be and gasped when he saw Henry standing with bruises to his forehead and muzzle.

He ushered the lawyer inside, cupping his paw under the wolf's chin to inspect the bruises. He looked a fright, and Charles feared this might be the handiwork of his alter ego. "Good lord! Look at you, Henry. What happened?"

Henry winced, but feigned a weak smile. "Charles, we must talk. In private," he briefly nodded his muzzle towards Jessica, who took obvious offence.

"Of course." He nodded to Jessica. "Please excuse us."

Jessica wrinkled her nose and left without issue, her tail lashing out behind her.

"Who did this to you?" A brief flashback to the night before told Charles that he already knew.

"A man. I believe he meant to murder a member of the well-to-do. I caught him off guard and I fear he would have done away with me as well. For reasons I do not understand, he hesitated. He ran away, but not before leaving his mark." He put a paw to his cheek, grimacing at the tender flesh beneath his fur.

"Oh Henry, I'm so sorry. How did you come across such a sight? Did you see his face?"

"Last night," Henry wrung his paws, the tips of his ears turning red as he recalled the night of their engagement. "I heard a noise at the door. Though I expected to see you leave, the man I saw walking down the alley shortly thereafter was not the man I expected to see. He was taller, broader, and had a jacket remarkably like yours, but it rode too high on his shoulders. A suspicious looking character, so I followed him, and thank the Lord that I did. When it looked like he might murder that poor fellow with his cane I threw myself against him. I laid eyes upon him, and there was something terribly unsettling about his features. He looked rabid and feral, as though he belonged in the wild. He struck me before disappearing into the night and that was the last I saw him. He had long gone before any police arrived."

By the time Henry finished telling his story, Charles was white-knuckled. How dare he put Henry in danger like that. There was no question. He had to put a stop to this.

"Henry," his mouth dried up and he feared his voice may crack under the pressure of asking his friend yet another dangerous task. "I'm running out of time. If you see that man again, I pray you'll find the strength to kill him. You must, or everyone will be in danger."

"Charles, I must say I'm getting cold feet about this whole proposal. You are suggesting I take someone's life! My conscience would never allow me to do such a thing, not without the direst of circumstances."

"Try to understand the gravity of the situation. This man is a monster, he must not be allowed to live!"

"How can I possibly understand when you've done nothing to explain it? You must tell me what's going on so I can help you. Please," he begged, taking the fox's hands. "Tell me so I can help you."

Charles pulled his hands away and tucked them into his lap. "I wish I could Henry. Believe me when I tell you that it is better that you do not understand. You have witnessed what this man will do at even the slightest of provocations. I have reason to suspect he has murdered once before, and he will do it once again. I am so sorry that I must ask this of you, but this man is very dangerous."

"The burdens you must put on me, Charles." Henry rubbed at his temples, being mindful of the gash on his forehead.

"I am sorry, Henry."

Henry stooped his muzzle, shaking his head. "Only for you, my friend."

Charles sighed with relief. In the lull of conversation, his mind was quickly brought back to his work. The cure was his only hope for a peaceful resolution, but it was still so far out of his reach.

"I fear I must return to work, Henry. I am so sorry for your wounds."

"It was not your fault," Henry replied.

"I am not so sure," he muttered in return.

Charles stood from his chair to hold the door for his friend turned lover. As distressed as he might have been, he could not neglect his manners.

Henry stood at the door, facing Charles. "Whatever troubles you, I pray it passes soon, then we may put these crazy conspiracies to bed."

Charles sighed. "As do I."

The portly wolf put a paw to Charles chin and leaned up to give him a peck on the muzzle. Charles turned his muzzle, giving his lip a gentle lick as he inhaled the subtle, dusty scent.

A gentle breeze passed through the doorway. "Good day, my friend. I hope when next we meet that it is on better terms."

Henry nodded and laid a paw on the door frame on his way out. "Charles, where did you disappear to last night?"

"I must get to my work, Henry."

Henry nodded his goodbye, leaving just as Jess entered the room again. She waited until Henry was fully out of site before she began making a horrendous clatter with the pots and dishes.

Charles closed the door out of fear that the street may be able to hear before turning to her. "Jessica, please be careful!"

She threw a rag at the fox, hitting him square in the chest, leaving a large damp spot on his shirt. He grabbed the wet rag and set it on the table, sticking his tongue out at the uncomfortable feeling it left on his paw.

"Jess, what in the devil has gotten into you? You've been acting queer since I came upstairs."

"Queer indeed," she shouted with such volume that the neighbors were sure to hear. "How long have you been hiding that one? Best of friends, indeed!"

"The company I keep is my decision alone. I assure you that Henry is fine company and that my romantic life is no business of yours!"

The vixen glared at him with a fiery hatred. Her lips curled up, baring teeth, and her ears did not rise beyond the crest of her head. "Forgive me," she screamed, "for possibly believing otherwise. I daresay you will not need to worry about me meddling in your affairs any longer!"

Without another word she stormed from the room, slamming the door to the guest room.

There was no time for this. Repercussions would be dealt with later, but for now he had to finish his work. Lives depended on it.

Charles didn't dare leave the safety of his basement for days. He barely slept, for fear the wolf within him would awaken. Jessica had not been seen since their fight. The silence was a welcome change, even though the tea was not nearly as sweet. Every couple of days, only when he became faint, would he remember to eat.

Charles rubbed the sleep from his eyes, wondering when the last time he'd had a hot meal was. He wondered where Jessica had been for the past few days. The smells of roast beef and gravy no longer wafted downstairs. Maybe she'd really left?

Words blurred in front of him. He could no longer think straight, and his thoughts kept wandering to Jessica. The floorboards no longer squeaked, or perhaps they did and he no longer heard them.

He dipped his quill and ventured upstairs, finding the kitchen empty and unused. Some things had been moved from their original places, but the stove was cold and the blinds had been drawn.

Outside Jessica's room, he pressed an ear and could hear shuffling from within. He took a deep breath and rapped on the door. "Jess, are you in there?"

"Not for you, Mr. Jacklyn." His ear picked up a light sniffle and his stomach knotted.

"Jess, come out... please."

There was silence, then the door opened. Her eyes were red and she used a napkin to dab at her nose.

"Please, sit and have tea with me?"

Charles fumbled with the controls on the stove, spilling water onto the stovetop. "Where's the tea... Oh drat," he mumbled, spilling tea over the counter.

He reached for the teabags and started placing them back in their cup when he felt a paw touch him, and he looked over to see Jessica's sympathetic smile.

"Let me help you," she offered. "Can you get the milk and sugar?"

Charles nodded. Surely he could manage that.

"I should know better than to leave you along for so long. How did you ever manage to feed yourself?" Jessica barked a laugh, lighting the stove and moving the kettle from the counter to the burner.

She sat a comfortable distance away from Charles, with him at the other side of the table.

"I'm sorry."

Jessica folded her paws in front of her. "For what, exactly?" She neither smiled, nor frowned. Charles knew she wanted him to say it.

"I haven't been fair to you, and I've been negligent in letting you know when I appreciate your company. Imagine my surprise to find that a lady as fair as yourself fancied the company of an old fox like me."

Jessica's ears perked for one moment, and then they were down again, her expression neutral.

Charles raised a finger to speak when the kettle started whistling. He stood to grab it, but Jessica was already on her feet, pulling cups out of the cupboard and taking the kettle off the stove.

Charles' stepped behind her to grab the sugar and brushed against her tail. They nearly bumped noses when they both turned to look at each other and caught each other's gaze.

The breath left Charles as he stared into the vixen's chestnut brown eyes. Her own frown dissolved into a smile as the two of them turned towards each other.

"I don't want us to be cross with each other." Charles nudged his nose against the vixen's ear. "I've missed you, Jess. Though I don't always know how to show it," he admitted.

Jess tilted her muzzle up and gave a brief nibble to Charles' lower lip. "Who would you be without your flaws?"

The water sat chilling on the stove and raspy moans filled the room as Charles nibbled down Jessica's neck, holding her with slender arms. Her dress sat discarded on the floor, and Charles' shirt was hung over the door.

They embraced each other, bare chests pressed together as Charles carefully nipped down her shoulder, careful paws caressing her back and just above her hips.

Jessica breathed his name and draped her arms over his shoulders, giving herself to him in this spontaneous moment of passion.

Charles' erection strained against his pants. His muzzle moved lower, tongue lapping gently against her breasts before he took one of her nipples in his mouth. Jessica gasped and raked her claws over his back as he teased her pert nipple with his teeth.

With one paw on her back, he moved the other to her front, hooking her undergarments with a finger and editing them down towards her ankles. She panted in silent approval, spreading her legs when Charles slid a finger between her thighs.

Jessica gasped, writhing against the sheets before reaching a paw down to the fox's trousers, releasing the clasp of his belt.

With his pants on the floor, Charles knelt above Jessica, thinking briefly to his time with Charles. He had been ignoring the signs all these years, favoring the pursuit of knowledge over relationships, that he'd neglected the natural beauty in both of his closest friends.

He nudged his tip against Jessica's folds and watched her face fill with desire, easing in only after she nodded to him.

Claws raked Charles' back when he entered her. The soft warmth of her passage made him gasp, his body tensing as he felt himself sink within her. The spot where his knot would form was wrapped by her tender rose. He looked into her eyes as they flickered with desire, watching that flicker burst into a flame as her warmth squeezed around him.

The bed creaked as they rocked against each other with muzzles locked, their ill-feelings for each other forgotten. Hot breath rolled across each other's cheeks with steam rising from their bodies, and beads of condensation rolling off of the window as the cold autumn afternoon crept through the window of Charles's bedroom. Each thrust felt more intense than the last, just like it had with Henry.

A spark of regret chilled him when he realized that his quest for knowledge needn't have been so lonely. Wrapped up in his own world, he'd been blind to those who truly cared for him. He'd been such a fool, and he wondered how many fruitless cold nights in his basement could have been spent with one, or both of them, filling his life with warmth and love, as opposed to cold and loneliness.

Each thrust brought Charles closer, his knot throbbing against her folds. He wanted to fill her, to tie with her, and her paws clutching his hips and thrusting him forward seemed to agree.

Jessica's pitch heightened, her cries echoing against the walls as Charles pushed, her quivering sex giving way to his knot squeezing into Jessica's tunnel with a pop.

Her warm depths squeezed tightly around him as she clutched for purchase on Charles' shoulders. He snarled and grasped Jessica tightly to his chest as he filled her with his hot sticky seed.

They lay together, gasping for breath. Charles rolled to the side, still tied with the young vixen. They kissed and nuzzled together, sharing a yawn before settling in for the night. As he drifted to sleep, he noticed the absence of the other presence in his mind. Perhaps the wolf would leave him alone tonight. He could only hope.

"I've found it!" Charles exclaimed, holding a vial triumphantly into the air. A good night's rest had brought him clarity, and he could finally find the answer he'd been looking for.

With careful reserve he held the vial in front of his snout, inspecting it carefully.

The vial glowed dimly in the absence of light, throwing an eerie green glow on anything within a few feet.

The missing link between his sanity and complete loss of control, the solution that had taken him weeks to procure was finally within his grasp.

The aroma of it made him dizzy. It smelled strongly of sulphur and iron, with a sickly mix of a number of other chemicals. He plugged the end of the tube with a single finger and turned it upside down, saturating his finger in the rancid, green concoction.

It stung like acid and left a tickle at the back of his throat. "Medicine would not be medicine without the taste," he supposed.

He tipped the vial back and swallowed without a second thought. The vial shattered next to his feet when the taste overtook him. An inscrutable pain flooded his entire body. Charles hunched over the desk, feeling his limbs stretch out and his posture hunch forward.

With a cry he threw an arm across the desk, spilling papers and chemicals to the floor.

"No, no!"

This was wrong, this was all wrong! He could feel his feral instincts taking over. The wolf was coming out and there was desperately little he could do about it. Try as he might to resist, the wolf was far too strong now.

"Charles, are you alright?" Jessica called out. She must have been upstairs in the kitchen, drawn down by the sudden clatter.

No! He could only make strangled cries for help within his mind, now. *Don't come down!* His mouth gaped open but only a breathy snarl came out.

Jessica shrieked, lifting her paws to her muzzle as she turned the corner.

The transition was nearly complete. Charles's thoughts were being overpowered. If he tried hard enough, he would be able to wade through the onslaught of the wolf's consciousness, keeping oriented as best he could within a sea of hormones and murderous tendencies.

"Charles, what is happening to you?"

From behind his desk, the canine stood with his shoulders hunched over and his drool spilling out onto the scattered papers.

"Charlie isn't 'ere, Love," the wolf said with a dry laugh. "No... You can call me Jack."

Jessica gasped through her paw. "What have you done with Charles, you monster?"

Jack twisted his neck, joints popping and cracking. He shook his fur about and howled, the sounds echoing off the cellar walls. "He's alive, Dahling. Not for much longer, I'm afraid. Any last words you'd care to tell 'im, Love?"

She stomped towards the wolf, dress held in her paws with a viciously stern look on her face. "Give him back," she shouted.

The fox raised her hand to strike, but her speed was no match Jack's. He caught her wrist easily and pulled her against him, ignoring her shrieks and easily detaining her.

"Let me go!"

"Haw, that's cute. Yo'r comin' with me, Love."

Jack stepped over the shards of broken glass, taking Jessica up the stairs and out of the house. Night time had fallen, serving as the perfect cover. Though the vixen shrieked and pounded against Jack's back, they moved far too quickly for anyone to react in time, let alone see where they were going.

Jack lumbered down the street, holding Jessica over his shoulder with one arm and using the other as a way to balance, a cross between a feral and a civilized run.

210

"Put me down! Where are you taking me?"

"Charles' time is done," he snarled. "I'm tyin' up tha loose ends. That means, Love, that it's time ta do away with any meddling friends of his. You, and especially that oth'a little fuck toy a' his. Sorry it won't work out between you 'n him, by the way. Shame I can't keep a pret'y li'l ass like yours around, but them's tha' breaks," he said with a chuckle before continuing. "That fox may be weak, but he isn't stupid. He knew this day was comin' an' he warned that little faggot. I'll make sure he does not get a chance to keep his promises."

Jack stumbled over himself in the street, barely able to keep his hold on Jessica, who was still screaming and thrashing violently. Somewhere in the depths of Jack's mind, Charles was finding a way to fight back.

"Shut up," he yelled, loudly enough to wake any neighboring houses. "There's nothin' you can do to stop this! I'm only keepin' ya alive so you can watch your friends die by my hands!"

"Hold it right there, murderer! We've got you."

Jack turned to face the man behind him. A quaking shepherd in uniform stood with his gun out. He kept a wide, unpracticed stance and pointed his gun right at Jack. "Drop the girl and nobody has to get hurt!"

"Oh." Jack's lips curved up into a wry smile. "You mean like this pretty li'l thing right here?"

Jessica shrieked as Jack held her like a shield in front of the officer. She struggled, but she was no match for the overpowered behemoth that Jack had become.

"Drop the girl or I will shoot!" He responded, hands shaking on the trigger.

"Didn't yor mother ever tell ya not ta lie?" He held Jessica fast against his front. The cop was bluffing and he knew it.

"I mean it. Drop the girl!"

"Drop her, foul beast," another voice echoed from a nearby alleyway.

Henry rounded the corner with a pistol in hand. He held it out in front of him, shaking with nervousness and fear.

Henry! Charles cried from within the wolf's mind.

"Ah, Henry," Jack said with a sneer. "So glad you've saved me the trouble of tracking you down." The hunchbacked canine unceremoniously tucked the vixen under his arm and lumbered towards the smaller wolf.

"Stay back!" Henry shouted, holding the gun further out in front of him, still shaking visibly in his boots.

The fear in his eyes told Jack that Henry was not ready to pull the trigger. Jack smacked the gun from Henry's hand as it went off, the bullet finding its path through a nearby window. The pistol tumbled across the street and into the darkness.

"Pathetic," he laughed. "To think that Charles would put his trust in you, his only chance left in the world. Yo're just a short, fat, pathetic little wolf. I'm sorry I can't waste much time playing around with you tonight."

Jack raised his paw up into the air. "Prepare to meet your maker."

He struck Henry, throwing him off to the side with a sickening crack. The wolf rolled to a stop and did not get up.

Jessica shrieked and fought against the larger wolf. Her efforts phased him little. The police officer stood off to the side, still holding his gun, daring to shoot but unable to pull the trigger.

Jack curved his muzzle into a smile and stomped towards the shaking constable.

He continued to hold Jessica in harm's way. "Better pull the trigger," he said with unmasked glee. "Or are you afraid you'll hurt the little missus?"

The constable squeezed the trigger and the muzzle of the gun flared up with a loud bang that rang between the houses. Jack felt the rush of air past his left ear as the bullet sped off into the night.

He took another step towards the officer and smacked the gun from his hand. The officer stood dumb-founded in front of the beast, too slow to react when Jack grabbed him by the throat.

With his paw clamped tightly around the officer's windpipe, Jack lifted the wolf from the ground. The constable clawed at Jack's hand, struggling like a fish out of water.

"Ya shoulda just killed me," he laughed, his smile growing wider as the other wolf struggled, his efforts beginning to weaken. "It wouldn't have made a difference. Ya see, I'm just gonna to kill 'er anyway. You might have stood a chance against me if you just shot us both."

The constable continued to fight, clawing and grabbing at the larger wolf's hand until his movements stopped completely.

He threw the unconscious officer to the ground, bending to reach into his pouch for the cuffs that he carried on him. He dragged the toiling vixen to a nearby rail and cuffed her steady while he went to deal with more pressing matters.

By the time he turned towards where Henry's body lay, he was no longer there. The stout wolf was now on his feet, holding the gun tightly in his paws. Jack could see the white knuckles beneath Henry's fur as he stepped closer. "I'm going to tear your throat from that fat little body of yours," he said with a snarl.

No! Charles shouted from within his prison. For a moment, Jack halted. The wolf shook his head free of the meddling thoughts.

Learn your place, wretched fox! Jack shouted back within his mind at Charles. *You are going to watch me take care of your friends, and then I will take care of you permanently!*

Jack took another step and froze again. Charles was at the forefront, wrestling for control, trying desperately to gain power over the wolf. He would not let his other half bring harm to those he held dear.

What do you think you're doing?

I've let you bully me long enough, 'Jack.'

Charles fought for control against Jack. He was unprepared for the oppression that Jack's powerful conscience had, and was shoved to the back of his own mind.

"Learn your place!" Jack shouted again and held his head, forcing himself another couple of steps forward until he towered above the portly wolf. Jack raised his claws, ready to strike Henry down.

Henry stood his ground, quaking paws barely keeping a firm hold of his firearm. "I'll shoot!"

"Pathetic little thing." Jack laughed, shoving Charles to the back of his mind. "This is going to be too easy."

Jack tried to strike the fat wolf, but his arm would not move. He growled in frustration.

Charles was lashing out, desperate to regain control. The wolf thrashed about as they battled within Jack's body.

The wolf's features changed wildly, from gray hair to red and back, and his posture contorted into unnatural positions as they fought for power.

Henry watched, frozen, unable to make neither heads nor tails of the situation.

You can't do this! Yo're not strong enough without me!

I am, and I will not yield!

You've not seen the last of me, Charlie! If you defeat me now, I guarantee that you will see me in every shadow, in every dark room, and after every sunset. You'll never be free of me. I'll be rid of you and your friends!

You will never hurt them, you monster! I promise, I will be free of you, and I will find a cure for this wretched disease!

With one last shriek, Jack receded into the depths of Charles' mind. It seemed the fox was finally able to maintain control over the evil within him, but he couldn't tell for how long. The fur on his neck stopped bristling and he felt the rage within him subside. He looked to his friend whose fur was still bristled and bottle-brushed. He was still holding the gun, his hands trembling as he looked at the monster that stood before him.

Inner turmoil began to consume him. Jack would always be lurking in his mind, waiting for a moment of weakness such as sleep, or an intense moment of anger. His heart ached, because he knew he would never truly be free again. He needed to let this moment happen. He closed his eyes, and braced himself.

Henry pulled the trigger.

The gun's muzzle flashed briefly before Charles felt a searing pain rip through his chest and out his shoulder. He heard Jessica scream in the distance.

Charles fell to the ground, holding his chest. He gasped for air, finding it difficult to breathe, and the world around him blurred. His limbs shortened and his muzzle became more refined. His fox-like features returned to normal.

"I am free..." He whispered, the smile still faint on his muzzle. The wolf screamed in the back of his mind, cursing and begging for life.

"Charles?" The realization dawned on him, and Henry could not contain the horror in his face. "Charles, good lord! What have I done?"

The fox coughed blood into his paw. His breath quickly drew short, and soon he was unable to breathe at all.

"Charles, no. Charles, this isn't right! We'll get you help. Somebody, anybody!" Henry stooped to his knees and cradled the fox's slowly fading body. "Please, don't leave me!"

Charles' vision grew darker and words began to lose meaning. He listened to the last, fading cry of the evil within him.

Jack presence faded until Charles could no longer feel the evil within him. The struggle was finally over.

He no longer had to worry about hurting the ones he loved, and with his last few moments, he savored the solace, resting in his dear friends' arms.

"Charles, stay with me. We'll get you to a doctor!"

Jessica's screams drew closer, having just been freed from her cuffs. The officer had regained his consciousness and was standing several steps away. He only briefly made eye contact with Charles before looking away. Charles could read the sadness in his eyes and the stillness in his tail. The officer knew as he did: Charles did not have much time left.

"Charles, you can't leave us now! Someone call a doctor!"

The words were so very distant, as though he heard them through a long tunnel. Charles coughed blood onto the wolf's jacket. As disoriented as he was, he knew no doctor could save him.

In his last moments, he thought of his time with Henry, with Jessica. If only he would have taken the time to let them both know how he truly felt. So much time, wasted...

No amount of niceties were spared as Jessica and Henry grieved over Charles' weakening body. His grip on Henry's arm weakened, and Jessica became hysterical, her tears soaking into Charles' chest as the life began to leave his eyes.

With the sounds of sobbing and hysterical ramblings quickly growing faint in the background, and his body growing cold, he uttered one last "thank you," and closed his eyes.

Roland Jovaik

THE WANDER INN

Nogitsune Faux

Around the van, cold winds drove a near-blinding snow. The road was only just visible in the beams of the headlights; the driver pushed his head forward until his snout nearly met the windshield, as if trying to gain a clearer view of the road by proximity. Three others held to their seats as the van struggled forward.

"Dammit, I thought the weather was supposed to be partly cloudy with a slight chance of snow!" The kangaroo growled, his fingers keeping a death grip on the wheel as he slowed the van to a crawl, eyes keenly watching for any signs of traffic or obstructions.

"It was, Basil! You saw yourself this came from nowhere!" In the seat next to him, the cheetah passenger was furiously tapping on his phone and glaring at the weather app which showed a slight chance of snow. The cheetah's tail whipped furiously as well, his feet tapping in impatience.

"These are the mountains; it's not like storms give much warning." Behind the driver, a roan-furred deer was obviously trying to stay calm. He'd come along with his friends for a pleasant skiing trip, which was quickly becoming a nightmare. He was trying not to remember the horror stories that his grandparents had told him about avalanches and snowstorms, but he was failing as he watched the storm outside batter the van through the windows.

"That's real comforting, Jake," Basil said, his long ears twitching in agitation. The kangaroo had dropped another five miles an hour. He figured that at this rate they'd soon be pushing the van faster.

"At least you're taking it better than Abe." Next to Jake, a spider monkey was now using his glove covered feet as well as hands to grip the seat. His simian face was locked in an expression of pure terror.

"I told you we should have taken the bus like everyone else in the frat!" he screeched, locking his tail around the back of the seat as they reached another hairpin curve.

"Not helpful, Abe! Besides, you wanted to stay a few extra days just like the rest of us." the cheetah shouted, typing with increasing speed as he tried to find out any information on the storm. "Damn this is slow!"

"I'm surprised you can get reception at all, Zeph," Jake said.

"Well I fiddled with this enough to make a few modifications, but I'm down to one bar... and now it's gone."

There was a large gust of wind that rocked the van to and fro and Abe let out a piercing screech—all ears in the van twitched at the sound, "Smooth, Zeph, real smooth." Jake said, commenting on how easily the primate had freaked out.

"Isn't that a light on the side of the road?" From the very back of the van, a calm voice rose.

"Good eyes, Dover! I don't know how you saw it!" Basil immediately turned and followed the road towards the light which, as it got closer, took the form of a ski lodge. The storm started to ebb a bit, making it easier for Basil to find a parking spot in a sheltered area near the back. The five quickly gathered their suitcases from the car and rushed towards the front of the building. Just as they reached the doors, the storm resurged around them and they could all hear some very low rumbling in the distance.

"Avalanche!" shouted Jake, "Not close, but close enough!"

Zeph nodded. "Let's get in."

They rushed in and the first thing they noticed was the warm smell of pine and cider filling air. Inside, there were several large cushy seats around a low-laying table. A stone fireplace had a nice, cheerful fire roaring in it. Overhead there was a balcony and the exposed wooden beams of the steeply sloped roof.

Just beyond the fireplace, on either side, stood doors likely leading to stairs. To the very far right, a thick oak desk with a door to the side cut off the office area from the main. The five staggered towards the front desk, hoping that there would be no issue with them staying out the storm.

Since there was no one in sight, Basil rang a brass service bell, and a figure waddled up from somewhere in the back. He was dressed like a lumberjack, with a plaid, red shirt and blue overalls. His muzzle and head sported a shaggy mane that was several shades darker than the thick red fur that covered the rest of him. His pointy, black-tipped ears and thick, white-tipped tail marked him as a fox, though a huge one. He stood well over any of them, a wooden pipe in his muzzle.

"Can I help ya boys?" he drawled out, his dark green eyes glistening merrily.

"We need a place to stay until this storm lets up Mr.... uh?" Basil looked the fox over for a form of identification.

"Gus. Just Gus. And ya'll are?"

"I'm Basil, the deer is Jake, the monkey is Abe, the cheetah is Zeph, and the sea otter is Dover."

"Welcome to th' Wander Inn. I'm afraid I'm th' only one here right now, but I'm willin' ta help ya'll get settled. This here storm might be around some time."

"Um, okay, but we didn't bring a lot of money with us. Do you have an ATM?"

"Heh, 'fraid not Basil, but don'tcha worry about it. I can make out fine helpin' ya'll out. It's only neighborly."

Basil's ears twitched as Gus talked. He couldn't quite place the accent, but he smiled at the idea of free room and board, "Oh thanks! We'll find some way to repay you for this!"

Gus chuckled as he grabbed five old-fashioned room keys from beneath the desk and moved out to the main area. Along with his overalls, he was wearing thick, brown boots—though he had obviously not been out with them recently. "I'm sure ya'll will. Now 'iffen ya follow me I'll show ya to yer rooms. After ya unpack just head on down here again and I'll show ya to the dinin' room."

The five followed Gus as he led them through the door to the left of the fireplace. There was a short hallway with windows showing the now inky blackness outside. Basil shivered at the thought of anyone trapped out there. At the end of the hall was a rounded stairwell that winded its way upwards.

"How do you have electricity with this storm?" Zeph asked as they reached the first landing of the stairs. The balcony extended all the way around over the top. At the end of the balcony facing them was a thick oak door that Gus unlocked to allow his guests further in.

"I've got an alternative way of powerin' this old place, Zeph." Gus smiled and moved through the door. Beyond lay a long hallway with a nice, hardwood floor. At the very far end there was a glass door that had snow slowly climbing up. Basil counted out twenty doors, each matching the oak one that lead in. Gus gave them each a key to one of the rooms, ranging from 101 through 105. "Now, I can take special orders for dinner once ya'll have finished gettin' settled in."

"Thanks so much for all this, Gus!" Basil said, shaking the fox's paw. The fox just rubbed the back of his head with the other paw and the keener noses of the group could smell his pleasant embarrassment.

"Aw, now ya'll are gonna give me a big head!" he chuckled and left them.

Basil went into room, across the hall from where Jack was placed. Zeph was roomed next to Basil, and Abe traded rooms with Dover so he could be closer to the stairs. Dover just shrugged and went into room 105. It was almost like an apartment. At one end was a stone fireplace, a wide swath of plain marble floor around it leading to the welcoming light-hardwood floor. Along either wall was a blue plush couch and chair. Short, dark-wood tables with golden table lamps were at each end of the couches. On the right, the room opened to a kitchen area complete with refrigerator, stove, dishwasher, and light-wood table with four chairs. To his left, he saw another room with the same hardwood floor.

He moved towards it the room, and poked his head in. On the wall to his right there were windows with thick blinds and dressers. There was a large, royal blue bed was placed along the middle of the back wall. Like in the living room, dark-wood tables stood on either side of it with identical golden lamps. Finally, he saw a that there was a bathroom to his left, with a tiled floor all around a toilet, sink, and bathtub, though they were not crowded together.

Dover started unpacking his clothes, though he kept having a nagging feeling that something was missing. He double-checked through his underwear, socks, pants and shirts before looking for his comb, travel toothbrush, toothpaste, shampoo, and nail clippers. Finding everything in order, Dover sat on the bed a moment to consider what he might have left behind. As he looked around the room he realized that there was no TV.

"Huh, how odd," Dover got up and double-checked the other rooms. No television, radio, or even USB cable presented itself. Still, there were several modern appliances. Dover shrugged; he had never been to a ski lodge before—perhaps there was no TV so the guests would be encouraged to actually get out of the room. Computers were also so often wireless, that there would be no need for any cables. Shrugging off the continuing feeling that something was not quite right, Dover went to the dressers. To his surprise, he easily reached the top. Being a sea otter, he stood only four and a half feet tall. Dover was used to using only the middle and bottom doors; it was nice to be able to use the upper ones for a change. He finished his unpacking, realizing as he went through the apartment that somehow everything seemed perfectly sized for him. He wondered if Gus had deliberately given each of them rooms that would match their sizes. It wouldn't be the first hotel that offered different sized rooms for species. Smiling, he straightened out his blue t-shirt and left the room. All the others left their rooms almost immediately after, causing the five to chuckle at the odd coincidence.

"Looks like all our stomachs decided to cooperate for dinner together," Jack said.

"Looks like," agreed Basil. "Let's not keep them waiting."

The five arrived in the lounge downstairs, its warm, cheerful light and warm, comforting scent made Dover smile. Gus was seated in one of the chairs, smoking his pipe and smiling. He rose when he saw the five.

"Well, that didn't take ya much time. I guess ya must all be right hungry, right? Well, the kitchen's this away." Gus led them through the door on the right-hand side of the fireplace. At the end of another short hallway, they entered the dining room. It was a huge place with golden wood along the walls and floors. The tables and chairs were made from the same dark wood and were placed in groups with booth-like walls between them. Dover noted that the chairs were extra-large to accommodate bigger guests and they had plush looking cushions on them.

There was only one table with plates placed on it, and the five headed to it. Dover wasn't sure he'd be able to comfortably sit at the table, but to his surprise it and the chair seemed to be the perfect size for him. Of course, it also seemed to be the perfect size for everyone else as well, even though its surface seemed perfectly flat. After shaking his head from dizziness at the contradictory sight, Dover saw that Gus had provided each of them a menu. Dover picked it up, and his vision blurred for a moment, the text in front of him almost seeming to swirl and distort before it finally cleared. He chalked it up to low blood sugar so he didn't think much of it. But when he looked over the menu he was surprised to see most of his favorite dishes were on it, even the stranger ones like fried salamander. It was almost like the menu was made just for him.

All the others seemed to have found a favorite dish too, though, as they said them each aloud along with their drinks he couldn't remember seeing the items on his own menu. Dover wondered if Gus had given them menus based on their species, but the otter wondered how the fox knew where they were going to sit. He glanced over the menu and decided to get something easy on his stomach after that long daunting car ride.

"I'll have the fish on rice with a pineapple marinade and a raspberry iced tea." The sea otter announced when it was his turn.

"An excellent choice! I do love a well-fried fish myself. Of course, I'm a fairly eclectic eater!" Gus laughed and patted his round belly. The five friends chuckled.

"Would you like us to help you with the clean-up later?" Dover asked.

Gus looked startled, but then smiled, "Nah, thanks, I can handle things."

"Well, maybe you'll join us, then? I hate to think of you eating alone."

Gus smiled softly, then shook his head. "Nah, I'm okay, but it was sweet of ya to ask."

After he waddled off, Dover found himself being stared at by his friends.

"Are you crazy?! What was that all about?!" Abe was the first to speak.

"He's here alone with no help and no one to talk to. He's letting us have free room and board. I think the least we can do to repay his generosity is to help out or eat with him."

Basil's ears flipped positions. "Damn, now you've got me feeling guilty."

"You did the right thing," said Jake.

"Hey, with my speed I could have had the dishes cleaned before we ate!" Zeph joked.

"Yeah, amazing, just imagine the dishes being clean before we ate," said Basil.

"Well I think you're all nuts! I don't see why we should do anything. I'm certainly not!"

Dover was about to tell Abe off, when Basil quickly changed the subject, the five of them returning to pleasant conversation as they waited for the fox to return.

When the fox returned sometime later he was carrying the dishes on trays. He was amazingly balanced, and was able to delicately maneuver them down. He served them back in the same order in which they'd been placed. Dover's was the last and as Gus put it down, he could swear the bear-ish fox winked at him. Fortunately, everyone seemed too occupied eating to notice Dover's slight scent change of confusion and desire.

The fish was absolutely perfect, and Dover was hoping that Gus was well-supplied with them. The others all seemed very content with their suppers too. Once they finished, Gus returned to pick up the plates and everyone ordered a desert except Dover. He excused himself for a minute to find the bathroom. Instead, he followed Gus into the kitchen. Gus was just finishing putting the dishes in a dish washer, and he turned around.

"I figured ya'd follow. I do appreciate th' offer, but as ya can see I can take care of things pretty well on my own."

"I still don't think it's right. I mean, you must be pretty lonely."

Gus shrugged, "Well, 'iffen I was before I ain't now. Right now I have ya'll as my guests. Now, do ya want a desert too? I could see ya practically droolin' over somethin.'"

Dover chuckled, "Maybe there is, but I'm not telling you it unless you agree to eat with me. I'd be a lousy guest if I didn't take into consideration my host."

Gus's face softened and Dover could swear the big fox's eyes started to water. He looked like he was about to say something when, Abe called from outside the restroom, "Yo Dover! Didja fall in or what?!"

Dover peeped his head out the kitchen door to look at the monkey and said, "Wrong place, banana breath."

Abe shook his head, "Don't be such a goody two shoes. If he wants to cater to us, let him cater to us!"

Gus moved forward, forcing Dover out of the kitchen, "Yer friend was just about to put in a last-minute request for a dessert. He'll be joinin' ya and the others in a minute."

Abe smiled, "Okay. Just don't forget I love sprinkles on my banana split!"

Dover shook his head as Abe left, "I can never get him. When he's scared he's wimpy, otherwise he acts like a jerk."

"I've known a lot of folks like that. Usually there's somethin' they missed out on early in life that leaves them feelin' vulnerable if they ain't in control. Sometimes it seems like they really want to be under someone else's control but are afraid to admit it."

"Maybe, but that doesn't make it right."

Gus shrugged, "People sometimes change over time. Now about that dessert."

Dover laughed, "The chocolate-honey-peanut-butter ice cream, please." He grinned toothily and Gus laughed.

"Damn, another of my favorites! Well, I just can't refuse an offer to eat that! I'll make yer friends some things, then I'll be out with two orders."

Dover smiled and almost hugged Gus before remembering what happened the last time he did that to another guy. He instead shook Gus's paw and ran off to the dining room. Gus smiled as the otter bounded off.

In the end, everyone except Abe joined Gus and Dover as they ate dessert. Gus, having a dishwasher, insisted that none of them needed to help. After the harrowing day and wonderful meal, a good night's sleep seemed like the perfect way to end things.

As he laid down on the comfy waterbed (a completely surprising, yet very welcome bit of furnishing), Dover wondered about Gus. He could reasonably believe that with the encroaching storm, Gus had dismissed all the staff and stayed behind to take care of any traveler in need, but there was something very strange about the place overall. The more Dover thought, the harder it became to explain everything.

Well, mom and dad always did say I thought too much. Dover thought, chuckling as he cuddled and squirmed under the blankets. The surface of the bed felt good against his webbed paws and feet, and he didn't even have an issue positioning his tail. As he started to doze off, the last thoughts he had drifted to Gus, and Dover felt his cock poke out a bit from his sheath. His nose twitched the bristly hairs on his upper lip wiggled as he sniffed the air. He could smell his own embarrassment, even a twinge of his disdain for being alone, Dover wondered if he'd have the courage to approach the large fox, and even more how the fox would react.

He wasn't sure when the door opened, but Dover was awakened by a faint light from it. He rose from the bed, and walked towards the light, entering the hallway. It wasn't until he was halfway down the steps that Dover realized, almost as an aside, that he was naked. The fireplace was still crackling merrily, but in one of the huge seats Dover could see Gus sitting, smoking his pipe. He was completely naked as well, his huge, furred body seeming to fill the room. Dover couldn't help but approach the massive figure.

"Well, like what ya see?" Gus motioned to his body, smiling lustily. His tail was wagging slowly and Dover could smell a thick, manly scent wafting into the air. It was only matched by the manliness of his body, that fox had a red patch of thick curly chest hair, which formed into a treasure trail that went all the way down to his crotch, those white balls and hard pink cock sticking out like a sore thumb against all that red. The otter's shaft reacted by rising to the occasion.

Dover felt himself drawn in, the coffee colored sea otter's feet moving across that hard wood floor to that massive fox. Gus stood up, then picked Dover up and kissed him on the muzzle. Dover tingled as he kissed back, hugging what he could of the fox's thick neck, his short legs dangling as that large fox held him close, his stiff shaft pressing into the fox's soft belly.

"Damn yer a good kisser," Gus chuckled and placed the otter on the ground. The tip of Gus's cock was nearly level with the top of Dover's head. It was a good six inches and at least half an inch thick. Before Dover could do anything Gus said, "Would you like to see me get even bigger?"

Dover looked up and nodded. As he watched, Gus grew a couple more feet in height, his furry body gaining more muscle but retaining a layer of soft fat for a nice, cuddly look. The fox's ears became tipped with lynx-like tufts and Dover could see he now had three large tails poking out behind him. The greatest change, however, was to Gus's equipment. His cock was now nearly as large and thick as Dover's body and his balls were the size of Dover's head. A thick, manly scent came from Gus's groin and Dover lost all sense of restraint.

He stepped closer, letting that massive shaft press against his smaller frame, the huge fox lurking over him as that penis rubbed into his soft fur. He wrapped his arms around that massive member, squeezing it against him as his own shaft pressed into those low hanging balls. He leaned forward, his tongue sliding across the head of that other man's shaft, his tongue twitching as the salty manly taste rolled across his tongue. Gus chuckled, "Careful now, if you keep that up you'll end up all wet and sticky."

Dover, however, had ceased to care. He wanted Gus badly, and stroked the length of the cock with his body, his tail weighing down behind him as he squirmed. Up and down he went, slowly stroking until...

A bright light stopped Dover cold. He shot up and looked around and realized he was still in his hotel room. The storm had passed, leaving nothing but pure white snow behind. Feeling vaguely cheated, Dover left bed with a major morning wood. He then proceeded to the bathroom where a hot shower, some soap, and very few strokes managed to relieve the otter of his sexual frustrations.

Going downstairs, Dover saw the others sitting around in the main room. "It took you long enough to wake up!" Abe called out.

"I guess I was more tired than I thought. Has everyone had breakfast already?"

"Yep, and Gus showed us some other places. There's a game room that Abe and I plan to go to while Jake and Basil will be heading to a gym," said Zeph.

"Sounds like a plan. Is Gus still in the kitchen?" Dover approached the door.

"Yeah, your boyfriend is still in back," Abe chuckled, laughing more as Dover's scent of embarrassment wafted across the room.

Jake and Basil crossed their arms and scowled. Zeph whacked Abe on the head. "Not cool."

"Sheesh! A guy can't even joke around here!" Abe left the room through the same door they went in for dinner. Dover noticed a turn near the end of the short hall he hadn't seen before. He waved to his friends as they went down it while Dover went into the dining room. Gus was seated at the table closest to the kitchen. He rose as Dover approached.

"Have a nice sleep?"

"Yeah, a real nice one." Dover shuffled a bit as the bear-like fox approached, a manly scent accompanying him.

"I bet yer hungry. Anythin' ya might like?"

For an instant, Dover's eyes fell to Gus's crotch, wondering if there really was a treasure trail that led there. "Um, not sure. What do you have?"

"Well, my favorite is peanut butter pancakes with chocolate milk."

"Sounds good! Have you eaten too?"

"Nope. I figured ya might wanna have someone ta eat with."

Dover smiled and went into the kitchen with Gus, helping out with ingredients. The fox smiled at the otter, "So, ya got anyone special?"

Dover could smell his anxiety fill the air from that question, "No, not yet. It's a little hard sometimes."

Gus chuckled, "I hear ya. Ya never know if the guy or gal will like ya."

"You—um—dated guys?"

Gus smiled gently, "Yup. Some of my better dates were guys. Course, there's always a chance the guy might not like ya askin.'"

Dover nodded, "Yeah. I've had a couple nasty encounters, though most guys are fairly nice about it. I still haven't figure out a good way to approach someone outside that Knotz app."

The two went to a nearby table and started eating. A comfortable silence fell between the two of them. "Are you looking for anyone Gus? I mean you're a really handsome guy."

"Maybe." Gus winked and touched Dover's furry paw, "it might depend on who asked."

Considering getting scent-masker, Dover touched Gus's paw in return, gently rubbing it. "Well, I'd like to get to know you better. We could write one another, maybe call?"

"Well, you're always welcome ta stay here. But I've got a confession ta make," Gus paused and took a swig of his chocolate milk.

Dover could scent Gus's scent change, it shifted from a coy lust, to an anxious scent, like he had something important to say. "There's something different about you—about here—isn't there? Ever since we came I've been having this feeling like something's just a bit off."

"That's one way of puttin' it." The fox paused, as if working up the courage to finally say. "Dover, I'm a mage."

The sea otter looked at him inquisitive for a moment. "You mean like a wiccan?" he asked, wondering why the fox was so worked up about sharing his beliefs with him.

The fox chuckled, "No, no. My magic is far more real and stronger than that. Let me show you..." The fox took his index finger and placed it on the fork in front of him. His finger glowed softly for a moment, and the fork shrunk into a tiny metal ball, before it lurched and popped out an amphibian head and legs. The tiny metal frog leapt around the table, bouncing from place to place, before finally landing in the fox's drink with a splash and turning back into a fork.

"Well that certainly explains a lot... like why everything always seems to become my size or how you just so happen to have every one of my favorite foods in stock." Dover was somehow not surprised. "But why are you telling me this?"

"Yup, that's the reason. And well, I think yer a mage too, otherwise ya wouldn't be takin' this so calmly. This whole place is my creation an' I move it around from time ta time. This time I was here in the middle of the mountains. When I found out there was a storm, I figured I might be able ta save some folks."

"That makes sense. You did save us. Does this happen all the time?"

"Nah, most of the time I just go somewhere and nothin' happens much. It's hard ta explain, but I knew somethin' was different this time. My main problem is figurin' out what ta do with yer friends now."

Dover frowned. "What do you mean? Can't they just leave once the roads clear up?"

"Well, yeah they could, but I mean right now they're gonna be pretty bored."

"Couldn't you magic the road clean or something?"

Gus chuckled, "Yer a lot like me Dover, always lookin' fer practical magic. There's probably a couple different things I normally could do ta help them out. The problem is the magic ain't workin' right when I cast it."

"What do you mean? How can your own magic not work the way you want?"

"Well, my magic has been goin' haywire ever since ya showed up. Yer magic is still locked inside of ya, and it's making most of my spells not work like they should. I can do simple things like that frog, or the menu tricks. But most'a the bigger stuff like clearing the road isn't working."

"So what do we need to do?" Dover asked.

"Well... there's one thin' I can do. I could activate that magic inside of you, but I gotta warn ya... when someone like us is activated, it has a habit of affectin' the people around us. It won't hurt yer friends, it will help them really, but still it's gonna change them. Yer new magic will seep into them, and bring out their hidden desires and/or the things inside of them they aren't proud of to the surface. It'll cause some changes in them both physically and mentally. Most of it can be reversed, but whatever it is they need helped with is gonna stick."

Gus continued. "This also has ta be a onetime only offer. I bet ya understand, releasing people into the world with knowledge of magic could lead ta all sorts of consequences. So if you decide not to become a mage, when we finish this talk, I'll have ta wipe your memory. We'll just go back ta' talkin' like we was before I showed ya my little magic trick, and yerself and yer friends will be more than welcome ta' wait until the roads get cleared up before I send ya on your way."

Dover sat back in his chair, just taking in what the fox had just told him. "Before I answer, just let me ask something." The otter shifted, "if I chose not to do this, and let you take away my memories, I'm not going to know this place of yours moves around, will I? So if I leave without becoming a mage, I'm never going to be able to see you again, will I?"

Gus nodded, "Yeah, I can't have ya realizing I'm magic, and ya'd get suspicious if I had ya meet me and my home in different places all the time."

Dover reached out, and took the fox's larger paw into his own. "Then I guess I can't really say no." He said, grinning from ear to ear under his bristly whispers.

Gus returned the smile, "Alright, let's get started."

Dover nodded slowly, "So what can I do?"

"Just stand up, and hold still." The big fox said as he reassuringly squeezed the otter's webbed paw. They both stood up and Gus walked over to Dover. The large fox cupped the smaller creature's head in his paw, before looking down into the sea otter's eyes with his own green orbs. He smiled tenderly, his finger rubbing the otter's cheek, before he reached up with his other paw, placed his finger to Dover's forehead, and whispered something under his breath.

There was a pulse of energy, like a large gust of wind, which shot out all around them, surging through the house, and working its way towards the creatures in the ski lodge. Dover's eyes glowed with a bright white, before he fainted, falling into the large fox's waiting arms.

Jake and Basil admired the gym; it was clean and provided a good view of the beautiful mountains. Besides the usual equipment, there was a large pool to swim in as well as an indoor tennis court. They had just finished their workouts and showers and were about to head out when they noticed there was a sauna room.

"Strange. I didn't see that coming in," said Jake.

"It's a bit off to the side, so it's more obvious when you're leaving. I wonder if it's any good."

"You would want to get all hot and steamy after a nice shower."

"It's not like we couldn't shower again. Besides, when was the last time you were in one?"

"Too long ago," Jake replied. "Well, we might as well try it and see. The worse that can happen is our fur stays fizzled for a few hours."

Basil laughed and the two went into the steam room. It had an antechamber that provided towels and shelves where the two could leave their clothes. There was a faint scent in the air, nothing either could identify, but which seemed very invigorating. The two reached for the towels, then stopped. They both felt a strange tingle across their skin cleared as the new mage's magic started to take effect, it seeped into them, and made their vision blur for just a second before it cleared.

"Hey Baz, you see any reason we ought to wear these?" Jake's scent of embarrassment was obvious, but then he could smell Basil's, too.

"Strange, I was just about to ask you that. I guess that's the answer. It's not like we haven't seen one another naked before."

"It's not like you've got anything to be embarrassed about either," teased Jake.

"This coming from the guy who has the flattest abs in the West."

Golden wood benches formed a circle around the center where the steam would rise from. Basil and Jake took seats opposite one another. As Jake turned on the controls and set the time, Basil noticed there were several herbal-smelling crystals in containers near the hot rock container. He noticed a little sign that said, "To activate, please place inside the rock box." Choosing a few, he placed them in the center before Jake pressed the activate button. The box started to heat up, and then Basil poured some water over them and a large plume of steam rose into the wooden sauna.

He sat down, and then Jake noticed the containers with the crystals. "Hmm, want me to pause it so we can add some of those in?"

"Already added."

"You do think of everything, don't you?"

"Well, maybe not everything."

The two chuckled and relaxed as a colored steam started to fill the room. Along with it rose a strange, almost wild scent.

"Damn, that's nice," said Basil.

"Mmm, yeah. It makes me think of woods and fields in the wild."

The cloud soon became too thick to see through, leaving only general vague outlines. Basil soon found his sheath starting to stir, his cock rising from it and throbbing above his balls, but somehow he didn't care. He took his cock into his paw, and he began stroking it. He relaxed, leaning back into the wooden wall behind him. He knew he should feel worried about his friend seeing him. He'd always tried so hard to hide his lust for the other male after all. The years they'd been friends, he'd never let his friend catch on, he'd even dabbed on large amounts of scent masker to make sure his friend could never smell his lust.

Jake was so caught up in self-pleasure that he hardly noticed the feeling of growth in his muscles or that his antlers were feeling just a bit heavier. He could see his friend's outline through the mist; he found his mind wandering, wondering what that kangaroo would look like stroking his cock, that golden body sweating as he panted and squirmed.

Meanwhile Basil was trying to bring himself to a climax—to no avail. His whole body felt nice and warmly relaxed. He could swear he was getting bigger, but he also found he didn't care. He rubbed his paws over his whole body, feeling the massive muscles beneath his fur. He was beginning to find it hard to form coherent thoughts, but he was sure of one thing—he wanted sex badly.

"Hey, Baz," a deep, almost primal voice came from within the fog. Somehow Basil recognized it as Jake's.

"Yeah, Jake?" his own voice sounded an octave deeper than usual, but that was fine. He thought, men ought to have deep, sexy voices.

"I need to jack off and can't."

"I've got the same problem. Wanna help one another?"

In silent agreement, the two massive figures rose and met on the bench opposite the door. They should have been surprised to see one another, given they were both nearly eight feet tall and rippling with thick muscles. The kangaroo now sported a goatee his ears were flopped over from the new piercings that had sprouted at the end. The deer had huge, moose-like antlers with a thick beard and similarly long, wild hair.

The two of them looked at one another, their eyes tracing over their new muscular bodies, they both wondered how they'd managed to fit in the room, it almost seemed to change to fit their massive size. Basil reached out, his fingers sliding across his friend's thigh as he looked at the throbbing pole of flesh rising between them.

"So are we really going to do this?" He asked before he met with the deer's eyes once again.

Jake looked back at him, his heart thumping as he reached out and repeated what the kangaroo had just done to him. "Well... I know I would, but are you sure you want to?" His ear's folded back against his skull that had those new large antlers mounted atop it.

"I... I think I have to. I always just pretended like it wasn't there, but there's something about this place that makes me see it now. I want you Jake. I want to be more than just your friend; I want us

to become something new." The kangaroo said with a soft smile as his thick tail flicked against the bench behind him.

Jake smiled back, and he said, "I think I'd like that too."

Basil made the first move, his paw reached out and he slid his fingers across that pulsing shaft, letting it twitch under them. Jack and Basil looked each other in the eyes and then they slowly leaned in, their lips meeting and joining in the kiss they'd both long denied themselves.

They slid in close as they kissed, those two muscular bodies rubbing against one another as Jack reached down and took his friend's cock into his paw. They started to slowly stroke one another, their paws sliding up and down those new massive shafts. They groaned as they felt one of their tongues brush against the others, their eyes closed. The heat of the sauna surrounded them, the steam starting to diminish, leaving just the heat to seep into their fur.

Basil felt Jake lean into him, guiding him to lay with his back down on the bench. That kangaroo happily did so, watching as that bulking deer straddled his hips. He reached up, his fingers tracing over his new set of chiseled abs, they were so thick that they would have put most gym rats to shame. He shuddered as he felt them moving under the deer's fur, going from soft to hard as steel as his friend flexed from his touch.

Pre-cum drooled down their shafts, their large balls pumping it out in a steady stream as Basil reached forward and playfully ran his finger across the large deer's tip, getting a deep primal growl from him. Basil slid his paw down his friend's cock, before wrapping his paw around both of their shafts. Basil looked up at that muscular deer as he gripped the bench with one paw, and then started to slowly thrust against his friend's cock.

"Oh Jake," the kangaroo moaned as he squeezed down on their shaft as his friend bred his cock against his own. He wrapped his legs around Jake's waist, and squeezed him in close, feeling his friend's ass flex as he thrusted forward.

"Aguh! I can't take it anymore," the deer growled. "I have to know what you taste like. I want to suck you off, Basil."

"Only if I get to suck you off at the same time," the kangaroo said with a playful growl in his voice.

"Deal."

With that Jake stood up, turned around, and then straddled his friend's head. The playful kangaroo leaned his muzzle up and kissing over those low hanging orbs, before taking them into his muzzle and starting to suck. Jake just let him have his fun for the moment as he stroked his throbbing rod, his eyes watching as Basil's twitched and those big balls churned below it. He licked his lips and leaned forward, his balls slipping out of the kangaroo's muzzle with a lewd pop, before he leaned in and grabbed a hold of the kangaroo's shaft. The deer gave it a few strokes, before he leaned forward, wrapped his lips around the tip, and then slid down over that other male's shaft.

Basil could feel the kangaroo nosing at the spot where his sheath had pooled around his dick, and he groaned as the kangaroo slid his tongue along the underside of his shaft, before finally taking the tip in his muzzle and sliding his head down on that shaft. They began to bob their heads up and down, each of them groaning as the taste of their friend's flesh danced across their tongues.

Jake moved his heavy antlered head up and down as he bounced along that kangaroo's flesh, his lips wrapped over his teeth as he squeezed down on it, groaning as he felt that kangaroo's pre splash the back of his throat. The sauna filled with the scent of their musk, only fueling their arousal. They groaned, the kangaroo thrusting softly in and out of his friend's muzzle, as he sucked on that deer's cock. He could feel those heavy balls grinding against his chin as he reached up and cupped Jake's ass with his paws, feeling them as he moved his hips up and down and bred his friend's muzzle.

The two of them acted in perfect unison as if they'd practiced this for years; each felt their orgasms inching closer, both knowing the second they tasted the other's cum their lives would never be the same. They both took a deep breath, and then it happened. Their balls pulled up and warm gushes of cum squirted into each other's muzzles, that salty manly taste rolling across their tongues and each of them took great care not to waste a single drop.

"I'm telling ya Zeph—this is the life! No work, no worries, free food and board! It's too bad that chump Dover keeps trying to ruin it for us."

Zeph frowned at Abe. The simian was using his hands and feet to play at the controls for the video game. Zeph pretty well matched him, but he wished that Abe would shut up about the inn. Personally, Zeph thought that Dover was trying to do the right thing and agreed with the otter.

"Dover does have a point."

Abe shrugged. There was a surge of energy that washed over them, the two of them not noticing it as they continued playing the screen changed, glowing and pulsing in a slow, rhythmic way. It called to them, it drew in their attention, making them focus on it and nothing else, not even the passage of time. They carried on like this for several minutes, static leaping through their fur as they watched the pretty lights. It wasn't until about thirty minutes later that the game came back on, and they started to play again as if nothing had happened.

"Is it me or is it getting hot in here?" Abe asked and, without waiting for an answer, started taking off his shirt and shorts.

"Maybe a little." Zeph followed suit, taking off his shoes and socks, carefully folding his shirt and shorts into a pile while Abe simply threw his aside. Strangely, Zeph was completely comfortable with this. Abe didn't seem to mind either. The two kept on playing on the controllers, the colors from before flashing every now and again, interrupting the game, but neither of them noticing.

As he played, Zeph noticed his toes were getting longer and more finger-like. It was strange, but somehow seemed completely natural. Once his big toes had turned into thumbs, he grasped a second set of controls like Abe was using and kept playing at the imaginary game.

240

Abe felt a little strange, as though his stomach were pushing out. As he watched, his limbs slowly started to thicken. He kept on playing, though, even as his feet started to thicken and he lost mobility. Finally, he dropped the controls his feet held as they changed into something more akin to what an elephant would have.

"Yeah, I'd just love a life where I didn't have ta do anything."

"Doesn't sound much like a life to me, I like being active," Zeph felt strangely detached as he watched Abe continue to change, the simian's body getting fatter and larger, slowly swelling as he played. His own body was feeling much more lithe and nimble, even if there was a strange feeling of growth on his head, as if he was gaining a mane.

"Nah, it'd be...uh...great. Just sorta standin' around doin' nothin' all day..." Abe was just sitting, staring at the TV, a slight line of drool forming at the edge of his mouth. Zeph stopped playing and watched as Abe changed more. He was definitely getting fatter and larger, his eyes almost level with Zeph's. He rubbed his belly with his hands, then moaned as he felt a filling sensation in his balls.

His orbs started the size of Ping-Pong balls, but as Zeph watched they slowly swelled to the size of oranges, then to that of cantaloupes. They hung thick and low—Abe's member long and hard above them. Abe's fur started to gain darker spots, and his shoulders slowly started to slump down. It wasn't long before he was standing on all fours, his arms changing into legs and his hands turning into thick, rounded feet.

Abe's face started to thicken, his cheeks slowly turning into jowls. There was an increasingly dull look in his eyes. Two horns started to grow from his head and his ears slowly started to lengthen and look donkey-like.

"Uh, Abe, are you okay? You're looking a bit dumber."

"Huuuuuh? Oooh dumb...good. Thinkin' too much work," Abe smiled dully and gave out a low similar to a cow's. Zeph shook his head at how far Abe had gone for laziness—his body and head resembled a feral hippopotamus, with cow-like spots, tail, and horns.

"You are a complete moron Abe, and I don't mean just your current lack of IQ," Zeph shook his head while Abe just mooed. Zeph put on his clothes and tied his hair in a ponytail. He left his shoes off to let his hand-like feet feel the ground and left the room to see if anyone else might have an idea what to do with Abe. As he moved, Zeph decided to try running on all fours and found he could easily. Leaping and running, Zeph reveled in his athletic body and wondered if Jake and Basil would mind a third person in the gym.

The main lounge was an interesting sight. A giant moose and kangaroo were sitting on a love seat, cuddling one another happily. They had jock straps on and nothing else. Their massively muscled, furred bodies seemed almost incapable of the delicate fondling they were giving one another. Across from them sat what looked like a cross between a cheetah and a spider monkey. He had placed his long hair in a ponytail and was wearing a form-fitting shirt and shorts. His hand-like feet were bare.

"Hey guys, where's Abe?" Dover and Gus were surveying the room and grinning. Dover had always wondered if Basil and Jake were gay or at least bi.

"Last I saw banana breath, he'd changed into a cross between a feral hippo and cow. He's also dumbed down to the point that he can't even talk—something about it being too much work," Zeph explained with disgust.

"It might be a good idea ta check in on him; no tellin' what'll happen ta someone that lazy," said Gus.

The five went into the room to find Abe still in there. He was chewing on some grass growing from the floor. His body had grown rounder to the point of immobility, and he seemed to have gained a dinosaur-like tail as well. As they watched, his feet seemed to be taking root while plant-like leaves were slowly replacing his fur.

"Well, that just figures!" said Gus, shaking his head. "An' after that he'll probably change inta stone," Gus added.

"What happens then?" asked Dover anxiously. Abe was becoming increasingly bushy by the minute, loosing distinguishing features as he changed into a plant.

"We'll just have to carve him out again," Gus said and smiled reassuringly at the otter. "He's not the first this has happened to."

Even as Abe's head became little more than an oddly shaped bunch of foliage, his lower half slowly lost its color and leaves, turning slate gray. The five watched as the plant slowly changed into a large boulder, rounding out so that there was no way to tell head from tail.

"Well, that was anticlimactic," said Zeph. "I'm going to the gym to exercise. Not that I don't feel sorry for banana breath, but he brought it on himself and I don't see that there's anything we can do to help him." With that Zeph dashed off down the hall.

"I hate to say it, but Zeph's right. Jake and I will be in the gym exercising. Let us know if there's any change."

"We may even use some of the equipment," Jake said and winked, walking arm in arm with Basil down the hall.

"So now what?"

"Well, now we get to find out what karma decides to do with Abe," Gus smiled gently, "This is gonna be your task, your first act of magic. There are some things you oughtta know. First, once ya unleash yer magic it'll turn ya into yer true self." As he said this, Gus grew larger and more bearish, his ears became tipped with lynx-like tufts and two new tails formed behind him. A very noticeable bulge formed in Gus's crotch. "Course, besidin' the physical stuff ya'll might gain some other changes to."

"Like what?"

"I didn't always talk like this ya know. I always had a thing fer Southern-style accents. Unfortunately, I never had a particular favorite, so now I sound like someone with a real bad phony accent."

"I was wondering about that. Now you've got me worried—I've always liked surfer lingo!"

Gus chuckled, "Then ya'll probably end up talkin' like one, but probably not that accurately. Anyway, the first thing is ta relax an' concentrate. Close yer eyes and feel inside ya."

Dover did as he was told and relaxed. As he became calm he could feel a stirring within himself, like a fish waiting to be caught. Otterly instinct took over and he went after the feeling until he caught it.

"That's just great! Now open yer eyes."

Dover looked and saw his paws were glowing blue, "Wow! This is amazing! Will my paws always glow when I use magic?"

"Not if ya'll don't want 'em to. It's easy enough ta suppress, but let's just leave that fer another day. Right now ya just need ta feel around Abe and get him mobile again."

Carefully, Dover started touching the boulder and somehow could feel where and what needed changed. Slowly he began to sculpt with the blue fire on his paws, and as he did he could feel his own body slowly changing as well. Trying to ignore the odd, yet pleasant sensations, Dover concentrated on the overall feel of the boulder. He slowly sculpted out the general shapes of legs and arms, hands, feet and head. As he worked, he realized the figure resembled a cross between a bear and an ape—an unexpected, yet somehow appropriate, figure.

Gus watched as Dover slowly changed. He was getting taller overall, his tail, feet and paws growing larger. As Dover finished the first run-through of the sculpture, he now stood equal to Gus in height. His clothing had changed to fit his figure but had not changed in style yet.

Now Dover felt along the figure more carefully, teasing out a tail, creating hands and hand-like feet. He could somehow easily turn it over to create a nice pot-belly and moobs as well as a well-endowed area for equipment. Little details like fur began to show through on the body as he sculpted it into shape, taking time on each section until he felt it was finished.

The sea otter's body kept changing as he channeled the magical energies. Gus watched as his fur started changing from dark brown to a sandy tan. His shoes changed into flip-flops and his pants turned into torn Daisy Dukes. As Dover continued to sculpt his shirt began to shrink, then vanished, leaving his lithe upper body completely revealed. A shark's tooth necklace formed around Dover's neck and Gus noted with satisfaction that there was a significant bulge forming in Dover's crotch.

The figure's head was still rough and lumpish, so Dover took time to tease it out, forming a thick brow ridge and a muzzle mixed with ursine and primate features. The last details he received were a pair of small, cow-like horns on the figure's head as well as a thick majestic mane. Looking at the figure critically, he felt it somehow suited Abe. The bear-ape looked real enough to breathe.

Dover gained a nice, thick head of blond hair and gentle sea-blue eyes. An earring appeared in each ear, and some dark brown stripes appeared on his arms, back, and legs, lending the final touches to his more obvious changes. He turned to Gus and said, "What now? I mean how do I make him live?"

"Just concentrate, ya'll are doin' just fine."

Dover nodded and closed his eyes. He focused on the form below him, imagining it warm and real and breathing. Suddenly he felt a rush of energy pass through him and into the still figure, causing it to go from grey to a dark brown black.

Abe stirred and blinked his eyes at Dover, "Aw Dov, now why ya gotta go an' wake me up fer? I wuz havin' such a nice dream!" The figure grumbled and groused, scratching it's furry behind as it slowly waddled out of the room.

"Duuuuude! That was, like, a totally gnarly rush!" Dover said, jumping excitedly until he realized what just came out of his mouth. His eyes grew wide, "Dude, did that, like, just come from me?! Aw man! I sound, like, totally ridiculous!"

Gus chuckled, "That's what I thought, but there's no gettin' around it. Ya'll got a real nice body out of the deal, though." He smiled as the room changed around them, showing full-length mirrors. Dover's eyes went wide again as he saw his body. He looked it over from top to bottom, even finding he could bend himself in ways he never thought possible.

"Dude, this is, like totally gnarly! Well, except for, like, the fact that I, like, sound like an idiot. Am I, like, even using the, like totally right words?"

"Probably not. Magic seems to take a perverse pleasure in makin' folks sound like livin' stereotypes. I wouldn't worry about it too much." Gus smiled and moved to hug Dover close to him. Dover smiled and cuddled with the bearish fox, slowly unbuttoning his shirt.

"I, can, like, totally get used to this," he said and leaned in to kiss.

Gus and Dover lay in bed next to one another, their naked furred forms cuddling gently. Both had happy smiles on their faces.

"So, like, what's next?"

"Well, iffen ya'll wanna stay here ya can. Yer friends will probably be wantin' ta leave pretty soon, now that I was able to clear the road."

"Like, how is Abe even gonna explain, like what happened to him?"

Gus shrugged, "His folk'll see him and it'll be like he's always been that way. The others will be the same, though how much they'll keep I can't say. Abe'll keep everythin'. I had a friend just like him once an' did the same thing you did. No one seemed ta notice, though."

"So how come you were, like, so totally worried?"

"Mainly cause while the physical stuff gets a magic pass, nothin' else does. A friend of mine was in the closet, after he got exposed he went out and got kicked out by his family. He ended up alright, but it wasn't fun."

Dover nodded, "Jake and Basil have, like, been best friends forever. Their parents are, like, totally cool with gays."

Gus smiled, "Then that should make everythin' just about right."

246

"You sure you wanna stay Dov?" Jake asked again. He looked more like a regular buck again, if on the buff side. He still had a wild mane of hair, a beard, and his antlers were unusually thick.

"Yeah, I'll be, like totally cool here dude!"

"Just be sure to text us!" Basil smiled and hugged Dover. Like Jake he was a more reasonable six and a half feet, but he had retained the relative musculature and all other features. Zeph was zipping in and out with the luggage, handing it to Abe, who was actually cooperative with carrying it. Neither had changed again at all, and Dover thought they both looked better and happier in their new forms.

"Fer sure! And don't forget I'm, like, totally coming back to college after winter break dude!" Dover chuckled and gave Jake, Abe, and Zeph hugs before they headed out to the car and drove away. After he finished waving, Dover turned to Gus, "Think they'll be okay dude?"

"They'll be just fine. I made th' road nice an' clear fer them. I put a couple protection spells on them just fer good measure too."

Dover smiles, "I'm, like, totally looking forward to what gnarly things you can teach me!" Dover paused, "Like, whoever invented the word 'gnarly' should, like, totally be hung out to dry!"

Gus chuckled, "I can sympathize, it ain't easy soundin' talkin' like this all the time either. But ya'll do sound cute." He smiled and kissed Dover on the cheek, a kiss tenderly returned.

"Do you ever, like, get lonely here? I mean you didn't have anyone but us."

"Sometimes. I know that some mages like ta set up demesnes where they get some followers. Bein' immortal an' all it can help pass the time."

"Oh, so, like Circe's island is, like, totally real?"

"Oh yes, and in more than one realm too. Maybe the two of us can set up our own eventually; it could be a lot of fun."

Dover nodded and hugged Gus. Whatever happened in the future, he'd be happy as long as he had Gus with him.

Papa Panda and the Selfie

Kodiak Malone

Papa Panda leaned back and scratched his chest idly. His shirtless torso flexed a bit as he wriggled to get more comfortable in the unfamiliar desk chair. He was in the back room of Orson's Pub, the local bar he frequented, and was relaxing after helping the owner clean up. The panda's white furred belly was distended from a big meal, and he smiled contentedly as he clicked through the various images on the computer's desktop.

"Enjoying my collection?" a voice rumbled over the panda's shoulder. Papa turned and lifted his blue baseball cap a bit to admire Orson, the large, heavy set polar bear male who was standing at the door holding a cup of coffee. He had a thick black goatee that stood out against his creamy white fur, and wasn't wearing a stitch of clothing, which was just the way Papa Panda liked his men.

"It's extensive, I'll give you that Orson," Papa said, switching to another folder of pictures while eyeing the polar bear as the bartender's cock started to rise to attention. "Sure this is okay to have on your work computer?"

"It's a work and play computer," Orson chuckled as he lumbered over to the chair and rested a big hand on Papa Panda's shoulder, "that's a perk of owning your own bar. The boss can't get mad at you for looking at porn on the job."

"That, and all the sex you get to have with your customers," said the panda, his black patched eyes twinkling in amusement as the polar bear began rubbing his shoulders.

"Well, you've always helped with that crowd," said Orson as he leaned down and chewed on Papa's round ear while looking at the screen. "A little bit of your magic always gets them in the right mood. Still don't know how you pull it off. Like last week, I never expected an orgy to break out on the pool tables. Though, I think my favorite part was after closing Papa. Getting a one on one fuck session with you is always the best."

"We should do it more often," Papa Panda said. His jeans were tenting from the polar bear's proximity and touch as Orson reached down and tweaked the panda's right nipple. The big ursine was intent on having another one on one session tonight it seemed. "There's a reason I like coming to this bar," the panda rumbled as the big polar bear fondled him.

"Besides it being the only game in town," Orson quipped, his blunt claws dragging through the panda's chest fur.

"No, there are two other bars in town," said Papa Panda with a small grin, pretending to play hard to get by paying attention to the computer just to tease his horny friend some.

"Right, like you'd go to either of those dives," the polar bear snorted as he leaned against Papa's side, rubbing his growing erection into the sitting panda's shoulder. "They aren't as big as mine," Orson fondled his own balls as he said that, smirking at the panda. "Or as gay friendly as mine, and they wouldn't appreciate it if you started an orgy," Orson said with a smirk. He followed Papa's gaze to the screen, "Find any guys on there you like?"

"You know me, Orson; I prefer my guys in the flesh and fur," said Papa Panda, scrolling down slowly and enjoying the images in front of him. They were mainly pictures of human men, guys with substantial frames, thick beards, and mustaches who would be called bears by people who hadn't met Papa Panda or one of his... projects like Orson before. Some had on leather, rubber, or flannel, but most were simply posing naked. Almost all the humans sported erections, and every once in a while Papa would find an image of a truly ursine fellow like himself and Orson. He enjoyed those the most. "Though, it seems there are plenty of good looking men online. You know any of these guys?"

"Yeah I chat with some of them and do web cam stuff," said Orson with a grin as he hugged the panda. "You really should get a computer and internet connection. Bring yourself online more."

Papa Panda stopped at an image of a large grizzly bear he recognized, a real bear like him and Orson were. He was posing in leather next to a motorcycle, a thick cigar stuck in his mouth as one big bear paw stroked his rod. The bruin was another of Papa's creations, like Orson had been once.

"I see Zee is doing well after his change," Papa muttered, idly unzipping his jeans. The grizzly bear had come a long way from being an uptight jock who had once insulted Papa Panda for parking to close to his precious ride. Papa had managed to fix that uptight part with a thick cock up the ass and a liberal dose of Papa's own creative and highly transformative juices.

The photograph of Zee was a lot more professional looking than most of the snap shots Orson had collected were, and it was followed by a whole photo shoot of the bear posing with his motorcycle. Papa licked his black lips and his cock jumped a bit as he reached the last of the set, which featured Zee's ample rump pointed at the camera, his big dick pulled back so you could see it drooling across the back of the bike as if inviting you to go for a ride. The panda bear gave a low rumble, remembering how the grizzly bear's ass had felt when he'd first turned the overconfident jerk of a man into a real bear. It had felt even better than Orson's paw gripping his dick through his underwear did now.

"Yeah, Zee joined a group of motorcycle guys a while back and one of them is a photographer. He's got the entire gang doing photos like that, all gay for pay site stuff." Orson indicated several hairy tattooed humans after Zee, "Though I don't know how true that bit of marketing is now. I sent an email to him a while back when I found him online. I was hoping to get a discount but Zee said no, apparently the site pays for a lot of stuff and it's helping him get into the pants of most of the gang. Worth the price, though, don't you think? Course most humans just see a particularly big and hairy human when they look at Zee, but it is still hot to think that some people can see what he really is now. I've got a few videos of him hooking up or getting one of the gang to blow him. Want to see?"

"Maybe later," The panda smirked a bit as Orson leaned in close, his paw now really working the panda's dick through his briefs. The polar bear's own cock was grinding against Papa's shoulder. "I get enough real life action. I don't need a computer to get off. I don't really even know why I got one of them smartphones, it is fun to play that game with those grumpy birds, but I don't really need all this tech."

"Yeah, but you're missing out on so many hot porn sites," Orson growled a bit and nuzzled the panda's neck, his fingers continuing to tease the panda. He knew Papa wouldn't play hard to get forever, and it was fun to play along with the black and white bear, "or better yet, you could make one of your own."

"Thought I already had a porn site," Papa Panda growled lustily, a wet spot appearing on his underwear as his cock began to leak pre due to the polar bear's attention.

"No," Orson corrected him, "that's just a forum for all of the guys you've changed into bears. We use it to chat and hook up with each other. And talk about you behind your back, since you never come on."

Papa Panda ignored that last comment as his eyes settled on a folder of image that wasn't mixed in with the others, but was sitting off to the side on Orson's desktop. He double clicked the folder and grinned a bit as the pictures began to display, "Hmm, now this is one guy that doesn't belong with the rest."

Orson glanced at the screen, which displayed a picture of a small-fry human with red hair who couldn't be more than twenty five, and Papa Panda felt it as the polar bear's dick jumped at the sight of him. The pictures were clearly from a selfie photo shoot in the guy's bathroom, but they still showed off a lot. The human was not in great shape, but he had a really handsome face under a mop of red hair. He had no body hair beyond some pubic bush, a clean shaven face, and even had freckles on his cheeks. The polar bear snorted, his black nostrils flaring as he looked down at Papa, trying unsuccessfully to cover his reaction. "Oh, I just saved those by accident."

"Sure you did," Papa Panda said, shifting in the chair and grabbing Orson's erection. The barkeep's dick was at full mast and leaking at the sight of the scrawny redhead. "Who is he?"

"Him?" Orson grunted, feeling the big hand on his cock. "Just some guy from a straight dating site I go on sometimes. I like trawling for closet cases to mess with. You wouldn't believe how funny that can be, hooking up with a 'straight' dude." The polar bear huffed as his teasing strokes where returned with interest by the panda. "Either they get all flustered and shy when another guy actually shows up, or they either go all religious on you. They usually try and get me to change my wicked ways."

Both bruins chuckled at that, their paws each rubbing the other's erection. Orson was especially hard as he talked, eyes locked on the freckled young man on the screen. "Either way, they usually try and flirt with me, and they're so cute when we finally hook up. Even naked and covered in lube, they can't spit out the words for what they want me to do to them." The polar bear grinned, flexing his chest as Papa began rubbing a paw across his pecs. "I'm a big guy thanks to you, so I don't have much to worry about if one of them freaking out on me. Do you remember Freddy?"

Papa's head tilted a bit, thinking. "Was he the guy with a big black beard that went down to his naval?" Papa gestured with one hand from Orson's chin down to his white furred belly. That hand then began to scratch Orson's belly, making it shake above the polar bear's hard-on as Papa kept up his stroking. "The one who was a serious nudist who liked to hike only wearing his boots?" asked Papa Panda, thinking back to a recent Freddy he had helped by turning him into a real bear, instead of just the mountain man look alike he had been.

"That's the one." Orson panted, his big frame starting to tense up as the panda's paws began really working him over. Papa grinned and kept up his stroking, signaling for the bear to keep talking. "Well," Orson licked his nose, "before Freddy met you, he was a big ol' closet case like that guy. I saw him on the dating site, and then spotted him in the bar. He would sneak into the bar some nights, get drunk like he was trying to forget something, and then duck out when things got hot and heavy. But he kept coming back, kept creeping on my patrons. He obviously needed a push, so I invited him to come to the bar on a night you were around. I sent him lots of pictures of you being, well you." Papa chuckled at this, and the polar bear groaned as his nipples were tweaked.

"I do that once in a while to closet cases just to see how they'll react to you. Normally they don't show up, but I know they're jacking it to the pictures. But Freddy showed, and you set him on the right path." The big polar bear grinned as Papa continued working his shaft with one paw, a shudder running up the white bear's spine. "Now he's got a new hobby, getting guys to blow him on hikes and loving cock."

"I do good work," Papa Panda muttered, gauging how quickly he was stroking the polar bear's big cock so that Orson wouldn't get off too soon, but was left hanging on the edge as they talked. Papa didn't want the night to be a short one after all. "So you bring in guys to have me change 'em?"

"Most times no," said Orson with a shudder as Papa began teasing his nipples more, "I know you like to make that choice and you hate being tricked into a transforming a guy. I think we all remember Thomas and that little stunt he tried, but once in a while I get lucky and find a guy you'd like to see grow fur. Anyway, that's just a random guy's pics I saved. That small-fry is clearly not interested in a big manly guy like me."

"Hmm that's a shame," Papa Panda hummed a bit as he squeezed Orson's cock, still looking at the picture. The polar bear was staring at the red head and panting hard, hanging right on the edge as Papa teased his dick. "He should appreciate big thick slabs of man-meat like this."

"It's not like I post up pictures of just my cock," Orson said disdainfully, "I got more to offer then that. I like showing off the entire package."

"And he didn't like the package?" asked Papa with mock surprise.

"He did not," Orson said, trying to keep his voice steady, but it was hard to keep a poker face when being edge. "He said he wasn't into guys. Can you believe someone turning down a big, masculine guy like me?" The polar bear sounded indignant, but Papa could sense there was more too it.

"Now that is a real shame," said Papa Panda, nodding his head and starting to smile. "A crying shame really," the black and white bear said as Orson became more and more tense as his thick dick was tugged by Papa Panda's paw. The big white bear was just about to lose it when Papa Panda let go of his dick suddenly, leaving him panting for more. "Someone should teach that cub how much fun big masculine guys can be." Papa Panda held up his smart phone as Orson looked down at him in frustration, the polar bear's hard-on dripping pre onto the panda's belly. "Any chance you can show me how to put pictures on here and send emails?"

Nicolas Land rolled his eyes as he paged through email from work on his company smartphone. It was mostly junk, the usual emails about things that didn't concern him, inter-office drama, and memos about bake sales or toy drives. Of course, hidden in that mess of emails were a few things that did actual require his attention, but Nicolas was glad he wasn't the only guy on tech support duty for this business. Having to deal with all of this idiocy alone would have been too much. He loosened his tie and dropped it on the counter as he headed into the kitchen.

He set the phone down beside his tie and got himself a glass of water. His roommate Jasper wasn't in the apartment; he had left for a business trip for a few days. Nicolas wasn't sure what to do now that he had the place to himself. A common joke was to walk around naked but that wasn't really his sort of thing. Still, as much as Jasper was a close friend, Nicolas did want to take advantage of the freedom of having the apartment all to himself.

His phone beeped at him, alerting him that he had gotten another email. Running his hand through his short puffy red hair, he sighed. He grabbed his phone off the counter and noticed right off the bat that the email was to his private address, and it had clearly not been sent from a work address either. *PapaPanda? What a weird handle,* Nicolas thought as he previewed the message. There were attachments, naturally, so it was probably spam saying it could make his dick bigger. Still... he was curious; normally he didn't share his personal email around and he didn't get much spam...

On a whim Nicolas opened the email. He quickly scanned the body of the text which was just a telephone number and a short message saying to call whoever this Papa Panda was. Below the note, one of the image attachments popped up.

It was a picture of himself, the one naked pic that Nicolas had used for that dating site he'd joined a few months ago. It was, admittedly, not a great picture. He was standing in front of his bathroom sink, red hair puffy and curled over his eyes, and clearly in need of a trim. He preferred his hair as short as possible, but he'd been trying to impress some ladies with the bad boy look. It hadn't worked. Nor had taking off his clothes. That just showed off why his dress shirts for work always felt so baggy, he was skinny as a rail with nobly knees and elbows that stuck way out. Several of the girls he had tried to chat up had commented that the sink was dirty. Honestly who paid attention to details like that in pictures like these? Well, besides those girls and whoever sent this email. Not that he had any luck at getting laid since joining that site. Nicolas preferred not to think about his romantic prospects. The curse of being a tech geek he supposed.

Then, unbidden, the second image attachment loaded up. Nicolas stared at it for a moment, not comprehending the image.

In the second image a much large man was in the exact same pose he had been in the first. Nicolas drew the phone closer to his face and his eyes widened as he realized that despite the size difference, this too was a picture of himself.

It was weird. The pose was the same, the bathroom was the same. Even the dirty sink was the same. Nicolas was certain it was picture of himself, but he was a lot bigger. And big was the only adjective that he felt fit this second picture. That version of himself was huge, with a big belly, a rounded face, and big powerful arms. Everywhere Nicolas was skinny and nobly, this version of himself was muscular and fat. Even his dick was bigger, hanging much lower over a pair of fat balls covered in red hair. He was hairier, too. He was just covered in red pubic hair. Nicolas couldn't stop looking at the picture. His eyes traced over the image, surprised and dismayed by it, and yet drawn to keep looking.

Fuck, he thought, *I look hot.*

Nicolas paused, confused. What? Where did that thought come from? He looked like some hairy fatso posing like a faggot.

Yeah, but that is pretty hot. Nicolas looked confident and strong in the picture, and he liked how his cock was nice and thick.

Nicolas screwed up his face. Why did he care how thick his cock was in some crazy weird photo-shopped picture?

Because it's hot.

"No, wait," he said to himself. Nichols blinked a bit and began to turn away from the image on his phone, but something caught his eye. His facial hair, well the picture's hair, was a lot thicker than his own wispy attempts at a beard had ever been. Unlike the unruly body hair covering the rest of his picture self, his beard was neatly trimmed and looked a lot better than any beard he'd been able to grow in real life.

Nicolas's eyes roamed that smiling, round face and that perfect red beard. The beard was nicely trimmed to frame his cheeks and he had a mustache under his nose, but no amount of trimming could hide how thick and full bodied that beard was on that face.

As he stared at that beard, wishing he could grow one like it, his face started to prickle slightly.

Nicolas ignored the sensation, staring at the little screen, zooming in on that full bodied beard. As he did so, little red hairs started to sprout across Nicolas's upper lip, far thicker than they had ever been before. They quickly grow into a mustache covering his upper lip, and the stubble began growing on his cheeks and chin, the hairs thickening into a full bushy bright red beard that matched the image on the screen.

The young man stared in stunned fascination at the version of his on the phone, unable to look away, and not fully realizing what had happened to his real life face.

As he looked at that jolly smiling face, Nicolas felt his cheeks widen and thicken. His face puffed out, growing fatter to match the jolly smile on the little screen. In a daze, Nicolas zoomed back out to see the whole picture, and his eyes drifted from the face to the rest of his photo-shopped body.

He was a lot rounder and bigger. A lot bigger, with some serious muscle on him, yet Nicolas looked cuddly somehow because of how the extra weight softened his body. As Nicolas's own face finished changing to match the digital version of himself, the changes followed the young man's gaze, spreading downward.

His neck grew thick with muscle, new hairs sprouting down his back to give him a nice coating of red fuzz below his dress shirt. Nicolas's collar began growing tight as he continued staring, his arms and shoulders expanding to match the swell of muscle that his selfie had. The young IT specialist marveled at how strong his doppelganger's bearish body looked, not fully comprehending that his own arms were now straining the fabric of his shirt as they grew to match.

His stomach expanded next, pushing out and sagging a bit as it distended the white cotton. His shirt grew increasingly tighter and tighter, struggling to contain the increased weight as Nicolas continued to fill out the once baggy shirt. His belt creaked and groaned, and Nicolas grunted in sudden discomfort from the clothes hugging his body, straining under his growing mass. A button popped off his dress shirt and flung itself to the floor, and a seem in one of his sleeves ripped as he moved an arm.

"I need to get better clothes," Nicolas mumbled to himself as he continued to remain transfixed by the image on his phone. He undid his belt without thinking as his hips began to widen, his body bulking out to sustain the muscle and fat he now sported. His eyes stayed transfixed on the phone as he took off his shirt, his biceps tearing the thin fabric as his arms flexed, switching the phone from hand to hand to other as he stripped so he never took his eyes off the screen.

The shirt dropped on the floor, forgotten, but he didn't get to his pants quickly enough to save them, and the button snapped off due to the sheer girth of his widening hips. Pressure caused the zipper to split, and they pooled to the floor around his ankles as his legs flexed, beginning to grow to match his thick arms.

Nicolas could only assume even his feet were bigger in the image, and so he kicked off his shoes quickly just before they swelled to match his now much larger size. Nicolas continued to stare at his massive girth in the photo as he stepped out of his ruined pants, his butt widening to proportionally match his new weight.

The young man had to admire the confidence this digital version of himself had. He looked so much bigger and manlier. *Sexier. Was that right?* he wondered hazily. *Yeah sexy, that's the word. With a big belly like that and that manly hair, I'd look so damn sexy.* He grunted slightly and his eyes finally went to the crotch of the man in the photo.

Naturally with his eyes lingering on his own photo-shopped crotch, it didn't take long for Nicolas's real balls and shaft to swell up, and the final piece of clothing Nicolas wore began to strain under the pressure. The young man stared in envy at the big dick of the 'other' man, unaware that the front of his own briefs was growing tight. Not from an erection, but from sheer pressure as his growing bugle as his package swelled to match the massive man he was becoming.

Soon the cotton of his underwear shredded and the elastic snapped, giving way to Nicolas's growing body and hanging in tatters around him, no longer covering his fat new dick. The thick soft shaft hung down over heavy nuts, which grew bigger and heavier until they matched the image and looked large even on his massive testosterone fueled frame.

Man the guy in the photo is hairy, Nicolas thought, staring at the picture which matched the thick red pubic bush he now had in real life.

This other version of himself had Sasquatch levels of fuzz over his beer belly, chest, arms, and legs. Nicolas's beard thickened some more, as did the hair on his head, growing to match the unruly mop in the photo. His arm pits grew thick red patches of hair, as the red pelt of body hair swept down his arms, which soon matched the manly, hairy arms of the strange photograph he couldn't take his eyes off of. His legs grew a forest of red hair right along with them, and a bushy tuft of red hair sprouted in the center of his chest, lightly covering his brand new pectoral muscles.

At first, just a simple treasure trail started to grow up to his belly button, but it soon thickened and widened, making sure that anyone looking at him naked would have their eyes drawn right down to his thickly furred groin and the forest of hair that framed his now massive cock and balls. The hair only stopped growing when Nicholas was as hairy as the image, if not more so.

With that final change in place, Nicolas found he could look away from the image, and he did so chuckling. A warm glow filled his body, which tingled as he was just waking up. *What a weird email to get*, he thought in a dazed sort of way. Whoever had done these photo edits was really talented. They had taken his selfie and turned it into a real bear of a man, and they'd done a magnificent job of it.

Still, it was a very strange thing to get. He turned off the phone and set it down as his large hand idly scratched at his stomach a finger feeling his deep recess of a belly button then going lower to feel and scratch his crotch, idly fondling himself.

Nicolas stopped scratching his dick as it slowly dawned on him just how hairy he felt down there. How much bigger his stomach looked from this angle. The young man's cock jumped in his hand as he looked down at his massive hairy body, and the difference in the size of his dick brought reality crashing down on Nicolas.

With a bellow, he snatched up his phone and rushed to the bathroom to look in the mirror. "What the fuck?!" he shouted at his reflection. Staring back at him from the mirror was the spitting image of the very hairy, and very large, man from the photo. He waved a now large hand a few times to test whether it was really his reflection. He twisted his body back and forth, staring in shock at his bearded face and hairy large body. His tattered underwear creaked and shifted as he moved, hanging off his wide hips like a loincloth, until his cock shifted underneath it, growing bigger, blood pumping into it at the sight of his new body. Why was he getting turned on by his own freaky reflection? What the hell had happened? *This is insane!* Nicolas thought desperately.

Picking up his phone, Nicolas quickly reopened that strange email. Nicolas opened up the first image, the actual selfie he had taken months ago and stared at it. He looked it over in detail, just like he had the photo-shopped one, and then glanced back up at the mirror. There was no change this time however.

He tried shaking his phone, his now big fingers sliding over the screen, zooming in and out on the picture of his old self to no affect. Finally with an exacerbated sigh Nicolas looked back at his bathroom mirror in stunned disbelief. How had this happened without him even realizing it? He'd put on a hundred pounds of fat and muscle, no two hundred at least, without even noticing it. As one hand patted his large stomach he looked at the email on his phone again. Maybe he should have paid more attention to the body of that letter.

With a flick of his new fingers, Nicolas scroll back to the top of the email. The text read:

Hello Cub, I saw your selfie on the Match and Mingle website and I thought I could help you out. Clearly you need to learn how to take a picture of yourself so I made a few improvements with the help of a friend.

Yours,

~Papa Panda

"Well that's fucking vague," Nicolas grunted, only now registering how much deeper his voice was.

Under the signature was the phone number he had seen before. Maybe if he called he could straighten this all out? Dialing it quickly he waited as the phone rang and rang. Part of Nicolas realized that something was gone horribly wrong, that his body had radically changed, but he wasn't actually that freaked out by all this. It hadn't hurt after all. His hand continued to stroke under his belly, feeling the thick, curly red pubic hair there as he waited for the call to connect.

"Hello," a deep voice rumbled on the other side of the phone. Nicolas shuddered at the sound of that voice, his new body trembling at how powerful and masculine it was. The tone of the man's voice alone was enough to make his cock twitch and pulse in the air in front of him. "How can I help you Cub?"

"Yeah, uh..." Nicolas said as the dazed head rush he'd felt before returned, and his hand continued to rub his stomach, running back and forth over the overhang cleft of his belly over and over again. The voice on the other side rumbled softly, and Nicolas shook his head to clear it. Staying as focused as he could manage, he said quickly, "my name is Nicolas and, uh, I got an email with this phone number on it."

"Oh? Tell me Cub," the deep voice chuckled, "What was in the email?"

"Well, uh, ya see there were these two photos..." and Nicolas was suddenly unsure of how to explain his strange situation as he looked at his other self the mirror.

"Go on Nick," said the voice, "Tell ol' Papa Panda about these photos."

"Well, first there was this photo of me I'd posted on a dating site," Nicolas said and he waited for a second to hear a response from Papa Panda, wondering if he should have corrected the deep voiced man that his name wasn't Nick. When Papa said nothing, Nicolas mumbled, "and then there was another one of, uh, well, I guess of me too?"

Papa Panda had a deep, rumbling laugh that made Nicolas's dick jump, and the younger man's free hand dipped lower to squeeze his growing flesh. "You guess?" Papa said, "Don't be a silly little cub Nick, it either was you or it wasn't. They can't both be you after all; it's one or the other."

"Well it's just the other picture was, uh…" Nicolas coughed a bit suppressing a grunt as he felt his thick cock swelling in his grasp, while the tattered shreds of his underwear clung to his hips. The sensation of his own hairy arm pressing into his new, big hairy belly sent a thrill up Nicolas's spine. Mind wandering Nicholas thought, *Man, Papa's voice is sexy. I wonder if he's as sexy in person.* What, no, that didn't seem right… he didn't think guys were sexy. Nicolas grunted, and felt his cock disagree with that statement. It pulsed with arousal as Nicolas forced himself to keep talking, "Well it was me but… different looking."

"Different how cub?" asked Papa Panda. Nicolas looked at the mirror seeing the thick python of meat in his hand as it twitched, big and heavy between his tree-trunk like legs. He slowly gripped and squeezed his tool, staring at himself in the mirror. The deep voice shocked him out of his trance, but he kept stroking his meat, "go on Nick tell your Papa."

"Bigger," Nick grunted feeling his penis thicken, "hairier, fatter."

"Bet it turned you on seeing it," said Papa Panda, "really gave you a thrill and made you hard."

"What?" Nicolas let go of his cock and shook his head, confusion flooding his thoughts again, "no it didn't Papa."

"Sure it did," Papa Panda's rich deep voice soothed the younger man from the other end of the phone call. "I bet it was a huge turn on seeing such a big masculine version of yourself on your phone, all hairy and thick just showing off his fat hairy big body. I hear a bit of an echo. I bet you're in the bathroom, Nick. Bet you're looking at yourself in a mirror right now, and its turning you on. Ain't it, Cub?"

Fuck, I look hot, had been the first thought in Nicolas's head when he saw the picture. *Hadn't it?* He thought now, his mind jumbled. *It must have been me thinking that.* Nick finally said, "Well, okay sure it was hot Papa, but that isn't the point."

"Then what is?" asked Papa Panda and Nicolas could hear in his voice the man was grinning, "Wait, I know cub you called because you wanted to talk to the guy who made you so manly looking? You needed to talk to the guy who turned you on."

"Yeah!" Nicolas exclaimed and then just as quickly corrected himself, "I mean no. You said that wrong. Guy's don't, um, don't turn me on."

"Don't they, Nick?" asked the voice on the other end of the line, and Nick's cock twitched as Papa kept speaking. Nicolas's big hand began to slowly stroke his shaft again in time with the words, "The thought of big hairy guys don't turn you on? Big guy's flexing their muscles. Beards on their faces smoking stogies and feeling their bodies doesn't arouse you? You really want to tell me the thought of guys with bodies like the one you have now don't just make your pecker beg to be stroked? That you can go without thinking about those big bodies with hard erect dicks without salivating?"

Nicolas felt a trickle of drool escaping from his lips at the thought of having a big thick cock in front of him, swinging back and forth between the legs of a big hairy man. Fuck that was so hot. He squeezed his shaft again and slowly stroked it as precum bubbled from the head. "C'mon Papa that's not fair, you just sent me this hot pic, that's all it is," he said weakly.

"You and I both know that's not all it is, Cub. You're turned on by my voice. You find me hot, sexy. You want me," said Papa Panda confidently.

Nick stammered out, "N—no."

"Please," Papa said in a disregarding tone. "You're jacking your rod right now," said Papa Panda definitively just as Nick squeezed his shaft and felt his big balls start to bounce with his stroking hand.

"No, I'm not," Nick lied unconvincingly, "I don't jack off to guy's voices."

"Sure you are," said Papa Panda chuckling throatily sending another shiver of pleasure through Nick's body, "Ya know, I'm jacking off hearing your voice. Jerkin' off to a guy's voice is only natural."

"You are?" Nicolas felt a thrill of sexual arousal coursing through him at the thought of a big man like Papa Panda jacking off to his voice. Whatever Nicolas had intended to say to Papa when he'd first called the older man was now completely forgotten.

"Sure am," said Papa with obvious pleasure, "I'm squeezing my shaft right now Cub, teasing the head a bit with a big fat thumb. You doing the same?"

"You know it Papa," Nick blurted out unthinkingly as he tugged on his schlong, using his thick finger on to feel the head of his shaft and spread the pre around the dark red head.

Nick heard a slurping sound, followed by Papa saying, "Why don't you do what I just did and lick some of that precum off your fingers?"

Nick didn't see any reason not to, and so he raise his hand to his face and licked the goo off of his fingers and hand, watching himself do so in the mirror. When he was done, Nicolas said aloud, "Why did I do that?" Confused thoughts rushed through his head as the strange taste coated his tongue.

"Because you're a good cub who follows orders, Nick" said Papa Panda with a growl, "you know you love big guys. Bet after we're done this phone call you'll start looking for pictures of big manly guys."

"You're right I will," Nicolas nodded his head in the affirmative, the expression on his bearded hairy face returning to the softer, happy smile he'd worn while licking his fingers, and he went back to slowly jacking off.

"Thinking about big horny masculine guy's turns you on to no end," said Papa confidently, "it's one of the reasons you just had to call me. Doesn't it Nick?"

"Sure is," Nicolas said with another grin, and this time the name Nick no longer sounded unfamiliar or strange when Papa said it.

"You love the idea of them fucking you in the ass," said Papa Panda.

"I do?" Nicolas was bewildered for a moment. Papa Panda had been right so far. He was clearly right about everything... that was why he was Papa Panda... right? Still, he wasn't so sure about that last directive.

"Oh you know it," said Papa Panda with a growl, sensing the hesitation in the younger man. "Take that hand off your cock, lick your finger nice and wet, and shove a finger inside your ass, Cub. Now Nick."

Nick did as he was told without thinking, savoring the taste of his precum again as he licked his finger. Then he reached a hand back behind him, twisting with difficulty because of how big his body was now. He had to lean forward over the sink and rest his belly, which was at just the right height, as if the counter had been made to be a shelf for his new belly bulge. *Or... it's the other way around...* Before he could really think more about that or what he was doing, the new Nick slid his slick finger around his hair lined pucker, and slowly started to push it inside of his own hole. He moaned loudly as he felt that fat digit slid into those tight, warm, and previously virgin depths.

"See? What did your Papa Panda tell you? You love it," said Papa Panda's firm deep voice, "Now, just imagine that finger is a big cock inside of you. Sliding in and out of you, fucking you good before busting a huge nut inside of you, squeezing your hips before sliding out so another cock can slip in and fuck your needy hole a second time."

"Sounds so hot," Nick breathed heavily, fingering himself as he thought of what it would feel like to be taken like that. Nick's fat dick rubbed against the front of his bathroom counter as he imagined what it would be like to feel a string of guys sharing his hole, and he fumbled with the phone for a moment before putting

Papa on speaker phone so he could finger and jerk himself off as he listened to Papa Panda speak.

"Almost as hot as sucking some of them off as the others fuck you, ain't it Nick?" said the voice on the phone.

"Almost," Nick nodded eagerly, his face a mask of sudden excitement. "I bet sucking them off is tastier and faster. Gotta make sure to please all the guys after all, and if one hole is being filled I might as well fill the other too." That thought, of having both his mouth and his ass full of dick, made nick's cock throb in his hand.

"You sure do," said Papa Panda, "course after this phone call, you're gonna need to go buy a dildo to shove up your ass."

"I really do," Nick nodded his bearded head, face twisted with concentration as he thought. "I got to... got to train myself up, don't I Papa? Be ready for it when I finally get proper fucked."

"That's right cub. You gotta get ready. Know what else you need?" asked Papa Panda.

"What Papa?" Nick asked desperately, any trace of hesitation and resistance gone from his voice now. He wanted, no *needed*, to know what Papa Panda wanted for him next.

"You need a tattoo Cub," growled Papa, and Nick could hear the other man's voice catch as Papa continued jerking himself off. That sound made Nick's own hands work harder, stroking and fingering himself to Papa's voice.

"I do? I do! What... what should I get?" asked Nick, curious about what tattoos he should mark his body with to please this man.

"Clearly you need a bear pride triangle, considering how much you're jacking off to hairy guys and thinking about them fucking you," said Papa Panda.

"Bear pride, Sir?" asked Nick, but before Papa could answer an image of a brown and white striped flag flashed into Nick's mind, and now the red haired young cub could only nod and groan at the idea of a nice bear flag colored triangular tramp stamp in the middle of his back, pointing down as his now eager hole.

"Of course cub," Papa Panda chuckled over the phone, the sound sending a jolt through the red haired younger man's body. "After all, you're a big ol' horny gay bear. Craving a good fuck, needing a big cock in your mouth, and jerking off, that's all you are now Nick." Papa's voice grew deep and rough, and there was a hitch in the way he spoke, as if he were forcing the words out. "A big, horny bear..."

Nick grunted, and his mind focused on those words. *A big, horny gay bear. A fucking, jerking off, cum drinker who needed to be filled. Fuck, that's what I am.* Nick felt his ears give an odd twitch, and the red haired man stared in fascination at his reflection as his ears twitched suddenly grew! They became bigger and rounder, growing gray-tinged white hair. No... it was fur! Nick grunted and rubbed his cock watching as the two large, white bear ears shifted upwards on his skull, settling into a place that looked... right somehow. He wiggled them and squeezed his achingly hard dick again with a moan. "Yes, Papa!" he practically shouted.

"In fact, the more turned on your get right now at the idea of showing your pride, in being a big ol' horny gay bear, the hairier you'll get." Papa Panda intoned from the other side of the phone.

Nick growled loudly, jerking himself off furiously at the thought of men fucking him one after another, of how proud he would be to get fucked like that, of Papa Panda fucking him like that, and across his body, Nick's newly acquired thick red body hair started to grow again.

It started on his forearms, the bushy red hair multiplying, growing a pale grey white as the hair covered every inch of his skin and became thick fur. The fur grew across his legs the same way, and began spreading up his limbs to his chest and belly. The white fur was thicker and shorter than his pubic hair, which remained the bright red color they had always been. The treasure trail down his belly and thick red pubic hair was enhanced by the new white fur that was spreading over his body, the contrast making the remaining red pop out against a forest of white.

Nick staggered upright, leaning back against the wall as white fur washed across his body up to his neckline. His nipples stood

out bright pink amid the white fur, and they were hard as Nick stopped fingering and jerking himself to pinch them, staring at his changing body and muttering to himself, "So horny. Fuck. Love the idea of being a big bear." Nick mumbled that over and over again, pinching and twisting his nipples, looking at his changing body in fascination, "Big manly bear. So proud of being a bear..."

"You sure are Cub. Bet you're letting the beast out fully now, aren't you? Why don't you jerk on that big meaty cock some more, use it to show your ursine pride, and let those hands and feet of yours become proper paws," said Papa Panda huffed as he spoke, and Nick could hear soft slapping sounds of a paw against hard flesh. He knew Papa Panda was jerking his big thick dick to all this as well, and that made the younger man even hornier.

Nick's big, white furred hands reached down and squeezed his cock, feeling the thick log of a schlong pulsing between his fingers. The contrast of the soft white fur of his legs and his thick bush of red pubic fur just turned him on even more. He stroked himself and squeezed his cock, staring at his hands as he tugged on his shaft. As he did, his nails thickened and turned into black claws. His fingers got fatter, sensitive and soft black pads forming on the underside. The shift to paw pads brought heightened sensation to nick's touch, and he moaned as he jerked himself furiously. His body felt so massive and powerful, and he felt his whole body tensing up as the hands holding Nick's dick grew into big, thick paws. His feet became larger and heavier too, forming the same claws and pads his hands had.

"You're almost there Nick," Papa panda growled, his voice echoing in the bathroom from the little cell phone on the counter top. "Just a little more cub, and you'll be a big horny bear for good."

Nick shuddered, his body twitching as the gray-white fur crept up his neck finally, his cock massive and flopping back and forth as he jacked off.

His beard remained the bright stark red his body hair had always been, but his nose turned a steel gray and the tip darkened. His nostrils flared and grew larger, and suddenly Nick could smell his own arousal. *Fuck. So big. So Horny,* he thought in a rush. *So close...*

Nick jacked his rod as his lips turned black and his nose grew bigger and bigger, his tongue feeling too large for his mouth as it slid out over his black lips and sharp teeth. Fuck his tongue would be so big and perfect for really sucking a lot of guys off. Fuck. His face started to push out as he grunted and growled, moaning as his voice deepened further, if that was possible. Nick's face twisted, pushing out into a big broad polar bear muzzle with a bright red beard. The fur on his face seemed to quiver, settling, and with that the final change was complete, Nick's eyes opened wide as he stared at his new ursine self and he moaned, "Fuck, I'm near the edge Papa!"

"Bet you are cub," the confident voice said over the phone, "So am I. Let's go over together. Blow your wad for Papa. Become a big gay bear for me, Nick."

"FUCK!" Nick roared as he heard those words, and it was a true bear's roar that shook his whole body. There was a sense somehow that this was the last part of all this, that by cumming now he'd be sealing the deal and making himself a big horny gay bear for good. Not that Nick minded one little bit.

His thick cock pulsed, and rope after rope of thick warm bear cum burst out of his dick, hitting the sink, the floor, and the mirror. Nick jerked his cock wildly, covering his clawed, paw-like hands, densely furred belly, and muscular chest. Nick breathed in deeply, and his new nose flared as he smelled his own arousal and orgasm. It was amazing, the most incredible, full bodied climax of his whole life.

It took many long minutes of breathing deeply, his thoughts taking forever to clear after so intense an orgasm, for Nick to finally say, "That wasn't exactly the reason I called."

"You enjoyed it," Papa Panda grunted.

"You know it Papa," Nick tweaked a big pink nipple with his clawed fingers, staring at himself in the mirror. "Why'd you do it through? Send me that photo in the email? I never met... we've never talked before. I would have remembered your voice."

Papa Panda gave a low, throaty chuckle. "Well, I had some help finding you from a polar bear friend of mine named Orson. He's the one who found your picture online."

"A fellow polar bear?" asked Nick with a growl, saying the first thing that popped into his head. "Hot!"

"Oh? You turned into a polar bear? Interesting, Orson will be pleased to hear that," said Papa Panda with some satisfaction.

"You didn't know Papa?" asked Nick with some surprise, his paw playing with his thick cock which was still drooling a bit. He could feel his large balls hanging heavy and somehow he knew he would be ready to go another round in only a few minutes. "Fuck I'm horny," Nick muttered, cupping his low hangers to support them.

"Doing this thing over the phone can be difficult sometimes. I don't always know the ursine that will pop out. " Papa Panda explained, "that's why I normally do it in person, but I figured you weren't going to come to meet me without some convincing. And you're horny because a bear should be horny."

Nick licked a few thick ropes of cum off his fingers, savoring the taste, and then peered down at his nose. It was now much longer, and easier to see than it had been before. "Going to be hard going out in public with a snout, Papa," Nick muttered.

"Don't worry cub, that's part of the charm," Papa Panda growled, laughing a bit, "unless they're sensitive to this sort of thing, humans will only see you as a human. A big hairy human, but that's just sexy. Right?"

"You know it," Nick nodded looking at the mess in the bathroom, "going to have to clean all this up."

"Use your tongue," Papa Panda ordered him, "lick up every drop you can. You do love cum after all."

"Fuck, I sure do," Nick drooled a bit and then teased his nipple again, "I might need to cum a few more times first."

"Save it, cub. After you clean up, go get your dildo, and use that to cum next."

Nick felt a thrill run up his spine as he thought about the dildo he'd promised to buy, and then looked at his huge dick. "I'm gonna have to stretch myself out good so I can take you, aren't I? I want your dick inside me so bad..."

"Don't rush cub, you'll get it soon enough. But that's for later. For now, clean up and play with your new body. After you've had some time to adjust, you can come down to Orson's Pub. I want to see my handiwork," said Papa Panda with a growl of lust. "And you can meet Orson when you do."

There was a ping from his phone, and Nick picked it up with a shaking paw. He opened the latest email, staring in fascination at an image of an older, beefy, and very handsome polar bear. The young new cub took a deep breath, staring at the picture. It had obviously just been taken, and the polar bear's chest was covered in what Nick just knew was Papa Panda's fresh cum. "Oh, I look forward to meeting him, Papa," said the young, red haired and newly minted polar bear. Which was true, Nick had never seen a man who looked so good before.

They said goodbye and Nick dropped to his knees, beginning to clean up his own jizz as he thought about the big, white furred bear he would soon get to know very well.

274

WEAPON

James L. Steele

The man on the operating table slowly opened his eyes. His pupils squeezed shut, trying to cut out the intense whiteness. White ceiling, white walls, white tiles on the ceiling. The room was so white he couldn't distinguish where the ceiling ended and the walls began. His eyes wandered around the room for a while. Eventually he could make out the faint shadows that were the lines separating the walls from the floor and ceiling.

The man became aware of his arms. His legs. The slight chill that started at his armpits and spread across his chest, down each leg and arm. He tried to move his head, but it was held in place.

He moved his eyes back and forth, tried to look down his body. He only saw himself in his peripheral vision, but what he saw he recognized. He was naked on a padded, hospital bed. His wrists, ankles and abdomen were strapped down. He tried to move his head, but again something was holding it still. The more he felt the resisting force, the more it felt like a metal clamp. He balled his fists and tried to raise them. He tried to lift his legs. The restraints were so tight he couldn't even lift them off the mattress.

The man opened his mouth and tried to speak, but his mind was moving in slow motion, and his voice was a bubble of slime trying to squeeze out of his lungs. He moved his mouth, tried to moan, but nothing was coming out. For some reason this made the man panic, though he wasn't sure why.

He writhed under his restraints, trying to move anything, trying to reach the clamps that held his wrists with his fingers, but they were so taut he couldn't even rotate his wrist. His chest was held down so tight he couldn't arch his back. His breathing was partially blocked.

He could not look around the room. His only view was what was right in front of his eyes. The man writhed harder, trying to move, straining to speak, trying to reach out and feel something. He turned his head a millimeter in all directions and strained his eyeballs to look around the room. He could accept the restraints holding him down, he could accept his nudity, but he could not accept that he was blind to most of the room.

As he struggled and writhed and tried to look around, his mouth was working and his voice started to come to him.

"Wrrhh!" ... "Wwwhh" ... "WWAAAHHH!"

The sounds weren't much, but they were sounds, and he could still speak if he tried.

"WWAAAARR!" ... "RRRUAAA"

He continued exercising his mouth and vocal cords, teaching them how to work together, teaching his brain how to form words again. His struggle against his restraints matched his inward struggle to force his voice to work.

"WWhhheeerr aahh aaayyee." He panted a few times.

"Wwhheere... ah... aayye." His body settled down now that his voice was coming back.

"Hellloo... Heelll... Heeelll"

He realized he couldn't stop slurring his words. His brain was moving at regular speed but the rest of his body was still in slow motion, and this sent him into another frenzy of writhing and struggling under his restraints.

"HEEEE-OOO! HEEEEEWWW! WHE-MM-AYYE!!!!"

He relaxed again, completely exhausted. He wanted to scream out and demand to know where he was, who was there, what they were doing to him. As he pondered the words he wanted his mouth to make, he slowly realized that he really didn't remember. He didn't remember any circumstances that could have landed him here. He didn't remember his name. The peripheral glance down his naked body was all he saw of himself, and now that he thought of it, he wasn't sure if he remembered what he looked like.

What was his name? What did he look like? Where had he come from? He sensed he should know these things, but he couldn't force the memories. They were there. Answers to these questions were on the tip of his tongue, but they wouldn't rise out of his subconscious.

He settled down on the bed again. He didn't want to. Doing so implied he was lying down and accepting where he was. But he was tired. His body was moving slower than his mind sensed it should. He wanted to fight it, but as resilient as his mind was, his body was so tired. His mouth made weak noises, which his brain sensed should be loud enough to shake the room.

"Hhhheell… sssmmnnn heelllll mmmm. Nnnnmmm" and on and on. Over and over. He abandoned force and settled for persistence. Maybe if he kept it up long enough his body would catch up to his mind.

After a long time, he heard a soft clang from somewhere. He stopped talking and listened. Footsteps and crinkling plastic echoed around the room. The sounds came closer and closer. Then a plastic figure slid into his vision. The man recognized it instantly as a clean suit. Behind the person in the suit would be an accordion-like appendage connecting him to the world outside the room.

The figure in the plastic suit reached down his arm and did something. It held a needle up. The needle had a little blood on it.

"The I.V. slipped out," came a faint, male voice inside the plastic suit. "Reinserting."

The man struggled under his restraints again, trying to project his voice, but all that came out was more mumbles and slurred syllables. The plastic suit's hand dipped below his vision, the man felt something slip in his arm, and a moment later he went black.

The man's eyes flew open as he sensed something was in the room with him. He was lying on his back in the hospital bed, but this time there was nothing holding him down. He looked left—

His head wasn't clamped in place! He took full advantage of his mobility and looked all around. A dozen plastic suits were walking around. Most were yellow, and these suits were accordion-attached to the far wall. Two suits were blue, and two others were red. These weren't attached to the wall, but they were attached to tubes coming out of the ceiling. Surgical equipment lay on various tables, and he was under a very intense light. There was also a robotic surgical arm poised over his skull.

"He's awake!"

The man's head turned in the direction of the faint female voice. The plastic sounds synchronized as all the suits turned simultaneously to look at him. Quickly the man swung his legs off the table and dropped to his feet.

BLOODY HELL!

His legs were deformed. He couldn't think of how to put it in words, but they did not look right. The man sensed he should be terrified, but he wasn't. This strange disconnect within his own mind was unsettling and confusing, but at the moment he couldn't remember how to be confused or unsettled.

They were curved backwards, forcing him to stand on his toes. Surprisingly, he stood quite easily on them. Now that he saw them in action they reminded him of a dog's hind legs.

He stood as straight as his legs would allow, but something was wrong with his back as well. His back was curved forward, and he couldn't stand as straight as he thought he should.

The suits slowly backed away from him. Some held their hands up.

Who are you?! What are you doing to me?! Why can't I remember my name?!!

The man thought all this. In his mind he was screaming it at the top of his lungs, but all that came out was "HHrrgguumm?! HRRAA?! WHAHALAAHHHH?!"

278

Why can't I speak?! Oh God why can't I speak?! Let me out of here!

He muttered more inarticulate growls, croaks and whines, and meanwhile the plastic suits were backing away from him. The accordion suits were folding back to the far wall, which the man now noticed was a two-way mirror.

The floor was made of smooth plastic. So smooth he had a hard time standing upright. The man looked around at the retreating plastic suits, filling with undirected rage. He wasn't sure why he was furious or afraid, but lingering in the back of his mind he had a feeling there was something he was supposed to remember, and these people had taken that from him.

The man relaxed his posture. In the mirror he looked like he was stooping over, slouching, but his spine and legs felt like he was standing upright. Yes, this felt like a natural position—his default posture. He set his sight on one of the yellow suits slowly retreating from him. A dim revelation lit up in the back of his mind: through those suits lay his way out.

Still hunched upright, the man ran towards the yellow suit, yelling and growling. His new legs had a different muscle structure, and the small feet allowed him to run faster than he thought possible. His posture helped with this as well. It felt good to run at full speed. The yellow suit backed up faster, flailing its arms, as if that would speed up its retreat.

The man leaped off the ground, his new leg muscles propelling him high in the air, almost touching the ceiling, and landed on the yellow suit's chest. The yellow suit fell over onto its back, arms in front of it, yelling various screams and shouts muffled by the plastic.

The man hacked away at the suit as if he had claws. He bit down on the plastic... And was disappointed that the material didn't rip in his jaws. He sensed it should, so why wasn't it?

Didn't matter; he was going to get into that suit! He looked at the short length of accordion attaching it to the wall. He jumped off the suit itself and started pulling and biting at the accordion.

It didn't give, or rip, or tear. The man was frustrated. He felt it should tear in his teeth, or his hands should rip it apart. Then the man wondered why he sensed it should be working. He didn't have claws or teeth that would tear anything, so where did the expectation come from?

He became aware of rustling plastic around him. The suits connected to the wall with accordion appendages were against the wall, now vacant of their occupants. The remaining four suits, the ones that weren't connected to the wall but to hoses on the ceiling, were still in the room. Two were on the far side of the room, the other two were holding needles in their hands and were approaching him.

His eyes glanced over the table and the tray of equipment. The surgical equipment! There'd be knives in those tools! The man walked on his toes towards the two suits with needles. He felt light, springy. Completely free to move however he wanted. He liked his new legs and posture. They streamlined his body for forward movement. Time to test that.

The plastic suits flanked him. The man recognized the move and didn't let them. He ran straight for one of the suits. The suit held the needle up. At the last instant the man leaped through the air, grabbed the plastic tube connecting the suit to the ceiling and held onto it as he landed on the floor. He landed firmly on his toes. The thin tube had come with him. The man let go of the tube, and it retracted into the ceiling, pulling taut above the suit.

The man dashed to the table. He looked over the tools and sure enough there were many knives. He picked two of them up and held one in each hand. He didn't pause to show the suits what he had; he leaped straight for one of the suits again. The suit ran for him, holding the needle out.

The suit threw the needle at him like a dart. The man saw it coming and sprang off the floor into the air. He caught the hose connecting the suit to the ceiling and cut it. A rush of moist air hit the man's face as it escaped from both the hose and the suit.

"Shit!" came a radio-quality voice from inside the plastic.

The man landed lightly on his feet and ran straight for the accordion suit hanging limply from the mirror that ran the length of the whole wall. He stabbed the yellow suit with one of the knives. The knife penetrated with no effort, and he gouged the suit through three layers of plastic. Another rush of air hit his face as the smells of the non-sterilized outside world filled his lungs. He dropped the knives on the floor and spread open the rips with his bare hands.

He had just poked his head through the tear when suddenly he felt dizzy. Chills spread over his body like third degree burns. His nose itched and began leaking. Every joint in his body burned and he dropped to his knees, still trying to crawl out, but now it was becoming hard to move.

"God damn it!" came a radio voice behind him. The man felt a plastic hand on his shoulder, a needle enter his skin. "He's contaminated!"

"What is it? What's the matter?"

"He has no immune system! It had to be destroyed prior to phase two or his body wouldn't accept the new DNA."

"A two-week setback, maximum. Get him to decon. Have antibiotics standing by and I want that anesthesiologist's head on a silver platter."

The man felt sleepy. He couldn't move. The voices faded. The fresh air smelled so good.

I want to go home... There is a war to... fight...

The mirror on the ceiling reflected the view of his entire body back down to him. The room he was in was tiny, white, and clean. The only feature on the wall was a single door on the far side of the room, which the man couldn't see unless he turned his eyes all the way down and strained.

His body restraints were visible in the mirror. He was held down not by straps, but by metal prongs which were buried into his skeleton, holding him down by the bones themselves. A tube was coming out his throat. He felt another in his anus, and a catheter in his urethra.

His legs were even more deformed now. His feet once had recognizable toes. Now he didn't know what they resembled. His whole body was lined with small incisions and needle marks. An ugly, red scar ran around his scalp. He wanted to move. He wanted to break free. But nothing would move. His mind was a haze.

It happened over several days. Maybe weeks. His face elongated at the mouth, nose and lips fusing together part way and jutted out in front of him. Two small nubs became visible on the top of his head, and his ears receded three-quarters of the way back into his skull. His toes took on a new shape, as well as his fingers. All twenty of them felt like they had something stuck inside of them. Something solid.

The man's mouth tingled. His legs tingled. His arms tingled. His face, head, neck, chest and everything else tingled. A very dim flicker of consciousness thought this should hurt, but it didn't. The nubs growing from the top of his head felt good. The strange thing happening with his toes felt good. Even the metal bars holding his bones stationary felt really, really good.

He felt too good to go to sleep. The man stared at himself for hours. Days. Weeks. His body was changing. He watched it happen. His nose and mouth were indeed merging and it happened in spurts. For hours nothing would happen, then all of a sudden something would move. It was always too quick to see it consciously, but the end result was obvious.

The same thing was happening with his fingers and toes. They were changing. Shifting positions. Something inside was growing. His arms and legs were also changing. The muscles were crawling around underneath his skin. He watched his chest muscles expand gradually. He watched his arm muscles slowly bulk up. Veins rose to the surface and puckered up as the growing muscle pushed them harder against the skin.

His leg muscles grew the fastest. He watched these in real time, not in long stretches of inactivity followed by bursts of change.

He watched them expand. He watched them separate, bulk out, separate again, grow even more. His chest and arms swelled. His skin stretched to accommodate the new mass. His bones stretched and grew.

It felt so good. The bones growing, the muscles expanding, the things growing out of his skull, the things growing at the tips of his fingers and toes, whatever was growing inside his mouth. For hours at a time he lay on the bed with an erection. Even that looked different than he remembered.

Days, weeks, months...

Lying on the bed, watching himself grow in the mirror.

The nubs at the top of his skull grew into large ears. The ears that had once been on the side of his head had long disappeared into his skull. His mouth and nose were joined together at the end of a long muzzle.

Something wiggled out from the tips of his fingers and toes. One at a time, claws poked through the skin of all ten of his fingers and toes. Blood ran down his feet and hands as they bored their way out.

Now as he stared at the mirror he noticed fewer changes. The pleasure had waned long ago, and his body seemed solid again. No movement, no shifting, no bones growing and realigning.

He settled back down, relaxed, when suddenly his whole body ignited in pleasure. Hair was growing from everywhere on him, from the tips of his toes to the top of his new ears. It grew in so fast he watched it from sprout to finish. The fur was a muted mix of brown and black with a cream underbelly. His backside tingled and surged him with even more pleasure. Something was growing there, but he couldn't see it.

It felt so good his eyes rolled to the back of his head, completely awash in ecstasy.

The man opened his eyes. The colors of the room were muted shades of grey and brown. He couldn't remember being in a room that wasn't white, and the sensation was disorienting.

The man noticed he was seated in a chair of some sorts. Something about the chair he was sitting in struck him as unusual, but he couldn't expand on the feeling. After all, he'd never seen a chair before, so how would he know?

The chair was all metal, and it was built specifically to accommodate his posture. His arms and legs were held in place with metal straps. The man looked around the grey and brown room, now realizing he was free to move his head. Three of the four sides of the room had mirrors that took up almost the entire wall. His reflection stunned him.

The man had gotten used to a thin, pale, hairless figure staring back at him. What was seated in the chair looked nothing like what he was used to seeing, even though he'd watched the transition from one to the other. An enormous brown and black canine sat in the chair in the mirror. His arms and legs were strapped down by thick, metal strips. He remembered his former human face. It was flat and drawn back, as if in retreat. The canine face that looked back at him from the mirror was pointed directly at him. Everything from the eyes to the angle of the snout pointed forward in attack. He opened his mouth. Two rows of large, canine teeth lined his mouth.

God... I'm hideous...

The thought was very faint. As soon as the idea surfaced, it drowned, leaving the man a little curious where that strange, soundless voice had come from.

Lying on the floor elsewhere in the room were large pieces of metal. One of them had the digits 200 stamped directly into its side. Another was labeled 500. The last was labeled 1,000. In the center of the room was a table.

The man leaned forward. Suddenly his nose caught something. He didn't know what it was, but the smell made him want to go to it. He strained forward, sniffing it, lifting his hands and trying to walk. Something was on that table. He could see it, smell it, almost taste it, but he couldn't reach it.

The creature in the mirror practically doubled in size as every muscle on his body flexed and struggled in the chair. He was growing frustrated— the chair was holding him back and he had to get to the scent!

The man settled himself and breathed. The creature in the mirror paused as well, massive chest heaving in and out under his coat of fur.

He looked down at his arm. The wrist was restrained by an inch-thick bar of solid metal. He lifted his wrist again it, forearm muscle bulking out his fur as it moved under the metal and pushed up.

A distant connection rose up in his mind: The metal wasn't too thick. He could break it.

The man turned his arm over and curled. His wrist pushed against the metal. At first nothing happened, but then he felt the metal give. This encouraged him to curl his arm up harder. He glanced at the creature in the mirror. His face was cinched up in a snarl, bicep and forearm flexed to their maximums, veins popping out, visible even under his fur.

The man's expression dipped slightly. Was that him? He didn't feel like he was snarling, or angry, or exerting any effort right now. Before he could think on it, the metal bent. He flexed harder, pulled harder. The metal whined and bent and warped. Finally it snapped, and his arm was free.

As soon as he broke the metal and saw his arm free, his body swooned in a powerful feeling of ecstasy. He flexed his other arm, pulled up against the metal, flexed as hard as he could. The metal whined and bent until it broke.

He did the same with his legs, but forced them to move outwards at the same time. The braces on his ankles groaned and snapped easily, and the man leaped out of the chair and ran for the table.

A pile of bloody meat was on the metal table. Mixed into the meat was an extra scent. The scent was arousing and his mouth began to water. Desire to extinguish it overwhelmed him. He opened his mouth, grabbed a hunk off the pile and tore it free. He turned his mouth up and gulped it down.

More pleasure.

Sweet bliss came from snuffing out that scent. It wasn't coming from the meat itself, but from something mixed into it. The man opened his mouth, grabbed the rest and gulped the remainder. The bliss intensified.

When the meat was gone he turned his nose to a new source of scent. It was coming from one of the pieces of metal, the one labeled 200. He crouched closer to it, scenting the air around it. The meat scent hadn't been there earlier; only after he finished the meat on the table.

He walked around it, looking for the source. He found nothing on any side of the small block. He smelled the top. The only other place it could be coming from was underneath.

The man crouched down and gripped the block on both sides with his clawed hands. The pads on his palms gripped the smooth metal firmly. He tried to push, but the block wouldn't move in that direction. He flexed his legs and lifted. The block rose easily, and he threw it aside. It clanged on the floor and slid a ways before coming to a halt. There was a small cavity beneath where the block had been. In the cavity was more bloody meat mixed with some artificial odor. The man reached in with his snout and devoured the meat straight from the hole.

He looked in the mirror as he chewed the last bite. The creature in the mirror was covered in blood, matting the fur. He didn't feel like that creature. Briefly he thought he saw a human figure move as a shadow behind the mirror, but as soon as he thought he saw it, it was gone. He forgot about it.

The scent was back! Instantly he was up, walking in his half-crouched stance, like a permanent stalk, and following his nose to the new source of scent. It was under the block of 500 metal.

He wrapped his paws around this one, lifted with his legs. This block took much more effort to lift, but it felt so good to lift he continued to raise it above his head, working every muscle in his body. This felt even better. He watched himself lift the block in the mirror. The creature in the mirror looked fierce, strong, powerful. The man didn't feel that way, and yet his body was soaked in pleasure from lifting the block. He set it down gently and gorged on the meat in the cavity beneath the block.

Before he even finished the meal, the scent reemerged. His snout and head rose from the cavity and pointed him straight at the final block of metal. The 1,000.

He rose slightly and ran to it. He watched himself run out the corner of his eye. The creature in the mirror was stalking, running silently on his pawpads. His head never moved, his tail was straight out behind him, keeping his balance.

He stopped in front of the block, crouched down and picked it up. His muscles had to work harder than ever. The creature in the mirror was snarling and straining and flexing his muscles. It felt good to lift this block! Better than eating the meat. His legs did the initial lifting. He raised it over his chest, and his arms, chest and shoulders got involved. He lifted it over his head and held it there. The enormous creature in the mirror was holding the block over his head, muzzle and chest fur matted with blood.

He threw the block aside. It crashed into the floor, made a hole in the tiles and sank out of sight. The man crouched down and devoured the meat in the cavity. Midway through the meal he looked up at himself in the mirror, chewing and swallowing the meat, blood dripping off his muzzle and onto his chest fur. His fur was matted down enough that he could see the definition of his pectoral muscles.

The man reached down, grabbed the last piece and stood up, watching himself eat it. The creature in the mirror chewed up the meat. He liked the way his fur looked when it was caked in blood. He liked the way his body felt when he was lifting the blocks and breaking the metal off the chair.

As he chewed, his mind made the connection. The creature in the mirror was him. He was the creature. He was strong. He was powerful and enormous. That was him. He was proud to be the creature in the mirror.

He swallowed the rest of the meat and looked around the room. No new scents. No more blocks. The room now looked a disarrayed mess, especially with the hole in the floor.

He felt proud of that hole. He wanted to make another one. He walked to the 200 block, picked it up—

He paused. It was so light now. He let go of it gently and held it with one hand. He lifted it over his head with one arm. It felt good to do it with one hand. He lifted it with the other arm a few times. Then he tossed it across the room. It smashed into the floor, making a crater in the tile. His tail wagged back and forth.

He found the 500 block of metal, picked it up and tossed it. Another hole in the floor appeared. He ran to the block, lifted it out of the hole and tossed it again. And again. And again. The block was too easy.

He noticed the chair. It looked like it was welded to the floor. He grabbed it and pushed. The metal legs whined and groaned. The resistance made his muscles work hard again, which made him feel good. He wanted more resistance. He pushed and pulled and twisted. The chair finally bent and snapped free from its welding and he threw it across the room. It plunged through the mirror. It shattered and collapsed in a cascade of reflective glass.

When the glass settled, the creature was staring into another room. There were people standing in the room behind the mirror. All of them were against the wall, shielding themselves from the glass. None had hit them, but they were clearly shaken. The creature smelled shock and fear from them.

The creature heard a sound from his right. A door that had been recessed into the wall was swinging open. In walked a man dressed in business casual attire. Another man stood behind him. They did not smell afraid. The creature stood up straight, which still meant he was crouching, all features pointed forward in attack. Their scents did not change.

"Very good," said the one in front. "Your body has assimilated the modifications. Come with us now. Time to step up your olfactory and auditory senses."

The creature understood none of these words. All he sensed was the tone of the sounds. They sounded confident, but not threatening. He respected that. A distant impulse made him hate these men. He sensed he should escape from these horrible men for doing what they did to him.

But nothing these men did to him had harmed him. In fact, it felt good! He wanted more! He ignored the impulse and strode to the men at the door. They stepped to the side and let him pass. The one at the back closed the door. They led the creature down a long corridor.

The creature's mind awoke. The air in the room was different than the air he fell asleep in, and he raised his head instantly and looked around. The creature was curled up in front of a large hallway. The air smelled unfamiliar. He turned his head and looked behind him at a solid wall. No doors. No mirrors.

The creature stood up and scented the air deeper. Everything smelled different now. Scents that had been muted before were loud and obvious now, from the odor of the tile in the floor, to the foam in the ceiling tiles. He smelled metal in the ceiling. His ears picked up a faint trickle of water running through those pipes. The wall in front of him funneled into a hallway, which smelled of metal and concrete.

Suddenly he smelled it. That scent... The one he had to destroy! He looked around him, but the source of the scent was out of eyesight. Something about it... He craned his neck forward, taking in the air in shallow puffs. Every breath he took added the faint scents together and made them more noticeable.

He wanted to find where that scent was coming from. The creature walked into the funnel. The smell of metal and concrete surrounded him, making it difficult to pick out. He walked down the hall until he came to a doorway. Peering around the corner, the passageway extended in both directions, turned corners. There was another door just a ways down the left passage.

He pulled his head back and looked further down the passage he was in. It, too, curved that way. Curious...

And the scent... It was here. Very faint, but detectable. The creature raised his nose upwards and took in the air in short breaths. Each breath added the faint scents together more and more until it became loud enough. When he stopped breathing, the scent began to fall apart and fade in volume. That's when he realized the scent wasn't coming from the air. It was coming from the floor.

The creature stooped down and inhaled the air coming off the floor. He had to inhale the floor many times to add the smell up enough for him to identify it through the tile's odor, but it was there.

The scent didn't veer down this corridor. It continued straight down the corridor he was in. The creature stood up and walked straight. He turned the corner, followed it to another intersection. Here the hallway broke off into four different directions, each way turned a corner and disappeared.

The creature bent down and scented the entrance of each hallway. Since the scent was still fresh in his mind he didn't have to smell the floor for very long. He found the path where the scent had gone, turned and followed it.

The creature followed it down several more turns and hallways. By now he didn't need to bend down and scent the floor to find it. It was so fresh in his nose that all he had to do was inhale the air coming off the floor to find where the scent wasn't. It was growing stronger. This made the creature feel a sense of urgency, and he ran down the corridors, pausing at gaps and turns, decided where the scent went and ran down that hall.

The hallways and doors were identical to the eye. The only sense that led him anywhere was his nose. Using it made him feel good. Running made him feel good. The scent was strong now, which meant he was close to the source. He was running at full speed, pivoting on his paw and turning sharp corners without slowing down at all. The scent led him. He didn't have to think anymore. His nose did all the leading. It felt good. The hallways and doors twisted and turned in and around each other. The scent path was practically visible to the eye by now.

The creature turned a corner, and suddenly the hallway opened up. A large slab of meat rested in a corner. He crouched and leapt at the meat. He sank his teeth into the hunk. He tore it to pieces and swallowed them one at a time. Wave after wave of pleasure spread through the creature.

A faint sound came from his right. He turned his head and looked up. A door had opened, and in stepped those same two men from last time. The creature's stance softened. His tail lowered.

"Congratulations," said one. "You made it through the maze. Come with me. There's more to do."

The creature's tail wagged, and he walked with the men out of the room into another with a metallic scent.

The creature had a 1,000 block in his hand. He lifted it over his head, paused then lowered it. He then lifted his other hand over his head. It, too, held a 1,000 block. He alternated arms, lifting the blocks again and again, over and over.

As he did he looked at himself in the mirror. He thought he looked good before, but when he woke up in this room he was even bigger! All he could think of was picking up the blocks again and finding out how much he could lift this time. Already the 1,000 blocks were starting to feel light.

He held both blocks over his head, squeezed his legs and lifted the blocks with his legs. He lifted them again and again, watching himself in the mirror. After a while he felt compelled to lie on his back and use his chest to lift the blocks. As many ways as he could. Every muscle squeezed pleasure into his body and made him want to lift more.

He was once again in the large room with many mirrors, but this time there had been no meat under the blocks. The reward seemed to be his new ability to lift the blocks themselves.

It had taken forever. After the men led him from the concrete hallways into the metallic room, he had been strapped down in a bed, bars inserted into his bones to keep him still, and left there for a very long time. There was another mirror in the ceiling, and he watched himself grow again. Slowly, but noticeably, he grew to twice his size, and it felt even better this time. Now he could lift the 1,000 blocks as easily as he'd once been able to lift the 200 blocks. It felt so good he hadn't stopped since he woke up.

And now he smelled humans behind the mirrors. He heard their voices.

"He's been lifting those things for hours..."

"That's good. Means the DNA is working, as well as the neural repathing."

"How soon until he's ready for deployment?"

"Only one last attribute to test, regeneration. If it works as expected, he could be in the field by Friday."

The creature understood none of these words. He didn't care. He felt so good and he never wanted to stop.

Hours later a door opened. The creature was lifting the weights outward using his shoulders, relishing the powerful feeling it gave him. He turned his head to look. The same two men were standing at the door.

Tail wagging, the creature dropped the weights, making two more holes in the floor and pranced to the door to meet them.

"Hey, big guy," said the first man. "Six hours. That's long enough. You're almost ready. Next test is right this way."

The creature hopped around, tail wagging, eager to go with the men.

The creature woke up on his back. His nose told him he was in an empty space surrounded by metal walls and the usual tile floors.

There were two men in the room. Their scents mixed together. Both reeked of fear, but one of them reeked of...

The creature rolled to a crouching position and looked around. The room was jet black. His eyes showed him sharp outlines of everything in the room. What his eyes couldn't make out, his nose filled in.

His arm felt different. He looked down at it. Though it was pure black in the room, he could still see it was a completely different color. He reached up and felt it. It had no fur and it smelled new compared to the rest of his body. Hairless and discolored.

He heard a shriek coming from the other side of the room. The creature's ears turned to face it. His head turned to match his ears. He stalked silently to the source of the scent, towards the outlines of the two men. They were both walking around, feeling the walls.

"What was that?" said one. "Something's in here with us... It's moving."

"Shut up!"

"I'm serious! Don't you smell it? Smells like a dog."

"All I can smell is you. Jesus, don't they have showers in England?!"

"I don't know what it is. I just woke up in this room and I'm covered in this smelly liquid. And I'm tellin' you there's something in here!"

"Just stay away from me! I'm gettin' outta here, and whatever trick this is to get me talk won't work."

"I don't know where we are either! That's the problem with you people. You're so bloody paranoid, think everyone's out to get you, the world conspired to bring America down."

"Everyone in the world wanted the U.S. to collapse! They figured if we were gone, that'd free all the resources for them, and you goddamned Brits were the cheerleading the whole thing!"

"Let's just find an exit!"

They were on opposite sides of the circular, metallic room. The creature had plenty of time to take in their scents. Drink their fear. The one on his left had a nice, neutral scent. But the one on the right... His scent pulled the creature to him. He was covered in that scent he had to destroy. He walked on his pads towards the man on the right, who was groping and feeling the walls in wide circles from his feet up to as high as he could reach.

"We were your allies," said man on the left, "and you led the fight to bring America down! We fought back!"

"No one brought the U.S. down. Other nations surpassed you in innovation. The world started buying their products instead, down went your economy, and your bloody government didn't do shit about it except convince you the world conspired to bring you down. You could've adapted to the change, but instead you sulked and blamed everyone else. The world hates you because you started the attacks! Don't blame us!" The man on the right slapped the wall with his palm. "These walls are solid metal. Where in God's name are we?"

"If you think this is gonna get me to talk, you're wrong." He raised his voice. "You hear that you damn Brits!? I ain't tellin' you shit!"

The man's voice grated the creature's ears, but he liked his scent. The man on the right, however, made the creature furious. He hated that scent! He now stood in arm's reach of the man. A low growl escaped his throat. The man feeling the wall stopped dead still.

"Did you hear that?" he said.

"I did... It came from across the room."

"I think it's right next to me." The man slowly rose to full height and looked towards the center of the chamber. "Smells like a bloody dog."

The creature couldn't take it anymore. As the man's fear rose, it affected his scent and aggravated him further. His voice began to shake and that made him want this man dead. He growled again. The man froze.

"Nice doggie...?" he said.

The creature's mouth watered. He snarled and lunged at the man. His body slammed into the wall and flailed against it. The creature buried his teeth in his soft neck, his teeth piercing a hard tube of flesh, before he pulled back and popped it free. The man choked and squirmed and fell face first on the floor.

The other man was now running along the walls, frantically searching for an exit, panting and crying. The creature turned and ran towards the man. He stopped and stood over his shoulder, taking in his scent and breath. The man clenched his eyes closed and cried.

The creature disliked the fear in his scent... But he didn't have to destroy it, and he hadn't stopped him, so he liked this man. He licked him on the forehead, turned around and walked away. The man shriveled up and curled into himself against the wall.

About a minute later, bright light streamed into the room, casting everything in stark light and shadow.

"Mother fu...h..." panted the cowering man as he gazed at the creature standing just a few paces in front of him.

The two men walked in through the doorway. The creature's tail wagged and he pranced to meet them.

"Final test complete, big guy," said the first man. "You're ready."

The creature jumped up and down through the doorway, urging them to lead him to another metallic room and do something else to him.

The creature's eyes opened to complete darkness. The scent of the air was wrong. There was no metal or tile. He rolled to his feet and stood up quickly. He held his nose high and scented the area. The creature couldn't place any of the scents. He'd never smelled these things before.

Everything around him was alive. The thing jutting up from the ground in front of him was full of life. There was no metal anywhere. He looked around for a mirror, but there were no walls. The room was endless. He looked up. The ceiling was so high he couldn't see it. Having no limits on his environment was disorienting.

Curious, he walked up to the tree, scenting up its trunk. The tree was alive. Living things were crawling around inside and outside. Above and below. The ground felt wrong. It wasn't solid tile or plastic, but soft and a little spongy. He bent down, scented the ground. He smelled a multitude of scents staining the ground by his feet. His nose was drawn to them and he took them all in.

He took short, quick breaths over the dirt, letting the weak scents build up in his nose. Gradually he caught that scent... The one he had to destroy... It was coming from a place quite a distance from here. His body aligned itself in that direction and he ran with it. His powerful legs propelled him across the land, up the steep hill. His sensitive eyes helped him avoid the trees and branches.

Gradually he realized there was no wall. There were no mirrors. The air... He vaguely remembered smelling this air before, once, a long time ago, when he feared the people in the plastic suits and tried cutting open a suit to escape. The air that rushed over his face now was the same. He was outside the metal walls. Away from the men behind mirrors.

Now he felt what it was like to use his body to its fullest! His legs carried him fast and light. His nimble feet changed his direction with the slightest pivot, avoiding obstacles. His nose kept him oriented with the scent, which pulled him uphill.

He crested the hill and stopped. Before him was more metal scent, but this was different. It didn't smell like the metal rooms he'd lived in. This smelled lighter, more airy...

He approached it, scenting it. It was simple lines of metal pulled between posts about five paces apart. A light hum emitted from the lines. He recognized the hum as electricity, but he never heard or felt electricity this strong before. The creature lowered his nose closer to the lines, scenting it. The feeling of so much electricity was curious, and he wanted to be closer to it—

Pressure—line pulling him into it—intense pleasure rushing through him!

The creature mustered enough control to back away from the line. He breathed heavily, still unsure of what just happened. It felt good, but the creature didn't like how he lost control of his body.

He backed away, looking left and right. The metal lines continued onward in both directions, each rounding corners and continuing on. Beyond the metal lines was a large complex of buildings.

And the scent he had to destroy.

The creature's face curled up in a snarl. He jumped, testing his leap compared to the height of the lines of metal. He landed softly on his feet, crouched down and jumped again. The second jump his legs cleared the top line. Just knowing he could jump over a fence this high made the creature feel good.

He backed up a few steps, ran to the fence and leaped into the air. His legs propelled him up and out in a large arc, he cleared the lines easily and landed softly on his feet.

The ground was asphalt inside the lines. The scent was stronger here. The creature scented the air, letting it add up until he didn't need to smell it consciously to follow it.

His muscles flexed, his face cinched up, his legs propelled him in its direction, snarling and drooling in anticipation of that scent's source on his tongue, in his belly. Something told him immense pleasure waited for him when he destroyed this scent. He bounded straight for the buildings.

"What the hell—""Holy fucking—""—God—""—is that!?"

The creature stopped short without sliding on the ground, turned and faced the source of the noises. Three men wearing uniforms were standing a ways off from him. They were staring at him in awe, reeking of fear. One of them stank of urine.

All three men reached for their guns. Two of them were shaking too much to even find their pistols, but the oldest of the three found it and aimed it straight at the creature. Three loud, sharp sounds came from the pistol one of the men was holding. The creature felt pressure on his chest for an instant, and then intense pleasure. Oh, it felt good!

These men were stopping him from finding the scent. He hated them. The creature dropped to all fours and charged towards the group, never making a sound. They fired again. Pressure on his chest changed to pleasure and the creature wanted them dead more than anything else in the world.

He sped up and landed on the man who had shot at him. The man was pinned face up under his paws, struggling and screaming. The creature bent down, clamped his muzzle around his throat and silenced his screams.

"Intruder! Intruder! Unknown threat! Full alarm!"

pop-pop-pop-pop

The creature turned his head and looked at the other two men. One was talking into something in front of his mouth. The other was shooting at the creature.

pop-pop

The creature stood still, blood dripping down his muzzle and onto his chest. Every pop sound was followed by a light wave of pleasure. His erection stirred in his sheath, and he raised one of his arms, hoping to encourage the man to shoot him in the belly.

He did.

pop-pop-pop-click-click

Three shots of pleasure on his stomach. The creature lifted his head back and panted in ecstasy.

click-click-click

"Shit!"

A moment later a loud siren sounded. The creature's ears swiveled forward. He felt vibrations of footsteps. If these few men were trying to stop him from reaching the scent, others would do the same.

"Outside, third quadrant, Ashton is dead, Reilly just unloaded his clip into the thing and it didn't even flinch!"

The creature turned, coiled up and leapt at the men. He landed, pinning one of them under each paw. He chewed out the talker's neck first, then buried his muzzle in the shooter's neck. Their blood tasted good. When he was sure they wouldn't stop him from finding the scent, the creature leaped off their lifeless bodies and bounded to a large doorway.

Something felt different as he ran. He felt like there were tiny pieces of metal in him, brushing against his muscles as he ran. Every step he took made him feel good. So good... He wanted to keep running, keep feeling the joy.

He stopped at the door. He remembered men swinging these doors open, but he didn't know how. He pounded on the door. The metal bent with his fists, and he remembered the chair and metal restraints. He braced himself against the door and pushed. The metal heaved and groaned and puckered inward until finally something snapped and the warped door careened into the hallway inside.

The creature stood in the doorframe and let out a growl. The pleasure he got from breaking that door was so intense, and the little pieces of metal buried in his muscles added spice to it.

He allowed himself only a moment to swim in the joy before the scent overtook his nose again. He bounded on all fours down the hallway, letting the scent decide which direction to go. The corridors were exactly like the concrete and metal maze he navigated before, so this was easy and familiar. He turned several corners. The scent he was tracking wasn't getting any stronger, but he stayed with it, not letting any of the other scents or sounds distract him.

The creature rounded a corner and halted, rearing back on his hind legs. Down this hallway was a team of two dozen men, all reeking of determination and confidence.

"Fire!" shouted a man in the rear.

Loud blasts and pops filled the creature's ears. A dozen pricks hit his body simultaneously, washing his mind out.

"Oh my God..." someone said.

The creature looked down at them. Smoke was leaking from the tips of their guns. Fear leaked out of their bodies.

"Fire at will!" shouted the man in the back.

The shots rang out again, but this time they weren't synchronized. Pellets pierced his hide, knocking him off balance briefly as they impacted. They felt so good the creature's tongue fell out the side of his mouth. Gradually the firing stopped. More fear leaked out of the men in the hallway. The creature looked down at them. He snarled.

"Retreat! Retreat!"

The men stood up and backed away. A couple of them fired at the creature. He dropped to all fours and ran headlong into the crowd. He didn't have time to taste their blood; he settled for stepping on them, breaking their necks, arms, shoulders and legs as he passed. For the talker at the front of the retreat, the creature jumped and landed on his back. It cracked, and the creature bounded onward down the hall.

He ran through the entire building, following that scent. He ran into many men trying to shoot him, and though he wanted to stand still and swim in the pleasure of being shot, they were slowing him down, keeping him from destroying that scent, so he ran past them, breaking their bones so they wouldn't bother him later.

He rounded a corner. A man threw something down the hall at him. It exploded a few paces from the creature. Thousands of shards hit him in the chest and legs. The creature stood still, relishing in the pleasure of it. The man threw another one, and again the creature didn't want to be slowed down, so he ran past the exploding pieces of metal, leaped on the man and continued.

The scent wasn't in this building. The creature found the nearest window and smashed through it. He was three stories up, and the pavement rushed to meet him. Alarms sounded from loudspeakers all around him. People were scrambling about, filling the cold air with panic, which made the creature happy. He landed hard on all fours, making a few cracks in the asphalt, but the creature felt as if he'd just hopped off a chair to the floor. He dashed to another building, smashed the door in and followed the scent again. It was stronger in here.

He had an extra problem. There were so many pieces of metal stuck in him that every step he took was orgasmic. He was having a hard time moving through all the pleasure. He wanted to lie down and let the erotic joy take him, but he kept following that scent.

More men were in this building than before, and the creature didn't even let them make a move. He killed them all as he ran by. He turned corners into rooms, searching for the scent. Some of the men who got in his way threw smoking bombs at him, but it didn't slow him down at all. Still others threw pods filled with acidic liquid in them. Fur and skin melted off parts of his body as he passed through the clouds of acid, and it made him feel good, but the men were only in the way, trying to distract him.

This building had multiple levels underground, and he followed the scent down five floors down. He could smell damp concrete and soil just behind the walls, but the scent he was looking for was here. It was getting closer! The scent down here was more recent, and it pulled him faster down the levels.

The creature burst into a room. No one was here, but the scent had been in this room. He was about to turn around and follow the scent again when his eyes caught a glimpse of something familiar. There was a mirror in here. He ran into the room and stood in front of it.

He was covered head to toe in blood. Most of his fur was missing. Large chunks of skin were missing, revealing the muscle underneath. His body was riddled with holes and bleeding gashes.

They felt good. He felt powerful. Strong. As he watched, some of the fur was growing back. The skin that lined the edges of the holes was growing inward. It itched, and felt good. Confidence renewed, the creature turned from the mirror and ran back into the hall.

He felt footsteps behind him. He spun around. A man was leaping in the air, swinging an ax. The blade disappeared into the creature's chest. The creature tipped over and crashed on his back.

Moments later another man appeared, stood over him and swung another ax down on his arm. He chopped his shoulder once. Twice. Three times. His shoulder and arm fell free from his body.

The creature's eyes rolled back in his head. He wanted to get up and find the scent, but this felt better than being shot! The same man hacked off one of the creature's legs in the same way, taking ten swings before it was completely severed.

The creature ejaculated.

"Oh my God..." said the man holding the ax.

"Get the head! The head!" shouted the other.

The creature's eyes opened. Something clicked in place. He didn't understand the words, but he did recognize there was danger if he let them bring the ax to his neck. He rolled over and grabbed the ax-man by the leg. The man's eyes swelled to three times their size and he dropped the ax. He squeezed the man's thigh. Bones snapped. The man screamed and cried. The creature squeezed harder. His hand clenched together, and he let go. The man fell to the ground, whimpering and crying helplessly. He crawled away.

The other man was reaching for the ax, but the creature raised his remaining leg and kicked him in the stomach. The other man fell backwards and rolled around on the floor, spitting blood.

The creature lay still. Something inside him told him he should.

A tingling sensation began from his severed shoulder and leg. Blood shot from the holes where his arm and leg had been. The creature writhed and moaned. His penis swelled up again. He turned his head to watch what was happening. A bone was growing from his shoulder socket. He looked down just as a bone shot out of his body where his leg had been severed.

Muscle and flesh grew from the hole. Blood shot out and covered the walls and floor. His penis was completely out its sheath and throbbing. Multiple bones grew at once. Flesh grew rapidly to cover the new bones.

The erection throbbed. A knot at the base swelled.

New fingers were starting to grow on the new arm. New toes were sprouting on the foot. The claws were growing inside the flesh of the toes. They pushed through solid skin and muscle and emerged in sprays of blood.

The creature ejaculated again.

The pleasure waned. The creature lay on the floor panting for a moment. Suddenly the scent hit him. He rolled to his feet and crouched on the blood-soaked floor. Both men were still here, looking up at him in awe. The creature looked at himself. His arm and leg were hairless. The skin was a different color than the rest of his body. But they were just as muscular and functional as his old limbs had been.

The creature was hungry now. He crouched over the man with the broken leg, tore his neck free, chewed the flesh and swallowed. He pulled off an arm and a leg with one hand and ran down the hallway, chewing the meat.

Though the alarm was still sounding, he didn't meet a single person. The scent was strong in this building, so the scent he was looking for must be here. He descended three more levels. The scent became stronger than ever. He turned a corner and entered a large chamber. One man in a uniform was standing in front of him. He held nothing in his hand.

His scent! His horrible scent! HIM!

The creature charged.

POW—SPLIFF!

The creature's legs gave out from the pleasure of being shot. He slid on his stomach across the floor. His prey ran out of the way.

This felt different. The pleasure was coming straight from his head. They shot him in the head with something... And it was still in there. He reached back and felt it. There was a long, metal rod sticking out of his skull. It was attached to a wire. The creature looked behind him. The wire ran the entire length of the room and was attached to an enormous box. Standing at the box was another man. The creature rolled upright and charged for him.

A wave of electricity surged through his brain. His muscles vibrated. His legs turned to jelly and he collapsed on his stomach.

So much pleasure...

The creature lay on the floor, brain swimming in bliss. His limbs were stiff and immobile, but felt like they were flailing in all directions.

...so good...

304

The two men approached and looked down at him. The creature hated them. He wanted to destroy them. He tried to move, but his muscles weren't responding. He tried to think, but nothing happened. Everything felt so good.

"Maximum voltage," said one of the men.

The second man disappeared. The creature looked at the face of the man he wanted to kill. Even with his mind drowning in pleasure he wanted this man dead. Even more pleasure awaited him when he destroyed this man's scent. In his mind the creature was snarling, but none of the appropriate muscles responded.

Then, his arms stiffened and tensed even more. His mind squeezed in on itself. The world turned black.

The creature lay on a bed. This bed wasn't nearly as comfortable or well-designed as the beds he was used to. Those beds felt like they were designed especially for him. This bed felt like it was worn out years before he ever lay his back on it. It was propped up partway, facing a plastic window cut into a wall. A metal prong protruded from the back of his head. There were no bars or straps or needles holding him down. Only the metal prong humming directly into his skull.

The hum of electricity filled the creature's head and danced inside him from his chest to his toes. He felt calm. At ease with everything. He still wanted to destroy all the foul scents that surrounded him in this building. Those scents were keeping him from destroying the scent he had to reach, but he felt so good he couldn't move at all.

The room smelled different. It didn't smell of sterilized metal and mirrors. This room smelled like many people had been in it before. Various medical instruments lay on tables and trays. He smelled them in drawers and desks all around the room. There were other beds in this room, all recently emptied.

Hour by hour people walked by the window, stood and stared at him. He heard their whispers clearly through the plastic and brick walls. They were always a mixture of fascination, hate, curiosity and fear. The creature wanted to destroy all of them, but his muscles weren't responding to this desire.

He watched the people. They walked by and looked at him. No one entered the room, but many lingered at the window for a long time, studying him, speaking to each other about him, giving off their foul scents.

Hours and hours.

Men finally entered the room. They had needles. They had knives. They injected things into him, injected things out of him. They cut fur from his body. It grew back in minutes, and they watched in amazement. They cut through the fur and pierced the skin. They cut off larger and larger chunks, then stood back and watched the skin grow back.

One of the men took a large knife and sawed one of the creature's fingers off. The creature's tail would have wagged if it could, anticipating the feeling that would follow. One of the men clicked his watch, and they observed the bone grow out of his hand, muscle and flesh twist and build up around it, out and out and out until the whole finger had grown back. The fur was the last to return. The creature moaned and panted the whole time. He hoped they'd cut off his whole leg again, or an arm. It felt even better when those grew back. The man clicked his watch.

"Forty-eight seconds."

"Incredible..."

The men wheeled in a large machine. It spun around the creature. Many other devices came and went. Many different men. The creature wanted to kill them all, but he didn't want to move either.

More people walked by the plastic window. More men came in and examined him. They talked to each other in front of him, and the creature felt every word. They were fascinated and curious.

Hours.

Days.

Days.

He'd been alone for a long time.

Then, a familiar man stepped in front of the window, looking in on him. The air vents above carried his scent to the creature. He wanted to kill this man. Above all else he had to destroy his scent! The creature tried to get up. He tried to move his legs, but nothing responded. Every time he tried to move, his thoughts were interrupted by the pleasure humming deep in his skull. The creature lay still. He had never moved, even though in his mind he was struggling and fighting and writhing on the bed to stand up and attack.

"Lieutenant Westing?" asked the man.

He paused, as if expecting something to happen.

"Marty?" he said, and waited.

A while later, a second man walked up next to the creature's prey. He was holding a clipboard.

"Is that the report?" said his prey. "What in God's name is this?"

The man with the clipboard looked through the plastic at the creature and spoke. "There's no doubt about it. That is Lieutenant Westing. Residual DNA testing confirms traces of his human chromosomes... alongside canine genes as well."

They were both looking through the plastic at him. Their scents were remorseful instead of terrified.

"God..." said the prey. "He was captured by the Americans last year. He's still in the official P.O.W. list issued last month. Is the biological study complete?"

"Yes, sir."

"Well, lay it on me."

"Where do I begin?"

"Just pick a place."

The person next to his prey held a thick stack of papers up to his face. He flipped through them.

"His DNA has been rewritten multiple times. It looks like the Americans used several different kinds of canine genes as the baseline for the initial phase. After that, they went back and hand-spliced the genetic sequences for his hearing and olfactory. Possibly the muscle structure. It looks like it's been augmented two different times."

"And the self-regeneration?"

"Yes, that." He flipped a few dozen pages, stopped and read for a moment. "Every cell in his body is a stem cell. His cells recognize when, say, a finger is missing, and know how to grow it back."

"How is that possible?"

"It's light years ahead of our gene research. But it's obvious they haven't perfected the technique for their soldiers to use. The process must be incredibly painful, as all of the lieutenant's pain receptors have been rewired directly into the pleasure center of his brain."

"What?"

"Yes, sir. It would've been one of the first things they did. This kind of physical change... There'd be no sleeping through it. The pain would be so great it would wake anyone out of the deepest coma. He was awake for the whole process. And it must've felt really good. His gonads produce no sperm, but they pump out testosterone in ridiculous quantities. His adrenal glands are also hyper-stimulated, probably to keep the senses sharp."

"But why? Can you tell me why?"

He lowered the papers to his side and stared at the creature. "This is not a science experiment, sir. This thing is a biological weapon. Missiles and bombs are nearly useless these days, so it's reasonable to conclude the Americans set out to create a weapon that can follow its target quickly and stealthily, adapt to any situation, and be unpredictable. Canines are much more maneuverable than the human body, and the canine body and brain structure can better handle the sharper senses. They began with a human brain to retain the intelligence and innate knowledge of human environments. His dense muscle structure doubles as body armor. But that's not all."

"It gets worse?"

"Yes, sir." He briefly consulted the papers again. "His olfactory and auditory senses are tied directly to a specific clump of cells in his reasoning center. This cluster is not natural. It was pieced together deliberately, programming him to seek and destroy a specific scent. The lieutenant's brain activity peaks whenever you're around, sir. In a nutshell, you're his target, General Stagris. Every modification done to his body is aimed at maximizing survival through the most brutal attacks just to get to you. His brain is designed so his only purpose in life is to track his target and kill it. He'll never stop until he finishes his goal. When he does, his brain is programmed to overload his pleasure center, then the immune system severs the nerves to the medulla and cannibalizes the cells to destroy his DNA. And if he should die before reaching his goal, we're pretty sure his immune system will destroy the body, too."

"Didn't expect us to figure a way to capture him alive, did they?" said the General.

They were both silent for a while.

"This war has been in stalemate for twenty years," his prey continued. "They're too scared to use the Bomb. Everyone has defenses that can intercept all ballistic attacks—they've been useless for decades. Every nation has the antigens for biological and viral weapons. For years all the Americans could do was demonize the world, posture and make threats. So what do they do? They create a living, breathing weapon as unpredictable as life itself, designed to feel no pain as it suffers through its suicide mission."

They both stared at the creature for a while longer.

"Was the lieutenant married?" said the prey.

"Yes, sir. I took the liberty of looking her up. Gloria Westing, also a lieutenant."

"She's enlisted?"

"Correct, sir. Apparently they met on a base in the Middle East five years ago and decided to say vows. Managed to transfer together the last three deployments."

"Somebody had a few friends in command..." He sighed. "Bring her here. Fast as you can. Let's find out if there's any part of lieutenant Westing left in there."

The other man nodded and walked out from the view of the window. The General leaned closer to the window, still peering at the creature.

In his mind the creature was writhing and kicking his legs and running and breaking through the window and chewing this man's throat out. But he only lay still in bed.

Days and days and hours and days... Still silence and humming. No one had come to the window since the General walked away. No one came in to poke or prod or cut anything off him.

Then, a woman walked in front of the window, wearing standard military clothes. Just behind her was the General, leading her to the window. He stood against the wall and let her approach the window alone.

"Marty...?" she said.

She turned around, looked at the General.

"He can hear you. These walls aren't soundproof. And his hearing is hundreds of times more sensitive than ours."

She turned and looked at him again. Her face was contorted in a mix of disgust and curiosity. And even hope.

"Is that really him?"

"The DNA tests confirm it. There's just enough of your husband's DNA left to match it up."

"What's that thing he's hooked up to?"

"The power grid. When he invaded the base, bullets didn't stop him. Two of my men cut off an arm and a leg, and they both grew back in about two minutes. We figured his brain had been rewired to feel pleasure instead of pain, so we're injecting current directly into his brain. It keeps his pleasure center occupied and disrupts motor functions."

"That can't be my husband..."

"That's why I brought you here, lieutenant. We want you to meet him. We'll be watching for any change in brain activity."

He walked behind her, to a small door next to the window. A lock turned, a bolt unlatched, and the door swung inwards. The General held the door for her. The woman walked away from the window, behind the wall and reappeared in the door. She took a couple deep breaths and slowly approached the bed. The General closed the door and stood in front of it, arms folded. She stood next to the bed, looking down at him. The creature could only move his eyes and look at her.

"Marty?" she whispered.

Her breath washed over the creature. It stank. He stirred in his mind, willing himself to get up, but all he could do was lie still.

"Do you know who I am?"

The creature blinked.

She looked at his eyes for a while. She squinted at them, as if trying to read something written on his pupils. Tears shined at the corners of her eyes. She raised her arms from her sides and leaned on the bed.

"What did those bastards do to you?"

She leaned harder on the bed. She looked closer at his muzzle. She raised an arm. She held it over his chest, hesitated, then placed her hand gently on his chest. The creature writhed and flailed and grabbed her face and twisted her head off... In his mind. She was between him and his prey. She had to die.

She rubbed his chest. Her hand migrated up to his face. She held his muzzle in her hand, turned his head slightly to look at her directly. The creature felt his arms and neck rising up to meet her neck and rip it open, but nothing was moving.

She said many more things. She kept talking. Kept feeling him, stroking his fur back and forth. He didn't hear her anymore. He just wanted her hand off his chest and her scent extinguished so he could reach his prey.

Finally, the General placed a hand on her shoulder. She turned to face him.

"I'm sorry, soldier. But the doctors have told me that brain activity has increased. The pattern matches what he feels when he catches my scent."

She turned to him again. Her jaw was clenched and tears shimmered at the corners of her eyes but never escaped.

"He wants to kill us."

She clutched the mattress, then spun around and stormed out of the room, behind the wall, past the window and out of sight. The General remained there for a moment, eyeing him.

"I know what the doctors say, but I don't believe them. You're still in there. Somewhere. And I know you're not going to understand this, lieutenant, but I am so sorry. I promise I have a plan. It will give them what they deserve, and it will make amends for what they took from you."

He turned around and walked out the door, closing and locking it behind him.

The creature was up, smashing in the door, running on all fours to catch up to the General, grabbing his body and silencing that scent forever...

The creature lay still in the pleasant hum. The scent of the women lingered in the room. He breathed it in, nose twitching. The longer he breathed it, the more familiar it seemed, but his prey's scent also lingered in the room and the thought was quickly buried beneath desire to destroy it.

Days.

Weeks.

Months.

Men and women entered the room often, extracting tissue and blood and other fluids from him day and night. Many times he lost consciousness, falling into a waking sleep. Men and women poked and prodded and cut pieces off him. Those parts grew back, and it felt as wonderful as ever.

They moved him from room to room often. They switched beds a dozen times. More people came and observed him. More men talked about him while they looked at him.

In the beginning, the creature willed himself to get up and kill them, but as the months passed, the less intense the desire to break free and kill them to get to his prey became.

The hum of electricity never stopped. The gentle massage in his brain that wrapped his body in joy was ever present, and with the desire to kill everyone slowly decreasing, he was free to enjoy it without the impulse getting in the way. It had brought him pleasure before, but gradually he forgot it ever had.

Then, one day, the General and a doctor walked in the room, leaving the door open. The doctor walked around one side of the creature's bed, the General walked around the other side.

The doctor raised the bed until the creature lay upright. He reached behind the creature's head and—

The humming stopped.

Enormous pain gripped his body as the rod slid out of his skull. The creature had never felt this before and he didn't like the feeling. Immediately the doctor wrapped the creature's head in a bandage. The creature moved his arm again. He spread his toes. He looked at the General.

The General smiled.

The creature swung his legs off the bed and stood on the floor. He stretched to his full height, towering over this man. His prey. His...

He felt nothing.

The General's scent. The doctor's scent. They surrounded him, filled his head. He felt no reflex to kill it. Nothing. The creature stood still, looking at the General.

"Hello, Marty. I'd like you to meet someone."

Through the door walked in...

The creature thought he was looking in a mirror. Another furred creature walked through the door, arms held by two men in camouflage uniforms. She walked skittish and unsteady, scenting the air and looking around as if expecting everything to reach out and attack her.

One of the uniformed men closed and locked the door. When they did they stood still about five paces away from the creature. The creature's eyes met the female creature's eyes, and they stared at each other.

"This is Gloria," said the General.

The creature turned and looked down at the man. Strangely, he felt nothing, so he stood still.

"We've been working on you, Marty. It's taken nine months, but we not only reverse engineered the technique used to create you, we removed most of the programming they added. The nerve complexes that made you want to kill me and everyone who stood between. Everything we could do to give control of your mind back to you."

He walked up to the female. To Gloria.

"Your wife didn't need much persuading, especially when I told her the mission I had in mind for both of you. We extracted your DNA and applied the same changes to her. Everything you have, she has. Indestructible, unstoppable."

The General stepped forward and stood between them.

"The timing couldn't have been better. Since I've been playing dead for the better part of a year, the Americans think their plan worked. They have begun dropping more canines like you on the British Isles. We have more than a dozen confirmed sightings and attacks. I anticipated this move."

The General had begun pacing back and forth across the room, voice growing more and more menacing and angry.

"We are capturing these creatures, taking them to our secured labs and modifying them as we have modified you. The enemy doesn't know we're on to them, and they probably didn't think we could figure it out."

The words were not entirely lost on the creature now. Somehow, in a way he couldn't remember consciously, they made sense. Yes... Someone had done this to him. People... He couldn't escape... They turned him into this. He loved what he'd become. He really did... But... They did something to him, and because he couldn't remember what, or why it should anger him, it enraged him even more.

He looked at the female before him. Gloria. She smelled nice. He walked closer to her, scenting her air from this distance. Her scent was so familiar. He felt like he should remember it, but the memory was not there anymore. The emotion it produced still was. This person was the anchor who kept him sane no matter what he saw in the field, what horrors he witnessed in whatever hellish place he deployed. He couldn't imagine a day without her. She walked closer to him, also scenting him. Her body language told him she felt the same way.

Their noses touched. They reached out and touched each other. The touch turned into an embrace. An overwhelming desire to protect her filled him up. Her scent expressed she was filled with a similar desire. They agreed.

The creature looked at the General. He was smiling.

"We reconnected your pain receptors to allow you to survive long term, but when you regenerate after injury, they will shut off completely. We will do the same for the ones we capture as well, then drop them over American soil. Both of you are going to do your country a great service. Give them a real enemy to fight. Give them hell, lieutenants. That's your mission."

The creature didn't catch every word, but in a subconscious way, he understood. The idea excited him. If any of those people came near his mate, he'd kill them. He'd kill them until their scents were so far away they'd never be a threat again.

Yes, sir.

The creature rose higher. He wasn't sure where that thought came from, but it felt good.

Marty.

He looked over his mate's shoulder at his vague reflection in the plastic window.

That's me... Marty.

For the first time in as long as he could remember, it felt right.

About the Authors

Ianus J. Wolf:

Ianus J. Wolf is a writer of furry fiction across a few genres including horror, erotica, noir, and others. His stories have been seen in *Will of the Alpha*, *FANG Volume 5*, and *Abandoned Places* from FurPlanet to name a few. He is also the editor of *Pulp!* and the *Trick or Treat* series from Rabbit Valley. Currently he lives in the Seattle area with his mates and two lovable dogs. He's always happy to hear from people who have read his work by any of the methods listed below.

The writer can be found at:
Email: ianusjwolf@gmail.com
Twitter: @IanusJWolf
Furaffinity: IanusJWolf
SoFurry: IanusJWolf

Richard Coombs

I come from a small island off the coast of Maine where I learned an appreciation for storytelling thanks to a huge amount of time spent around a campfire, just listening to others tell stories, whether real or fake. This, combined with a fascination for animals with human traits led me to start putting pen to paper and seeing just what might spill out of my head and onto the page.

The writer can be found at:
Email: Goombasa@aol.com
Twitter: @Goombasa

Ajax B. Coriander

Ajax B. Coriander is a Saint Bernard who has been writing furry fiction for almost half of his life. He has worked on one other anthology project prior to this, and he has been punished in a few anthologies. He is his most active on FA, but he tries to keep his galleries mirrored on every furry site.

The writer can be found at:
Email: ajaxwrites@gmail.com
Twitter: @saintajax33
Furaffinity: saintajax
SoFurry: saintajax33
Inkbunny: saintajax33

Whyte Yoté

Whyte Yoté has been writing erotic furry fiction since 1995 when he was probably far too young to be doing such a thing, and he has been seriously pursuing his craft since 2000. His works have appeared multiple times in *FANG*, *ROAR* and *Heat* magazine, as well as the anthologies *X*, *The Fortune Teller's Poem*, *Holidays*, *Will of the Alpha* and *Trick or Treat*. When he's not writing, he… oh wait, nevermind. He juggles personal work with anthology submissions as well as commissions and collaborations. He currently lives in Sacramento with writer/graphic designer Tym, his forever boyfriend since 2004.

The writer can be found at:
Email: whyte.yote@yahoo.com
Twitter: @whyteyote
Furaffinity: whyteyote
SoFurry: WhyteYote
Inkbunny: WhyteYote

Apollo Wolf

A recent transplant to Michigan, Apollo enjoys spending summers near the lake and hates winters just about anywhere. With a vivid imagination, Apollo has been transforming people and places for years and occasionally writes some of it down.

The writer can be found at:
Email: apollo_wolf@yahoo.com
Furaffinity: apollowolf
SoFurry: apollo wolf

Roland Jovaik

Roland is a humble ferret that resides in the great Canadian prairies. When he's not tinkering with electronics, you can usually find him behind a keyboard, writing the next installment in his series of bitter-sweet stories. Writing found its way into his blood at an early youth and has refused to lose hold well into his adulthood. You can find some of his most recent stories in anthologies such as *ROAR Volume 5, FANG Volume 5, Trick or Treat* 1 and 2, and *Pulp!*.

The writer can be found at:
Email: rolandferret@gmail.com
Website: www.fangsandfonts.com
Twitter: @rolandferret
Furaffinity: roland

Nogitsune Faux

He lives in eastern Ohio in one of the rustier parts of the Rust Belt. He's always loved reading and writing and have wanted to be published for a while. He is hoping this will give me the courage to write even more.

The writer can be found at:
Email: brenner.mike@gmail.com

Kodiak Malone

Kodiak Malone lives in Minnesota and enjoys a good pipe, snowy cold evenings, and thinking up different ways to transmute and transform people in stories. He thinks everyone should relax and have a great time whenever possible and he hopes you enjoyed his story.

The writer can be found at:
Furaffinity: kodiakmalone

James Steele

James L. Steele is a writer in Ohio. He is often asked to sum up his life's story in a single paragraph. James is very depressed by how easy this is. He has been published in various anthologies and magazines, including: *Solarcide, Allasso, Different Words Different Skins v.2, Tall Tales with Short Cocks v.2, Bourbon Penn*, and *Fictionvale*. His sci-fi novel, *Huvek*, is published through FurPlanet.

The writer can be found at:
Email: JLSteeleAuthor@aol.com
Website: www.JamesLSteele.com | DaydreamingInText.blogspot.com
Twitter: @JLSteeleAuthor
Furaffinity: JLS

Kuma

Born in San Antonio Texas, I've been drawing longer than I could walk or talk, discovering from an early age I had an affinity for it. Taking inspiration from things such as Disney and Square-Enix as well as always having a strong interest in transformation, all of which have been a primary focus in my artwork.

The artist can be found at:
Website: http://www.furaffinity.net/user/kuma/

Andres Cyanni Halden

Andres Cyanni Halden writes fantasy, romance, and contemporary fiction, all of which involve talking animals in some way. He has finished a fantasy trilogy, and his short stories have appeared in several anthologies, including *The Fortune Teller's Poem* and *Holidays*. You can probably spot him lurking around tables at conventions, signing any book handed to him. All of his published work can be purchased through www.FurPlanet.com.